THE PAŃĆATANTRA

Tradition ascribes the *Pańćatantra* to Viṣṇu Śarma whose exis- tance has not been conclusively established. Legend has it that Viṣṇu Śarma was one of the names of Viṣṇugupta Cāṇakya, the author of the Arthaśāstra. However, there is no evidence to show that the author of the Arthaśāstra also wrote a Nitiśāstra, the term used to describe the *Pańćatantra*. Viṣṇu Śarma was apparently a celebrated teacher living in Mahilāropya. At the age of eighty, he undertook to educate three very refractory princes, in six months, in the art of governance. The stories he used as teaching aids form the *Pańćatantra*.

CHANDRA RAJAN studied Sanskrit from the age of nine, in the time-honoured manner, with a pandit in Madras. She went to St Stephen's College, Delhi, where she had a distinguished aca- demic record and took degrees in English and Sanskrit. Trained early in Carnatic music, she studied Western music in New York. She has taught English at Lady Sri Ram College, Delhi University, and at the University of Western Ontario, London, Canada. Her publications include *Winged Words*; *Re-Visions*, a volume of verse; and *Kālidāsa: The Loom of Time* published by Penguin India in 1989. Chandra Rajan is currently working on a children's version of the *Pańćatantra* and a translation and criti- cal study of Bāna's famous prose romance, *Kādambari*, and a series of tales belonging to the Vikramaditya cycle: *The Goblin Tales*, also known as the *Vetālapańćavimśati*. She is also involved in a long-term project for the Sahitya Akademi – a translation of the complete works of Kālidāsa.

VIṢṆU ŚARMA

The Panćatantra

Translated from the Sanskrit with an Introduction by
CHANDRA RAJAN

PENGUIN BOOKS

PENGUIN BOOKS

Published by the Penguin Group
Penguin Books Ltd, 80 Strand, London WC2R 0RL, England
Penguin Group (USA) Inc., 375 Hudson Street, New York, New York 10014, USA
Penguin Group (Canada), 90 Eglinton Avenue East, Suite 700, Toronto, Ontario, Canada M4P 2Y3
(a division of Pearson Penguin Canada Inc.)
Penguin Ireland, 25 St Stephen's Green, Dublin 2, Ireland (a division of Penguin Books Ltd)
Penguin Group (Australia), 250 Camberwell Road, Camberwell,
Victoria 3124, Australia (a division of Pearson Australia Group Pty Ltd)
Penguin Books India Pvt Ltd, 11 Community Centre,
Panchsheel Park, New Delhi – 110 017, India
Penguin Group (NZ), cnr Airborne and Rosedale Roads, Albany,
Auckland 1310, New Zealand (a division of Pearson New Zealand Ltd)
Penguin Books (South Africa) (Pty) Ltd, 24 Sturdee Avenue,
Rosebank, Johannesburg 2196, South Africa

Penguin Books Ltd, Registered Offices: 80 Strand, London WC2R 0RL, England

www.penguin.com

First published by Penguin Books India 1993
Published in Penguin Classics 2006

014

Copyright © Chandra Rajan, 1993
All rights reserved

ISBN-13: 978-0-140-45520-5
ISBN-10: 0-140-45520-5

www.greenpenguin.co.uk

To Tangerina,
a great lady of elegance,
sensitivity and intelligence,
and to her delightful family,
special in individual ways:
I have learnt much from them.

Key to the Pronunciation of Sanskrit Words

Vowels:

The line on top of a vowel indicates that it is long.

a   (short) as the u in b*u*t
ā   (long) as the a in f*a*r
i   (short) as the i in s*i*t
ī   (long) as the ee in sw*ee*t
u   (short) as the u in p*u*t
ū   (long) as the oo in c*oo*l
ṛ   with a dot is a vowel like the i in f*i*rst or u in f*u*rther
e   is always a long vowel like a in m*a*te
ai as the i in p*i*le
o   is always long as the o in p*o*le
ow as the ow in *o*wl

Consonants:

k, b and p are the same as in English
kh is aspirated
g   as in *g*oat
gh is aspirated
ć   is ch as in *ch*urch or *c*ello
ćh is aspirated as in *chh*ota
j   as in *j*ewel
jh is aspirated
ṭ and ḍ are hard when dotted below as in *t*alk and *d*ot
ṭṭ is the aspirated sound
ḍḍ is aspirated
ṇ   when dotted is a dental; the tongue has to curl back to touch the palate.
ṅ   as in ki*n*g
t   undotted is a th as in *th*ermal
th is aspirated
d   undotted is a soft sound—there is no corresponding English sound, the Russian 'da' is the closest.
dh is aspirated
ph and bh are aspirated
The Sanskrit v is an English w
There are three sibilants in Sanskrit: S as in song, as in *sh*over and a palatal Ś which is in between, e.g. Śiva.

Contents

Foreword

The authorship, dates and provenance of ancient Sanskrit texts have always been problematic. The *Pañćatantra* is no exception. And in this case the problem is further complicated by the fact that the work belongs to the age-old oral tradition of which storytelling is an important part.

Storytelling has its origins in pre-literate societies of the distant past, where it was a communal activity. No story is ever 'told' the same way twice; no song is ever 'sung' the same way twice. Names and dates are difficult to pin accurately and securely to works in the oral tradition.

The author of the *Pañćatantra* is a storyteller of hoary antiquity, an almost legendary figure like Vyāsa (a word that literally means 'compiler' or 'editor') whom tradition declares to be the author of the *Mahābhārata*. In fact we know a little more about the author of the *Mahābhārata* than we do about the author of the *Pañćatantra*. Tradition ascribes this fabulous work to one Viṣṇu Śarma. But we know nothing about this gifted author who, judging from the artistry displayed in the text he is credited with having composed, brought storytelling to such heights of sophistication; who in fact created a literary genre of storytelling; who had many imitators over the centuries, none of them his equal.

Sometimes the name Viṣṇu Śarma is given as one of the names of Viṣṇugupta Ćāṇakya (son of Ćaṇaka), the author of the *Arthaśāstra*. But there is no evidence to show that the author of the *Arthaśāstra* also wrote a *Nitiśāstra*, the term used to describe the *Pañćatantra*; there is nothing to prove the contrary either.

Who then is Viṣṇu Śarma? His name occurs in the *Preamble* to the text, nowhere else. He is a celebrated teacher living in Mahilāropya, a place unidentified except by H. H. Wilson who suggests that it might be Mayilāpura, Peacock City, now part of the capital of Tamil Nadu. As he says of himself, he is eighty years of age, has no worldly desires and concerns; and he is successful in educating three very refractory princes in six months time through storytelling, so that they become expert in the art of government. Then he fades away leaving behind an impersonal voice. This is not much to go upon. And what little there is about Viṣṇu Śarma is all in the text; it is part of the story-book world.

We are therefore left with two possibilities to consider in relation to the identity of the author of the *Pañcatantra*. Viṣṇu Śarma might have been the name of the storyteller/author who had the imagination and the artistry to first shape a floating body of tales—popular and moral tales, fairytales and folklore—into the artistic whole with the complex and unique structure and well-defined purpose that the *Pañcatantra* is. The names of the storytellers who went before him and who come after have perhaps been subsumed under his revered name—not an uncommon practice in India, as in the case of the *Mahābhārata* and of the *Nātya Śāstra* of Bharatamuni. It is reasonable therefore, to consider a multiple authorship for the *Pañcatantra*.

The other possibility is that Viṣṇu Śarma is himself a fictional character like the numerous characters, human and nonhuman in the *Pañcatantra* that have delighted children of all ages in all places at all times, and still continue to do so. It is noteworthy that there is an anonymous narrator in the *Preamble* to the text, who introduces Viṣṇu Śarma, the first of a series of narrators, (perhaps an archetypal storyteller) and the three princes, the very first audience (see pp. xlviii–il of the introduction). Who this anonymous narrator was we shall never know. And we have been pushed into a region of anonymity.

Anonymity is a distinctive feature of much of Indian art in the past. We have therefore to rest content with the realization that we do not know who the author of the *Pañcatantra* is, where he lived and composed his great work, and when. Tradition is important in oral transmission. But tradition says little here; it merely provides an ascription, a name.

What's in a name, one might ask: a great deal if they are the names of the delightful characters in the *Pañcatantra*. Nearly all the names in this work are descriptive of some essential trait, physical or otherwise of the characters. For instance, *Piṅgalaka,*

Tawny, the lion in the frame story of Book I, is so named because of the reddish-brown coat of lions, but another lion is named *Mandamati*, Dimwit (I. *Dimwit and the Hare*), because he meets his end on account of his stupidity. *Sūčīmukha*, Needlebeak (IV. *The Officious Sparrow*) aptly describes a weaver bird, and so on. The choice of names is deliberate, as in some of the novels of Thomas Hardy, and adds to the total meaning of the story. I have therefore translated most of them. In a few cases, the Sanskrit names have been retained, because they are untranslatable, for example, Nāduka in the tale of 'The Preposterous Lie', (I. tale 29); or because the name sounds silly or cumbrous in English—Mahilāropya, City Ornamented with women, Yajnadatta, Gift of Sacrifice (I. *The Grateful Beasts and the Ungrateful Man*).

The names of the two jackals, *Karaṭaka* and *Damanaka*, in the frame story of Book I form a special case of some interest. I have called them Wary and Wily; these are not translations of the Sanskrit names. In English these two names would be Little Crow and Little Tamer, neither of which convey what the Sanskrit names express so well. *Karaṭa* is one of the many words in Sanskrit for a crow. It is a common belief that the crow is the most intelligent of birds, wise, shrewd, cautious, with good judgement; just the qualities we see in the first jackal whom I have named Wary. (The suffix *'ka'* denotes the diminutive form of a word). Whether the second jackal, *Damanaka*, is a 'tamer' is highly doubtful; but wily he certainly is; a mean and conniving rascal. And the name Wily seemed appropriate, in contrast to Wary.

Dharma and *niti* are two all-embracing words that cannot be translated by a single English word. In most contexts where the word occurs I have translated *dharma* as the Law; the moral law of the universe in its physical and ethical aspects which implies the existence of order at all levels. *Niti*, I have rendered by the phrase, 'living wisely and well in the truest sense of these terms'. These two important terms have been fully explained in the introduction, on pp. xlii, xliii and xlv.

I conclude this foreword with a few words on the jacket design. It is a reproduction of an illustration in a manuscript copy

of the original *Kalila wa Dimnah*, the Arabic version of the
Pañćatantra done in Iran in AD 870 (see p.xv of the introduction
for details). This manuscript in Arabic script dates from 897 H (AD
1491) and has recently been acquired by the National Museum,
New Delhi. It was inscribed and illustrated somewhere in India.
The illustration is for the frame story of Book III of the
Pañćatantra—Of Crows and Owls.

I take this opportunity to express my thanks to Dr Naseem
Akhtar, Keeper, Manuscripts Section, the National Museum,
New Delhi, for showing me this manuscript copy of the original
Kalila wa Dimnah and for arranging to provide the slide for the
jacket design.

Makara Samkrānti, Vikrama 2050   *Chandra Rajan*
(14 January 1993)
New Delhi.

xiv

Introduction

Since then, this work on wise conduct (nitiśāstra[1]) has become celebrated as an excellent means of awakening young minds. It has travelled far and wide over this earth.

This is how the *Preamble* (*Kathamukha*) of the *Pañcatantra* speaks of itself before it closes with the traditional *phalaśruti* (*Preamble.* 3), the declaration of benefits that are gained by the proper study of a text. And this is no idle claim, but a claim amply justified. For this work, the product of the genius of Viṣṇu Śarma, has indeed travelled far and wide over the globe in many guises—translations, transcreations and adaptations.

As Johannes Hertel who spent many years in the study and editing of the textual corpus of the *Pañcatantra* writes in the Preface (p. vii) to his *Das Panchatantra* (1914):

> This book treats of the history of a work which has made an unparalleled triumphal progress from its native land over all the civilized parts of the globe and which for more than fifteen hundred years has delighted young and old, educated and uneducated, rich and poor, high and low, and still delights them. Even the greatest obstacles—whether of language or customs or religion—have not been able to check that triumphal progress.

That is a fair and accurate assessment of the extraordinary

---

*   Key to quotations from and references to the translation of the text: The books or *tantras* are referred to by roman numerals; the tales and verses by Indian numerals in universal use; lines of prose in the translation are referred to by using points and plus and minus signs after a verse number; eg. II.3.-6 refers to the sixth prose line before verse 3 and II.3.+2 to the second line after verse 3.

popularity of this fabulous work. According to Hertel, there are more than 200 versions of the *Pañcatantra* in fifty languages, most of them non-Indian. Carried by scholars from the land of its origin to other lands and peoples, as many Indian texts were during the early centuries AD, the *Pañcatantra* started on its 'triumphal progress' before AD 570, initially as a version in Pehlevi (Middle Persian) during the reign of Khosro Anushirvan (AD 550–578), Emperor of Iran. This version was executed under the Emperor's orders by his court physician, Burzoë. The original Pehlevi version was unfortunately lost, but not before a Syriac version by a priest named Bud, in AD 570, had been done entitled *Kalilag wa Dimnag*, followed by one in Arabic, the *Kalilah wa Dimnah* by Abdallah Ibn al-Moqaffa, a Zoroastrian convert to Islam, AD 750. The two words in the titles, Kalilag-Kalilah and Dimnag-Dimnah, are Arabizations of the names of the two jackals in the Sanskrit original—*Karaṭaka* and *Damanaka*—in the frame story of Book I, *Estrangement of Friends*; Wary and Wily in our translation.

The Arabic version is the parent of nearly all the European versions of the *Pañcatantra* known generally in medieval Europe as *The Fables of Bidpai*. Between AD eleventh and eighteenth centuries, versions of the *Pañcatantra* had been made in Greek, Latin, German, Spanish, French, English, Armenian and Slavonic languages; and Hebrew and Malay. A more or less complete table of the *Pañcatantra* versions in medieval Europe can be found in the 1938 reprint of the Elizabethan version by Sir Thomas North (published by David Nutt, Strand, London—Bibliotheque de Carabas).

Immediately after the invention of printing, the German version, *Das der Buch Beyspiele* (1483), was published, making the *Pañcatantra* one of the earliest works to be printed. An Italian version in two parts by one Doni[2](*La Moral Philosophia*, 1552) caught the eye and the imagination of Sir Thomas North (the translator of *Plutarch's Lives*). He made a version of the first part in fine Elizabethan English. This was published in 1570, a full thousand years after Viṣṇu Śarma's famous book of moral and political instruction through stories, left its native land to travel to the Persian court. North's translation (of Doni) was entitled *The Fables of Bidpai: The Morall Philosophie of Doni.*

The initial phase of the *Pancatantra*'s 'triumphal progress' over the globe, is itself a 'story'; a miniature romance in fact. The *Pancatantra* was the earliest work to travel outside India. Individual stories that this work had in common with the *Jātaka Tales* had already spread far beyond the shores of India, long before the *Pancatantra* set out on its travels. The *Jātaka Tales* is a collection of tales about the Buddha's nativity and his many incarnations as *Bodhisattva*, some in non-human forms. The Buddha is believed to have come down to earth many times, to redeem mankind by teaching the *dhamma*, (Pali for *dharma*), the Law or the Right Path. In the ancient world, stories and legends migrated, carried like silks, spices, ivory, gems and other rich commodities, from port to port and caravanserai to caravanserai by merchants and travellers, soldiers and sailors.

The story of the 'book of stories' probably formed part of the lost Pehlevi redaction of the *Pancatantra* by Burzoë (AD 570), perhaps as a prologue. It was carried over into the Arabic version of the Pehlevi text, *Kalilah wa Dimnah*, and into the European versions based on it. It forms part of Sir Thomas North's *The Fables of Bidpai: The Morall Philosophie of Doni* (1570), as 'The Argument of the Booke'.[3] The following is a brief account of the story.

Once, Khosro Anushirvan (Anestres Castri, in North), King of Iran (Edon) was presented a book which contained among other things the secret to raise the dead by means of an elixir (*rasāyana*[4] in Sanskrit). The book explained how the elixir was extracted from herbs and trees growing on the high mountains of India. The king, eager to find out the truth about this elixir sent his chief minister and treasurer, Burzoë, to India, providing him with a great deal of gold and silver to defray the expenses of the long and arduous journey, and with letters to the courts of many monarchs in India, requesting their help. Burzoë, on reaching India, received all the help he needed and with the wisest and most learned sages began combing the mountains for the herbs and trees mentioned in the book. But to no avail, for no extract had the power of restoring the dead to life. Burzoë and the learned

Indian sages were driven to the conclusion that everything that had been written about the elixir in the book, 'was false and untrue'.

Burzoë, greatly distressed, consulted the learned sages as to what he could do to not return empty-handed to his king. Then 'a famous philosopher', who had also searched long and in vain for the Elixir of Life only to discover in the end that the elixir was in truth a book, showed Burzoë a copy of it. This philosopher also explained the allegory contained in the first book, the one presented to the King of Iran, which started Burzoë on his travels, as follows: The high mountains were the wise and learned men of lofty intellect; the trees and herbs their various writings and the wisdom extracted from these writings the Elixir of Life that revived the dead intelligence and buried thoughts of 'the ignorant and unlearned'.

Burzoë asked for a copy of that book which was 'alwayes in the handes of those Kings, for that it was ful of Morall Philosophy' and permission to translate it into his own tongue for his king. And so 'with the helpe and knoledge of all those learned philosophers', Burzoë rendered the famous book into Pehlevi and returned home with it.

King Khosro Anushirvan studied the book deeply and was so impressed by the wisdom it contained that he began to collect books with great diligence and sought out learned men to come and live in his court. Then he built a great library in his palace, in which the book he esteemed so highly—the *Pañcatantra*—was given the place of honour, 'being of examples and instructions for man's life, and also of Justice and the feare of God . . . .'

Burzoë is reported to have asked as his sole reward, the honour of having his life and exploits form part of the book he had brought back from India; which it certainly has. A happy ending indeed, to Burzoë's travels and travail; the pity is that his own version of the original Sanskrit text he used (also lost), is lost to posterity.

Judging from the English versions of the *Pañcatantra*, that of Sir Thomas North which is several removes from the Arabic version, *Kalilah wa Dimnah*, and the recent translation of the same text by Thomas B. Irving,[5] it would appear that Burzoë or al-Moqaffa[6] was much more of a moralist than the venerable Indian sage Bidpai whom we know as Viṣṇu Śarma. Indeed, we might suspect that the Persian and Arab and their medieval European successors in the transmission of the *Pañcatantra* were attracted to the work by the 'moral philosophy' that it contained. The tales might have been regarded as incidental to the message. Whereas, in fact, what makes the *Pañcatantra* a unique work and fascinating to study, is the intricacy of its structure: the art and artistry with which the tales are interwoven with the discourse; the skilful blend of narrative and dialogue with maxim and precept; the over-arching frame in which the tales and everything else are set, as we shall see later in the introduction. Another interesting feature of this very ancient work is the presence of a dual perspective—entertainment and edification. And an element of inconclusiveness in Book I which takes up almost half of the text, further adds to its literary merits.

The *Pañcatantra* has not only been enormously popular as an entertaining (and instructive) work of fiction, it has also had great influence on world literature as no other work of Indian literature has had. Arthur Macdonell points to its 'extraordinary influence on the narrative works of the whole Middle Ages' in Europe, and to the enrichment it brought into the literature of the those languages in which versions of the work were made (*India's Past*; p. 122). Because of its great antiquity and its extensive migrations, traces of its influence might be detected in works of literature so widely separated in time and place as *The Arabian Nights*, the *Gesta Romanorum*, Boccacio's *Decameron* and Chaucer's *Canterbury Tales*, *The Fables* of La Fontaine, some stories of Grimm, and in the most unlikeliest of places, the Br'er Rabbit stories[7] current in the southern United States. However, if we are to pick the two works that display an unmistakable and notable influence of the *Pañcatantra*, they would be *The Arabian Nights* and La Fontaine's *Fables*. La Fontaine acknowledges his debt to our text when he expressly states in his preface to the second edition of *The Fables* (1678), that the greater part of the new material was 'derived from the Indian sage Pilpay', whose work is regarded 'as earlier than Aesop's'.

As we have seen, the name of 'the Indian sage' appears in some European versions as Bidpai. Strange indeed are the ways in which Indian names of places and persons appear metamorphosed in other languages in other lands. It is not easy to detect the original form of this name, Pilpay-Bidpai under its linguistic disguises. A. B. Keith[8] and Thomas B. Irving[9] (translator of the *Kalilah wa Dimnah*), suggest that it is a corruption of the Sanskrit name Vidyāpati. But it might just as well be the odd transformation of Vājapeyi,[10] an honorific title assumed by Brāhmaṇas who had successfully performed the great *vājapeya* sacrifice of the Vedas.

Within the country the popularity of the *Pañcatantra* down the centuries has been unsurpassed, as the many recensions of the work in Sanskrit (Hertel lists twenty-five), and the numerous translations into other Indian languages indicate.

Individual stories belonging to it which might have originally come out of folklore have passed back into that vast body of folktales current to this day, often without any knowledge of the work (the *Pañcatantra*) that the specific story or stories were once a part of. Works of fiction written later, such as Dandin's *Dasakumāracharitam* (*The Tale of Ten Princes*) and *Sukasaptati* (*Seventy Tales Told by The Parrot*), employ the frame structure of the *Pañcatantra*.

Like the great epic[11] the *Mahābhārata*, the *Pañcatantra* belongs to the rich, age-old oral literature of India. Even after it was committed to writing at some point in its transmission the work retains some of the characteristics of its origin as an oral text. We find certain formulaic phrases: 'as it is told'; 'as we have heard'; 'and then he said'. The use of two or three and sometimes several maxims or illustrations to make a point as in I.69, might also be a feature of patterns of *speech* rather than *writing*.

Because it belongs to the oral tradition of storytelling, the *Pañcatantra* has undergone continuous and constant revision. For it has been narrated repeatedly, countless number of times over the long period of nearly two millennia. In the quadrangles and pillared corridors of temples, in the palaces of princes and mansions of wealthy merchants, in fairgrounds and market squares under makeshift awnings and under the spreading banyan tree in villages, wherever skilled and celebrated storytellers gathered a group of eager listeners round them, this very popular work must have been narrated. Kālidāsa mentions 'village-elders/well-versed in the Udayana-tales', and 'skilful storytellers' who 'entertain their visiting kin', 'recounting old tales'. (*Meghadūtam*)

Music might have been a part of the narration: singing, drums and a primitive lute like the one still used by wandering minstrels and performers in the oral tradition. Miming and dance might also have been part of a storytelling session, as they still do in the country, forming part of the performances of contemporary storytellers such as the fabulous Teejan Bai and others. These have always been part of the storytelling tradition.[12] An example in the West of a story told to the accompaniment of music is that of the narration of *Peter and the Wolf*, with music by Prokofiev.

Since a text in the oral tradition is not *fixed* as a printed text is, a storyteller has some scope for inventiveness and a certain freedom to exercise his imagination. Working within certain given parameters, he can introduce changes by varying the details of narrative and dialogue; by expanding or condensing the discourse; by altering the point of view and so on. A skilled storyteller is both creator and narrator. By making revisions in the oral text handed down to him he exercises his rights as a creator while preserving the continuity of the tradition.

It might be assumed that revisions in an oral text are made with an eye to *relevance* to the place and time of narrator and audience.[13] The narrator or *storyteller* has a relationship with his audience and establishes a rapport with it that are denied the *storywriter*. He can improvise on the spur of the moment, adding something, leaving out something else because he has an instant feedback.

Any retelling of a work so popular in the country as the *Pañcatantra* would inevitably be different from 'the original', the

Ur-*Pañcatantra* (which we do not have),[14] in ways both subtle and substantive. The revisions lend an air of contemporaneity to the happenings of a distant past and introduce freshness into the telling of old tales, giving them new life. This is the way of all oral transmission.

Some of the retellings of the *Pañcatantra* would have been committed to writing, giving rise to the many recensions of the text that we now have. The various recensions do not present a uniform text. They do not all have the same stories. The stories they have in common are not always placed in the same order, or even in the same book. A few stories are transposed from one book into another. Maxims and illustrations vary. The reasons for the changes that we see in the different recensions of the text can be explained by the fact that a talented storyteller would not be content to tell a story as it has been told before; as it has been handed down to him. He revises. He leaves the impress of his sensibility and imagination, his observations of the manners and morals of men and women, and his comments on the vicissitudes of life.

We see the process of revision at work in the *Pūrṇabhadra* recension[15] on which the translation of this volume is based. This is a relatively late text of the *Pañcatantra* and is dated AD 1199. It was edited by Johannes Hertel and published as vol. XI of the Harvard Oriental Series, in 1915.

Pūrṇabhadra's text is longer because it includes stories not found in some other recensions; e.g. the pathetic tale of the pair of turtle-doves (III. *The Dove who sacrificed himself*). The discourses on ethics and policy are wide-ranging and elaborate. It has a number of lyrical and elegiac verses not found, for example, in very popular editions of the *Pañcatantra*.[16] To give a couple of examples, we have the following verse which is a part of the lamentation of Lively, the bull, whose world has crumbled faced with the treachery of his friend and lord:

> *Where Yamunā flows with deep blue water and sapphire-*
> *sparkles of glittering sands,*
> *there, in those depths, lies submerged the dark blue snake;*
> *coiling mass glossy as collyrium.*

Who would track him down there? Unless . . .
he is betrayed by gleams of brilliant star-gems clustered in the
circlets of his hoods?
By virtues raised to lofty heights,
by those same virtues the noble fall.

(I.289)

And in Book II, we have Goldy's litany of sorrows which concludes his parodic paean to Lust (*Tṛṣṇā*, consuming thirst); I quote the second of two verses:

Of foul stinking water I have drunk;
of clumps of mown grass I have made my bed;
grievous parting from my beloved I have endured;
with pain rising from deep down in my loins,
I have cringed and spoken humbly to strangers;
Footweary I have trudged and even crossed the seas;
a half-a-skull-bowl I have carried around.
Is there anything else you'd have me do, O, Desire.
Then for God's sake command me quickly
and be done with me.

(II.101)

There is a poignancy in these utterances. A strong personal note is struck and we forget that these lines are spoken by a poor bull facing certain death, and a humble mole burrowing in the ground who having lost his winter's store of food, bewails his lot. For a mole, food stored away is wealth; it is precious. These passages also indicate the sympathy felt by whoever introduced them into the text, for the lowliest of creatures. This sympathy (or empathy) is a distinctive feature of the *Pañcatantra*.

If we glance at the extra-Indian versions of the *Pañcatantra*, the manner in which revisions are carried out in them with an eye to *relevance* is seen very clearly. Though these versions are often described as 'translations', it is clear that they are by no means 'faithful' translations. They are more in the nature of adaptations. The Arabic version (*Kalilah wa Dimnah*) on which most of the

European versions are based makes substantive changes to the original text as we have it in India and introduces changes suited to the mores of another culture and religion. Since both the original Sanskrit text of the work and Burzoë's Pehlevi version, the first extra-Indian version—to the best of our knowledge—are lost, it is hard to tell at which point in the transmission changes came in. Therefore, the Arabic version of the AD eighth century has to be taken as the point of reference.

A sizeable part of the *Pancatantra* in an early form (or recension) is embedded in the *Kalilah wa Dimnah* within material drawn from other sources: stories, parables, homilies and the like. Since the Sanskrit text of which Burzoë made his Pehlevi version in AD 570 is lost, we cannot tell whether it *was* the original or a recension. In the case of a text in the oral tradition it is hard to fix on the original, pristine form in which it emerged from the hand of its author. The parts taken in and translated are mainly Book I, *Estrangement of Friends*, and a number of stories from the other four books. Names of the characters human and non-human, and of the locale, are changed, which is to be expected. For instance the bull, *Sanjivaka*, Lively, is called Shatrabah (Arabic), Senestra (Latin), Chiarino (Italian and North); *Pingalaka*, Tawny, remains anonymous; the two jackals, *Karataka*, *Damanaka* are Kalilag-Kalilah, Dimnag-Dimnah (old Syriac-Arabic), Celile-Dimna (Latin), Belile-Dimna (Spanish). Then strangely enough in the Italian and North they are changed into an anonymous ass and mule. There are numerous other changes of names and place names. But there are some drastic changes. For example, Book I has a sequel entitled *The Trial of Dimnah*. Dimnah is the treacherous jackal, *Damanaka*, Wily in our translation. The trial proceedings are initiated by the Queen Mother, the lion's mother, and a leopard minister is the chief witness in the court. Dimnah, the villain is tried, sentenced and executed. In North, the villainous mule is flayed alive, its flesh fed to the ravens and the bones offered up as a sacrifice in pious memory of the noble bull who was slain unjustly. Crime is punished and justice meted out in a cruel manner. But what is interesting to note, is that no blame attaches to the gullible lion.

The minister pays dearly, but the prince goes scot-free with not a word of censure spoken at any point in the narrative. These changes have been carried over into the European versions where further changes and adaptations seem to have been made at more than one level of transmission of the *Pañćatantra* text. The line of descent of the *Fables of Bidpai* is as follows: Arabic to Hebrew then into Latin; from Latin into other languages, mainly Spanish, from which Doni's Italian version and North's translation of it derive.

The conclusion of Book I with the trial and execution of the villainous jackal that are part of the extra-Indian versions is totally different from that in the *Pañćatantra* corpus and wholly alien to the spirit of the Indian work. It is also contrary to the objectives set out in the *Preamble* of the work—the education of princes; the 'awakening of their young minds'; the teaching of *niti*. Presumably it was not part of *the original* or of the text that Burzoë used for his Pehlevi version. Otherwise it would have shown up in one or other of the recensions of the text. It is highly probable that it was introduced into the Pehlevi text to adapt the original to a different culture so that it conformed to the mores and tastes of another society: Islamic society.

In certain recensions which Kale seems to have used, the lion, Tawny is consoled by Wily's predictably specious arguments and carries on, forgetting his grief and continuing to rule his kingdom with the two-timing Wily as minister. It is business as usual, it seems. On the other hand, the conclusion in the Pūrṇabhadra recension is different; it is inconclusive. Wily does not replace the noble Lively as chief minister. Wary, having waited for his friend (or brother?) Wily to return, seeks him out and finds him in the lion's presence. '*Seating himself beside the lion*', Wary now addresses Wily. The last words in Book I (429. -9, to the end, 436. +8) are given to Wary and not to Wily as in the other recensions referred to above.

Now, Wary is on centre-stage for the first time in the narrative. Up to now he has stood outside of the action, on the sidelines as it were. A minister out of office as noted at the beginning of the frame story of Book I, he keeps his distance from the court, watching the events as they take shape, from a vantage point on the periphery. He has made observations to Wily from time to time, disagreeing with the latter; or drawing his friend out shrewdly as if to unmask Wily's inmost thoughts, though not all his plans. Wary serves as a kind of sounding-board for his friend. Sometimes he makes a remark that seems ingenuous on the surface but is in fact made tongue-in-cheek. 'Can success really follow on a well-devised plan . . . ,' he asks Wily, 'Even if it is a deceitful plan?' (I.193.+1 to 3). And though he is well-versed in statecraft, as we realize at the end of Book I, Wary makes an observation or asks Wily a question as if he wants to know and learn. In fact, he is leading Wily on; e.g. I.153.+1, 'Evils?' queried Wary. 'What are these evils . . . ?' And Wily gives him and the audience the benefit of a long exposition on an aspect of polity—dangers to a state. Wary now eggs him on to disclose the bent of his mind. 'Your Honour has no power. How then can Lord Tawny be separated from Lively?' In reply, Wily hints that he is planning on doing some 'dirty tricks' (part of a scheming politician's 'stock-in-trade'); a clever ruse.

Wary is set up as a foil to Wily. Cautious, well-versed in statecraft, and learned, he articulates the principles that ought to govern the proper and rightful exercise of sovereignty, and the proper administration of the state by ministers and other high officials, as they are set down in the treatises; and of which Wily makes such a travesty (I. 345 to 349) In these verses two views are juxtaposed, of the politician and the statesman. To Wily, expediency, in the pejorative sense of the term, is the governing principle in all matters. For, in his world, expediency as prescribed in texts on polity and statecraft is not devising and carrying out a policy that is in the best interests of the state—the subjects and the ruler—but in his own personal interests, that is, self-aggrandizement. Wary's is the other voice that articulates the ethical concerns in the text. And he begins doing this after the first round of the fight to death of Tawny and Lively, lion and bull, monarch and minister (I. 353.-9 to 375). In this long passage of verse and prose, Wary is outspoken and tells Wily in a forthright manner what he had only subtly hinted at before.

From the point of view of structure, Wary's questions and observations that convey his misgivings, provide the opening for the 'emboxed' tales—the tales set within the frame story. They also give the author a way of introducing the discourses on ethics and polity and of marshalling opposing sets of opinions and arguments. We see that in Book III, such discourses and setting forth of different points of view on policy are also present, but handled with less art and artistry.

In the concluding portion of the narrative in the frame story of Book I, Wary lays out the guiding principles that the monarch and minister are expected to follow—*Nīti*. The *Pañcatantra* is a *nītiśāstra*, but it is not simply a manual of instruction for princes and others. It is much more than that; otherwise it would not have retained the sustained and continuing appeal it has had for more than two millennia. It is a *nītiśāstra* of the type of which the *Mahābhārata* is the supreme example. It poses questions and problems that arise daily in the lives of all, princes or peasant. These are presented in real life situations that demand solutions. Saints, villains, fools, learned persons, rogues, decent men and women—it is a vast gallery—and it is their actions that are held up in a mirror.

Nīti is a word like some others in Sanskrit, *dharma* for example, that is impossible to render into English by the use of a single word. It comprises meanings that convey several closely linked ideas. In fact it signifies an attitude and conduct that expresses and represents a whole way of life. The concept of *nīti* would include carrying out duties and obligations, familial and socio-political, and the exercise of practical wisdom in affairs private and public: the wisdom not of a saint or a sage but the wisdom that has to govern the thinking and conduct of persons who are of the world, and who are in the world. *Nīti* would entail resolute action taken after careful scrutiny and due deliberation. A discriminating judgement has to be brought to bear on all issues, problems and situations. Stark distinctions of black and white, right and wrong, good and evil can seldom be made in the sphere of human actions, though they are being made all the time. And this is specially true in the case of princes, rulers, administrators and the like. An all-round and harmonious development of human powers is the basis of *nīti*; obsessions have no part in it, but good sense and good feeling do. To live wisely and well in the truest sense of these two terms—*that* is *niti*.

The *Pañcatantra* might have been originally designed for the use of monarchs as a mirror for princes, a pattern for a just ruler in the art of government and in the conduct of his private life and relationships. Because the private and the public areas of living are both parts of a whole, the two cannot be separated and compartmentalized. *Niti* applies at all levels. Further, this work goes beyond the education of princes. It is meant for all men and women. Many of the tales are about ordinary people going about the normal business of living rightly or wrongly.

In the colophon of our text, the redactor, Pūrṇabhadra, characterizes Viṣṇu Śarma's work as a manual on the art of government—*nripanītiśāstra*, (also known as *rājanītiśāstra*)—thus somewhat limiting its validity and applicability. It suggests that *nripanīti* or *rājanīti*, the wise conduct of rulers is a category of conduct separate and on its own. That is not so. It is Wily who, as we remember, draws a stark distinction between 'the nature and norms of the commoner' and those of princes whose policy is 'protean', assuming 'many forms like a courtesan'. (I.428)

> *What are vices in ordinary men,*
> *those very vices are virtues in kings.*
>
> (I. 427.3,4)

But the text clearly indicates that *niti* applies to all persons.

Wary's last speech addressed to monarch and minister and to the audience is like an epilogue spoken before the curtain comes down on a quasi-tragic drama. He is even-handed in apportioning blame and proffering good counsel. The responsibilities of both ruler and minister are spelled out clearly and emphatically. The epilogue sums up the essence of what has been stated and exemplified many times already in the narrative through precept and story.

There is a short but perhaps significant phrase in the sentence that Wary speaks before he begins castigating Wily severely (I. 428. +1, 2). It describes Wary thus: 'Seated properly

beside the lion, he addressed himself to Wily'.[17] Does that
suggest that Wary might have become Tawny's chief minister?
We cannot say, because, the text is open-ended. Questions are
raised in our minds and uncertainties surface. It is not certain
whether the ruler, Tawny, saw the wisdom couched in the words
of the elder statesman, Wary and profited by it or not. Up to now
Tawny has been a weak and irresolute ruler, gullible and easy to
manipulate, though he certainly possesses some fine qualities:
magnanimity, loyalty and a basic sense of right and wrong. But
he is wanting in judgement and in Wary's words, 'a person whose
mind retreats before the persuasive speech of others'. He is not
'master of his own thinking, uninfluenced by other
pressures . . . . ' (I. 436. +1, 2). And, needless to say, Wily is
extremely clever and knows the texts on statecraft well enough
to use them to his own advantage. The question to ask therefore
is, whether the prince (Tawny) remained as he was, unchanged
by any part of his experience; or did he weigh the two opposed
sets of views placed before him in the last scene, one, callously
opportunistic by Wily (I. 427.-2 to 428), and the other, by Wary,
wise and well thought out, pointing out the qualities necessary
in a wise and loyal minister and a wise and discerning ruler. The
firefly is not fire; what is false appears to be true; the true seems
false. So do not be deceived by appearances but look carefully
into the rights and wrongs of a case. A crafty retainer might be
motivated by sheer self-interest and therefore a monarch should
consult several ministers, deliberate over their counsel and come
to his own decision. This is the gist of Wary's cautionary
comments to his king, Tawny. This is the way of *nīti*. Did Tawny
follow *nīti*?

The text does not impose an ending, narratively or
otherwise. It leaves it open to listeners and readers to ponder over
the matter and wrestle with the disturbing possibilities. I suggest
that this inconclusiveness is deliberate; Viṣṇu Śarma (in this
recension) has a purpose in so doing, as I shall endeavour to show
presently.

There are other doubts and uncertainties that surface. Some
of Wary's comments and the despair he is plunged into suggest

two possibilities; that the lion may not have survived as ruler, or
that he may not have survived at all. 'Seeing his master in a
pitiable condition', Wary laments, 'Alas, alas! What calamity is
this that has befallen our lord . . . all from listening to evil
counsel!' He adds that by listening to 'the counsels of base men',
rulers 'enter the cage of evils thronged by *rivals*'. (I. 364. +1 to 2;
365). He also says: 'By your actions, sir, you have brought
disorder and confusion into this whole forest-domain.' (I.353.-4
to -2) An ill-considered and unjust act has repercussions in the
whole kingdom. But that is not all. The downfall of the minister
(Wily), and his family is also hinted at. 'The pity of it however is,
that you have striven hard to bring about not only the destruction
of your own family but of our master as well. Since you have thus
chosen to reduce our lord even to this *pitiable condition*, it is clear
that you care for no one but *yourself*'. (I. 399 +1 to 5). Even this,
self-interest, is at risk. For,

> *Expert in recounting the vices of others,*
> *devoted to praise of his own virtues,*
> *skilled in engineering everyone's ruin,*
> *the villain—wills his own retribution.*
>
> (I. 397)

Wary's many comments suggest a general ruination of ruler and
state, as a possibility.

The three princes who are the first of the many audiences
that the *Pañcatantra* has addressed itself to, would have listened
carefully to the epilogue, for it contains the final words, the advice
that the first narrator/storyteller leaves his audience with.
Questions would have been raised in their minds as they have
been in ours; disturbing questions pointing the way to several
possibilities that have been suggested in the previous pages. If at
this point, we look carefully at the words spoken by Viṣṇu Śarma
to the king at the start of the work, we are on to something
significant. The eighty-year-old teacher proclaims that if he did
not succeed in making the princes gain *unrivalled knowledge* and
understanding of *nīti* in six months' time, the king would be at

liberty to boot him out in disgrace. A tall claim and preposterous? An incredible one indeed, but only if we were to take the 'lion-roar' of the venerable teacher at its face value and interpret it literally. But, obviously, we are not meant to do that. For to do so would be to make Viṣṇu Śarma's claim an idle boast, and not a 'lion-roar'. The king himself who had a lot more at stake than we (the readers) have, kept an open mind, very wisely. The opening lines of the *Preamble* gives us a character sketch of the king: a powerful monarch of a prosperous and extensive kingdom; brave and learned; a warrior and scholar.

Three words used in the *Preamble* give us a clue. *Buddhiprabodhanam*, awakening of the intellect; *prabuddhah*, with their intellect fully awakened—both depth and extensive range of understanding are signified by the prefix 'pra'; and *avabodhanartham*, for the purpose of awakening the intellect. *Buddhi* signifies not merely the intellect; it includes understanding and signifies the whole intellective process. All three point to one aim—the *awakening* of the mind or intellect and understanding. Viṣṇu Śarma's objective is not providing formal instruction in polity and allied branches of knowledge and learning, using perhaps traditional methods of which learning by rote of definitions, precepts, illustrations is a part, as implied in the statement of the king's ministers that it takes twelve years to master the 'science of words'—grammar. That has been tried and failed, as we gather from the opening section of the *Preamble*, *reading between the lines*. It appears that instructors have come and gone but the princes have remained 'unlettered' and ignorant. I have used a qualifying phrase here—'reading between the lines'—advisedly, because in the storytelling tradition, every detail in the narrative is not spelled out. The reason being that the storyteller has another language that he makes good use of: gesture, stance, facial expression and tone of voice. A curling of the lip, an arching of the eyebrows, widening or narrowing of the eyes, a sob or sneer or little laugh, these speak volumes. A story writer does not have this 'other' language. He/she has only words. It is noticeable that the text frequently or nearly always uses formulaic phrases such as: 'then he said'; 'and he replied';

'she asked', and so on. *How* it was said—wryly, ingenuously, with disbelief or sarcasm—is not stated. The context might in places indicate the particular nuance, or it might not. Without the body-language, ambivalence arises. For example, in the following lines: 'Whereupon, Wary observed, "Why, in that case, if Your Honour is such a man, one who has made his decision, go ahead; work towards accomplishing your goal; and good luck,"' (I.215.-15 to -13), is Wary, in responding to his friend (or brother?) Wily's observation that he had a stratagem to sow discord between the two friends, the lion and the bull, and had decided to use it, being ironic or ingenuous or indifferent? Or is he genuinely unaware of the lengths to which Wily would go to get what he wanted? This ambivalence provides scope for different interpretations of character in the storytelling tradition.

The image of 'the noble bird', 'the swan', that separates milk from the water it is mixed with, is significant, because it conveys the idea that the princes should be taught only what is *essential*. What Minister Goodsense implies here is that the dead wood that forms a good part of all academic curricula in all systems of education, would only burden the minds of the princes, blunt their intelligence and dull their interest in learning.

The princes (and we ought to be clear on this point), are not stupid; they are 'unlettered' and ignorant. As the king, their father says, 'they lack judgement', being 'averse to learning'. How to *awaken* their intelligence is the problem the king faces, and he puts it to his council of ministers that some way of awakening the intelligence of the princes has to be found in the interests of the kingdom.

'To *awaken* the intelligence': this is Viṣṇu Śarma's objective. He has to *educate* the princes to fit them for their future high office and all the responsibilities it carries. They have to become able and wise rulers of great kingdoms like their father. The *Preamble* opens with a description of King Amara Śakti as a warrior, a scholar well-versed and expert in all branches of polity and economics, and accomplished in all the arts. In short, the king is a rounded and versatile man; an ideal ruler. This passage is composed in an ornate and elaborate style with long compounds that sets it apart from the simple narrative and dialogue that follow. It draws attention to itself; it directs the reader to pay attention; for this is a pen-picture of the ideal king.

Viṣṇu Śarma, on his part, is confident that he will succeed in the task he has set himself. This is suggested by the word he uses to describe his solemn promise to the king—'lion-roar'. His confidence is based on his recognition that the princes need a different system of education which he would provide. Viṣṇu Śarma's pedagogy is different; it is new. His aim is to teach the princes *how* to think, not *what* to think.

> 'With mere book-learning men remain fools;
> the man who acts using his knowledge, he is wise.'

(II.109.1,2)

says Slowcoach, the tortoise to his friend Goldy, the mole. Further, 'mere book learning' without practical good sense, might even turn out dangerous, as the tale of the four Brāhmanas exemplifies. Three of them who prided themselves on their superb scholarship and their mastery over 'all branches of learning', put together the skeleton of a lion, clothed it with skin and flesh and revived it by breathing life into the carcass, only to be killed by the lion. Whereas, the fourth Brāhmana whom they had sneered at because he had only common sense and no pretensions to scholarship, climbed up a tree before the lion was revived and lived to tell the tale (V. *The Scholars who brought a dead lion to life*).

To fulfil his task of educating the young princes, Viṣṇu Śarma devises a novel method of instruction which uses life and its varied experiences as the textbook. He presents real life situations and problems in the guise of stories that would rouse and sustain the interest of his pupils while teasing them into thought. It is to be presumed that once the princes had been trained to think and use their minds constructively, they were bound to develop an interest in acquiring knowledge. So many texts are referred to and quoted from in the tales that any intelligent person would be possessed by a desire to know more about them and get to read them. It is all a matter of using the right method and opening windows to an intelligent person.

In a deep sense, storytelling is theatre, with one man or woman playing several roles. The young princes watch how the characters in the tales, both human and non-human think, feel, and act in situations many of which would be similar to situations that they would find themselves in at one time or another, as rulers. They see how they should or should not act when faced by problems arising in their public and private lives. The motivations of those who surround princes—ministers, retainers, attendants, parasites and family—are laid bare. As men and women from all walks of life pass before their mind's eye, the princes also acquire a knowledge of the conduct and actions of ordinary people, their future subjects. As the frame story of Book I which begins the storytelling session, is set in *Mahilāropya*, their own city and their father's capital, it is a familiar scene; and yet not quite familiar because it is distanced from their world by being placed in another time—a story-book time.

The city is described in a passage that sets it apart from the narrative following, by the use of the ornate style with long compounds and a passive construction that we have already noted. Seven long compound words and two short phrases which, split up, take a whole paragraph in the English rendering, present this fabulous city to the audience. It is a story-book world.

The *Pañcatantra* is not strictly theatre in the technical sense as it is generally defined and accepted.[18] There are differences between formal theatre and the kind of theatre involved in the technique and practices of storytelling. For one thing, this work paces itself in a leisurely and relaxed manner. It pauses at certain points in the narrative, some crucial, to interrupt the narrative flow and introduce a new tale: e.g., the tale of the former captivity of Speckle, the deer, is introduced at the moment he lies trapped and in imminent danger (II. tale 9). A maxim is stated, or a short passage of dialogue with a comment on the power of Fate, as in this case, and a tale is introduced. This is part of the technique of storytelling by which wise counselling is combined with entertaining storytelling and ought not to be regarded as a defect as is sometimes done. No more than the spectacle of a coloratura,[19] stabbed to the heart, gasping out her life's breath in a series of trills and cadenzas and finally dying on a high C that fades gradually into silence, is a defect. It is part of the musical interest in an opera.

For another, the *Pañcatantra* deploys a vast variety of characters drawn from high life and low, town and country in the human world, and also brings within its ambit a whole new world—the world of nature with its own hierarchy of high and low, strong and weak, predator and prey. In both respects, the *Pañcatantra* is like the Indian epic with which it has a strong and close kinship.

The work represents society at many levels. But it does something more; and it does it in a highly self-conscious manner. It holds a mirror up to society. The tales are not entertainment, pure and simple. That is one part and an important part of the aims of the work. Edification or instruction is another, equally important. *Education* in the art of living wisely and well; *niti*, is one of its aims. The *Pañcatantra* has a dual perspective.

The *Pañcatantra* presents two worlds, one mirroring the other. We cannot see ourselves as we really are, truly and completely, except in a mirror as a reflection, flattering or otherwise. We have to stand back to look at ourselves, our conduct and our actions. Since we get overly involved in the daily motions of living, we do not always see a pattern and meaning in events and circumstances until we view it presented before us. And what is more, we see and understand it better when they are presented as happening elsewhere to others. And this the *Pañcatantra* does very effectively. The two worlds—human and non-human—dialogue with each other and/or comment on each other.

In addition to these two worlds, Book V introduces a third, a twilight world where elements of magic and dream-illusion, of the grotesque and macabre are present to create a tone and atmosphere different from that of the other books. Inhabiting the blurred landscape between reality and fantasy, this twilight world also holds up a mirror, a distorting one that is disturbing. Dreams crumble or turn into nightmares.

The narrative of the *Pañcatantra* moves constantly back and forth, from one world into the other. The frame story of Book I is the clearest illustration of this movement. Abandoned by man in his hour of distress, Lively, the noble bull, hobbles painfully to the lush meadows by the sacred river, Yamunā. Freed from man's yoke, he is soon restored to health and vigour and he roams joyously resembling 'Śiva's bull', with not a single human being in sight. The meadows bordering the sacred river, lush and 'emerald-green', is a place of freedom, joy and plentitude. It is paradisal. There are other similar paradisal 'spaces' in the work; for example in the frame stories of Books II and IV. In the former we have the idyllic haunts of the four friends, the mole, the crow, the tortoise and the deer, in shady groves by the shores of a great lake deep in the heart of a 'dense forest', far from the human world with its drought, famine and slaughter that Goldy, the mole, and Lightwing, the crow, flee from. In Book IV there is another idyllic spot, where a mighty rose-apple tree grows by the seashore, bearing a profusion of delicious ambrosial[20] fruit the year round. The ape, Redface, lives there until the wife of his friend, the crocodile, disrupts the peace and happiness of his world.

Lively's brief sojourn in the meadows by the sacred river is a blissful interregnum between his two stays in the forest-world. He has already been there once and met with the accident that left him limp and broken. He is drawn again into the forest-world where he finally meets his death. As we enter this 'other' world with Lively, we notice immediately that the two worlds of man and nature are astonishingly alike. The world of nature is a mirror-world.

Relationships between the two worlds are established by means of certain links. The social and political organization they have in common is notable as a link. There is a court in the forest, with a king and a hierarchy of office and of duties—the Four Circles or Mandalas. 'It is said,' speaks the narrator, 'in any city or capital . . . or any sort of community of people, there can be only one occupant of the lion's post.' (I. 5.-45 to -43) The lion's post is the seat of sovereignty surrounded by the other three circles or orders of hierarchy in a state. What these are is not quite clear.

The three orders could be ministers, courtiers or retainers, and attendants or menials. Or they could stand for court, city and country. The passage cited clearly draws an analogy between the human community and the natural community in the forest. The court of *Piṅgalaka* (Tawny), King of the Forest is like any other royal court. It is a paramount state with 'ministers, and others who were in his (the king's) secret counsels'; a royal retinue, assembly (*sabhā*—I. 234. 1, 2: 'Once acclaimed in the open Assembly as "Behold, here is a man of merit,"'), doorkeeper or chamberlain and attendants. The 'state' in the forests also has its share of power politics and the motivations lying behind the play of power politics: envy, greed, ambition, jockeying for royal favour and high position.

Another link between the two worlds and their societies is effected through projection. Human beings tend to project their own emotions (or the lack of it) on to the world of nature; to attribute to other forms of life traits of character and behaviour, and qualities noble or vicious, good or bad, that are essentially human; and quite mistakenly. This might be a way of entering into a relationship with 'the other'; of escaping from a solipsist world into an exploration of a different world. Expressions such as, 'brave as a lion', 'mean as a jackal', 'wise as an owl', 'vicious as a snake', come to mind. The tales of the *Pañcatantra* belie such confident and complacent assumptions that human beings make, often wrongly. The 'people' of woods and waters are not quite like us; but the point that the *Pañcatantra* tales make is that they are *people*. Tawny, when he is first introduced to us in the frame story of Book I, is presented as standing, frozen in his tracks, shaken and 'deeply troubled at heart' on hearing the tremendous bellowing of Lively, the bull. The King of Owls (Book III) is scarcely wise. The snake (I. *The Grateful Beasts and the Ungrateful Man*) is not vicious but actually grateful, wise and helpful.

The non-human characters in the *Pañcatantra* merely appear to be creatures of the world of nature, of woods and waters and hills. In fact they are human actors wearing masks. The masks are fairly transparent. They have to be for the text to fulfil the objectives it has set itself: education in the broadest sense of the term. The text exploits human perceptions of the non-human world, sometimes correct and frequently wrong, together with certain superficial similarities in behaviour—an animal reacts to something unusual like a sudden sound, it may be a light rustling or deafening bellowing, to become alert and wary as Tawny does when he hears Lively letting out thundering peals of sheer delight—to make identification of 'us' with the 'other' possible. Without this identification, the learning process for the princes and all others who listened to the storytellers of the past, and the readers who still 'listen' to the text as they read it, will not get off the ground. Viṣṇu Śarma requires that the princes look at the world of nature, at the same time bringing to bear on the tales, their culture-conditioned perceptions—the jackal is mean, the bull is noble, the turtle-dove is constant, and so on—as people and learn from it.

The world of nature functions as a metaphor for the human world. It is the basic image in the text and is employed consistently to sustain and convey the message. The natural world wears two faces: the *jungle*, where nature is red in tooth and claw and each one looks out for himself; and the *community* where co-existence prevails and each looks out for the other, as in the frame story of Book II, and in some of the sub-tales (Book I. *The Lapwing who defied the Ocean* and Book II. *The Mice that freed the Elephants*). In certain other subtales the members of a species band together against a common threat, or, several species work together to outwit a common enemy (Book I. *The Crow and the Serpent, Dim Wit and the Hare, The Sparrow and the Tusker* and Book II. *The Mice that freed the Elephants*). These are no doubt human perceptions. The stories are not about animals and their behaviour, their ways of bonding or banding together, or of their fighting. This is not to say that there is not close observation of animals and other non-human forms of life; for there is. And there is ample evidence in the stories of the understanding and the sympathy for them that flows out of close observation. It forms part of the characterizations of these extraordinary creatures, and accounts for the charm of the *Pancatantra* tales. But the main purpose of the work, or rather its avowed purpose, is something else; it is to inculcate *nīti* in the young princes and in others who come after them. 'Since then, this work on *nīti* (practical wisdom) has become celebrated as an excellent means of awakening and training young minds,' (*Preamble*. stanza 3. -2).

The natural world is human society transposed and thereby distanced. For example, Wily, the jackal in the frame story of Book I, *is* an ambitious, callously opportunistic politician out for what he can get. Longlegs, the lapwing (I. *The Lapwing who defied the Ocean*) is a person with an overweening sense of self-importance who pays for it; the eggs of the lapwing pair are stolen by the ocean. But the ocean is also humbled for acting with such arrogance as it does, pitting its tremendous power against a pitifully small bird standing on its shores, puffing out his puny chest in defiance. The donkey who claims to be a musicologist and wishes to sing under the moonlight, is simply a 'pompous ass'. He knows everything in the texts on music that a good singer ought to know; he lacks only one thing—a good voice (V. tale 5). On the other hand, no bird worth its salt would bother to pursue a vendetta with such determination as the sparrow does (I. tale 19); for that indeed, is a human trait.

Not for a single moment is the reader permitted to forget that this fabulous work by Viṣṇu Śarma is all about human beings; about human society and political organization; about human virtues, vices and foibles. It points to the nobility in man and to his baseness; to the heights he can scale and the depths to which he falls.

The text sets up prominent signposts at various points in the narrative to remind us of this. For instance, Lively, the bull is described as learned in many branches of knowledge and possesses a store of wisdom gained through his studies. And he is a good teacher too (I. 110.-12 to -6). Goldy, Lightwing, Slowcoach and Speckle, the four friends in the frame story of Book II, are also scholars with a fund of learning; the right kind of learning that is a judicious blend of book-learning with sound practical sense. They also have the right attitude to living. Each leads his separate life; but they meet daily under the pleasant shade of trees beside the lake to discuss matters relating to the

Law, economics, polity and other allied subjects (*dharma*, *artha*, etc.). Theirs is a community modelled on the forest-hermitages of ancient sages. Some of the dwellers of forest and lake have a keen wit and can turn a neat phrase. So well-educated are they with the ability to converse on a variety of subjects, quoting chapter and verse with such facility, that they could be the envy of many a specialist in the human world who cultivates his/her little patch of scholarship with assiduity, not looking over the hedge at other fields.

Talking animals and birds are present in Indian literature from earliest times. In the *Ṛg-Veda* (10: 108) Saramā, the hound of heaven, goes over the wild wastes of water as an ambassador to negotiate a trade deal for her masters (devas) with the *Paṇis* (merchants), and fails. The golden wild goose in the *Mahābhārata* story of King Nala and Princess Damayantī carries love-messages between the two which lead to their marriage. A bull, a wild goose and a diver instruct the Brāhmaṇa pupil, Satyakāma, in matters relating to the nature of Reality (*Ćandogya Upaniṣad*, IV: 5, 7, 8). In many ancient cultures, non-human forms of life, birds, animals and even trees were believed to have suprahuman abilities and powers; to possess a special kind of wisdom and to bear a special relationship to the sacred. Further, Indian thought and belief does not make a stark distinction between human and non-human orders of being. All are parts of a *whole*; all possess that spark of divinity that is in man.

In a literary tradition that springs from a world view such as the one outlined above, it is natural to put words of wisdom into the mouths of non-human characters. It is easy for the human and natural worlds to interact as smoothly as they do and comment on each other. Viṣṇu Śarma has a precedent in the examples cited to use animals, birds and other creatures of the world of nature as vehicles for instruction, both in the context of *realpolitik* and the larger ethical context. The concept of *nīti*, as discussed earlier is comprehensive and applies to the whole range of human action.

The *Pañcatantra* is even-handed in its criticism of the conduct and motives of people; merchants, tradesmen, monks, scholars,

judges; the uxorious husband and deceitful wife, the gluttonous
or feckless Brāhmaṇa and the cruel hunter, the rash and
imprudent and the cold and calculating; everyone gets a fair share
of criticism. Fools and knaves, the too-trusting and the conniving
person, are castigated equally sharply. The pompous and
garrulous are held up to ridicule. Princes and women, however,
come in for some trenchant criticism, perhaps only apparently.
There is a long and sharply-worded diatribe against women in
general in I. 138 to 146.

> *This whirlpool of suspicion, this mansion of immodesty, this*
> *city of audacity*
> *this sanctuary of errors, this home of a hundred deceits,*
>
> *
>
> *. . . this casket entire of tricks:—*
> *Who created this contraption called Woman? . . .*
> *To set Virtue and the Law at naught?*
>
> (I. 142)[21]

But the effect of this passionate castigation of the female sex is
somewhat changed by the fact that it forms part of a story told
by the villainous jackal, Wily, to illustrate his maxim that the ends
justify the means (I. *The Weaver's Unfaithful Wife*) and by the
further fact that it is put into the mouth of a holy man who is
worldly but not wise. A piece of moral criticism depends for its
efficacy on who the speaker is and what kind of a person he/she
is. As against this outburst against women, we have the stories
of the girl who is married to a snake (I. *The Maiden wedded to a
Snake*) and the princess who is married to the sick prince whose
life is being sucked out gradually by a snake in his belly (III. *The
Snake in the Prince's belly*) both of whom accept the husbands
chosen for them cheerfully and care for them; and of the female
turtle-dove who is a model of constancy and forgiveness (III. *The
Dove who sacrificed himself*).

  Never put your trust in creatures with horns or claws, men
who bear arms, women, flowing streams 'and the whole cursed
lot of princes', says Wary. For princes are like serpents,

formed coil upon coil,
encased in smooth, sinuous scales,
cruel, tortuous in movement,
menacingly fierce, savage . . .

(I. 49)

and they are like mountains, 'with ups and downs and hearts of stones' (I. 50. 1, 2). Their minds are houses full of hidden serpents, forests swarming with predators and beautiful pools where crocodiles lurk under the lotuses. The castigation of princes is surprisingly candid considering that this is a work written primarily for them.

Satire is perhaps too strong a word to use for the kind of corrective criticism we find in the *Pañćatantra*. Education might be a more appropriate term; for education includes both instruction and correction. The *Pañćatantra* is distinguished by two features which it is important to note. First, it does not set up impracticable ideals for men and women in a social and political context. Its main concern and the thrust of the work is to layout the way of *nīti*, living wisely and well in the truest sense of these two terms, through story and precept. Second, the conception of *nīti* is based on and articulates a very central and fundamental concept of Indian thought, that of the *purushārthas*: *dharma*, *artha* and *kāma*, the triple aims of human existence, on which society is grounded and which forms the framework for all human action and relationships. This threefold existential scheme provides the philosophical structure for the *Pañćatantra*.

Dharma has several meanings: the Law,[22] righteousness, duty, moral and social order, the inherent property or quality of a thing. *Artha* signifies the economy, all material resources and their management. *Kāma* is Desire in the broadest scene of the term, and Will. The three terms embrace the whole of an individual's life: the ethical and social, the material and economic and the emotional dimensions. A fourth goal, *moksa*, release or ultimate freedom from all worldly concerns and pursuits was posited, added at some later stage in the evolution of philosophical thought. But though this was present as an ultimate goal, it was to come at the end of an individual's life and perhaps not a goal for everyone except in an academic sense. In the *Pañcatantra* only one tale (not found in all recensions of the text), presents *mokṣa*—the tale of the turtle-doves (III. *The Dove who sacrificed himself*).

To outline these three aims of existence, I take up the first, *dharma*. *Dharma* is both absolute and relative. It is relative because the observance of *dharma* depends on an individual's place in the scheme of things and the duties pertaining to that place. *Dharma*, in the sense of the Law, prescribes duties, responsibilities and rights appropriate to an individual in the social order and station of life. For example, it is the *dharma* of a king and warrior to fight and shed blood in the defence of his land and people. If a ruler confronted by naked aggression is too weak and has scant resources to fight a powerful enemy, the Law recommends that he may resort to underhand means to protect himself, his kingdom and subjects. Book III of the text exemplifies this. Cloud Hue, King of Crows is a ruler who has to defend his kingdom and subjects against a cruel enemy. And he does this by employing a clever ruse suggested by his minister. Obviously, a private individual is not expected to rush out and burn his neighbour's home and family to avenge some wrongdoing, since he does have recourse to the law and the courts. On the other hand, the tale of the turtle-doves in the same book illustrates the observance of the principle of *dharma* in an absolute sense. Theirs is saintly conduct. Their reward is in the hereafter and their happiness is deferred until they are 'translated' into another life in another world. The meek and forgiving do not inherit this earth.

The principle of *dharma* operates at all levels of life, and not simply at the human level. The snake (I. *The Grateful Beasts and the Ungrateful Man*) tells the Brāhmaṇa who is terrified of helping him out of the well: 'Sir, we are not free agents; we would not bite a soul if we were not constrained to do so.' Venom is the inbuilt defence of certain creatures; it is an inherent quality in them, enabling them to survive.

Coming to the second goal of human existence which is *artha*, the acquisition of wealth and other material resources, it is perhaps pertinent to point out that Indian thought has in no way and at no time believed in or recommended the pursuit of an other-worldly objective to the exclusion of all else. To live in this world, wealth (or money) is needed. The *Pancatantra* states this need insistently and emphatically. To do without wealth, a person has to follow the path of the great sages and retreat into the forest or lonely mountain caves. That *is* an option for anyone who prefers it, in which case the individual is opting out of the socio-political world.

The text repeatedly expatiates on the evils of poverty, especially in Books II and V (II.68 to 75). 'Ha! A plague upon this poverty,' says Goldy, the mole when he has been deprived of all his wealth by the two monks, Crumplyear and Broadbottom. He has also lost his power and status as a consequence. Overnight he has become a beggar and without honour among his own people (II.76.-7 to 85). As he broods he exclaims bitterly: 'Alas! Poverty is the root of all evils.' Goldy continues to brood: 'Yes, beggary is as terrible as death,' he says. But in fact it is worse, much worse, for even a corpse knows well that 'a man is better dead than poor', (V.18) and would not exchange his lot with that of a beggar. The ills of poverty are put in a telling manner and with wit in this verse:

Wit, kindliness and modesty,
sweetness of speech and youthful beauty,
liveliness too and vitality;
freedom from sorrow, and joviality;
uprightness, knowledge of sacred texts;
the wisdom of the Preceptor of the Immortals;
purity as well of mind and body;
respect too for rules of right conduct:
all these fine attributes arise in people,
   once their belly-pot is full.

(V.73)

But money is not everything and it has no value in itself. It is a means to living wisely and well. It has to be put to good use for oneself and for others. The *Pañcatantra* does not recommend the uncontrolled pursuit of amassing wealth. The greater part of Book V is a criticism of greed. Further it warns against unprincipled methods of making money. What is earned is to be earned with honour and integrity and used well, giving to others and sharing.

> *You may have only a morsel yourself,*
> *why not give half of it to a suppliant?*

(II. 54. 1, 2)

> *The poor man can only offer his mite,*
> *but the reward he reaps, the Vedas say,*

(II. 55. 1, 2)

is as great as that which the rich gain by their munificence.

Finally, looking at the third goal, Desire and Will; again the *Pañcatantra* lays emphasis on the middle way, on moderation and restraint. Excessive desire in all forms is to be curbed; but to be without any desire is to lack success and achievement. The will to act, to achieve the right goals, to yoke all one's powers and abilities to worthwhile enterprises and persevere until success crowns a person's efforts, is manliness. To desire the good things of life that are lawful and do not injure others, brings happiness—family, friends, good company.

> *Those who enjoy happy times,*
> *friends with dear friends,*
> *lovers with their beloved,*
> *joyful with the joyous . . .*

(II. 162)

only they 'live life to the fullest; they are the salt of the earth'.

However, it is friendship that is given a special place, and set above all other relationships. It is singled out for high praise as one of the most important requisites for the good life. True friendship is possible only between equals and with noble minds who are good and wise and 'cherished for their learning, their refinement, their discipline' (II.179). Such friendships, close-knit like 'flesh and claw difficult to split' (or 'flesh and nail' in the human context) are a blessing, opening out trails in life's wilderness.

> *A chalice of trust and affection,*
> *a sanctuary from sorrow, anxiety and fear—*
> *Who created this priceless gem—a friend,*
> *a word of just two syllables—Mitra?*

(II. 194)

The frame story of Book II is a testimony to this true friendship. When Goldy comes with Lightwing to the great lake that is the home of Slowcoach, he is neurotic being ridden by obsessions. First, it is an obsession with gathering material resources (*artha*), then with the desire for vengeance and last, with a feeling of total despair brought on by acute shame. He is restored to health in the tranquillity of his surroundings and the company of good and wise friends.

The aim of the *Pañcatantra* is to inculcate the importance of a harmonious development of all the powers of man; to balance the needs and demands of the individual in society so that the ethical, social, material and emotional aspects of personality may be integrated and lead to a life that is lived wisely and well in the truest sense of these terms. This is *niti*. To be free from fear and want is the basic need. Other values are then built on it: giving and receiving, friendship and affection, kindliness and compassion for the needy and distressed, the intelligent use of learning and the rightful use of intelligence, the exercise of judgement and prudence, deliberation before acting, followed by resolute action, giving the best an individual can to succeed in worthwhile enterprises. This is the wisdom conveyed by the *Pañcatantra*, a gentle and practical wisdom. There is no prophetic fervour calling fire and brimstone down on the head of fool and knave; no strident notes are struck. The *Pañcatantra* sets forth a very civilized view of life; a noble way of living which man can aspire to. To characterize this work as unmoral or amoral as has been done at times, is to do it gross injustice. And now we shall examine the artistic form in which this noble and civilized view of life and the ability of human beings to achieve it, if only they had the will to do so, has been presented by Viṣṇu Śarma.

II

Storytelling is an ancient art in India going back to the earliest literature. It formed part of the rituals surrounding the great sacrifices performed during vedic and epic times. We know from the *Mahābhārata* that storytelling sessions were held in the intervals between the performance of sacrifices that often stretched over long periods of time, days, weeks, even months. Little stories are embedded in the Brāhmana literature[23] between explanations of the rituals of sacrifice. The stories of *Śakuntalā* and *Urvaśi-Purūravas*, which later provided Kālidāsa with the plots of two of his great plays, are found in the *Śatapatha Brāhmana*. The *Mahābhārata* is a veritable mine of stories. But the *Pañcatantra* and the *Jātaka Tales* to which we have already referred, are the oldest surviving works of fiction that form artistic and cohesive wholes. (The *Bṛhatkathā*[24] of Gunādhya has been lost; only parts of it are preserved, embedded in later works of fiction.) These two works, the *Pañcatantra* and the *Jātaka Tales* have many stories in common, which suggests that they have in part, a common source in some distant, undateable past, in the floating body of stories and legends current in societies from the very earliest times. These would be popular and moral tales, fairy and folk-tales and fables. Some of these stories common to the two works are depicted in the Bharhut friezes (second century BC). Stone is a more durable medium for art than birch bark and palm leaves, in spite of vandalism of many sorts that monumental architecture and stone sculpture have been subjected to in India in the long march of centuries.

Of the two works, the *Pañcatantra* has a unique structure. It is hardly accurate to describe it as a 'collection' of stories as is sometimes done. A collection of stories consists of single, individual tales, loosely strung together to form a continuous narrative at best, told usually by a single narrator. The *Pañcatantra*, on the other hand, is an artistic whole with a highly organized and complex structure with several narrators functioning at multiple levels of storytelling. It is an intricately designed text interweaving tales with maxims and precepts, discourse and debate.

The text has a frame story, the *Preamble*, with five narratives or books (*tantras*) set within it, each narrative or *tantra* having *its* own frame story, narrative, dialogue and discourse, and well-defined characters. Within the 'frame' or *tantra*[25] of each of the five books are set 'emboxed' stories (story within a story). An 'emboxed' story has one or more tales nesting within it, narrated by one or other character to others in that specific tale who form the audience. Each tale and subtale has therefore a narrator and an audience and dialogue, together with maxims and precepts and discourses on ethics and polity, all woven into the fabric of the narrative to form a rich pattern: e.g. the tales of *The Holy Man and Swindler*, and *Fair Mind and Foul Mind* (I.tales 4 and 27). In some cases, to complicate the structure further, the process of 'emboxing' is taken one step further, and then another: e.g. the tales of *The Lapwing who defied the Ocean*, and *Strong and the Naked Mendicant* (I. tales 16 and 23).

The pattern of structure of frame story-emboxed tale is repeated at several narrative levels in the *Panchatantra*. Thus, each *tantra* mirrors the structure of the work as a whole. The following diagram would clearly indicate how the text takes the audience into a series of story-book worlds, one after the other, and how each time the audience (listeners/readers) steps into layer after layer of storytelling. The examples are from Book I, tale 16.

PAÑCATANTRA

Ist level: Narrator, anonymous; audience, listeners/ readers at all times and in all places.

2nd level: Frame story of the king, the three princes and

Viṣṇu Śarma.

Narrator/storyteller and audience the same as at the Ist level.

3rd level: *Tantra* I; *Estrangement of Friends (Mitrabheda)*, Frame story—the merchant, his bull, Lively (*Sanjīvaka*), the lion, Tawny (King of the Forest, *Piṅgalaka*), and his ex-officials, the two jackals, Wary and Wily (*Karaṭaka, Damanaka*)

Narrator—Viṣṇu Śarma; audience—the three princes.

4th level: Emboxed tale 16—The Lapwing who defied the Ocean; Narrator—Wily, the jackal; audience—Lively, the bull.

5th level: Subtales in tale 16, (Four); narrators, (two); audience, (two);

i)   Subtale of The Turtle and the Geese

ii)   Forethought, Readywit and What-will-be-will-be

iii)   The Sparrow and the Tusker

Narrator—Chaste, the hen-lapwing

Audience—Long Legs, the cock-lapwing

iv)   The subtale of The Ancient Wild Goose and the Fowler

Narrator—a wise bird, friend of the lapwings

Audience—the concourse of birds.

6th level: Tale within subtale iv (5th level): The Lion and the lone Ram

Narrator—The Ancient Wild Goose: subtale iv

Audience—Garuḍa, King of Birds and the whole concourse of birds including the lapwings.

It is clear from the foregoing diagram that there is a multiplicity of narrators at several levels in the narrative, each with his/her immediate audience. In addition, they speak to a whole range of audiences beginning with the three princes and ending with the modern reader. Several points of view on fundamental concerns of life and conduct such as fate, free will, ethics and expediency are presented with a case being made for the validity of each point of view by telling a tale or tales. The variety of characters, the diversity of opinions expressed by them and the constant interaction of narrative and discourse, make the *Pancatantra* a densely textured and layered text. Behind all this diversity however, is the presence and voice of the ancient storyteller who sits at his loom, weaving all the richness spread before us. He provides the thread of unity.

Who is the weaver of these delightful and witty tales? The narrator of the prime frame story (the *Preamble* of the work) is anonymous. He is re-telling a work of fiction composed by one Viṣṇu Śarma whom he introduces in the *Preamble* together with the king of 'the southern lands', presumably the patron of the author and the three princes who form the first of a long series of audiences.

Nothing is known of a Viṣṇu Śarma except that he is said to be the author of the *Pancatantra*. The names Viṣṇugupta and Viṣṇu Śarma are associated with Ćāṇakya (a patronymic), author of the *Arthaśāstra*. But there is no proof that Viṣṇugupta Ćāṇakya, author of the *Arthaśāstra* also wrote a *nītiśāstra*, the *Pancatantra*. The question is whether Viṣṇu Śarma is himself a fictional character like those in the gallery of characters he created for the entertainment and edification of three young princes and all others since who love to hear a good tale well told. Or whether the name is symbolic like Vyāsa, the author of the *Mahābhārata*, or Bharata who composed the *Nātya Śāstra*, the classic work on dramaturgy, music and dance, and other ancient authors. Anonymity of artists and writers has been a feature of Indian art in the past. No one knows whose brush delineated the wistful beauty of the *apsarā* on the walls at Ajanta (cave 17); or the name of the genius in whose hands the hard rock of the Western Ghats became yielding as softest clay to create the wonder that is the Kailāsanātha temple at Ellora? Viṣṇu Śarma is a storyteller of hoary antiquity, almost legendary. Whoever the author was, he was a keen observer of the morals and manners of society at all levels; a careful and sympathetic observer of birds, animals and other dwellers of woods and waters; and an accomplished writer of prose and verse with a full command of many styles: the epigrammatic, lyrical, elegiac and rhetorical. Further, he is a man of enormous learning and philosophical outlook; and a writer of wit, humour and elegance. The tale of the bedbug and the wasp is a good example of the qualities named last (I. *Crawly, the bedbug and Drone, the wasp*)).

'And what, noble lady, is the right time and the right place?' asked Drone, adding, 'Being a newcomer, I am unfamiliar with the protocol of such matters.' Gentle irony is employed here to make fun of court etiquette.

That his learning is not pedantic but enters actively into the life of the imagination and colours his outlook on life is evident in his work. The following verse is a good example:

> *What is Knowledge, if having won her,*
> *firm control over passions fails to follow,*
> *or rightful use of Intelligence lost;*
> *if with Righteousness, Knowledge does not dwell,*
> *if She leads not to Serenity or Fame;*
> *if to have Her is to simply bandy*
> *Her name in this world—What use is She then?*

(I.361)

That the author was probably connected with some royal court, perhaps even a court official, is suggested by the tone of the work as a whole and by several passages specifically; e.g. I.23 to 28; 59 to 66. These indicate that here is a man who has observed the ways of courtiers and men who aspire to be royal favourites. It is not the kind of knowledge gleaned from books.

The *Pañćatantra* is a work of great art and artistry. Some of the rhetorical devices employed can be carried over into a translation; others not. There are several examples of the former; for instance the repetition of a single word or phrase to achieve an effect that is cumulative:

> *Lost are a hundred kindnesses*
> > *shown to the base;*
> *lost are a hundred wise maxims*
> > *spoken to fools;*

(I.239)

and so on, over two verses where examples are piled one on top of the other with the repetition of the phrase 'lost are a hundred' in the first stanza, and the single word 'lost' in the second. They come down like hammer blows to show the utter waste of the acts named in the two verses. Clauses are balanced antithetically or in a complementary manner:

> *Princes without retainers,*
> *retainers without princes;*
> *the situation cannot hold.*

(I.67)

and again,

> *Honey flows freely in her speech,*
> *deadly poison lurks in her heart.*

(I.141)

Or:

> *Easily filled is a tiny stream;*
> *easily filled the cupped paws of a mouse;*
> *easily pleased a scurvy fellow;*
> *he gives thanks for crumbs.*

(I.14)

And again:

> *A trouble to acquire; a trouble to protect;*
> *a trouble if it's lost; a trouble if it's spent;*
> *money is nothing but trouble;*
> *alas! From beginning to end.*

(I.119)

On the other hand, certain kinds of wordplay are untranslatable;

where words in Sanskrit have a sonic identity but are different in meaning (like the English word 'still'), or have their meanings changed by an affix or prefix.

The *Pañcatantra* is a work known in Sanskrit as *champū*, written in a mixture of verse and prose. The two forms are used for different and distinctive purposes. Verse is employed for articulating maxims, proverbs and precepts, sententiaea generally, and for conveying heightened emotion; prose for the narrative and dialogue. A verse, always identical, comes at the beginning and end of a tale, thus marking some kind of separation of the tale from the rest of the narrative. It lays out the content of the tale in brief and points out the moral. Generally the prose is simple and straightforward so as not to detract from the story-interest. Occasionally, a passage is written in an ornate style with long compounds, drawing attention to itself in various ways, as noted earlier.

The structure of the work with a frame story or several frame stories, one for each *tantra*—in a sense every tale and subtale is framed—and emboxing tales within it, has a precedent. The *Mahābhārata* is structured similarly with a grand frame and a second frame within it; the story of the epic itself and hundreds of other stories and legends are set within this second frame. But, the *Mahābhārata* as we now have it is vast and unwieldy, because its aim has been to be encyclopaedic. The kind of art and artistry of the *Pañcatantra* is not possible of accomplishment in a work like the former which is a saga of a people and their history and culture.

III

We now come to the date of this fabulous work, the *Pañcatantra*, which I have left to the last because dates are a marginal concern especially in texts that belong to oral literature. What the text says and how it says it are more important to examine and consider.

Hertel was of the opinion that 'the original' *Pañcatantra* was composed in Kashmir around 200 BC. (He is believed to have revised this date and placed it a few centuries later).

Regarding the provenance of the work, I would like to note

that the text itself begins the 'telling' in a place other than Kashmir—Mahilāropya in 'the southern lands'. Four out of the five frame stories are located 'in the southern lands' (Books I, II, III, V) and Book IV is placed 'by the shores of the great ocean where a mighty rose-apple tree grows'. That the prime frame story, the *Preamble*, is situated in the southern lands, seems quite significant.

Some of the 'emboxed' tales are located in places that are identifiable: Pāṭaliputra (Patna), Vardhamāna (Burdhwan), Kosala (a district of Uttar Pradesh). These place names might have been carried over with the specific tales originally current in those places which were taken into the *Pañcatantra* and reworked. But, generally, the stories are set in places that are described vaguely as, 'in a certain woodland'; 'by the edge of a certain pool'; 'in a lotus pool', or 'in a certain town or settlement', and so on. These are places in an undefinable landscape of the imagination that seems eminently right and proper to set stories in.

'Once upon a time . . . ' is how stories begin. As noted several times already, storytelling is part of the oral tradition. Precise dates are hard to fix in such cases. The one clear and precise date we have is that of the recension on which the translation in this volume is based, the redaction of the *Pañcatantra* by Pūrṇabhadra (AD 1199). And we have this date only because Pūrṇabhadra Sūri ('Sūri' is an honorific in Jain terminology, corresponding to guru and āchārya) states his own name, the name of his patron, Minister Soma and the date according to the Indian calendar, in the colophon of his text.

Another important point to consider is that in spite of Edgerton's *reconstruction*, we do not possess 'the original'. The text which Pūrṇabhadra used, viz *Tantrākhyāyikā*, is accepted by Hertel and others as pretty close to 'the original'. Texts in the oral tradition, of which the *Mahābhārata* is the supreme example have a habit of growing, like a tree; like a great, spreading banyan tree. This is true of the *Pañcatantra*; and the opening of Book II which sets the tone of the whole *tantra*, *Winning of Friends*, epitomizes the work itself.

'Oh! How was that?' asked the princes eagerly. And Viṣṇu Śarma began the tale.

'In the southern land flourished the city known as *Pramadāropya*.[26] Not too far away grew a lofty banyan tree with mighty trunk and branches providing a home for all creatures. As it has been said:

Deer recline in its shade;
birds in multitudes gather to roost,
darkening its dark-green canopy of leaves;
troops of monkeys cling to the trunk;
while hollows hum with insect-throngs;
flowers are boldly kissed by honey-bees:
Oh! What happiness its every limb showers
on assemblages of various creatures.
    Such a tree deserves all praise,
    others only burden the Earth.

(II.2)

PREAMBLE

PREAMBLE

OM

Salutations to Sarasvati, Divine Muse and Goddess of Wisdom

Viṣṇu Śarma, having delved into all the texts pertaining to matters of polity and worldly wisdom, and having pondered over the pith of the matters dealt in them, composed this work made up of five books of delectable stories.

And this is how it came about:

In the southern land flourished the city of Mahilāropya, where the great king, Amara Śakti[1] lived and ruled. Here was a king well-versed in all the known works on practical wisdom. Further, he had crossed over to the far shore of knowledge of all the many arts the world possessed. So many mighty princes kneeled to him that the mass of lustrous rays shooting forth from the gems set in their diadems, illumined his feet. This king had three sons; Vasu Śakti, Ugra Śakti, and Ananta Śakti.[2] They were supreme ignoramuses.

Seeing his sons totally averse to the very name of learning, the king one day summoned his ministers and spoke earnestly to them: 'Honourable counsellors,' he said, 'you well know that my sons, all three of them, have set their faces against learning. They lack proper judgement; when I see them, my kingdom, though free of thorns, brings me no happiness. For is it not aptly said:

> *Far better that a man have no sons born*   (1)
> *or, that born they die; though there be grief, it passes soon;*
> *But, to have living sons, who turn out fools,*
> *and obstinate fools at that, that indeed*
> *is a lifelong misery hard to bear.*

'Again, as the old saying goes:

> What good is a cow that neither calves nor yields milk   (2)
> What good is a son unlettered and stubborn to boot?

'Therefore, it is high time that something be done to deal with this situation. Some means have got to be adopted to awaken the intelligence of the princes; to rouse them from their present torpor.'

The king looked round at the ministers gathered there. Then each of them, in turn, rose and spoke; and they all said much the same thing; it went something like this, 'Your Majesty, the study of grammar takes twelve years. And when that has somehow been mastered, there are others to follow; the study of Law, sacred and secular, of polity and statecraft. These at least have to be tackled and mastered. Only then can the mind truly awaken and shine.'

A faint shadow of disappointment passed over the king's features. Then, one among them, Minister Goodsense,[3] rose up and spoke: 'Your Majesty, it is true that life is short, and it is beset by many obstacles. Knowledge knows no bounds, and it takes years to acquire it. Therefore, it is held that the essentials of knowledge have to be extracted and grasped, just as the noble bird, the swan, extracts the milk from the water it is mixed in. A short cut has to be found to educate the princes. Now, in our own city, my lord, lives the Brāhmana, Viṣṇu Śarma, a scholar par excellence who, according to the reputation he has among the body of students here, has mastery over several fields of learning. Why not entrust the princes to his care? He will, I am sure, make their minds blossom in no time.'

The king, highly pleased with Goodsense's counsel, sent for Viṣṇu Śarma at once. When the learned Brāhmana arrived, King Amara Śakti spoke to him most courteously. 'Your Reverence, I have three sons, all dunces of the first water, each one more dull-witted than the other. Their intelligence has to be awakened.

Do me a favour, sir, and take the princes in hand; teach them, instruct them, so that they become unsurpassed in their mastery over all matters relating to practical wisdom. And I shall reward you with a hundred grants of land, revered sir.'

To this request of the king, Viṣṇu Śarma replied, 'My lord, I do not sell my learning, not even for the gift of a hundred land-grants. Now hear me speak; I speak the simple, unvarnished truth. I have no craving for wealth, my lord. I am now eighty years of age, and my senses have turned away from their objects. But I shall do what you ask of me. If I do not teach your sons in such a manner that in six months time they do not have complete mastery over all the wide expanse of political and practical wisdom, then let my name be thrown away and forgotten. And Your Majesty may show me His Bare Royal Bottom. So let this day be noted and set down. In six months time, your sons will possess unsurpassed knowledge of all branches of practical wisdom. Hear! This is my lion-roar.'

The king was greatly astonished at hearing the Brāhmana's extraordinary claim. He sent for the princes and handed them over to Viṣṇu Śarma; a wave of relief swept over him. Viṣṇu Śarma accepted charge of them and took them home with him where he devised a system of education suited to the princes. He composed these five books of stories known as:

1. *Estrangement of Friends,*
2. *Winning of Friends,*
3. *Of Crows and Owls,*
4. *Loss of Gains,*
5. *Rash Deeds.*

With the aid of these tales, he instructed the princes. They too, learning through these stories, became in six months what Viṣṇu Śarma had promised they would. Since then, this work on practical wisdom has become celebrated as an excellent means of awakening and training young minds. It has travelled far and wide in this world. Why expatiate on its excellence? Suffice it to say:

Whoever always reads this work; (3)
whoever listens to it told;
he will never face defeat, no,
not even from the Lord of Gods,[4] Himself.

And this is the preamble to the work.

BOOK I

Estrangement of Friends

Now, we begin at the beginning with the first book of tales, the *Estrangement of Friends*.

> *Oh! What a beautiful friendship it was!* (1)
> *of noble bull and lion majestic—*
> *In the deep, dark woods it waxed and grew strong,*
>> *then—along came a jackal treacherous;*
>> *consumed by greed, he hacked it down.*
>>> *And—Alas! It died.*

And this is how it is told:

Once upon a time, in the southern land flourished the fair city of Mahilāropya, rivalling in splendour even Amarāvati, City of the Gods. Possessing all excellences that could possibly be imagined, it shone as the Earth's crest-jewel. Built in the shape of the peak of Kailāsa, it had lofty gates and high watchtowers plentifully stocked with many different kinds of weapons. Its main gateway, gigantic and decorated by beautiful, carved arches had a massive portal of solid wood, wide, fitted with strong bolts and crossbeams. In all, the city resembled nothing less than the fabled Indrakīla mountain. Numerous temples graced the city, placed as prescribed in the texts, in spacious squares formed by broad crossroads. Soaring ramparts resembling the towering ranges of the Himālayas, encircled by a deep moat, ringed the city.

In this beautiful city lived Vardhamāna,[1] the merchant-prince, endowed with ever so many fine qualities. The merit of his good works earned in many past lives had blessed him with immense wealth.

Once, in the dark of night, a sudden thought crossed Vardhamāna's mind and he lay musing after this fashion:

'Wealth, even an immense fortune, dwindles with constant use . . . as does the collyrium. On the other hand, even a modest fortune grows, if added to constantly—as an anthill does. So . . . even immense wealth should be made to grow; whatever remains unearned ought to be earned. Once earned it should be safe-guarded. What is guarded well ought to be increased: well-invested. Wealth guarded in the customary way of the world, that is, hoarded, can disappear in a flash—life is full of dangers. Further, wealth hoarded is as good as wealth not possessed. So wealth gained, should be safe-guarded, increased and made use of. For it is said:

> Let the wealth you earn circulate (2)
> and you keep it still.
> Water in a full tank, lacking an outlet
> spills over and goes to waste.

> Wealth lures wealth as tame elephants the wild; (3)
> wealth cannot be earned by wishful thinking;
> there can be no trade without wealth.

> The man who lets the wealth that Fortune showers on him, (4)
> sit idle, finds no happiness in this world,
> nor in the next. What is he then?
> A confounded fool performing a watchman's role.'

Having thus pondered over the matter, Vardhamāna came to a conclusion. He would travel. Having assembled his servants he collected a wagon-load of merchandise that would find a ready market in the city of Mathurā. He then fixed a day and time when the moon and stars were in auspicious positions. After receiving the blessings of his parents he set out, with the blowing of conches and music of pipes going before him, and his friends and kinsmen bringing up the rear. At the water's edge he bid goodbye to friends and kin and started on his journey to Mathurā.

Now, Vardhamāna possessed two noble bulls, white as clouds and bearing auspicious marks that augured good fortune.

Named Joyous and Lively,[2] they were yoked to the wagon loaded with merchandise.

In time the caravan reached a great forest; enchanting with densely clustering trees, dhava and acacia, sāl, flame-of-the-forest and numerous other beautiful flowering trees; awe-inspiring from the many powerful beasts that roamed it, elephant and bison, buffalo and wild boar, tiger, leopard and bear; delightful with herds of gazelles and bushy-tailed deer; abounding with rills that tumbled down the hillside; and possessing deep, dark glens and caves.

There misfortune struck the noble bull, Lively, when one of his feet chanced upon a patch of soft, wet mud at a certain spot where the far-flung spray of a rushing cascade fell continuously. Struggling under the weight of the heavy, overloaded wagon, the bull fell down, breaking the yoke. Seeing him collapse and lie sprawled on the path, the driver of the wagon jumped out in great consternation and rushed to report the matter to the merchant-prince who was riding not far behind. Bowing ceremoniously and folding his hands, he quavered, 'My lord, O my noble lord, it is Lively; wearied by the journey, he slipped and fell in the mud; he is lying prostrate.'

Hearing that, the merchant was plunged into dejection on account of Lively's sad plight. He broke journey and halted five nights, so that Lively could be cared for and get well. But when the bull showed no signs of recovery, the merchant set aside a supply of fodder for him, and detailed some of his servants to stay and look after the bull, exhorting them in the following manner:

'Now listen, fellows, take good care of Lively; if he recovers and lives, bring him along, and join me. If he dies, perform the last rites; cremate him, and join me.'

Having thus instructed his men, Vardhamāna proceeded on his journey as planned.

Then one day, Vardhamāna's men, fearful of the many dangers lurking in the great forest, decided to call it a day and abandon Lively to his fate. They quickly rejoined their master and told him the tale of how the bull had breathed his last. 'O master,'

11

they cried, 'Poor Lively is gone, dead; we did all we could. Then we performed his last rites and consigned him to the flames.' Oh! What a snivelling there was and blowing of noses and wiping of tears!

Vardhamāna heard it all in sorrow; for a moment he remained stunned with grief. Then, as duty bound, he performed all the prescribed ceremonies for the peace of the departed spirit and without encountering any further mishap reached Mathurā safely.

And now, what about poor Lively, alone, ill, and abandoned? Well, he was destined, through his own good fortune, to live out the allotted span of his life. Gradually, he recovered, restored and invigorated by the refreshing spray of the cascades. He then slowly got up on his feet and hobbled along, step by step, and finally reached the river Yamunā's green banks. Cropping the tender tips of the lush, emerald-green grass, in a few days, he grew sleek and plump like Lord Śiva's bull, sporting a magnificent hump and bouncing with energy. Every day he frisked around in the verdant meadows like a playful elephant and amused himself by charging the huge anthills, butting their pointed tops, goring them with the sharp tips of his horns.

It chanced that one day the lion, Tawny,[3] accompanied by a retinue of different kinds of animals, came down to the river to drink, when he heard the bull Lively's tremendous bellowing that sounded like the thundering of rainclouds. Instantly, Tawny froze in his tracks, deeply troubled at heart. However, concealing the true state of his emotions, Tawny withdrew, retiring into the vast circle formed by the spreading banyan tree not far from where he had stopped. There, he drew up his retinue in the formation commonly known as the Four Circles.

Dear Reader, since you are far removed in time and space from this ancient story-book world, permit me to explain what the Four Circles are. We have the Circle of the Lion, the Circle of Attendants, the Circle of Courtiers—those hangers-on who caw and crow—and the Circle of the Menials—the fetchers and carriers. As it is said, in any city or capital, town, village, or hamlet,

settlement, Brāhmana colony, border post, monastery or community of people, there can only be one occupant of the lion's
post. The Circle of Attendants comprises many; that of the
hangers-on, naturally, consists of myriads. And as for the fourth
circle, that of the 'others'—well, they mill around at the edge of
the forest—they are on the fringes, the periphery, so to speak.
Such is the hierarchy, high, middle, low. That is how it is, has
been, and will always be.

Tawny had his ministers, as well as others who were in his
secret counsels; true enough. But he enjoyed a kingship that may
be described as follows: he vaunted none of the external trappings
of royalty; no pomp and circumstance surrounded him; no royal
white umbrella or royal chariot; no ornate fans and flywhisks with
jewelled handles; no entourage of bards and wanton women
going before him, singing and dancing. He held his head high,
erect, from sheer pride and innate majesty: from his feeling of
indomitable daring; from his sense of uncompromising honour
and a fiery spirit that welled up from within. He exercised a
kingship that was free and sovereign; that brooked no rival and
disdained to be subject to another's will or authority. It was a
sovereignty that proclaimed its presence by haughtiness firmly
grounded in vehement passion; stemming from heroic fury. It
was a stranger to the kind of cringing speech that some practised.
It was not abject or timid; it never folded its hands in humble
obeisance. Fearlessness was its goal and it acted fearlessly to
reach its goal. It disdained flattery to gain its ends but always
displayed a magnificence that rested solely on manly strength,
resoluteness, self-esteem. Such was the kind of kingship that
Tawny exercised, serving no one, encumbered by no one.
Disinterested, it deemed the pleasure of benefiting others its own
reward; it was devoid of small-mindedness, of meanness of spirit.
It was a kingship by no means insignificant. Unconquered, it
enjoyed dominion without taking thought of building defences
and fortifications; or, of keeping accounts of revenue and ex-
penditure. There was no need for it to indulge in intrigue and
machinations. Tawny's kingship was a stranger to deviousness.

Easily roused to anger from possessing an overabundance of valour and endowed with an uncommon appetite for power, it would never scheme or work behind anyone's back. It was above suspicion. Above reproach, it easily brushed aside the malicious babblings of officious wives, and spurned their tears and wails. Without formal training in the use of weapons it acted to kill but with no desire to. It provided itself with adequate food and shelter without the aid of attendants. Tawny, regal, roamed the forests, unhesitating, unalarmed.

> *The King of Beasts, full of energy,* (5)
> *dwells in the woods, solitary*
> *without emblems of royalty;*
> *unlearned, untrained in polity,*
> *his superior strength gives him sovereignty;*
> *he rules, crowned simply by the words,*
> *O King! Hail! O King!*

> *No rite of consecration,* (6)
> *no sacred ablution*
> *do beasts of the forest perform*
> *to crown the lion as king.*

> *Earned by valour alone*
> *his deeds are quite well-known,*
> *sovereignty over beasts is his.*

> *Meat of tuskers moving slow, majestic,* (7)
> *drops of rut trickling, he relishes most;*
> *but if his favourite food comes not his way,*
> *still you'll never catch a lion eating hay.*

There were two jackals in Tawny's train, Wary and Wily, sons of ministers. They were out of a job and this is what started them consulting earnestly with each other. It was Wily who brought up the subject first, saying, 'Wary, my good friend, did you just see our lord, Tawny, coming this way for a drink? Why then is he standing over there looking quite dejected?'

And Wary replied, 'Yes, I did; but what of it? It's none of our business, is it? Or have you not heard of the saying:

He who pokes his nose where it does not belong,   (8)
    surely meets his end;
for that's what happened to the monkey who meddled
    with the wedge, my friend.'

'Ah!' exclaimed Wily, 'And how did that happen?' Upon which Wary began the story of *The Monkey and the Wedge*.

In a certain city, a merchant was having a temple built within a grove on the outskirts. Everyday, the master-builder and other artisans left for the city at noon to have their midday meal. One day, a band of monkeys descended upon that half-built temple. An enormous log of rosewood split by one of the carpenters, lay on one side, with a wedge of acacia-wood inserted at the top into the cleft. The monkeys romped around playing on the treetops, on the lofty rooftops and towers, and in the woodpile. One of them, whose downfall was on the cards, scampered out of idle curiosity on to the log and sat there wondering, 'Now, who on earth has gone and stuck a wedge in such an odd place?' Getting hold of the wedge with both hands, he started pulling and straining, trying to work it loose. He succeeded; suddenly, the wedge flew out; the split halves snapped shut. Now, you should know without being told as to what happened to the monkey's genitals dangling within the cleft below the spot where the wedge had been inserted.

'Therefore, I say to you,' remarked Wary, 'anyone with his wits about him is careful to mind his own business.'

And he added, 'We seem to do well enough on Lord Tawny's leavings.' To which Wily replied with some asperity, 'So, that's what it is, is it? To fill the belly is Your Honour's sole concern, then? No wish to perform any service of distinction? It is aptly said, though, that the wise embark on a career of service with kings for two reasons: to help one's friends and to harm one's foes. Who in this world does not take care of his belly?

To help one's friends and hurt one's foes (9)
  are proper ends of serving kings,
as the wise perceive. In this world,
  who does not heed the belly's call?

'Moreover:

One truly lives on whose life depends (10)
the livelihood of the many.
Birds too fill their bellies full
with several beakfuls of food.

If a man does not hold dear the well-being (11)
of parents, kin, dependants, and himself,
what good is his living in the world of men?
A crow too lives long eating ritual offerings.

Throw a dog a bone with barely meat on it — (12)
a sorry bit of stinking gristle and fat,
it hardly stills his hunger pangs,
yet he is content—
  But the lion—he whips aside
  the jackal that lands right in his lap—
  to chase a bull-elephant.
The meanest in the world
hankers after the recompense
he regards as his birthright.

Watch the dog— (13)
he wags his tail,
grovels at your feet,
rolls on the ground, baring his belly and his fangs.
The bull-elephant eyes his food,
toys with it,
and waits for a hundred cajoleries
He takes his time before he deigns to eat.

> *Easily filled is a tiny stream,* (14)
> *easily filled the cupped paws of a mouse;*
> *easily pleased is a scurvy fellow;*
> *he gives thanks for crumbs.*

> *If between what is good and proper, and what is not,* (15)
> *a man cannot discern;*
> *if from all commerce with Scripture's holy precepts,*
> *his mind is shut out;*
> *if to fill the belly is his sole aim,*
> *what difference then, between beast and man-beast?*

'And think too of this:

> *The grass-eating ox pulls the heavy wagon;* (16)
> *he draws the plough over ground rough and smooth;*
> *pure of birth, he labours for the good of the world;*
> *Can you compare a man-beast with the ox?'*

Wary pouted at this and remarked, 'But, we have no place at the court; we are not among the king's men. Why then should we involve ourselves in his business?'

Wily was quick to answer, 'Ah, my good chap; sometime or other, someone who is not the king's man, becomes one. For as we know:

> *By serving well the king,* (17)
> *one who's not the king's man becomes one;*
> *by failing to serve the king,*
> *another who is, falls from his place.*

> *By no man's smile is any man raised high;* (18)
> *by no man's frown is any man cast down;*
> *up or down, a man rises or falls in life,*
> *by the true worth of his actions and conduct.*

'Further:

> *With greatest effort are stones carried uphill;* (19)

17

and with the greatest ease do they tumble down;
so too with our own self, through Virtue and Vice.'

All that Wary could observe was, 'Well, then, what does Your Honour make of it?' Wily then explained, 'I guess our lord is afraid; surrounded by his retinue which is also cowering in fear, he stands dumbfounded.'

'And how would you know this, Wily?' asked Wary.

'What is there to know in this?' came Wily's pat reply.

> *'Any creature understands what is plainly said,*   (20)
> *an elephant, a horse, when driven, moves on;*
> *what is left unsaid, the learned, wise, infer.*
> *The intellect sees clearly revealed*
> *another's true intent and purpose,*
> *gains knowledge from expression of face and eyes,*
> *from tone of voice, from gait*
> *from gesture and deportment.*

'Before long, I shall have our master in my power, using my abilities of comprehension.'

Wary still demurred, 'But my dear chap, Wily, I'm sure you have not a clue to what it takes to serve a king. Now tell me something, how do you propose to gain power over our master, Lord Tawny?'

But Wily was not one to be put down; as always he was ready with an answer. 'Well, my dear chap, how can you say that I am unacquainted with the ways of the court, and, with the knowledge of serving a king? Have I not read and made completely my own the knowledge contained in the chapters of the sage Vyāsa's great epic, where the Pāṇḍava brothers arrive at the kingdom of Virāṭa, and enter into the service of the king there? And it has been aptly said:

> *What job is beyond the competent?*   (21)
> *What place too far for the adventurous?*
> *What land alien to the well-informed?*
> *To smooth talkers, who remains a stranger for long?'*

Wary objected, 'Supposing Your Honour is rebuffed by the king for forcing yourself on him, when you are not welcome? What then?' To which Wily replied, 'There you do have a point, my friend. But I am a person well aware of time and place; I can judge when the occasion is right. As we know:

> *Even the Lord of Learning*[4] *can make a slip;*   (22)
> *uttered on an inauspicious occasion*
> *his words, no doubt, will lack of persuasion,*
> *and more, act as extreme provocation.*

'Then again:

> *The wise and well-bred, though riding high in royal favour,*   (23)
> *will desist from sudden intrusion into the royal presence;*
> *as when the king is closeted in secret counsels,*
> *or occupied in intimate activities,*
> *or, when he's bewildered, dithering, at a loss how to act.*

'Or to put it another way:

> *No well-bred courtier, even one granted free access*   (24)
> *will ever dream of intruding at certain times:*
> *when the king is in conference,*
> *when his physician, or his barber,*
> *is in attendance on him,*
> *when he is at table, or in bed with a woman.*

> *A courtier in the palace should act with extreme caution;*   (25)
> *a pupil in his teacher's house, with respect and discretion;*
> *Those unmannerly who do not know their place,*
> *will soon meet with extinction like oil lamps*
> *lighted at dusk in dwellings of the poor.*

'What's also important:

> *Ascertain well beforehand, the royal mood,*   (26)
> *merry or sad, angry or otherwise;*

19

only then enter the palace, in modest attire,
bowing low, walking with slow, hesitant steps.

'And remember:

> A man might be lacking in learning and wisdom,   (27)
> or be of humble birth, or not well-commended;
> if he sticks close to the king, in constant service,
> never doubt that royal favour is his.
>
>> Kings and women and slender climbing vines,
>> cling to whatever they find close to them—
>> Such is the way of the world.

'Also:

> By careful scrutiny of his master's face   (28)
> for signs of anger or of grace;
> a servant slowly climbs on to his back,
> even if the monarch bucks and bolts.

'And further:

> The learned, the brave, and he who well knows how to   (29)
>   serve,
> these are the three who pluck the Flower of Gold in this
>   world.

'How does a man serve a king? Listen, then:

> The king's favourites and his well-wishers,   (30)
> especially those whose words carry weight—
> The wise man makes them his gateway
> to royal favour. There is no other way.

> The wise do not care to serve the king   (31)
> who cannot recognize each one's individual merit;
> such service is wholly barren of all fruit,
> like the tillage of a salt meadow.

Serve well a monarch worthy of service (32)
even if he lacks wealth and powers of state.
Your livelihood is thereby assured,
and in time you will enjoy the fruits.

The servant despises his lord, thinking— (33)
'this man, he does not deserve to be served.'
Why does he not despise himself for knowing
who deserves service and who does not.

The Queen Mother and the Royal Consort, (34)
the Crown Prince and the Chief Minister too.
The High Priest and the Royal Guard:
    these deserve a royal treatment.

He who stands in the forefront in battle, (35)
but walks behind the king in the city,
waits in the palace at the royal chamber-door:
    he is beloved of princes.

He who always greets the prince, when addressed, (36)
with the auspicious words, 'May you live long,'
who knows what should be done, what should not
and acts resolutely: he is beloved of princes.

He who directs wisely, royal gifts of wealth (37)
toward the deserving; who confidently wears
garments and other gifts from the prince to him:
    he is beloved of princes.

He who never returns insolent words (38)
even when taken to task by the prince;
checks his laughter in the royal presence;
    he is beloved of princes.

He who will not carry on intrigues (39)
with attendants of the royal harem,
or whisper with the monarch's consorts:
    he is beloved of princes.

He who will never step over the line, (40)
even in distressing situations,
thinking, 'I am secure in the king's favour,'
    he is beloved of princes.

He who endears himself to those dear to the lord of men (41)
and swears eternal enmity to his foes:
    he is beloved of princes.

He who does not consort with his royal master's foes, (42)
is not contentious, or spreads slander around:
    he is beloved of princes.

He who is fearless, regards the battlefield (43)
and holy sanctuary with the same eye;
to whom living in his native city
and sojourn abroad are the same:
    he is beloved of princes.

He who looks upon dice as Death's messenger, (44)
and drink as the Deadly Poison;[5]
who sees other men's wives simply as forms;
    he is beloved of princes.'

Wary, having listened to all of this, now asked, 'Sir, what will you say first when you are in our lord's presence? You'd better tell me that.'

And Wily answered,

'Words follow words; words spring from words (45)
even as seed begets more seed
with timely rains.

'What's more:

Men of learning and intellect, with skill using (46)
the various expedients of policy,
lay out clearly for their master's viewing

> danger that looms in unwise policy,
> and success that gleams in the wise, as well.

> Men of merit who can pursue such a course, (47)
> and in the Assembly earn for it
> high praise from the wise and virtuous elders,
> should nurture that talent and preserve it.

'And it is also said:

> If a man does not seek his master's fall (48)
> let him speak unbidden;
> this is the duty of the virtuous;
> any other course is contrary to the Law.'

Wary objected, saying, 'But, sir, it is so hard to gain the trust and goodwill of princes. You know the proverb:

> Princes are like serpents; (49)
> formed coil upon coil,
> encased in smooth, sinuous scales;
> cruel, tortuous in movement,
> menacingly fierce, savage,
> yielding only to magical arts.

> Princes are like mountains: (50)
> with ups and downs and hearts of stone;
> not low, or vile,
> but sought after by the low and vile;
> ever-haunted by the murderous,
> by those who delight to kill.

> Never put your trust in these: (51)
> creatures furnished with claws, or horns,
> men wearing armour, carrying arms,
> women, and also flowing streams,
> and the whole cursed lot of princes.'

To this Wily's reply was, 'True enough; you have a point, my friend; but:

A person's state of mind makes known (52)
what manner of man he is;
entering it, one with experience
quickly gains control over that man.

If the master gets angry, his man bends low, (53)
sings his praises, extols his largesse,
hates his foes, dotes on those he favours:
that's the sure way to win someone over
without recourse to magical arts.

'Albeit:

A man may excel in action, (54)
in knowledge, or in eloquence;
know your man; tailor your approach
to suit different dispositions.
But once you find your man lacks strength,
for god's sake, give him up at once.

Words should be used wisely and well; (55)
spoken where they would yield rich fruit.
Colours take the firmest hold
and brightest, on whitest cloth.

If a man should undertake something, lacking (56)
knowledge of resources and energies,
his best efforts will not shine forth, even as moonlight
on the Snow Mountain,[6] *though brilliant, does not.'*

Wary responded simply, 'If you are that confident, then go
and seek an audience with His Gracious Majesty; and may good
fortune attend you. Do as you think fit:

But act with due circumspection (57)
when you seek the king's protection.
For, our own well-being depends
on the fortunes of your own person.'

Wily then bowed to Wary, took leave of him, and set out in the direction where Tawny was.

When Tawny saw Wily approaching, he ordered his door-keeper with the words, 'Put your staff of office aside, sir, here comes Wily, the son of our long-time minister, and he has free access to us. Usher him forthwith and offer him a seat in the Second Circle as is his right.'

Wily now entered. Bowing low to Tawny, he accepted the seat offered to him. Tawny extended his right forepaw that gleamed with claws resembling thunderbolts, and asked graciously, 'Is all well with you, sir? We have not seen you for a long time.'

Wily answered, 'Though we are not entrusted with any official duties in the services of His Majesty, yet I thought that I should present myself at court at the proper time. For it is not that there is no occasion when I cannot be of some service to His Majesty:

> *Even a worthless bit of straw comes in handy* (58)
> *for the great ones to pick their teeth or scratch their ear;*
> *what to say then of the service a person*
> *endowed with speech and limbs can render, O King!*

'And let me add, my lord, that we who are the hereditary retainers of His Gracious Majesty, are duty bound to attend on our lord even in times of misfortune. There is no other way for us. A proverb also points out:

> *Servants and ornaments are to be placed* (59)
> *each in the position right for them:*
> *to say, 'I can do this, so I shall,' and fasten*
> *a crest-jewel on the foot—that's not done.*

> *A king may be of lofty lineage* (60)
> *descended of a long line of kings,*
> *he may be possessed of immense wealth;*
> *but he can never keep his retainers,*
> *if their merits he recognizes not.*

If he makes them equal to others not their equals,   (61)
if he honours them less than their equals,
if he appoints them in stations beneath them:
In all three cases retainers leave the king.

'And this too, is true:

A fine gem fit to grace a gold jewel,   (62)
if mounted in a cheap tin setting,
does not scream, nor refuses to gleam.
It's the jeweller who's put to shame.

A good judge of employees decides thus   (63)
'This one's intelligent; and loyal too:
that one's disloyal; that other is dull!'
Retainers flock in droves to such a king.

'Even now, His Majesty made a just remark, that he has not seen me at court for a long time. May it please him to know the reasons for my absence?

Where no distinction is made   (64)
between the right hand and the left,
there, no gentleman will care to stay
an instant, if he has another way.

Once retainers see the master treat   (65)
all alike and no distinctions make,
the persevering zeal for service there
of the diligent and skilled among them wanes.

In a place where no difference is perceived   (66)
between a priceless gem with eye of fire
and a fragment of pale crystal,
how can a gem-trade flourish there?

Princes without retainers,   (67)
retainers without princes,

the situation cannot hold;
a close relationship is theirs,
linked by mutual dependence.

'The truth is, that the excellence of a retainer flows from the merits of his lord. And the saying goes:

A horse, a weapon, a text, a lute,   (68)
a voice, a man and a woman—
  they perform ill, or well,
  according to who masters them.

'And further, it is not right to show contempt for me, thinking, "He is a mere jackal." For:

Silk is spun by the humble worm;   (69)
gold is born of rock;
the holy dūrvā-grass springs from cow's hair:
the lotus from mud;
the moon from the ocean,
the beetle from dung:
fire flashes out of wood,
the emerald from the serpent's hood;
orpiment comes from the bile of a cow.
A person of merit shines
by the light of his own rising merits.
Of what consequence is his birth?

'Moreover:

A mouse might be killed though born in your home,   (70)
  being the bringer of harm.
A cat, a stranger, might be welcomed with gifts,
  being the bringer of good.

'Another point to consider:

What good is one incompetent though loyal;   (71)

what good is one out to get you though he's strong;
know me to be strong and loyal as well:
and I do not deserve your scorn, O King.

Scorn not the wise who have understood highest truths: (72)
Wealth, like straw is light, She can never shackle them.
Lotus-fibre cannot hold fast the bull-elephant
striding in glorious intoxication,
Spring's fresh flow of rut darkening his cheeks.'

Tawny then remonstrated with Wily, 'O, no, no, don't talk like this; after all, you are the son of our long-time minister.'

Wily, somewhat mollified, spoke again, 'I have something of importance to say to you, my lord.'

'Well, my good chap, go ahead and tell me what's on your mind,' answered Tawny.

Wily, who had been leading up to this, replied, 'Why is it that our gracious master, having set out to drink at the river, turned back and retired to this spot?'

Tawny, however, concealed his real state of mind carefully, and gave a nonchalant reply, 'O that, that is nothing; nothing at all.'

'O well,' responded Wily, 'If it is not something to be mentioned, why then, let us leave it alone.

A man might confide some things to his wife, (73)
some to his close friends, and some to his son;
these deserve his trust: but not reveal
all matters to everyone in sight.'

Thereupon, Tawny began reflecting, 'Hm . . . this fellow appears trustworthy. I guess I can tell him what is on my mind. As the saying goes:

A true and tested friend, a faithful wife, (74)
a loyal servant, a powerful master,

> *disclosing his troubles to these*
> *a man discovers great relief.'*

'Hey, Wily,' Tawny addressed Wily. 'Did you by any chance hear a tremendous sound in the distance?'

'Yes, my lord, I did,' answered Wily. 'I did hear it; what of it?'

'Well, my good fellow, I intend to leave this forest,' said Tawny.

Wily replied, 'Whatever for, my lord?'

'Because,' replied Tawny, 'some extraordinary being has come into this forest: these prodigious sounds that we hear are made by him, no doubt. This being must possess a form and strength to match his voice; and valour to match his form and strength.'

'O, my lord,' replied Wily with a hint of a snort, 'what! My lord afraid of a mere sound? As the proverb says:

> *A bridge may be breached by water;* (75)
> *a secret too not well-guarded;*
> *Friendship by intrigue may be broken*
> *and a coward unmanned by words alone.*

'It's not right that our lord should abandon in a trice, this great forest whose possession has been in his family for generations and which has been inherited by him. As it is aptly said:

> *The wise man puts one foot forward* (76)
> *while he stands firm on the other:*
> *he'll not forsake his former home,*
> *until he finds another.*

'Moreover, here in this forest, we hear a variety of sounds . . . so many . . . mere sounds, that's all they are; they should not cause fear to anyone. We hear the rumbling of clouds, the whistling of wind in the reeds, we hear sounds of lutes and drums, big and small, sounds of conches and bells, of wagons and doors

29

creaking, sounds of axes and saws and similar implements—all kinds of sounds are heard here. One should not be afraid of them. It is pointed out that:

> *A king who summons up all his courage* (77)
> *to face the most savage of foes,*
> *advancing, drunk with fury,*
> *and will not yield, will never face defeat.*

'Again:

> *The Creator may rage,* (78)
> *unshaken stand the brave;*
> *summer may dry the lake,*
> *the great river flows ever full.*

'Also:

> *Joyous in prosperity,* (79)
> *not cast down in adversity,*
> *steadfast in battle,*
> *rarely does a mother bear such a son—*
> *the ornament of the three worlds.*

'Further:

> *A blade of grass bends low, powerless,* (80)
> *tosses about, light, lacking inner strength.*
> *A man who lacks a sense of honour and pride,*
> *is like a pitiful blade of grass.*

'Knowing this, my lord should muster up his courage and act firmly; not be afraid of mere sounds. His Majesty surely knows the story of the jackal and the battle-drum; as the jackal said:

> *At first I thought it stuffed with food—* (81)
> *I entered it:*

30

I found it but a thing of skin and wood.'

'Ah!' exclaimed Tawny, 'What's the story?' Then Wily began the tale of *The Jackal and the Battle-drum*.

In a certain region there lived a jackal who had hardly found anything to eat for days. His stomach pinched by hunger, his throat dry, he wandered around searching for food and chanced upon a battlefield of kings in the depths of a forest. Suddenly he stopped dead in his tracks—for he heard a great booming sound coming from somewhere in the vicinity. His heart pounded with fear; he was greatly troubled in mind. 'O all you powerful gods,' he cried, looking up at the skies. 'What kind of danger have I walked into unawares? I am as good as dead. I am done for right now, right this minute. What kind of sound is this? What sort of creature is making it?' He stood still, listened again, and then decided to investigate the source of the sounds. He walked gingerly in the direction of the sound and he saw a huge battle-drum, as large as the peak of a hill. And he thought to himself, 'Is this its natural voice? Or is someone causing this thing to sound?'

Now, when the tips of grass swaying in the wind brushed against the drum, it made the booming sound; at other times it remained silent. Sensing its helplessness, the jackal came close to it. Then out of curiosity he beat upon both sides of the drum. With intense joy he thought, 'What luck! After all this time food is practically dropping into my mouth. I'm certain that this huge thing is chockful of delicious meat and fat.'

Having come to this conclusion, he picked a spot on the drum, and gnawed a hole in it. As the hide was thick and tough, he was lucky not to break his teeth. He peered inside the drum and slowly entered it; but alas, he found nothing. No meat, no fat; the thing was just hollow. He stood and viewed it quizzically and then said:

'What an awesome sound it made, (82)

I thought it was stuffed full of food,
until I went in and found,
it's just a thing of skin and wood.'

The jackal clambered out and laughing at himself, said, 'I knew it; I knew it all the time.'

'Therefore I say to you, my lord, you should not be agitated by a mere sound.'

To which Tawny replied, somewhat petulantly, 'That's all very well, but just look at my retinue; seized with fear they simply want to take to their heels. How then can I screw up my courage, as you put it. Tell me.'

'It's not really their fault, my lord,' replied Wily. 'Like master, like servants. As the saying goes:

A horse, a weapon, and a text,   (83)
a lute, a voice, a man and a woman,
they acquit themselves ill or well,
according to the one who uses them.

'Calling up your valour and your manliness, my lord, just wait here at this very spot while I go and find out what sort of creature we have here; and return in a trice. After that we shall consider how to deal with it.'

Tawny was dismayed. 'What!' he exclaimed, 'Are you saying, sir, that you would dare go there?'

Wily answered promptly, 'Is it for a servant to hesitate when the master commands? As the proverb says:

A loyal retainer has no fear;   (84)
he will enter a torrent tumultuous
or even the vast ocean, perilous,
if that is his lord's command.

The retainer who stops to consider   (85)
whether his lord's command is dangerous,
or not, should never be considered
by kings, for a minister's post.'

32

Tawny responded, 'Well, my dear fellow, if that is how you feel, then go on your mission, and may good fortune go with you.'

Wily bowed low to his king and started on his way, taking the direction indicated by Lively's bellowing.

When Wily had taken his leave, Tawny began to have second thoughts. Troubled greatly at heart, he reflected, 'Alas! Alas! I am afraid I may not have acted wisely in this matter, putting my full trust in this fellow to the extent of disclosing my true state of mind. Who knows if Wily is not the sort of fellow who plays one against the other? He may well do me an ill turn if he bears a grudge for having been turned out of office previously. As the proverb points out:

> *Even those who are from fine families,* (86)
> *if once honoured by the king and then slighted,*
> *will at all times work towards his downfall.*

'Therefore, I think it is best in the circumstances, that I leave this particular spot and wait for Wily somewhere else . . . until it is clear as to how he may act. Who knows if the fellow might not lead that strange creature here to kill me. For it is said:

> *The weak, if wary and mistrustful,* (87)
> *can easily withstand the strongest;*
> *the strong who are foolish and trustful,*
> *may be overthrown by the weakest.'*

Having reached this conclusion, Tawny returned to another spot in the forest, where he waited all by himself, scanning the direction that Wily had taken.

In the meantime, Wily arrived at the place where Lively was romping happily. He took one look and exclaimed, 'Good god, this is just a bull.' Delighted by this discovery, Wily thought to himself, 'Oho! What luck. As matters have turned out, I think I can have Tawny completely in my power . . . by practising the policies of peace and friendship, or war and enmity, using this creature. It is indeed shrewdly observed:

> *Where the king finds himself in trouble,* (88)

33

> the minister is in clover.
> What wonder then if ministers wish to serve
> a king dogged by adversity.

'How true this is:

> As a man in perfect health   (89)
> disdains all doctors and drugs,
> so, a king free of troubles
> thinks little of his ministers.'

Musing thus, Wily turned around and proceeded to where he had left Tawny waiting for him.

Seeing Wily returning at a distance, Tawny at once assumed his former stance and expression. When the jackal approached his king, bowed low and took his seat, Tawny enquired, 'Well, sir, did you get a look at that creature?'

'O, yes, my lord, I did,' replied Wily. 'By the grace of Your Majesty, I did see him.'

'Is that the truth?' rasped out Tawny.

'O, my lord, could I possibly speak otherwise in His Gracious Majesty's presence? Is it not truly said, my lord:

> Even the smallest lie spoken before a king   (90)
>   has the gravest consequences;
> the ruin of the speaker's parent and teacher,
>   and that of the gods as well.

'For it is said:

> Blended of essences of all the gods,   (91)
>   a king is formed; so sages sing.
> Look upon him, therefore, as a god;
>   never speak an untruth to a king.

'It is also said:

> A king who is incarnate of all the gods,   (92)

34

is . . . mark this . . . yet a god with a difference;
you taste his pleasure, or, his displeasure,
right now and here . . . of the gods, hereafter.'

Tawny, a little restive, replied, 'All right, I guess you did see this creature. Anyway, the great and noble do not vent their anger on the lowly and weak. As you must have heard:

A hurricane does not uproot the pliant grass   (93)
that bends low before its fury;
it snaps only proud, lordly trees;
A man of might lets his valour speak
only to others of equal might.'

Wily answered, 'I knew this; I knew already that my lord would speak such words. Now to cut the matter short, let me inform His Majesty that I shall lead the strange creature into his presence, presently.'

Hearing this Tawny felt supremely happy; his face blossomed with delight like a lotus. Wily left straight away and once again bent his steps where Lively was and called out to him in a peremptory tone of voice.

'Hey there! You rascally bull. Come here, come here at once. Lord Tawny wishes to know why you keep up this bellowing, without ceasing and without a hint of fear.'

Lively looked at him, uncomprehending, and asked quite innocently, 'My good friend, who is this Tawny that you are talking about?' Hearing that, Wily, putting on an air of outraged surprise, exclaimed, 'Not know who he is! What, you mean to tell me that you don't as yet know of our Lord Tawny?' And he added with utter disdain, 'Well, well, you'll know soon enough—when you reap the consequences of your ignorance. Let me enlighten you. Celebrated by the name Tawny, he is a great lion; he is the King of Beasts. Possessed of enormous strength and power that are his sole wealth, his heart swelling with pride, his head held high, he stays even now there within the vast circle of that banyan tree, holding court.'

No sooner had Lively heard these words than he felt he had breathed his last. Drowned in the depths of despair, he spoke faintly, 'My good friend, you appear to be a kindly sort of person; and you do have a way with words. If you must absolutely take me there to your lord, at least do me this favour; ask your master to be gracious enough to grant me a safe-conduct.'

'Right you are,' said Wily, 'Well spoken, my friend . . . I see evidence of prudence here; and mind you, what you ask is eminently just. For as the wise remark:

> Earth's true extent may be compassed　　　　　　(94)
> that of the seas and mountains too;
> but the world of a king's mind and thoughts—
> that is beyond anyone's reach,
> anywhere, at any time.

'You stay right here, while I go to our lord; and after binding him by a promise, I shall return and escort you there.'

Wily then went straight to where Tawny was waiting for him. 'My lord, this is no ordinary creature. He is the sacred mount of the great Lord Śiva Himself. When I questioned him, my lord, what do you think he said . . . ?' Tawny was definitely uncomfortable. And Wily spoke in low, awed tones.

'"The Supreme Lord, highly pleased with me, has graciously granted me the right to graze here on the emerald-green meadows bordering the Yamuna. What more is there to say? The great Lord has bestowed this forest on me, as a playground." That's what he said, my lord.'

Tawny's mane quivered; he spoke trembling with fear, 'I know it now. Without the favour of the gods no creature can roam freely, fearlessly, in this lonely forest, grazing in the meadows, and bellowing with impunity . . . . But what did you say to him?'

Wily looked deprecatingly and then he said, 'What did I say to this creature, my lord? I told him a thing or two, without mincing words. "Now look, my dear chap," I said, "Tawny is the special mount of the fierce, warrior consort of Lord Śiva. This great forest is Lord Tawny's domain. And understand this—you

have come here as his guest. Tell you what; you must meet him
in brotherly affection; spend time with him, eat, drink, work and
play with him; do things together in one place as friends . . . ."
He agreed to everything that I said, but, he made a request, "See
that you get a safe-conduct for me from the master." Now my
lord should decide what is best in the circumstances.'

Tawny was delighted, 'Splendid, splendid, my wise servant;
you have spoken to him as if you knew my inmost thoughts. I
grant this chap a safe-conduct. Now, hurry along, man, and bring
this fellow straight here: but . . . listen . . . not until he has also
bound himself to me by some strong oath; take care; for it is aptly
said:

> *A kingdom is held firm by ministers,* (95)
> *who are tested and true, straight, resourceful,*
> *uccomplished and endowed with inner strength,*
> *as a temple is well-supported by pillars*
> *straight, strong, well-polished and firmly-grounded.*

> *Wisdom shows herself in actions;* (96)
> *a minister's in forging friendships;*
> *a physician's in healing life-threatening illness.*
> *Who is not wise when everything goes right?'*

Wily mused as he went to fetch Lively, 'Aha . . . . Things are
turning out well for me; our lord and master is gracious to me
now; he has been won over by my words. No one can be more
fortunate than I am at present.

> *Sweet as nectar is the fire's warmth in winter;* (97)
> *sweet as nectar is the sight of one's beloved;*
> *sweet as nectar is royal favour;*
> *sweet as nectar is food cooked in milk.'*

Approaching Lively, Wily addressed him deferentially, 'My
good friend, I have spoken about you to our master; and he is
pleased to grant you a safe-conduct. So you need have no fear;
approach him in all confidence. But there is one thing that you

37

have to keep in mind. You must always act in agreement with me; don't you get out of step thinking that now that you have the royal favour, you can slight me and act haughty. For my part, I shall work under your direction functioning as minister and shouldering the whole burden of administration. In this way, we shall both enjoy the benefits of royal fortune. You see how it is:

> *A sinful game . . . by unjust means* (98)
> *men make royal wealth their own;*
> *one drives the quarry from its lair,*
> *another strikes it down.*

> *Whoever is too haughty to pay* (99)
> *a royal attendant his honour due*
> *will find his footing insecure*
> *and fall from favour as Fine Tooth did.'*

'Really?' queried Lively; 'And how did that happen?' Upon which, Wily began the tale of *Fine Tooth and the Palace Sweeper*.

There was a city known as Prosperityville where lived a great merchant by the name of Fine Tooth, who was the governor of the city. He managed the administration of the city and the king's personal affairs so well that the citizenry was very well satisfied. As a matter of fact, no one had seen or ever heard of so clever and efficient an administrator. What usually happens is this:

> *Look after the ruler's interests,* (100)
> *and you earn the people's hatred;*
> *work then for the people's interests,*
> *you are shown the door by princes.*
> *In such a conflict, it is hard to find the man*
> *who deals out an even hand to ruler and ruled.*

While he was holding this high position, Fine Tooth, at one time had occasion to celebrate his daughter's marriage. He invited with all ceremony the whole citizenry, the king and his retinue and the royal household, received them with great honour and after treating them to a sumptuous banquet, bestowed rich gifts, fine garments and the like, on them. At the close of the festivities, Fine Tooth personally escorted the king and the royal household back to the palace, and offered the customary courtesies.

Now, there was one Bellowing Bull, a royal attendant, who served as the sweeper of the king's personal chambers. Though it was time for him to have gone home, that day, Bellowing Bull stayed on and occupied a seat that he was in no way entitled to, right in front of the seat reserved for the High Priest. When Fine Tooth noticed this inappropriate act, he caught Bellowing Bull by the scruff of his neck and threw him out. From that very instant, the humiliation he had suffered rankled so deeply in Bellowing Bull's mind that he could not sleep a wink at night. He brooded; he revolved plans in his mind to somehow or other topple Fine Tooth from royal favour. At other times he despaired of his ever being able to accomplish this, and told himself, 'Ah! Why am I letting this thing consume me to such an extent that my body is wasting away? There is nothing that I can do to harm this man. How excellently the proverb puts it:

> *If you cannot get your own back*   (101)
> *why in the world would you shamelessly*
> *rant and froth at the mouth; I ask you.*
> *The chick pea may hop up and down frantically;*
> *but will it crack the frying pan?'*

After some time, early one morning, Bellowing Bull was busy cleaning the floor near the royal bed, while the king was lying suspended between sleeping and waking. As he worked, he muttered, 'O gracious gods! Just look at Fine Tooth's impudence! He holds the Royal Consort in his arms.'

No sooner had the king heard these words than he sat bolt upright and cried out, 'Hey, hey! Bellowing Bull! What are you babbling there? Is this the truth? What? Our crowned queen! Embraced by Fine Tooth!'

'Oh! Pardon, my lord,' replied the sweeper. 'I really don't

39

know what I was saying. I am addicted to the vice of gambling, I must confess. All night I was awake playing dice. Though my hands are employed in the customary job of cleaning, I am so overcome by sleep that I can hardly keep my eyes open.'

The king grew jealous. He thought to himself, 'This fellow has free access everywhere in the palace . . . . So has Fine Tooth . . . . Who can tell? This fellow might have sometime or other witnessed our queen in the arms of Fine Tooth . . . . For it is said, that:

> *What a man watches or does*   (102)
> *or yearns for during the day*
> *he does the same at night in his sleep.*
> *He talks about it; he acts it out.*

'And again:

> *What a man keeps hidden deep in his heart,*   (103)
> *a good thought, or an evil, it will out,*
> *when he babbles in his sleep or in his cups.*

'Moreover:

> *The fool who thinks and tells himself:*   (104)
> *"How enamoured my love is of me,"*
> *he is eternally in her thrall,*
> *a pet bird, at her beck and call.'*

The king lamented thus, in many ways, for many days, until finally he withdrew his favour from Fine Tooth. Why spin a long tale? The king forbade Fine Tooth's entry to the palace.

Seeing that he was no longer high in the king's favour, Fine Tooth began reflecting on his situation. 'Alas,' he said to himself, 'How true are these statements:

> *Which man does Fortune not render proud?*   (105)
> *Which seeker after pleasure sees his troubles end?*
> *Whose heart is not shattered by a woman?*

40

Who indeed can claim he is beloved of kings?
Who does not fall into the clutches of Time?
Which cringing suppliant is held in high esteem?
Which man once caught in the subtle snares
of the wicked, escapes unharmed?

'And again:

Whoever saw or heard of these: (106)
cleanliness in a crow,
truth in a gambler,
forbearance in a serpent,
spent passion in a woman,
daring in a feeble fellow,
discernment in a drunkard
or friendship with a king?

'What's more, I have done no harm to the king; nor to anyone else for that matter. I have not acted in an unfriendly manner; no, not by a single word; and not even in my dreams. Why, then, why has the Lord of the Earth turned his face away from me?'

And Fine Tooth kept turning these thoughts over and over in his mind. Then, one day, noticing him at the palace being refused entry by the guards posted there, the sweeper, Bellowing Bull, laughed derisively, calling out loud to the palace guards, 'Hey there! Hey, hey, you guards! Take care. This is Fine Tooth himself; the man who was used to granting or denying favours to one and all. See that you fellows don't receive the same treatment I did . . . caught by the throat and thrown out on my ear.'

Light dawned on Fine Tooth. 'Ah! I see it all now quite clearly; whatever was done came about through Bellowing Bull's mischief . . . . Oh! How wise is the observation:

A man may be a base-born churl;   (107)
he may even be a fool;
lacking honour on top of it all;

but . . . *if he serves the king,*
he receives honour wherever he goes.

Or, he may be a coward, (108)
a mean contemptible fellow;
but . . . if he's the king's attendant,
he'll not stomach the least affront,
not from any man on earth.'

Bewailing his lot, Fine Tooth went home, disconcerted and his mind in a welter of anxious thoughts. That evening, he sent for Bellowing Bull. He presented the man with a pair of fine silken garments and then spoke courteously to him. 'Look, my friend, you should not think that I threw you out of the Royal Hall of Audience through sheer anger. I acted as I did only because I saw you seated in front of the royal priest, in a seat you were not entitled to. I punished you for misconduct.'

Bellowing Bull accepted the fine garments as if they were the cloths of heaven. Highly gratified, he said to Fine Tooth: 'I forgive you, great merchant; and note this, it will not be long before you see the returns for the great honour you have paid me today; and that will come in the form of the restoration of royal favour and other honours.'

With these words, Bellowing Bull rejoicing in his good fortune returned home. Seeing him leave, his face beaming with joy, Fine Tooth thought to himself,

'A scurvy knave and a pair of scales, (109)
they have one thing in common:
a trifle lifts them high up
a trifle dashes them down.'

A few days later, while cleaning the floor near the royal bed at dawn, as the king was lying half asleep and half awake, Bellowing Bull muttered: 'Our King, what fine judgement he displays . . . he eats cucumbers sitting on the toilet.'

Hearing this, the king sat up in amazement, 'What! Hey you! You rascal! Bellowing Bull! What is this nonsense? It is only because you are a menial working in my home that I refrain from throttling you, right now, this very instant. When have you ever seen me do such a thing . . . the thing you say you saw me do?'

'O, my lord,' replied the sweeper, humbly, 'Pardon, my gracious lord; a thousand pardons. I am an inveterate gambler; all night the dice kept me awake. Though I was cleaning the floor, I felt so drowsy that I must have dropped off to sleep. What I was mumbling in my sleep, I can't say: I don't know what it was, Gracious Majesty; pardon this wretch whom sleep has over-powered.'

The king fell to thinking: 'From the day I was born, I have not done such a thing . . . eating cucumbers, indeed, while answering the calls of nature. If this confounded dunderhead can babble such errant nonsense about me, what if . . . . What if the thing he said about poor Fine Tooth is also sheer rubbish? I am sure of it. How could I have treated him the way I did, stripping the unfortunate man of his position and honours. It is inconceivable that a man like him would ever be guilty of what this blockheaded sweeper alleged he was guilty of. And what's more; in the absence of Fine Tooth the affairs of state as well as the city's administration have all fared badly.'

The king then thought over the matter very carefully, looking at it from all angles. He then decided to send for Fine Tooth, presented him with fine garments and jewels from his own person, and reinstated Fine Tooth in his official position with all honours.

'That's why, my friend, I say to you,' concluded Wily, 'he who out of pride offends those who serve a king, pays for it.' To which Lively replied, 'My good friend, what you say is true. Let us do it the way you suggested.'

Lively being agreeable to the arrangement, Wily escorted him to Tawny's court and presented him, saying:

'Your Majesty, here is Lively; I was talking to you about him. I have brought him here; now it is for His Majesty to decide what should be done.'

Lively bowed with great reverence to the King of Beasts and stood respectfully before him. Thereupon, Tawny extended a massive paw furnished with claws gleaming like thunderbolts and with the utmost courtesy enquired after Lively's health. 'Is all well with Your Honour,' he asked, 'And how is it that you have come to live in this lonely and inhospitable forest?'

Lively then responded, recounting in detail all the events that happened after his separation from the merchant-prince, Vardhamāna. Tawny listened attentively and then said, Friend, don't be afraid; protected by the might of my arm, you may now live without fear or hindrance in our forest. But I'll mention this to you; it is best if you live, move and divert yourself not too far from me; for this forest is full of dangers; it swarms with ferocious beasts.'

Lively folded his paws, nodded and answered, 'As my lord commands.' The interview over to the satisfaction of both parties, Tawny made his way down to the river, drank his fill of the delicious water of the Yamunā, plunged into her cool waters and lazed a while; then he entered the deep woods to roam as his fancy took him.

Time passed in this way. Lively and Tawny spent a good deal of time together and became the best of friends, their mutual affection growing daily. Now, Lively possessed great intelligence and had developed profound wisdom, having studied and mastered many branches of learning. He spent much time and patience instructing Tawny so that in a short while, even a blockhead like the King of Beasts became wise and intelligent. From a creature of the woods practising the wild ways of the jungle, Tawny became civilized, versed in urban ways and manners. Why go on and on? The two friends were so close that they spent all their time together, talking and discussing between themselves, in private and unattended. All the other animals were kept at a distance and shut out of their private confabulations. Our two jackals did not even get a look-in. Lacking the strength of the lion and his skill in hunting and foraging, the animal community, including our two jackals, were unable to forage for themselves as needed. Not getting sufficient food they became lean and pinched with hunger; miserable, they gathered at one spot. As the saying goes:

> *As birds abandon a withered tree,* (110)
> *so too, retainers leave a king,*
> *though lofty and of noble descent,*
> *whose service is barren of benefits.*

Then again:

> *Even retainers of noble birth* (111)
> *and unimpeachable loyalty,*
> *who are held in high honour at court,*
> *are certain to leave the service of a king*
> *who breaks the thread of their livelihood.*

On the other hand:

> *Retainers will never abandon a king* (112)
> *even if he sternly takes them to task,*
> *if only he pays them well and pays in time.*

All things in this world live off one another, using many different strategies to do so, some peaceful, others not so peaceful. Think:

> *Rulers live off their lands,* (113)
> *physicians off the sick;*
> *merchants live off consumers,*
> *the learned off fools;*

> *Thieves live off the unwary,* (114)
> *almsmen off householders;*
> *harlots off pleasure-seekers,*
> *and workers off the whole world.*

> *Snares of many sorts are carefully set;* (115)
> *day and night they lie in wait, watchful,*
> *surviving by sheer strength—fish eating fish.*

The two jackals, Wary and Wily, deprived of their master's favour, lean and pinched by hunger, began to consult with each other. Wily, as usual, began, 'Sir Wary, it seems we are persons of no consequence at court. Moreover, Tawny hangs enamoured on each word that Lively utters; and to such an extent that he neglects his own affairs. As for the other royal retainers, they are all scattered, each one gone his own way. What's to be done?'

'I think you should speak to our master,' answered Wary. 'Even if your words fall on deaf ears, the master should be admonished so that he can draw back from the wrong course he is on. For as the wise observe:

> *A king should receive wise counsel from his ministers,* (116)
> *even if the counsel is not well-received,*
> *as Ambikā's son received from wise Vidura*
> *to turn him away from wrong policies.*

'And again:

> *An elephant in rut runs amok* (117)
> *and the keeper is to blame; a king*
> *rushes into error maddened by pride,*
> *the world points the finger at the prime minister.*

'And remember, my friend, it was you who brought this grass-eating creature to the notice of our master; and so doing, you were really carrying live coals in your bare hands.'

Wily answered, 'Yes, you are right: the fault is mine, not our master's. As the proverb points out:

> *The jackal caught in the duel of rams;* (118)
> *Red Planet's clever trap,*
> *the woman who acted as a go-between:*
> *the ruin of all three was of their own making.'*

Wary asked, 'How did that happen?' And Wily began the tales of *The Holy Man and the Swindler* and *The Weaver's Unfaithful Wife*.

In a certain region there was a sanctuary built in a secluded place;

in it lived an ascetic named Worshipful.[7] In course of time, he had
amassed a goodly fortune by selling the many finely-woven
cloths presented to him by various persons for whom he had at
one time or another performed sacrifices. Not trusting anyone,
Worshipful kept his worldly wealth tied in a knot at one corner
of his lower garment and tucked securely at the waist. Night and
day he guarded it this way; indeed, it is aptly said:

A trouble to acquire; a trouble to protect;   (119)
a trouble if it's lost; a trouble if it's spent;
money is nothing but trouble,
alas! From beginning to end.

Now a rogue named Red Planet[8] who lived by robbery had
been watching the ascetic. He noticed the treasure secured in a
knot at the waist and thought to himself. 'This treasure, now,
how can I steal it from this holy man? The sanctuary has solid
stone walls . . . that I cannot break into; the door is so high that
there is no way I can climb and enter within. So . . . the only way
to relieve the holy man of his treasure is to become his pupil, and
worm my way into his confidence. Once that is done and he begins
to trust me implicitly, I'll have him in my power. For it is aptly said:

One without ambition does not hold office;   (120)
one fallen out of love does not care to adorn himself;
one who lacks learning displays no eloquence;
one who is blunt in speech is never a cheat.'

Having deliberated over the matter, the swindler
approached the ascetic. Intoning the words, '*Om*, salutations to
Śiva,' he prostrated himself before the ascetic and spoke with
the utmost reverence, 'Holiness! Vain and unprofitable is human
existence; youth rushes past like a mountain torrent; life is no
better than a fire built with mere straw; what are pleasures but
shadows cast by clouds? Our relationships with children and
wives, with kin, friends and servants—all a dream. All this I have
understood only too well. Tell me what I have to do to cross this
sea that we call existence.'

Listening to Red Planet speak in this manner, Worshipful responded in earnest tones, 'My son, you are indeed blessed; so young in years, and such indifference to worldly things. As the saying goes:

> *He whose youth is calm and passionless,* (121)
> *he is truly a saint, that's my view;*
> *once the senses have lost their edge,*
> *who in the world is not at peace?*

'Moreover:

> *The senses age first, then the body,* (122)
> *in those blessed with virtue and piety;*
> *but in those who possess neither,*
> *body ages, senses never.*

'You have asked me about the ways and means of crossing this sea of mundane existence. So, come, listen to what I have to tell you:

> *A tiller of the soil, an outcaste with matted hair,* (123)
> *or any other man duly initiated*
> *with Śiva's mystical names and vows; whose body*
> *is marked with sacred ash becomes a twice-born pure.*

> *Uttering the six-syllabled chant mystical* (124)
> *let him place one single flower on Śiva's sacred symbol,*
> *and he is never born again.'*

When Red Planet heard these words, he clasped the ascetic's feet and spoke in a reverential tone to him, 'Your Holiness! Be gracious enough to initiate me into the sacred vows.'

Then Worshipful answered saying, 'My son, I am only too willing to bestow this favour on you. But remember, you should never enter my sanctuary at night, the reason being that it is a command laid upon ascetics who have renounced the world that they should not consort with anyone. This applies to me and to you as well. For it is said:

> A king is ruined by bad advice; (125)
> an ascetic by company;
> a child by fond indulgence;
> a Brāhmana by lack of learning;
> a noble line by evil sons;
> virtuous conduct by serving the base;
> friendship from want of regard;
> investment by mismanagement;
> affection from long absence;
> and a woman by drink;
> a farm too from neglect;
> wealth through misdirected charity.

'Therefore, after taking your vows, you should sleep in a thatched hut at the gates to the sanctuary.' Red Planet readily agreed, saying, 'Your Holiness, your word is law, for it is my sole means of transport to the other shore.'

So at bedtime, Worshipful duly administered the rite of consecration and accepted the swindler as his pupil. On his part, Red Planet massaged his preceptor's hands and feet, brought his writing materials and placed them ready at hand, and performed sundry little services that supremely gratified the ascetic. But at no time did Worshipful let go of his treasure tucked at his waist.

And so the days went by until Red Planet became somewhat restive and began to seriously reflect on the possibility of ever getting his hands on the ascetic's treasure. He told himself, 'Damn it; there seems to be no way I can make this holy man put his trust in me. What should I do then? Shall I knife him in broad daylight? Or simply butcher him as I would an animal?'

As he continued pondering over the options that he had, chance presented itself in an unexpected manner. One fine day, there arrived at the sanctuary, the son of one of Worshipful's old pupils, with an invitation. 'Your Holiness,' said the young visitor, 'I have been sent here to invite you to our house on the occasion of the investiture of the sacred thread for a young member of our family.'

As soon as he received this invitation, Worshipful set out with Red Planet accompanying him. On the way they came across a river. Removing the treasure from his waist and hiding it in the folds of his patched robe, Worshipful bathed and worshipped the deities; and then he addressed his pupil, 'Listen, Red Planet, I am afraid I have to step aside to answer the calls of nature. You watch over my robe and this crystal symbol of Lord Śiva.' So saying he went some distance. No sooner was his preceptor out of sight then Red Planet grabbed the ascetic's robe and ran away post-haste.

In the meantime, Worshipful, whose suspicions had been put to rest by the exemplary qualities of his pupil as he had carefully observed them, sat without a care in the world attending to his bodily needs. And as he sat, he saw a flock of ewes nearby and in their midst there was a pair of rams fighting. The rams would withdraw in great fury and then rush charging at each other, heads bent, forehead clashing against forehead, while streams of blood flowed profusely. A jackal passing by noticed this, and seized by a craving for flesh, he came trotting in and stood right in the middle of the fight between the two rams greedily lapping up the blood.

As he watched this little scene, Worshipful thought to himself, 'Dear, O dear, how stupid can this jackal be? If he happens to get caught at the very moment the two rams go for each other, will he not be crushed to death instantly? I haven't the least bit of doubt on this score.'

At the next deadly encounter of the two fiercely-butting rams, this is exactly what happened. The jackal, lusting after fresh blood was caught between the two heads as the rams charged and was killed instantaneously. 'Ah,' remarked Worshipful, 'The jackal was killed in the crossfire . . . .' Feeling a bit sorry for the poor dumb animal, he got up and returned to where he had left his treasure in his pupil's care.

As Worshipful came slowly picking his way back to the river bank he could see that Red Planet was not there. Washing himself and performing a purificatory rite in a hurry, he saw that his little treasure was gone. 'Alas, alas! I have been cheated,' he cried aloud and fell senseless on the ground. After a few moments, regaining consciousness, he rose from the ground, sobbing and breathing heavily, 'Ho there, ho, Red Planet, where are you? Where have you fled after cheating me like this? Reply, give me an answer . . . . ' Lamenting in this manner and muttering repeatedly, 'And we too, cheated by Red Planet . . . and we too . . .' Worshipful went along slowly, step by step, lamenting his fate all the while.

As he walked along, Worshipful noticed a weaver going with his wife to the nearby town to drink in the tavern. He stopped them saying to the weaver, 'My good man, listen, here I am, a guest approaching you at sundown. I do not know a single soul around here. So carry out the duties enjoined on you and let me have your hospitality. For it is said,

> A stranger at dusk must not turn back unwelcomed;   (126)
> householders who honour and serve a guest
> brought by the setting sun, themselves
> take on an aura of divinity.

'Moreover:

> Water, a pile of straw, and a place to sleep,   (127)
> kind words of welcome, these four things
> are never found wanting in the houses
> or mansions of the good and virtuous.

'And:

> By a gentle welcome the sacred fires are gratified,   (128)
> by the offering of a seat Indra is pleased,
> Kṛṣṇa by giving water to wash the feet
> and the Lord of Beings by the offering of food to eat.'

The weaver heeding these words, turned to his wife and said, 'My love, take this guest to our home. Give him water to wash his feet, offer him food to eat and a bed to sleep on; then wait for me. I shall be on my way to the town and will return presently with plenty of meat and drink for you.'

The wife agreed and walked back home accompanied by the ascetic. Her face glowed with happiness; for being a woman of easy morals, she had a certain man in mind, her lover by the name of Devadatta,[9] whom she planned to meet. How wisely is it observed, that:

> *A cloudy day in the dark half of the month,* (129)
> *with city streets hard to negotiate,*
> *and the husband travelling in distant lands—*
> *Happy times for a man-hungry woman!*

> *Amorous women greedy for stolen raptures* (130)
> *care a straw for the marriage-bed richly-spread*
> *and the arms of a tender, loving husband.*

Also:

> *Ever-hankering after another man,* (131)
> *the slut is always willing to accept*
> *the world's censure, and her family's fall,*
> *even a prison cell and life imperilled.*

Reaching her house, the weaver's wife dragged out an old broken-down cot and giving it to Worshipful said, 'Hey there, Holiness, I am just stepping out to pass the time of day with my good friend who has just returned from her village. I'll be back soon. Meanwhile you may stay here in our home, but please be careful.' Having said this, she went to her room, dressed herself in fine clothes, adorned herself and set out to meet her lover, Devadatta. But it turned out that at that very moment, her husband was on his way home, reeling drunk, his hair untied and floating wildly, stumbling at every step he took and holding a pitcher of liquor in his hands. The woman saw him and at once rushed home, quickly removed all her finery and appeared dressed as before. But the weaver had already noticed her walking rapidly somewhere dressed in all her finery. In addition, rumours about her character that were doing the rounds had already reached his ears. Deeply troubled at heart, he entered the house in a rage and questioned her, 'Hey! You whore, you wicked slut; where do you think you were off to?'

She replied coolly, 'Nowhere; since I left your side and came home I have not stirred from the house. What utter nonsense you talk! Completely stoned, is it? For it is said, and aptly too:

> *Delirium, trembling, tottering, falling down,* (132)
> *a constant patter of incoherent babbling,*
> *these are the sure signs of foul fevers, life-threatening,*
> *and of drunkenness as well.*

'Also:

> *Weakness of hands, casting off one's raiments,* (133)
> *angry flashes, waning of brightness, loss of power:*
> *these are tell-tale signs of a drunken state,*
> *and displayed by the setting sun as well.'*

The weaver listened to her railing and having already marked the change in her dress, now lashed out, 'You whore! Scandalous reports about your character have been reaching me for a long time now. Today I have direct proof of it and I shall punish you properly for it, that's for sure.' With these words, he cudgelled her roundly till her body grew limp; then he took some strong rope, tied her fast to the pillar, and drained of energy by intoxication, fell into a drunken sleep.

At this juncture, in came the woman's friend, the barber's wife, and making sure that the weaver was drowned in sleep, she spoke urgently to the woman, 'Listen, my dear friend, Devadatta is at the usual place expecting you. Go to him, go quickly.'

The weaver's wife retorted, 'Look at the state I am in; how on earth can I go and meet him? You go to my lover, explain the situation and say this to him: "In the state I am in at present how can I possibly come to meet you!"'

To which the barber's wife replied, 'Now, now, dear friend,

how can you talk like this? Is this the way to talk for a free-spirited woman who goes her own way? As you must have heard:

> *Those who like a camel resolve to reach out* (134)
> *for the luscious fruit inaccessible,*
> *who persevere until it lies in their grasp,*
> *their lives, I hold, are praiseworthy indeed.*

'Further:

> *When this world is rife with many different rumours,* (135)
> *and the other is uncertain at best;*
> *when you have snared another woman's husband,*
> *best count your blessings and enjoy your youth.*

'To clinch the matter:

> *Though luck may not be on her side,* (136)
> *though ill-favoured her man might be,*
> *a loose woman will still lie with her lover*
> *in secret, whatever it might cost her.'*

The weaver's wife observed drily, 'That's all very well indeed, but tell me, where can I go tied as I am with strong ropes; and on top of it, here lies my vicious husband right here.'

The barber's wife suggested a way out. 'Listen to me, this drunken sot lies dead to the world; he will not wake up until touched by the sun's rays. So, let me take your place; I'll untie the bonds that hold you. You go and have a good time with Devadatta, but come back quickly.'

Counselled in this manner by her friend, the weaver's wife left home to meet her lover. Moments later, the weaver, some-what mollified, heaved himself up out of his drunken stupor and called out to his wife. 'You there! You spitfire, will you promise that you will never again leave the house, or speak harshly to me? I'll untie you.'

The barber's wife remained silent, afraid that the difference in voice would give her away. The weaver repeated his offer; still the woman made no reply. Angered by her silence, the weaver got up, picked up a sharp knife, and cut off the woman's nose, yelling, 'All right, you wanton, you stay right there . . . and catch me trying again to be nice to you.' Babbling on like this, he dropped off to sleep again.

After a while, the weaver's wife, having enjoyed the delights of love to her heart's content with Devadatta, returned, and enquired of her friend. 'Hey! Friend, is everything all right with you? This wretch did not wake up while I was gone, I trust?'

'O yes, everything is fine except my nose,' exclaimed the barber's wife. 'Now, quick, untie me and let me go home before this man wakes up again. Who knows what he will do next; he may lop off my ears or some other part of me and mutilate me further.'

The weaver's wife untied the bonds, set her friend free and took her own place as before. Standing there, she began crying aloud in an abusive tone, taunting her husband. 'O, you great blockhead! Curse upon you! Do you think you can commit this sort of outrage on me . . . ? On one who is an example of a chaste wife . . . ? You think you can disfigure me . . . ? A model of faithfulness that I am? O, you guardians of the universe! Look down and hear:

> *All you that see and judge Man's moral life;*   (137)
> *Sun and Moon, Air and Fire, Earth and Sky,*
> *and Water, Death and the Human Will,*
> *Day and Night and their twin meeting points.*

'If I am chaste, let these divinities restore my nose to what it was. If I am not, if ever I have entertained the shadow of desire for another man, let them burn me to ashes.'

Having delivered this peroration, the woman addressed her husband once more, 'O, you vile wretch! Look. The power of my chastity is such that my severed nose has become whole again.'

The weaver picked up a firebrand and held it to her face. Lo and behold, he saw plainly that his wife's nose was whole, while a great pool of blood was spreading on the floor. In utter amazement, he untied the knots, released her at once and put her into good humour with a hundred cajoleries.

Worshipful, who had been watching everything that had gone on, now said to himself in utter amazement:

> 'Those texts on policy that Śukra knew (138)
> — Bṛhaspati knew them too — are I daresay
> not a whit superior to Woman's wit.
> How do we protect ourselves from women?

> Falsehood and daring, folly and deceit, (139)
> uncleanness of body and spirit too,
> excessive greed, and lack of compassion,
> these vices are inborn in women.

> Never fall a prey to proud Woman's charms; (140)
> never wish Woman's power to grow and thrive;
> let a man dote on her, straight she plays with him,
> as she would, with a pet bird whose wings are clipt.

> Honey flows freely in her speech; (141)
> deadly poison lurks in her heart.
> O taste the sweetness of her lower lip,
> but beat her on the chest with your fists.

> This whirlpool of suspicion, this mansion of immodesty, (142)
>   this city of audacity,
> this sanctuary of errors, this home of a hundred deceits,
>   this field sown with doubts and distrust,
> this creature hard to tame even by the best, bulls among men,
>   this casket entire of tricks—
> Who created this contraption called Woman? This nectar-
>   coated poison?
>
> To set virtue and the Law at naught?

> Hard breasts, tremulous glances, heaven in her face, (143)
>   sinuous tresses, generous loins,
> low, hesitant tones, constant murmur of conversation,
>   a heart too easily alarmed,

displaying enchantments in love—these excellences!
Extolled! A legion of blemishes!
Let beasts of the wild fawn on these doe-eyed creatures.

They laugh, they weep, to gain their own ends; (144)
they win the trust of others; trust no one themselves.
Let them be shunned therefore like burial-urns,
by all men of good conduct and noble birth.

The King of Beasts with tousled mane (145)
and gaping fierce-toothed jaws;
tuskers glistening with streams of rut;
men of great intellect, heroes in battle—
all turn yellow in the female's presence.

'That's not all:

Pretty on the outside; poisonous within; (146)
they resemble the Gunja's bright berries;
Women! O God! Who did create them?'

Pondering over such thoughts, the ascetic passed the long night with the greatest difficulty.

In the meantime, the go-between whose nose had been chopped off, went home and began to worry. 'What's to be done now? How shall I cover up this great hole in my face?'

While she spent the night anguishing over the situation, her husband was in the palace performing his barber's duties; he returned at dawn. Eager to start serving his customers among the townfolk, he stood in the doorway, and not wanting to waste any time, called out to his wife, 'Dearest, hand me my razor-case quickly; I am going into the city straight away to serve my customers there.'

A brilliant idea flashed across the disfigured woman's mind as she listened to her husband's words. She took one razor out of the case and threw it towards him. The husband, seeing that she had not handed him the entire case with all the razors in it, got very annoyed and flung the razor back in her direction.

Immediately, the wicked woman ran out of the house and set up such a hollering, flinging her hands up and sobbing bitterly. 'Oh! Oh! Protect me; just see what this vile wretch has done to me, a respectable and virtuous woman. He has severed my nose; protect me . . . .'

Presently, the king's officers of law appeared on the scene. They overpowered the barber, bound him securely with strong ropes, and marched him along with his disfigured wife to the court of the city magistrates. The magistrates sternly demanded, 'Fellow! Why have you done such violence to your wife?'

The poor man, utterly bewildered by this strange turn of events was thoroughly confused and could make no reply. At which, the jurors citing texts and following the injunctions laid down in the law, exclaimed:

> *'Altered speech, changing complexion,* (147)
> *eyes darting from side to side in alarm,*
> *drooping, broken in spirit: such a man*
> *having committed a crime is afraid of his own act.*

'And mark this:

> *The man who enters with faltering steps* (148)
> *and a face pale and drawn,*
> *whose forehead is covered in sweat,*
> *who greatly stutters and stammers,*
> *and stands trembling with eyes cast down . . .* (149)
> *scrutinizing with care these tell-tale signs,*
> *those skilled and well-trained know him*
> *to be guilty of wrongdoing.*

'On the other hand:

> *The man who appears in open court* (150)
> *calm and cheerful, with smiling face, defiant eye,*
> *and speaks in clear, firm tones with confident pride,*
> *know him to be true and upright.*

'We conclude from all this that this man is an evil character. Because he has done violence to a woman, he deserves capital punishment. Let him be taken away and impaled.'

As the barber was being led to the place of execution Worshipful saw him and went straight to the magistrates.

'O worthy sirs,' he exclaimed, 'This miserable barber is being unjustly taken away for execution; he is a man of good conduct. Listen to what I have to tell:

> *The jackal at the ram-fight,*   (151)
> *we too, by Red Planet tricked,*
> *the go-between who poked her nose*
> *where it did not rightly belong,*
> *we three cooked our goose ourselves.'*

The magistrates, astonished, asked the ascetic, 'Holiness! How did all this happen?'

Then Worshipful narrated the events of all three episodes in great detail. Having heard it all, wondering at the strange happenings, they set the barber free and delivered their judgement:

> *'A Brāhmana, a child, a woman, a sick man*   (152)
> *and an ascetic may not be put to death;*
> *if the offence be serious, the law lays down*
> *that disfigurement is proper punishment.*

'This woman had her nose cut off as a result of her own actions; now by order of the Court, she will have her ears cut off.' The court's judgement was carried out forthwith; and Worshipful reflecting on these two examples took heart and returned to the sanctuary.

And Wily concluded his tale saying, 'Now, my good friend, you know why I quoted that verse to you, the verse that went like this: "The jackal at the ram-fight and we by Red Planet ... " and so on.'

Wary then asked him, 'My good friend, as matters stand at present, what do you think we should do?'

'Well,' answered Wily, 'Even in these difficult times, some good idea is bound to come up in my mind by means of which I shall manage to embroil these two, Lively, the bull, and our royal lord. And mind you, there is something else; Lord Tawny has fallen into certain evils. For:

> *Monarchs are bound to fall into evils,*[10]   (153)
>   *and all through their own folly;*
> *they should then be resolutely restrained*
>   *by ministers versed in texts of polity.'*

'Evils?' queried Wary. 'What are these evils that you say our Lord Tawny has fallen into?'

'Ah!' answered Wily. 'There are seven evils listed; they are as follows:

> *Women, dice, hunting and drink,*   (154)
> *abusive speech, that's the fifth,*
> *punishment severe beyond reason,*
> *and rapine—that completes the seven.*

'In fact, there is but one single evil which may be named Addiction, possessing seven limbs.'

'Is there only one evil then,' enquired Wary, somewhat quizzically. 'Are there not others, alas!'

Wily agreed and prepared to explain. 'Oh yes, certainly; there are five fundamental evils.'

'I see,' responded Wary, 'and what may their characteristics be?'

Wily proceeded to expound the matter. 'The five evils are: absence or lack; unrest or rebellion; addiction; calamities; tactical inversions.

'To start with the first: when a king lacks the six requisites, which are ministers, land and subjects, fortresses, treasury, allies and punitive power, understand that he has fallen into the evil of absence or lack. Even the lack of one of these constituents characterizes the evil called Absence.

'When external elements such as subjects and ministers and internal elements such as one's inner being and nature are in a state of unrest or rebellion, severally, one after the other, or altogether at the same time, consider that state to be the second of the evils listed.

'The third evil I have already itemized for you, as women, dice, hunting, drink and the rest. Of these, note this; the first four, that is women, dice, hunting, drink, spring from desire and form a group—the desire-group; the other three, abusive speech and the rest, spring from anger and form the anger-group. Further, what has no immediate connection with desire may be perceived to operate in the anger-group. The characteristics of the desire-group are well-known. But the other, the anger-group, though threefold as we have seen, needs further elaboration.

'Abusive speech is the ill-considered and insufferable re-tailing of faults by one bearing ill-will towards another.

'The ruthless and unwarranted employment of torture of different kinds in putting a person to death is known as severity of punishment beyond all reason.

'Relentlessly plundering greed is rapine. Thus, we have the sevenfold evil known as Addiction.

'As for the evil described as calamity, it is eightfold: disasters that are acts of god; disasters caused by fire and water, by disease, plague and pestilence, by panic-flights, by famine and the very she-devil of a rain. The phrase 'she-devil of a rain' is used only for those cataclysmic, deluging rains. All these come under the heading of calamity.

'Now I come to the last evil, tactical inversions: in the employment in reverse of political expedients; which are six in number: peace or alliance, war or expansion, advance or pursuit, halting and holding position, falling back or seeking shelter, and the use of deceiving tactics. For instance, when a king goes to war instead of forging an alliance; when he seeks to make peace instead of going to war; and similarly acting in contrary fashion with regard to the other expedients of policy; wrong policy in short.

'Coming now to the specific case of our royal master, Tawny, the predominant evil besetting him, is the first on our list—Absence. So captivated is he by Lively that he takes no

61

thought of the six constituents that support the state: ministers and the rest. He has further adopted the code and practice of a grass-eater. But why go on bewailing the situation at great length? It is imperative that Lord Tawny should be freed from the bull, Lively's yoke. Where the lamp is absent, we have an absence of light.'

Wary observed somewhat drily, 'Your Honour has no power; how then can Lord Tawny be freed from Lively's yoke?'

But Wily was not to be put down. 'What you observe is true, certainly, my good friend; but . . .

> *Where sheer prowess cannot succeed* (155)
> *a clever ruse may accomplish the end;*
> *the hen-crow by means of a golden chain*
> *brought about the deadly black serpent's death.'*

'O really?' exclaimed Wary, 'and how did that come about?' Wary then began his tale, the tale of *The Crow and the Serpent*.

In a certain region there flourished a mighty banyan tree. A pair of crows built a comfortable nest in its branches and took up residence there. But no sooner had their eggs hatched than a deadly black serpent who had his home in a hollow in the tree trunk, crawled out and swallowed the chicks, even before they had a chance to grow their first feathers. Though he suffered untold grief from the injury perpetrated by that vicious serpent, the crow could not bring himself to abandon that banyan tree which for so long had provided him and his wife a home, and seek another tree. As the proverb says:

> *Crows, cowards, deer, these three,* (156)
> *will ne'er abandon their home;*
> *elephants, lions, and noble men, these three,*
> *faced with dishonour will always leave home.*

After sometime, the hen-crow fell at her husband's feet one day, and wept, 'O, my dear lord, so many of our children have been swallowed up by this wicked serpent; and I am indeed consumed by sorrow, losing all my children. I am dying to go elsewhere. Let us now seek refuge in some other tree. For, as we all know:

> *There is no friend like good health;*   (157)
> *there is no foe like sickness;*
> *no joy equals that of children;*
> *no pain equals that of hunger.*

'We also hear this:

> *If one's fields lie at the river's edge;*   (158)
> *if one's wife sleeps with another man;*
> *if one's home is haunted by serpents:*
> *how, O God! How can one find tranquillity!*

'In all truth, we are living here at the direst peril of our lives.'

With his whole body convulsed by boundless grief, the crow then replied, 'My dearest, we have lived for a long time in this tree; how can we abandon it? You know the saying:

> *A mouthful of grass, a pawful of water—*   (159)
> *where can a deer not live well and happy!*
> *But his native woods where he has lived so long,*
> *he'll never leave, though driven by dishonour.*

'And what's more, I tell you, I shall encompass the death of this evil-hearted and deadly enemy by some ruse or the other.'

The hen-crow then started expostulating with him, 'O my lord, this is a deadly serpent, one with a double row of fangs. How can you possibly hurt him?' To this the crow answered, 'Don't you worry, my dear. Although I am myself powerless to harm this wretch, I still have friends who are well-versed in the texts on political wisdom; they are skilled in devising strategies. Let me resort to them for advice. Then I can carry out whatever plan they suggest; and, in no time, this vicious creature will perish.'

Having spoken these words in burning indignation, the crow then flew off to another tree. At the base of that tree lived his best friend, the jackal. Hailing the jackal with great courtesy, the crow opened his heart to him and told him the whole sad story of his sorrow, concluding with these words, 'Now, my good friend, what would you suggest as the proper course to follow in the present circumstances? Our children's death is nothing but our own death warrant, you know.'

The jackal thought for a while and then spoke to his friend, the crow, 'Well, I have thought over the matter very carefully. Distress yourself no further. By his wanton cruelty, this black serpent, miserable wretch that he is, has only contrived his own impending death. For, it is aptly said:

> *Why need you think of ways and means*   (160)
> *to do harm to evildoers,*
> *when they are sure to fall on their own*
> *like trees that grow by the river's edge.*

'It is also well-known, how:

> *Having devoured a horde of fishes,*   (161)
> *the high, the low, and the in-between*
> *a certain crane through excessive greed,*
> *met his end in a crab's stranglehold.'*

'Ah!' exclaimed the crow, 'and how did that happen?' And the jackal began the tale of *The Crab and the Crane.*

Once, there was a crane who lived on one side of a certain lake. Being very old and hoping to hit upon an easy way of living off the fish in the lake, he stationed himself at the edge of the lake, pretending to be weak and infirm, and refraining from catching even the fishes that swam quite close to him.

A crab who also lived among the fishes, noticed this, and came up to the crane to ask, 'Hey! Uncle, how is it that today you do not seem to be engaged in your favourite pastime of gobbling fishes, as you always do?' To this the crane replied, 'Ah! As long as I could catch fish, I did so and I was well-nourished and content. I spent my days in comfort relishing all your delicious meat. But it now seems that in the near future, a terrible disaster is going to overwhelm all of you, as a consequence of which, in my old age, this pleasant existence of mine will also come to an end. Thinking upon this I have grown extremely dejected.'

'I see,' observed the crab; 'and now, tell me, Uncle, what kind of a terrible disaster are you talking about?'

The crane answered sadly, 'You see, just this morning, I heard a group of fishermen talking among themselves as they were walking by our lake. And this is what they said, "Look, friends, see this great lake that has a plentiful supply of fish; let us fish here tomorrow and the day after, casting our nets far and wide. Afterwards, we shall proceed to the deep lake that lies close to the city and fish there." Considering that in the circumstances, once all of you are destroyed, I myself can expect nothing but the termination of my own existence, my heart is filled with such sorrow that I have no mind to eat.'

Hearing the crane's wicked, dissembling speech, all the lake-dwellers were fearful for their lives, and trembling, began crying out to the crane, 'O Uncle! O Father! O brother and friend! O wise ancient one! If danger threatens, then, some means of averting that danger can be found. O, sir! It is up to you to save each one of us from the jaws of death.'

The wily crane then answered, 'My friends, what can I do? I am only a bird; how can I fight against human beings? But . . . there is one thing which lies within my powers . . . what I can do is to transport each of you from this vast expanse of water to another lake, immeasurably deep.'

Then all the dwellers in the lake, being completely fooled by the crane's deceitful words, crowded around him, clamouring and pleading, 'O friend, O dear Uncle, O kinsman devoid of all self-interest! Take me, take me first . . . . Ah! Has Your Honour not heard the following verse:

Imbued with a passion for benevolence, (162)
saints on earth, possessed of steadfast minds, cherish

*service to others alone, and count as nothing
even the sacrifice of their own life for a friend.'*

At this, the malevolent wretch laughed up his sleeve and congratulated himself, thinking, 'Ah! These fishes have been totally bamboozled by me; they have fallen into my clutches, and now, I can devour them with the greatest ease.' He made a show of assenting graciously to the request of the fishes. Picking them up, a few at a time in his beak, the crane flew to another spot, where on one side of a rough plateau of rocks he ate them quietly. With supreme satisfaction he went back and forth daily on these trips, constantly beguiling his victims with bits of false information.

One day, the crab, who was becoming increasingly agitated by the prospect of his impending death, crawled up to the crane and implored him repeatedly, 'O, Uncle, why aren't you saving me from the jaws of death?'

The crane listened and after a while started thinking, 'Well, well; I am just about fed up with this monotonous fare . . . fish day in and day out. Let me have a change of diet . . . a taste of crabmeat, delicious . . . out of this world.' With this thought, he grabbed the crab in his beak and flew up into the sky. After a while, the crab noticed that the crane had passed over many spots where there was water, avoiding them, and was now preparing to alight on a sunbaked ridge of rock; he asked, 'Uncle, Uncle, where is this fathomless lake that you talked so much about?'

And the crane laughed, taunting the crab with, 'Ah! A lake? There, don't you see those sun-scorched rocks . . . where, all those lake-dwelling friends of yours are resting comfortably? Soon, you will also find your rest there.'

As the crab looked down, what he saw was a huge slab of rock heaped high with fish bones . . . a hideous place of execution. And the crab said to himself: 'O, my god, what is this?

Friends appear foes; foes appear friends; (163)
  and all to gain their own ends;
a few are farsighted enough
  to tell the difference.

> *Better take a walk with a snake;*   (164)
>   *or share your home with rogues or foes;*
> *never put your trust in evil friends,*
>   *false, fickle and foolish.*

'These piles of bones lying around must be the bones of the fishes that this rascal has already devoured . . . no doubt on that score. My time seems to be up; what on earth can I do now? On the other hand why spend thought on it?

> *Even a parent or preceptor*   (165)
> *if launched upon the path of evil,*
> *in arrogance undiscerning of right and wrong,*
> *deserves punishment as the teachings say.*

'Moreover:

> *Fear danger while it's still to come;*   (166)
> *once you're face to face with danger,*
>   *strike hard, with no hesitation.*

'So, as this fellow is about to dash me on the rock, I shall grab hold of his neck with all four claws.' Even as the crane was about to do just that, he found himself firmly seized by the throat with the crab's claws squeezing it. Through sheer ignorance of how to get out of the crab's pincer-like grip, the crane got himself decapitated.

Then the crab crawled back painfully to the lake where the other fishes still lived, holding on tightly to the crane's slender neck, slender as a lotus-stalk. When the fishes asked in surprise, 'Brother, why have you returned?' the crab displayed the severed head like a trophy, and explained, 'You see, friends, this crane enticed the water-dwellers around here with his dissembling speech and carried them to a large rock not far from here, only to dash them on the rock and eat them at his pleasure. But, because I was destined to live longer, I saw through his tricks and told myself, "This fellow is a betrayer of the trusting." I got him and have brought his head and neck. Forget all your fears; all the water-dwellers will live safe and happy from now on.'

The jackal, who was the crow's friend, concluded with these words, 'Therefore, I say to you, "Having devoured a horde of fishes . . ." and so on.'

The crow now pleaded, 'Advise me, noble friend, how is that vicious black serpent to be destroyed?' To which the jackal, his friend, replied, 'Sir, go to a place frequented by royalty and great lords and be on the look out for a piece of jewellery, a gold chain, a string of pearls or any other ornament left lying around carelessly by some wealthy man or other. When you find it, pick it up and drop it in a place where the search for it and its recovery would result in the slaying of the deadly serpent.'

From that moment, the crow and his wife started flying around as their instincts prompted. Soon, the hen-crow chanced upon a lake where she saw the queen with her ladies in attendance bathing and playing in the water, having left their clothes, their chains of gold and necklaces of pearls and other jewels at the edge of the lake. The hen-crow swooped down, picked up a gold chain and flew off towards her own tree-home. Seeing her flying off, the royal chamberlain and some of the palace attendants armed with staves and cudgels immediately followed in hot pursuit. The crow quickly dropped the chain into the hollow where the serpent lived, flew off some distance and watched.

When the king's men climbed the tree, they came upon the black serpent holed up there, hissing, with expanded hood. They set upon it and cudgelled the cobra to death. Retrieving the gold chain they returned to the lake with a light heart. The crow and his wife lived happily ever after.

Wily concluded his tale with this comment: 'To get something done, a proper stratagem ought to be devised; and what's more:

> *In blind arrogance, men often mistakenly disdain* (167)
> *a weak foe; only to find that foe*
> *easily put down at first, soon growing unassailable*
> *like a disease that flares if not contained in time.*

'Nothing in this world is impossible to an intelligent person. As it is said:

> *An intelligent man possesses power;*   (168)
>   *what power does a fool possess?*
> *The raging lion in the wild woods*
>   *was laid low by a humble hare.'*

Wary asked with interest: 'And how did that happen?' Then Wily began the tale of *Dim Wit and the Hare*.

In a certain forest there lived a power-drunk lion named Dim Wit,[11] who ceaselessly hunted down the animals living in that forest. He could not set eyes on an animal without slaughtering it at once. Then all the animals of that forest assembled: antelopes and wild boars, wild buffaloes and wild bulls, hares and all others and went to the lion. With woebegone faces, heads bent low and knees rooted to the ground, they began to speak in humble tones: 'O, great lord! Enough of this killing of the animals living here; it is an extremely cruel and senseless slaughter; an act which is unlawful; which runs contrary to the writ of the world beyond. For we hear that:

> *The sinful acts the ignorant commit*   (169)
>   *for the sake of a single life,*
> *bring them only sorrows that extend*
>   *over a thousand recurring lives.*

'And again:

> *How can a wise man do such acts,*   (170)
> *by which he gains an ill repute,*
> *by which he loses public trust,*
> *and goes straight down to the infernal pit?*

'And then again:

> *For the sake of this wretched body alone,*   (171)
> *a thing perishable and ungrateful,*

a veritable sink of impurities,
do the ignorant commit sinful acts.

'Realizing this, Your Honour ought not to extirpate all our species in this manner. We on our part shall send one animal by turns, daily, for your food, if only our lord and master would stay at home and wait for it. This way neither our royal master's earthly existence nor our own species will come to an untimely end. This is the duty of monarchs; pray follow it. For it is aptly observed:

When the protector of the earth enjoys   (172)
his kingdom lightly, a little at a time,
as if he were tasting the Elixir of Life,
in the full knowledge of its resources,
then prosperity to the fullest extent is his.

The lord of the earth, who through folly,   (173)
slays his subjects as if they were goats,
derives satisfaction once only;
for him there is no second chance.

A king who aspires to great success,   (174)
should greatly strive to nurture his people
with gifts, honours, other marks of esteem,
as a gardener waters his tender sprouts.

As a cow is milked at the proper time,   (175)
as a vine needs to be watered first
before its flowers and fruit can be gathered,
so, too, subjects should be cared for well.

A king is a lamp, wealth, the oil   (176)
    gathered from the people.
Who has ever perceived him as shining
    lit by in-dwelling virtues radiant.

As the fine seedling flourishes   (177)
    nurtured with care to yield fruit in time,
    so, too, subjects well protected.

> *Gold, grain and gems and drinks of various sorts,* (178)
> *and whatever else kings enjoy*
> *all come from the people.*

> *Great monarchs prosper greatly,* (179)
> *working for the people's good.*
> *It's only in the people's ruin,*
> *they find their own ruin, without a doubt.'*

Dim Wit listened to his people attentively and answered, 'Well and truly spoken, sirs. But, let me make one thing quite clear. If one animal does not present himself here daily, where I sit waiting, then, I promise you, I shall set out and devour all of you.'

'Yes, so be it,' they choroused their assent. And with a great weight off their minds the animals began to roam in the forest without fear. Each day, at noon, an animal presented itself without fail before Dim Wit, for his midday meal; each species by turn providing one individual, grown old or unworldly, grief-stricken or fearful of losing wife or child.

One day it was the turn of a hare. When the assembly of animals had instructed him to go to the lion's lair, the hare set out, thinking as he went along, 'Now, how on earth is this vicious beast to be got rid of? Let's consider:

> *What is impossible if you have intelligence?* (180)
> *What is unachievable if your will is firm?*
> *Who will not fall prey to a sweet and smooth tongue?*
> *What is unattainable if you persevere?*

'I shall destroy that lion.'

Determined to do this, the hare proceeded very slowly, planning to arrive well beyond the appointed time; and with an anxious heart deliberating all the while as to how best to kill the lion. He finally arrived at the lion's lair at the close of day. As for the lion, he was in a murderous rage, his throat pinched by hunger and he was licking his chops, thinking, 'Oho! The very first thing that I'll do in the morning is to kill all the animals.'

As Dim Wit was contemplating this prospect, the hare drew near, walking slowly, step by step; he bowed low to the lion and stood respectfully. Seeing that the hare had been so long in coming and was pitiably thin and small as well, the lion, blazing with fury, burst out menacingly, 'Hey! you rascal! For one thing you are hardly a miserable mouthful; for another, it is long past my dinner-time. As a punishment for this grievous offence, I shall kill you straight away; and then in the morning I shall extirpate all the animals here, every one of them, do you hear?'

The hare bowed very low and in utmost humility quavered, 'O, my lord, the offence is not mine; nor is it any offence of the assembly of animals that this has happened. Patience, my lord, please listen and I shall tell you the real reason.'

The lion retorted grumpily, 'O, well, all right, tell me quickly, before you find yourself stuck between my fangs.'

The hare began, 'My lord, this morning the assembly of animals decided that it was the turn of the hares to provide your meal for the day. Seeing that I was rather small, they picked five other hares to accompany me. On our way, out sprang a lion, from a huge hollow in the ground and confronted us, demanding, "Where do you think you are going? Call upon your chosen deities; say your prayers." We stood terrified and then answered. "Sir, we are on our way to the lair of our lord, the lion, Dim Wit; according to our contract with our lord, we are his midday meal this day." And this other lion retorted, "Oh! Is that so? If there is a contract that the animals here have made, it should be a contract with me, since this forest in my domain. That Dim Wit you mentioned is an imposter. Call him out to come and meet me here; and come back quickly. There shall be a trial of strength between the two of us and whoever is the victor will be the king here; and he will have the right to eat the animals in this forest." Ordered by him, my lord, I have come to Your Majesty. This is the reason for the delay in my arrival. Your Majesty may now do what you think right.'

At these words, Dim Wit roared, saying, 'My good fellow, if this is so, come, show me that false lion, that imposter, so that by venting my anger against the animals on this fellow, I can regain my peace of mind. For it is wisely observed:

> *Land, friends, or gold are the triple fruits of war;* (181)
> *in the absence of even one of these*
> *a man is foolhardy to start a war.*

> *Where no rich booty awaits him;* (182)
> *where only defeat faces him;*
> *a wise man does not look for grounds*
> *that may give rise to a war.'*

The hare said, 'What you say is indeed true, my lord. Warriors fight when they see a threat to their territory. This fellow however, is safely holed up in a fortress. He emerged from his fortress and blocked our way, as you know. It is a fact that an enemy ensconced in a fortress, is a formidable enemy. As it is excellently noted:

> *Not a thousand elephants,* (183)
> *and not ten thousand horses,*
> *can furnish kings with the power*
> *that a single fortress can.*

> *A lone archer stationed on the ramparts* (184)
> *can hold his own against a hundred foes.*
> *Therefore it is that experts on statecraft*
> *sing the praises of a fortress secure.*

> *Of old, guided by his preceptor* (185)
> *Indra, fearing the Titan, Gold Robe,*
> *had a fortress framed and built for himself*
> *by the Divine Architect's[12] skill and powers.*

> *Then Indra bestowed the boon* (186)
> *that a king who held a fortress,*
> *a conqueror would be. Therefore,*
> *the earth abounds with fortresses.'*

Dim Wit listened to the words of the hare, and said, 'Ah! My good friend, show this imposter to me, even, if as you say, he is skulking within his fortress, so that I might kill him. For how aptly is it observed:

> *The mightiest of heroes* (187)
> *if he fails to nip disease in the bud*
> *or fell a foe the instant he rears his head,*
> *can expect to be struck down himself*
> *by disease or foe greatly grown in strength.*

'On the other hand:

> *A hero who goes forth girt in energy and pride,* (188)
> *having taken the measure of his own power and strength,*
> *   can single-handed smite his foes, even*
> *as the Bhṛgu Chief[13] hacked down the princes.'*

The hare demurred. 'That is all very well, my lord. But, even so, the lion that I saw earlier today was prodigiously strong. I really don't think it is wise on the part of our lord to go forth and seek him without being fully aware of his strength and prowess. As the proverb says:

> *To rush headlong in rash impatience* (189)
> *before measuring one's own strength and power*
> *against the other's is to court disaster,*
> *like the moth that plunges into a blazing fire.*

'And further:

> *If a weak man sets forth with great pride* (190)
> *   against a strong foe,*
> *like an elephant with broken tusks,*
> *   he beats a hasty retreat.'*

Dim Wit rasped out, 'And what business is it of yours? Just show me where that imposter is, hiding in his fortress.'

'As you wish, my lord,' replied the hare. 'Let His Majesty follow me.' And he set out leading the way.

In a little while they came to a well. The hare stopped and addressed Dim Wit; 'See, my lord: who can stand before Your Majesty's prowess? Seeing you approaching at a distance, this imposter has lost no time slipping into his fortress. Come: let me show this fellow to you, my lord.'

At these words, Dim Wit spoke with some impatience: 'Quick, show him to me quickly, my good friend.' And the hare pointed to the well. Dim Wit, whom we all know to be a complete idiot, looked down the well and seeing his own reflection in the water, let out a tremendous roar, which, resounding inside the well was magnified and came out at him twice as loud. 'Oh! What a powerful lion he is!' exclaimed Dim Wit and leaped headlong into the well, flinging himself on his own reflection; and thus he died.

The hare bounded back, exultant, to the assembly of animals. With unbounded joy, he apprised them of all that had taken place and the happy outcome of his mission. Profusely congratulated and praised by the grateful animals, the hare lived happily in that forest.

Wily concluded his tale with: 'So you see why I say to you: "He who has intelligence, has strength . . . " and so on.'

'Purely accidental,' retorted Wary, loftily, 'What is known as "the crow-palm fruit fallacy."[14] Granted, the hare did succeed in luring the lion to his death, but it is still unwise on the part of a weak person to practise deceit on the high and mighty and hope to get away with it.'

Wily retorted, 'Be that as it may: whether a person is powerful or powerless, he still has to take a crack at what he thinks is worth attempting. As the proverb puts it:

> *Fortune is surely his who constantly strives;*   (191)
> *it is cowards who wail, 'O, my fate, it's my fate.'*
> *Strike fate a blow; show your manliness*
> *using whatever strength you have:*
> *What matter if your efforts fail.*

'Another point: the gods themselves befriend those who are ready and persist in their efforts: as the following well illustrates:

> *When men are determined, gods come through for them;* (192)
> *as Viṣṇu, his discus and his divine mount*[15]
> *came at the weaver's call to help him in his fight.*

'And also:

> *A well-contrived stratagem* (193)
> *is beyond even Brahmā's*[16] *ken.*
> *The weaver assumed Viṣṇu's guise,*
> *and lay in the arms of the princess.'*

Wary pricked up his ears and asked, 'Oh! How did that happen? Can success really follow on a well-devised plan that is carried out cleverly and with determination? Even if it is a deceitful plan?' And Wily began the tale of *The Weaver and Princess Charming*.

In the eastern region known as Gauda, there was a flourishing city called White Lotuses, where lived two friends, a weaver and a chariot-maker. Being master craftsmen in their respective trades, they had amassed so much wealth that they kept no count of their spending. They dressed in the most expensive clothes, fine and richly coloured; adorned themselves with flower garlands of various sorts; chewed scented betel leaves and nuts; and were redolent of the fine perfumes of sparkling camphor, musk and aloes that were wafted around them. Daily, they worked at their trade for three watches and devoted the last watch to their personal care, after which they met every day in the public squares, or in temples and other such places that people resorted to: the theatre, assemblies, friends' houses where birthday feasts and banquets were held, halls where festivals and other events were being celebrated. They returned home at dusk. And so their days glided by.

Once, during a great festival, all the citizenry turned out in their finest, dressed in whatever garments and jewels they could afford and sauntered through the city meeting in temples and other public places that people normally resorted to. The two friends, the weaver and the chariot-maker were also out, dressed in beautiful clothes and jewellery. As they walked around, watching the finely-attired and beautifully adorned citizens milling around, they happened to pass by a great mansion, dazzling white. In an upper balcony sat the princess surrounded by her companions. Her twin breasts, firm and budding in the spring-time of youth, marked with beauty the space over her heart; her waist was slender, sloping charmingly down to compact hips; her hair, glossy and dark blue like rain clouds, flowed in gentle waves; golden circlets in her ears swayed lightly as if they were made to be swings for Love himself to dally in pleasure; her face was radiant with the delicate loveliness of a lotus freshly opened. Like blessed Sleep holding in her grasp the eyes of the whole world, she appeared as a vision before the two friends who gazed on her.

As he stood with his eyes riveted on that maiden of incompa-rable loveliness, the poor weaver was pierced right through his heart and mind by all the five arrows[17] of the mind-born god.[18] Summoning up all his firmness of mind, he somehow managed not to let his appearance and bearing betray his emotions and returned home, where, he saw only the princess in whichever direction he looked. Breathing out long, hot sighs, the lovesick weaver threw himself on the coverlet spread over the couch and lay there, thinking only of the princess and picturing her before his eyes as he had seen her earlier. And he murmured his longing in verse:

> 'Where beauty is, there virtues[19] dwell,   (194)
> > so poets say, neither true nor well:
> > seated in my heart
> > so close, and yet so far,
> formed in every limb of loveliness exquisite,
> > my beloved consumes my body.

'Or to see it differently:

> *One heart drooping shot through with yearning,*   (195)

the other by my beloved abducted,
yet another sustains my life:
    Say, how many hearts have I then!

'On the other hand:

If to the whole world, virtues are the cause (196)
of only happiness, then why in the world
does the happy blend of virtues
in this doe-eyed girl, burn me thus?

Whoever makes a place his home (197)
    will surely guard it well;
You live in my heart, my artless charmer!
    Yet you burn it cruelly, unrelenting.

The coral berry of her lower lip; (198)
those twin globes, her breasts,
rising high in the pride of youth;
her navel's hollow, and diminutive waist;
her hair by Nature's own hand curled:
    all these my mind contemplates;
and bitter pain through my frame surges,
all at once: that comes as no surprise:
but, that the curves of her cheeks
gleaming with lustre of pearls
should burn me over and over again—
Is there any justice in that?

Wearied after passion's ardent play (199)
will I be fortunate ever to rest
and sleep for the briefest moment
the sleep that follows love's celebration—
    my chest on her breasts moist with sandal paste
    and glowing like the globed temples of a tusker
    maddened by spring fever,
    while caged within her arms she holds me fast?

    If it is Destiny's Will (200)

that I be slain, are there no other means
to compass that end
but this doe-eyed girl?

If my eyes grow weary gazing out, (201)
teach these eyes too, O my heart,
that same magic whereby you see my beloved face to face
though far away she stays.
Even her sweet company sought after,
is certain to rouse intense anguish for you
—for you are all alone, my heart—
Those lost in themselves—they never find happiness;
blest are they who desire the happiness of others.

The moon's pearly lustre, she has stolen; (202)
but the moon is a dull, cold, clod;
Her eyes' glowing loveliness is that of the moon-lotus,
and that is not unpardonable, I guess;
that sportive gait an exuberant elephant displays—
the poor beast does not know, it is his no more:
From me, the slender beauty has carried away,
my heart, knowing—the more to marvel in that!

She appears everywhere; on the earth, (203)
in the sky; in the far corners of space.
I'll call her to mind with my life's last breath;
the lissom maid pervades my universe.

All states of mind are transitory, Buddha claimed, (204)
O what an untrue statement that!
Thinking perpetually upon my love,
the moments of my life are an eternity.'

Bitterly lamenting his fate in this manner, the weaver with his thoughts and feelings in a mad whirl, passed the night with great difficulty. The next day, at the customary hour, the chariot-maker, elegantly dressed, came to the weaver's house. What does he see but his friend sprawled on his unmade bed, breathing out long, burning sighs, his cheeks pale and tears trickling down. Seeing him in that state, the chariot-maker exclaimed, 'Oh! My friend! What is the matter with you? You are in such a state.' But the weaver, though his friend pressed him repeatedly to disclose what had gone wrong, would not speak out of embarrassment. Then the chariot-maker, in a fit of desperation, spoke this verse:

> 'He is no friend whose anger you fear; (205)
> nor is he a friend on whose words you hang
> for fear you know not where you stand;
> he is a friend whom you can trust,
> as you can trust your mother;
> what are others but mere acquaintances.'

Then the chariot-maker after feeling his friend's heart and other vital spots with a skilled hand, said, 'My friend; this is no ordinary fever that has brought you to this state; it is love's fever, I think.'

His friend's comment provided the weaver the opportunity to speak. He sat up and recited this verse:

> 'The man who discloses his grief (206)
> to a faithful wife, a loyal servant
> a sincere friend, or sensitive master,
> is bound to find relief.'

Having said this, the weaver recounted his whole, sad tale, in detail, from the moment he had set eyes on the princess.

The chariot-maker fell into deep thought; and then he asked his friend, 'Are you not afraid of transgressing the Law? You are an artisan, belonging to the class of traders and merchants—those who carry on business; the king belongs to the class of warriors, those who are rulers and administrators of the kingdom.'

The weaver replied immediately; 'The Law allows a warrior a third wife, as you well know. Who knows if the princess is not the daughter of a lady of my class, belonging to the business community. All I know is that I am head over heels in love with her. How well the poet[20] has expressed it:

I have no doubt that by the Law, a warrior's bride (207)
she can rightly be, for my noble heart yearns deeply for her,
when in doubt, the heart's truest prompting is
to the virtuous, unassailable authority.'

Realizing that nothing could change his friend's mind, the chariot-maker, who was in a quandary, remarked, 'My dear friend, what is to be done?' To which the weaver replied, 'How should I know? Because you are my friend, I have told you everything.' And he fell silent.

At last the chariot-maker said, 'Get up, my dear friend; have a bath; and give up this hopeless despondence. I shall think of some way of helping you, so that you will enjoy the delights of love with the princess.'

With his hopes revived by his friend's promise, the weaver now rose and went about the normal routine of his life. The following day, the chariot-maker returned, bearing a mechanical contraption fashioned like a bird; like the golden eagle that was the Lord Viṣṇu's mount. It was made of wood and gaily painted in different colours and had cleverly devised pegs to operate it in an unusually novel manner. He set it down and explained its working to the weaver.

'Look, my friend, here is this mechanical bird that I have constructed for you. See how it works; if you push these wooden pegs in, it will rise and fly wherever you wish to go. Then if you retract the pegs, the flying machine will begin to descend wherever you wish to dismount. Now, this very night when all the world is asleep you are going to use it. After you have attended to your bath and other preparations to get ready, I shall make use of my skill and knowledge to dress and adorn you in the guise of Lord Viṣṇu Himself. You will then mount this bird to fly to the palace and bring it down on the terrace adjoining the princess' own private apartment. Once there you may make

81

whatever arrangements you wish with the princess. I have already ascertained that she sleeps on the terrace, alone.'

Having instructed his friend, the chariot-maker left. The weaver passed the remaining hours of the day in a hundred fond imaginings. In the evening, he bathed, burnt incense whose smoke perfumed his whole body, dusted himself all over with fine sandalwood powder; rubbed his limbs with delicately scented creams; made his breath sweet and fragrant by chewing betel leaves and scented nuts; sprinkled flower fragrances on himself; and put on richly-dyed and perfumed silken garments with his friend's help. A diadem and other fine jewels and garlands of fragrant flowers completed the weaver's costume as Viṣṇu.

Meanwhile, the princess lay on her bed, alone with her thoughts, gazing up at the moon that drenched the terrace with its cool, ambrosial rays. Thoughts of love flitted lightheartedly through her mind. Suddenly, she saw the form of Lord Viṣṇu mounted on the divine eagle in the sky; the bird alighted on the terrace and the godlike form stepped out. The princess gazed on that form for an instant and then jumped up from her bed in a flurry; she fell at the feet of the divine personage, worshipped him and spoke in low, reverent tones, 'For what purpose am I graciously favoured by this divine vision, Supreme Lord? What service is required of me? Command me, Lord.'

Replying to the princess, the weaver spoke in sonorous, measured tones and with infinite tenderness, 'Gracious Lady! It is you who have brought me here.'

'Lord, what am I but a poor mortal maiden?' she replied.

'Oh, no, no,' replied the god, 'No mere mortal, my lady, but my true, divine consort, banished to earth by a dire curse. I have protected you until this day from all contact with a mortal man. Tonight, I shall wed you by the Gandharva[21] mode of marriage.'

Reflecting that this was a happy event far beyond her wildest dreams, the princess assented. 'Yes, Lord,' she whispered; and they became man and wife; the marriage was consummated.

The days flew by in paradisal bliss as the couple enjoyed all the raptures and delights of love; and their love grew fuller and richer day by day. And everyday before the night had run its full course, the weaver would rise, mount the bird, saying, 'My love, I have to return to the Realms of Light, to Vaikuṇṭa.' Bidding her a fond farewell, he would return home before daybreak and quickly slip into his house without being seen.

Then it happened that one day, the palace-guards in charge of the apartments of the princess noticed that she was seeing a man. Fearing for the safety of their lives if they ignored this fact, they went in great trepidation to the king. 'Great lord; assure us first of the safety of our persons and lives, for we have something of the utmost importance to convey to His Majesty.' When the king promised, 'Yes, you have my sworn word,' they began: 'Your Majesty, even though we have done our utmost to protect our gracious Princess Charming and to ensure that no man enters her apartments, we have noticed that the princess appears to be in love and to be meeting a lover. This is a matter beyond our control and competence. His Majesty has to decide what to do.'

The king was astounded; his mind was in a welter of anxious thoughts; and he reflected thus:

> 'A daughter is born' — *start of a world of worries:* (208)
> *'Find the fittest bridegroom'* — *the biggest problem of all:*
> *Once wed, will she be happy, or will she weep:*
> *'Father of a girl!'* — *just another name for grief.*

'Moreover:

> *No sooner born than her mother's heart she steals;* (209)
> *growing up she brings pain to loving hearts:*
> *given in marriage, she can still bring dishonour:*
> *Daughters! unavoidable disasters!*

'Similarly:

> *Having brought into the world his creation,* (210)
> *like a daughter, the poet too agonizes.*
> *Will it be read and judged by the worthy?*
> *Will it give them pleasure? And be free of faults?'*

83

Revolving such distressing thoughts in his mind, the king went to the queen and addressed her. 'My lady, pray listen carefully to what the attendants of the Royal Household have to report. Think who this man might be who has committed a treacherous act and incurred the wrath of the God of Death Himself.'

When the queen had heard what the attendants attached to the apartments of the princess said they had noted, she was extremely agitated; hastening to her daughter's private apartments, she looked carefully at the princess. Her daughter's lips were bruised by having been kissed with great ardour; there were nail-scratches present on her body.[22] The queen burst out in anger, 'You wicked girl! You spoiler of family honour! What's this that you have done? You have permitted the violation of your maidenly honour? Who is this man who has dared to come near you? Who has seen Death face to face, to do such a thing? Speak and tell me the whole truth.'

And the princess overwhelmed by shame bent her head and lowering her eyes, keeping them fixed on the floor, slowly retailed the recent events in her life: the coming of Lord Viṣṇu mounted on the celestial bird; his courting of her, and her marriage.

The queen's face, as she heard it all, blossomed with joy. With her face wreathed in smiles and her whole body thrilling with delight, she walked quickly to the king and addressed him, 'My lord, your prosperity waxes; indeed, you are blessed. The blessed Lord Viṣṇu Himself visits our darling daughter, nights. He has made her his bride by the Gandharva mode of marriage. Tonight, you and I shall see him with our own eyes: in the stillness of midnight we shall stand concealed in the window niche. But He does not exchange words with ordinary mortals.'

Hearing this the king's heart was close to bursting with joy. He passed the day with great difficulty, a day that seemed to stretch out like a hundred years. When night fell, he and the queen ensconced themselves secretly in the window niche with their eyes fixed on the sky. And as they waited, they saw a form descending from the sky; mounted on the divine Garuḍa, and appearing in the guise of Lord Viṣṇu; bearing all the emblems attributed to the Lord; holding in His four hands the lotus, the conch, the discus and the mace. Everything was as Lord Viṣṇu is depicted and described.

Happiness flowed through the king's whole frame; he felt as if he had been immersed in a pool of divine ambrosia. Turning to the queen, he said, 'My queen, who in this whole wide world is more blessed than you or I, for the Supreme Lord Viṣṇu himself waits in love on our beloved child. All the hopes and desires that we cherished deep in our hearts for her, are now completely fulfilled. Further, through the greatness of our son-in-law, I can now bring the entire earth under my royal sway.'

At this juncture, the emissaries of Emperor Valorous,[23] Overlord of the South, who ruled over nine times ninety lakhs[24] of villages, arrived at the capital of Princess Charming's father, to collect the annual tribute due to their master. The king, however, puffed up with pride at having obtained Lord Viṣṇu Himself as his son-in-law, did not receive the emissaries with the respect they merited and the customary honours due to them. Vexed by the treatment they received, the emissaries complained indignantly, 'O king, the stipulated date for rendering tribute due to our emperor is long past. Does this mean that Your Majesty is withholding the tribute due to the emperor? It appears that Your Majesty has of late somehow come into possession of an un-expected source of power that is not of this world,' they added with irony and continued, 'Sir, this will surely make Your Majesty incur the wrath of Emperor Valorous, which, let us inform you, is like the blazing storm winds compounded with the poison of the dreaded serpent in the ocean depths and resembles nothing other than the Destroyer Time,[25] Itself.'

When the king, father of Princess Charming, heard this, all he said was, 'Go to hell,' and had them shown out contemptuously. The emissaries returned to their own land and reported all that had happened to their master, exaggerating the facts a hundred thousandfold, so as to kindle his wrath. Emperor Valorous at once had his forces assembled and lost no time in setting into motion his campaign against the rebellious vassal. He set out at the head of his fourfold army,[26] surrounded by feudatory princes and his retainers. As he started, he exclaimed in great rage:

> *'This king may enter the ocean depths;*   (211)
> *or climb Mount Meru,[27] by Indra protected;*
> *but, I swear, I will not fail to slay him,*
> *vile wretch that he is: this is my sworn oath.'*

By long, uninterrupted marches, the emperor quickly reached the eastern kingdom of Gauda; and he began laying waste his enemy's lands. The people of the outlying regions of Gauda, who survived the carnage, fled to the capital; rushing to the palace gates they clamoured for help, cursing their king. But all this outcry did not in the least bother him.

In the following days, when Emperor Valorous with his powerful army drew near the gates of the capital itself, the City of White Lotuses, and started laying siege to it, the council of ministers with the royal priest and leading dignitaries of the city came to the king and petitioned him, pleading, 'Lord, a powerful enemy is at the gates, laying siege to our capital. How can Your Majesty sit unconcerned as if nothing has happened?'

The king, perfectly at ease, answered, 'Honourable sirs, relax, remain calm; there is no need to be agitated. I have already thought up a plan to slay this enemy; and, gentlemen, what I have in mind to destroy his power, you will all know soon enough—at dawn tomorrow.' He then issued orders to have the city's gateways and ramparts well-manned and heavily guarded. Then, he sent for his daughter. Receiving her with all royal honours, he spoke tenderly to Princess Charming: 'My beloved child, banking on your husband's prowess, we have let matters come to a point where hostilities between ourselves and our foe are already afoot. I think you had better speak to the Supreme Lord Viṣṇu, when he comes to you tonight, that in the morning our enemy ought to be destroyed.'

When her husband came that night, Princess Charming told him what her father had said. The weaver listened to her words and then smiling indulgently, reassured her, 'Gracious Lady, this battle of mortals! What is it but a mere trifle, of little consequence! In the dim, distant past it has been child's play for me to slay the powerful Titans, great potentates, such as Gold Robe, my uncle, known as the Slayer, the twins, Honey and Honey-Comb, and others . . . thousands of them who possessed magical powers and could make themselves invincible, change shapes and so on. So go to the king and tell His Majesty, "Be of good cheer; at dawn, Viṣṇu will let fly his discus on Your Honour's enemy and destroy him with all his forces." Bursting with great pride, Princess Charming repaired to her father and told him what her husband had promised.

The king, mightily pleased, summoned the guard at his chamber-door and ordered him to instruct the town-crier to make a proclamation in the city by drumbeat, to this effect: 'In the battle tomorrow at dawn, when Valorous, the emperor, is slain, our citizens may keep as their own, whatever they are able to find and seize by themselves in the enemy's camp: grain, gold, elephants, horses, weapons and other treasures.'

When the citizens heard this proclamation made by drumbeat, they were transported with joy and they talked among themselves, 'O, how powerful is our lord, the king. Look how he stands firm, calm and collected, even when the mighty army of the enemy stands outside our city gates. There is not a shred of doubt that our king will annihilate the enemy forces in the morning.'

And here in the palace, our weaver, all thoughts of love-making fled, sat deeply despondent, pondering over the critical situation he was in; and taking counsel with himself, he meditated, 'O, Lord, what should I do now? I could simply get into my flying machine and fly away somewhere; in that case, I lose this pearl among women, my bride, forever. And on top of it, Valorous, victorious in battle, will kill my poor father-in-law, enter the royal apartments and carry off my wife. That must not be. Therefore, I have to accept the challenge and do battle. Death is certain and with it the extinction of all my hopes and desires. In any case, it is death to lose my bride and live without her. Why go on like this? Either way, it is certain death. Think no further; better choose the best way; do what is noble and worthy. Moreover, it is quite possible that the enemy, seeing me in the guise of Lord Viṣṇu and mounted on the divine Garuḍa, may think it is the god himself in person, and flee in terror—who knows! And is it not aptly said:

> *In danger or dire straits, or in misery,*   (212)
> *the great and noble should ever courage display.*
> *Raised high by daring, undaunted,*
> *they surmount hardship with hardihood.'*

When the weaver had come to the decision that he would stand and fight, the divine bird, son of Vinatā,[28] went at once to Lord Viṣṇu, abiding in the Realms of Light, known as Vaikuṇṭṭa, and spoke, 'Great Lord, there is a great city on earth, known by the name of White Lotuses. There, a weaver, assuming the guise of Your Divine Self, loves the daughter of the king. The sovereign of the southern lands, who is far more powerful than the king who rules in the City of White Lotuses, has arrived at the capital to extirpate this king. The weaver on his part, stands firmly resolved to aid his father-in-law. Now, I am putting this forward: if the weaver is killed in this battle, then it will be bandied around in the world of mortals, that Lord Viṣṇu was killed in battle by the Overlord of the Southern lands. Lord, if such rumours persist in the world of mortals, what will follow is that the performance of sacrifices and other religious rites and ceremonies will disappear off the face of the earth. Heretics will be encouraged to destroy temples and shrines. The devotees of the Lord and the mendicants who bear the triple staff will forsake their religious orders and observances. In view of these possible developments, it is for the Lord to pronounce His decision.'

Then Lord Viṣṇu having reflected deeply on the matter, turned to Garuḍa and addressed him in solemn tones. 'O, King of Birds, you have spoken well; now, hear me. This weaver has a spark of divinity in him. Further, it is ordained that he will be the slayer of the powerful monarch Valorous. The only way to

accomplish that purpose is this battle; and you and I have to aid
the weaver. Therefore a part of me shall enter his mortal frame:
you should infuse part of your divine power into his wooden
bird-mount and my discus should impart part of its power into
his fake-discus.' Garuḍa answered readily, 'So be it.'

In the meantime, on earth, the weaver inspired by Lord
Viṣṇu, instructed Princess Charming, 'Gracious Lady, now that I
am all prepared and ready to do battle, see that all arrangements
for the auspicious ceremonies performed on the eve of battle, are
made.'

The weaver was dressed in full battle-array. The mark of
victory made with red sandal-paste was placed on his forehead;
prayers were offered, the gods honoured, and the hero's sanctified offering for victory made up of yellow orpiment, black
mustard seeds, flowers and other auspicious articles was
accepted by the weaver.

Dawn appeared. The thousand-rayed god, the sun, gracious
friend to lotuses, rose, shining like a bright jewel set on the bridal
forehead of the eastern sky. Martial trumpets rent the air; battle
drums sounded roll after thunderous roll rousing all hearts,
setting them thirsting for victory; and the king of Gauḍa rode out
of the city through the great gateway to take his appointed place
on the battlefield, where the two opposing armies were already
drawn up in battle formation. The foot soldiers went into action
first.

At that moment, the weaver mounted his bird-vehicle and
from the terrace of the palace that glowed bright as moonlight,
he scattered largesse, as was customary, on the crowds gathered
in the square below: gold and silver coins, precious jewels and
other articles of value. Watched by the citizens with unbounded
curiosity, the weaver riding his bird then flew straight up into the
vault of the sky, cheered by the people who paid homage to him.
He circled the city and then sped towards the battlefield. Poised
over his army, the weaver put Lord Viṣṇu's magnificent conch to
his lips and blew hard.

One blast of that conch was enough to strike terror into the
enemy's army. Elephants and horses and the great princes who

rode them, warriors in chariots, foot soldiers, all reeled in fear and confusion, repeatedly voiding urine and excrement. Some, unable to endure the torment, fled the field shrieking as if they were demented; others fell in a dead faint, or rolled on the ground; yet others stood transfixed in terror, their eyes riveted on the sky.

All the Immortals arrived on the scene, consumed by curiosity, to view this strange battle. The Lord of the Immortals, amazed, then spoke to Brahmā, the Creator. 'Lord, is this some mighty war with Titans and powerful enemies of the gods, that the Supreme Lord Viṣṇu Himself is present here to do battle, mounted on Garuḍa, the foe of serpents?'

Thus addressed, the Creator reflected:

> *'Never will Viṣṇu let fly on mortals* (213)
> *His discus red with the blood it has drunk*
> *striking the foes of the Immortal Gods.*
> *The lion will never use his mighty paw*
> *that fells great tuskers, to swat flies.*

'Then, what strange occurrence is this?' And the Creator Himself was lost in wonder, which is why I said previously:

> *Even the Creator does not see through* (214)
> *a well-devised piece of fraud.*
> *For the weaver in Viṣṇu's guise,*
> *did indeed embrace the princess.*

As the gathered Immortals watched with mounting curiosity, the weaver flung his discus, which cut Emperor Valorous in two and immediately returned to the weaver's hand. Aghast at this, all the kings and princes who were allies of the emperor leaped off their mounts and chariots and fell prostrate before the Viṣṇu-form; their heads and knees, their arms and hands were bent low in obeisance as they implored the victor: 'Lord, a leaderless army is lost. Bearing this in mind, spare our lives. Command us. Tell us what is expected of us, now.'

To that whole vast princely host pleading in such words, the

Viṣṇu-form spoke reassuringly: 'Let Your Lordships have no fear from this moment. Whatever this king, Strong Armour of Gauḍa commands you to do, do that, obeying him at all times unhesitatingly.'

'We shall, Lord,' answered all the princes gathered there, willingly accepting the command of the Viṣṇu-form.

Thereupon, the weaver bestowed on King Strong Armour all the enemy's possessions: men, elephants, horses, chariots, and various other treasures. Having done that he lived happily ever after with the princess, enjoying all imaginable pleasures.

'And this is why I say, "Once a man has made his decision . . . " and so on and so forth,' observed Wily.

Whereupon Wary observed, 'Why, in that case, if Your Honour is such a man, one who has made his decision, go ahead; work towards accomplishing our cherished goal; and good luck.'

Wily then took his leave and sought an audience with Tawny. Having bowed low, he seated himself in his appointed place. The lion then addressed him, 'Your Honour, how is it that we have not seen you around for a long time now?'

'My lord, some urgent business that touches our lord and master closely, has come up today,' replied Wily. 'Though it is an unpleasant piece of information, I have come here to acquaint His Majesty of it because it concerns his well-being. To be the bearer of bad tidings is never the wish of royal retainers; rather, it is the fear that through neglect timely action might not be undertaken to deal with the situation, that makes them speak. For it is aptly said:

> *Men holding high office in the state* (215)
> *speak when questioned, if they are well-wishers;*
> *out of loyalty to the master,*
> *that springs from excess of affection.*

'Further:

> *It is easy to find men, O King,* (216)
> *who always speak what is only pleasant to hear.*

But one willing to speak, or listen to what is wholesome,
though unpleasant—Ah! That man is hard to find!'

Because Wily seemed to speak with such earnestness, Tawny enquired of him most courteously, 'What is it that Your Honour wishes to speak to me about?'

Wily answered with alacrity, 'Ah! My lord, it is about Lively. Having succeeded in gaining your complete trust, he now has designs upon your life, which on occasion he has conveyed to me in secret because of the great trust he reposes in me. He has spoken thus, "Listen, I have scrutinized the strengths and weaknesses of your master and gauged the state of his Three Powers[29] as well. I plan therefore to kill him; I can seize his sovereignty for myself with the utmost ease." This is the day Lively has picked to carry out his plan. As you are our hereditary lord and master, I have hastened to acquaint Your Highness with this.'

Tawny remained speechless at this, stunned by the terrible blow that had hit him like a bolt of lightning. Having correctly grasped Tawny's state of mind from his appearance, Wily continued, 'Alas! This is indeed the worst evil that can spoil a chief minister's career. How true is the saying:

> *When minister or monarch climbs to dizzying heights* (217)
> *Goddess Fortune stands on both feet holding them up—*
> *A load unendurable for a woman—*
> *Alas! She lets go of one or the other.*

'For, indeed:

> *A broken thorn, a shaky tooth, a wicked minister—* (218)
> *O, what a blessed relief to pull them out by their roots.*

'And again:

> *When monarchs place a single minister* (219)
> *sole authority in matters of state,*
> *he waxes proud, infatuated with power;*
> *pride breeds scorn for service under another;*

92

scorn provides a foothold deep in his heart
for the craving to win independence;
and for that independence's sake,
he practises against his master's life.

'As it is, my lord, Lively manages the business of the state as he pleases, without let or hindrance. Therefore, it is in the fitness of things that:

> *A minister however faithful at heart* (220)
> *who in the course of his duties, rides roughshod*
> *over obligations to consult with his lord,*
> *is not to be looked upon with favour*
> *by a king concerned for his own future well-being.*

'But such is the nature of rulers that:

> *Those who do good out of affection sincere* (221)
> *yet somehow earn unpopularity;*
> *others who do harm by practising guile*
> *gain nothing less than full-throated acclaim.*
> *The wavering moods of princes failing to find*
> *a stable resting-place, elude our grasp;*
> *the nature of service, the duties thereof*
> *inscrutable in the extreme, are ever*
> *beyond reach of even seer or sorcerer.'*

Tawny having listened to Wily's comments, replied, 'After all, Lively is my servant. How can he possibly entertain any hostility towards me?'

Wily retorted with some asperity, 'He may be a servant, or he may be not; that proves nothing one way or the other. Indeed it is aptly said:

> *There can be no royal functionary* (222)
> *who does not aspire to royalty;*
> *so long as he has no power of his own,*
> *he is content to pay court to another.'*

To which the lion replied, 'Good friend, even so, I cannot find it in my heart to turn against Lively. For:

> *Who in the world does not love his body*   (223)
> *however tainted by defects it might be;*
> *once dear, a person remains always dear,*
> *no matter what offences he's guilty of.*

'And,

> *Disagreeable his actions might be,*   (224)
> *harsh and cruel his speech as well;*
> *at all times, a person dear to one,*
> *will ever cause the heart to fill with joy.'*

Wily retorted, 'Ah! isn't that precisely the trouble with elevation to greatness, though? He whom the master made his mainstay, on whom he put his whole trust to the exclusion of all his other subjects, he is the very person who now aims to be master himself. Is it not true then:

> *A man may be of mean or of noble birth,*   (225)
> *once the royal eye looks on him with too much favour,*
> *he finds himself beguiled by the charms*
> *of Her Ladyship, Royal Sovereignty.*

'Therefore, my lord, this Lively who is the current favourite should be out of favour on account of his treachery; he should be rejected. For indeed, it is excellently spoken:

> *A kinsman of honour most worthy,*   (226)
> *a son or brother or friend dearly loved,*
> *who turns his face away from rectitude through folly*
> *deserves rejection by those who seek success.*
>> *Widely-known in the world is this saying — women*
>>> *sing it too:*
>> *'What use are rings of gold if they make your ears sore!'*

94

'And in case my lord thinks, "Lively . . . he is of enormous bulk . . . he might be of great service to me" —that too, I submit, is a false assumption.

> *What use is a fractious tusker*   (227)
> *that will not serve the king?*
> *A man may be fat, a man may be lean;*
> *he is best who gets things done right.*

'Perhaps His Majesty's heart is moved by compassion for Lively; that is not politic either. For it is well-known:

> *A man who leaves the righteous path*   (228)
> *to pursue an unrighteous course,*
> *will in time fall on evil times*
> *and reap the bitter fruit of remorse.*

> *Let a man but fail to accept advice*   (229)
> *most excellent offered by friends,*
> *he will in no time fall from his place*
> *and come under the sway of his foes.*

'It is a fact that:

> *Although maxims of practical wisdom justly state*   (230)
> *what may be done and what may not, the low and vulgar*
> *in their loose thinking pay no heed, as if they lacked for*
>
>   *ears,*
> *but pursue the wrong course without let or hindrance.*

'Moreover:

> *Where one will speak and one will listen*   (231)
> *to counsel beneficial in the end*
> *though harsh and hateful at the time,*
> *there prosperity delights to dwell.*

'In addition:

> *For ministers appointed to high office,*   (232)

to mislead princes whose spies serve as their eyes
is neither right nor wise.
Bear. therefore with what's unpleasant, or pleasant, O King;
advice both pleasing and salutary is hard to find.

Never should a newcomer be favoured (233)
at the cost of slighting the family retainer;
no weapon is more effective than this
in sowing dissension in the realm.'

To this, the lion replied, 'No, no, my good friend, pray do
not say such things; for it is well-known that:

Once acclaimed in the open Assembly (234)
as, 'Behold, here is a man of merit',
he must not be cried down as lacking all merit
for fear of one's convictions appearing shaky.

'And what's more, considering I granted him sanctuary at the
time Lively came to me as a suppliant, how then can he now prove
so ungrateful?'

Wily at once retorted:

'Does a scoundrel require provocation (235)
to fly into a great rage?
Or a saint need kindness to make him calm?
Isn't it just the same with lime and sugarcane?
It is the inherent nature of each
to produce its own flavour distinctive.

'And this too is true:

Try your very best to honour a rogue (236)
he will still remain true to his nature.
You may have a dog sweated,
or rubbed with musk if you choose,
his tail still remains curled.

'And I say more:

> *Even small favours shown to men* (237)
> *richly blessed with a wealth of merits, look great;*
> *The moon's rays are enhanced, indeed*
> *when they shine over the peaks of Snow Mountain.*[30]

'Whereas:

> *The favours of the meritorious* (238)
> *bestowed on those devoid of merit*
> *perish like moonbeams falling on the peaks*
> *of the Mountain of Black Resin in the darkness of night.*

'And what's more:

> *Lost are a hundred kindnesses* (239)
> *   shown to the base;*
> *lost are a hundred wise maxims*
> *   spoken to fools;*
> *lost are a hundred words of advice*
> *   on the incorrigible;*
> *lost are a hundred sage observations*
> *   on the dull-witted.*

> *Lost are gifts heaped on the undeserving;* (240)
> *lost is benefaction on the mean-spirited.*
> *lost are good deeds on the ungrateful;*
> *lost is courtesy on those unused to it.*

'Add to this, my lord:

> *A cry in the wilderness;* (241)
> *rubbing perfume on a corpse;*
> *planting lotuses on dry ground;*
> *incessant rain o'er salt-marshes,*
> *adorning the faces of the blind—*
> *like these is speaking good sense to fools.*

'What's more:

> *To persist in milking a bull, thinking:* (242)
> *'O! What a great udder, it must be a cow':*
> *To embrace a eunuch, exclaiming:*
> *'Ah! A young maiden of elegant charm':*
> *To pick up a bit of glass cut to catch light*
> *and sparkle, mistaking it for a sapphire:*
> > *O! How vain and useless!*
> *So is the delight in serving the witless*
> *that is born of blind affection for them.*

'Therefore, our good counsel should never be brushed aside by our lord and master. As the oft-quoted saying goes:

> *What tiger, monkey, snake advised,* (243)
> *I did not follow: And therefore*
> *have I now been brought to this pass*
> *by the tricks of this scurvy fellow.'*

Tawny asked, 'And how did that happen?'

Then, Wily began his tale—the tale of *The Grateful Beasts and the Ungrateful Man*.

In a certain town there lived a Brāhmana named Yajnadatta.[31] His wife, worn down by grinding poverty reproached him daily, saying, 'O Brāhmana! You sluggard! You stone-heart! Can't you see the children suffering, pinched by hunger? Yet you sit there, and not a care in the world? Go, go and find something to do . . . to provide food for us . . . anything that's within your power . . . and come back quickly . . . .'

Finally, tired of listening to his wife's daily complaints, the Brāhmana decided to go on a long journey and left home. In a few days he found himself entering a great forest. Wandering about in it, he soon grew parched with thirst and started searching for water. He chanced upon a spot where there was a well, overgrown with long grass. Peering into it, he saw down at the bottom a tiger, a monkey, a snake and a man. They saw him too.

The tiger was the first to react; 'Ah! Here comes a man,' the tiger thought to himself; and he called out, 'O noble soul! The saving of life is the noblest of virtues; consider that and pray pull me out so that I may once more live happily in the midst of wife and children, kinsfolk and dear friends.'

Yajnadatta answered, 'Ah! The very mention of your name strikes terror into the hearts of all living beings. I am afraid of you, I swear.'

But the tiger did not give up, and spoke again,

> *'The slayer of a Brāhmana, a drunkard,*   (244)
> *an impotent man, a breaker of vows,*
> *a traitor—for all these the wise prescribe*
> *rites of atonement—for the ungrateful, none.'*

And he added, 'I bind myself with the triple oath. Therefore, there is no reason for you to fear me. Be merciful and help me out.'

The Brāhmana communed with himself, thus, 'Well, if misfortune strikes one as a result of saving a life, then so be it; and count it a blessing.' Coming to this conclusion, Yajnadatta pulled the tiger out of the well.

Now it was the monkey's turn, 'O virtuous man! I beg you; please help me out too.' Heeding the monkey's plea, the Brāhmana pulled him out.

Next the snake spoke, 'O Twice-born![32] Please help me out too.' And the Brāhmana hearing those words, said, 'Good Heavens! Simply the mention of your name makes every one quake with fear; how much more to touch you.'

'Sir, we are not free agents,' answered the snake, 'we would not bite a soul if we were not constrained to do so. But to reassure you, I shall bind myself with the triple oath; do not be afraid of me.'

The snake swore his oath and the Brāhmana lifted him out. Then they all advised him earnestly saying, 'Listen, you see that fellow down there. He is the repository of a legion of evils. Don't help him to get out of the well. Beware; don't trust him an inch.'

The tiger, as he was preparing to return home, said, 'You see yonder, sir, that mountain with many peaks? That's where my home is, in a ravine on the north slope. You should come there sometime and do me the honour of a visit, so that I may have the opportunity to return your kindness. I would be reluctant to carry forward into my next birth, the debt I owe you in this.' With these words he set off towards his home.

The monkey now told the Brāhmana, 'Sir, my home is also in that same region, near a cave beside a mountain torrent. Do visit me there, without fail.' And he bounded off in that direction.

The snake then spoke, 'Whenever you are in dire need of any sort, just think of me.' And he slid away in the direction he had come from.

All this time the man in the well had been shouting, calling for help, 'O Brāhmana, good sir, help me, pull me out please.'

At last the Brāhmana relented, thinking, 'After all, he is a man even as I am.' And out of pity he helped the man out of the well.

'I am a goldsmith, sir,' said the man as soon as he had got up safely, 'and I live at Bhṛgu-Kaccha.[33] Any time you have gold to be worked into ornaments, just bring it to me.' And the goldsmith walked away towards his native city.

The Brāhmana continued roaming in the forest, looking and searching, but found nothing whatsoever; so he turned his steps toward home. On the way he remembered the monkey's invitation; he went there and found the monkey at home. The monkey welcomed him and offered the most delicious fruit, sweet as ambrosia. When Yajnadatta had eaten his fill and was refreshed, the monkey said, 'Friend, if this fruit serves your needs in any way, don't hesitate to come here daily and visit me; and you'll receive it.' The grateful Brāhmana responded warmly, 'Your Honour has served me in full measure, nothing lacking. But there is one little favour I would ask of you; would you direct me to the tiger's home?'

The monkey took him along to where the tiger lived. Recognizing Yajnadatta at once, the tiger, eager to repay the former's kindness, brought out a necklace and other ornaments of wrought gold and explained, 'Sir, sometime back, a certain prince whose horse had run away with him came here alone. When he was within range of my spring, I killed him and removed all this from his person. I have looked after these and kept them safely for you. Here, accept these gifts and then continue on your journey as you please.'

Yajnadatta accepted the tiger's gifts and as he walked, he recalled the goldsmith's parting words. 'Yes, that's where I shall go next; I'm sure the goldsmith will help me by selling these ornaments of gold.' So he did.

The goldsmith received the Brāhmana with great respect, offering him all due hospitality: water for washing his feet, the customary guest-offering of milk, honey and other appropriate articles; and offered the Brāhmana a comfortable seat. Then, having feasted him with fine food and drink and provided whatever else seemed needed to refresh a weary guest, the goldsmith said, 'Command me, Your Honour; what can I do for you?'

'I have some gold which I would like you to sell for me, if you will,' replied Yajnadatta

'Show it to me,' said the goldsmith; the Brāhmana did so.

The moment the goldsmith set eyes on the ornaments, he thought to himself, 'Hey, what's this? These are the very same ornaments I had made sometime back for our prince.' Examining the ornaments and making sure that that was indeed the case, the goldsmith said, 'Wait right here, sir, while I go and show these to someone.' He then hurried to the palace and showed the jewels to the king who exclaimed in surprise, 'Where on earth did you get these?'

'A Brāhmana has come to my house as a guest; he brought these with him, my lord,' answered the goldsmith.

At once the king's mind started working, 'So, this is the villain who killed my son. He will reap the fruit of his evil deed.' And the king called to the guards and issued orders, 'Go, seize this accursed Brāhmana, bind him fast and at the first light of dawn, have him impaled.'

When the Brāhmana found himself seized and bound in fetters, he at once thought of the snake who appeared before him the moment he was remembered and said, 'Sir, what service can I render you?'

'Release me from these fetters, my friend,' he replied.

The snake told him, 'This is what I shall do. I shall go to the palace and bite the king's beloved wife. Not all the charms and incantations of mighty magic-workers, nor all the medicines and salves that expert physicians use as antidotes against poisons can have any effect to neutralize my poison. I shall see to that; nothing but the touch of your hands will be able to revive the queen. Then they would have to release you.'

Having made this promise, the snake slid quickly to the palace and bit the queen. She fell lifeless. Then there was such an uproar in the palace; wails of despair went up; the whole city was plunged into gloom and confusion; all sorts of experts were summoned or sent for. And they all came, hurrying: magic-workers and exorcists, persons who used bird-charms against snake bites; physicians skilled in the knowledge and use of different antidotes for snake-venom; even persons from other lands who were versed in the lore of poisons arrived at the palace. They all tried their best, using all the skills they possessed, applying salves, administering every treatment they knew of or muttering incantations and devising charms. But to no avail. The queen lay in the grip of the deadly poison. Finally a proclamation was made throughout the city by beat of drums. Hearing it the Brāhmana volunteered, 'I think I can neutralize the poison and revive the queen.' No sooner had the words left his mouth than the guards freed Yajnadatta, took him to the palace and ushered him into the royal presence.

'Sir, can you restore the queen to life?' asked the king. The Brāhmana went to the queen's bedside and by the touch of his hands neutralized the poison and brought her back to life. The king was overjoyed at seeing his dear wife restored to life and health; grateful, he paid Yajñadatta great honour, treated him royally and then asked him courteously, 'Sir, please tell me the truth; how did you come by all this gold?'

Thereupon, the Brāhmana related the whole story in detail, right from the start. The king, now in possession of all the facts, immediately ordered the goldsmith's arrest and rewarded the Brāhmana with the gift of a thousand villages and also made him the prime minister. Yajnadatta brought his family over. By taking charge of all matters of state and administering the kingdom well and by performing many sacrifices and amassing spiritual merit, he lived in great happiness surrounded by family and friends, enjoying all the comforts that life could provide.

'Therefore I say, my lord, "What tiger, monkey, snake, advised . . . ."' And Wily continued,

> 'A kinsman or friend, an elder,[34] or king,　　　(245)
> pursuing a wrong path ought to be restrained.
> Fail to correct his ways, and you find yourself
> eventually being controlled by his will.

'My lord, Lively is clearly a traitor; but:

> The bounden duty of the benevolent　　　(246)
> is to painstakingly save friends bent on evil;
> this is the true and only righteous way;
> any other way the wise declare unrighteous.

'For we know this:

> He is kindly who preserves a pure act from violation;　　　(247)
> 　　She is a true wife who displays compliance;
> he who is honoured by the learned is esteemed intelligent;
> 　　true greatness is that which does not breed arrogance;
> Only he finds peace who is not tormented by greed;
> 　　he is truly a friend who does not exploit a friend;
> 　he is a man who is not cast down in adversity.

'As well, my lord:

> A man may sleep with his head in the fire,　　　(248)
> or even rest on a couch of serpents,

103

> *but never should he hold in high regard*
> *a good friend who is hell-bent on evil.*

'This evil in the shape of Lively's society has turned out detrimental in three ways[35] to His Majesty. If His Majesty disregards our good counsel which has been articulated clearly in a number of ways, and if he chooses to go his own way as he pleases, then the minister can in no way bear the blame, in case His Majesty comes to grief in the future. For it is wisely observed that:

> *When a king driven by passions reckons not*   (249)
> *what is good and what is proper but charges around*
> *wherever his fancy leads him, swollen with pride,*
> *he plunges down misery's dark ravine*
>   *like an excited bull-elephant.*
> *Then, heedless of his own disorderliness*
> *he turns on his ministers to cast blame on them.'*

Tawny then interjected, 'In these circumstances, my good friend, should Lively not be cautioned?'

'Cautioned, my lord? Good heavens! What kind of policy is that?' retorted Wily. 'For it is known that:

> *You caution a man, and straight out of fear*   (250)
>   *he dissembles, or, he decides to strike.*
> *Have no doubt; it is most impolitic*
>   *to caution a foe by word or by act.'*

Tawny demurred, saying, 'But . . . listen, Lively is a grass-eater; as for us, we are flesh-eaters. What harm can he do to us?'

'That is the point,' replied Wily. 'Yes, he is a grass-eater, Lively is; and yes, Your Majesty is a flesh-eater. So, he is food; Your Majesty is the eater of that food. Besides, this fellow, if he cannot himself wreak harm, is sure to find someone who can and incite him to do so. For is it not rightly said:

> *A scurvy fellow, though weak and powerless*   (251)

104

can still set another on to plot against the world.
The whetstone by itself cannot cut,
but it sharpens the blade of the sword that can.'

To this argument the lion objected, 'I cannot really see how that is possible.'

Said Wily, 'Why, Your Majesty is perpetually battling with numerous animals: rutting bull-elephants, wild bulls, buffaloes, wild boars, tigers, leopards; Your Majesty's body is covered by wounds and scars made by the onslaught of tooth and claw and charging horns of these creatures. As for this fellow, Lively, he is constantly at your side and he scatters his dung and urine everywhere. Out of this mixture worms will breed. Being in close contact with your body these worms will find weak points in it, wounds, fissures, breaks in the hide, to enter and bore deep inside. And then what? Your Majesty is done for. For it is said:

> *Never grant asylum to any person*   (252)
> *whose character is not known to you.*
> *It was Drone's mistake, we know,*
> *that led to poor Crawly's death.'*

'O, is that so?' asked Tawny, 'And how did that happen?'
Then Wily began the tale of *Crawly, the bedbug and Drone, the wasp.*

In the inner apartments of the palace of a certain king there stood a couch incomparable, furnished with all imaginable beauties and comforts. A coverlet was spread over it and at one particular spot on the coverlet lived a bedbug named Crawly.[36] Surrounded by her large extended family of sons and daughters, and their sons and daughters, and sundry other kin, she bit the king when he was fast asleep and sucked his blood. Richly fed by blood she grew really plump; she was a striking bedbug indeed.

As she was living thus comfortably, one fine day, a wasp named Drone came wafted in by a breeze and dropped on the couch. Drone derived supreme satisfaction resting on that couch. Overspread with a most exquisitely fine coverlet and with double cushions, the couch felt exceedingly soft, soft as the broad, sandy banks of the river Gaṅgā; and it was perfumed with a rare fragrance. Captivated by its delightful feel, Drone hopped here and there and all over the couch and as luck would have it, at one point he encountered Crawly who was taken aback and spoke sternly, 'Hey, you there, where have you come from? Landing like this into a residence only fit for princes, eh? Leave, get out at once.'

Drone replied, 'O noble lady, please, please do not speak like this. For:

> Fire is most revered by Brāhmanas;   (253)
> Brāhmanas are the most revered of all classes;
> the husband is the only one revered by women:
> a guest is most revered by the whole world.

'I am your guest. Now, I have tasted the blood of all four classes: priests and teachers, warriors and rulers, merchants and traders, peasants and workers. I find their blood thin and salty, slimy and not nourishing in the least. The person to whom this couch belongs however, must have vital fluids coursing through his body that are delectable without doubt, and sweet as ambrosia. I guess his blood must be disease-free and healthful from the constant and consistent efforts of physicians to maintain the balance of the humours, wind, bile, phlegm, with the use of herbal and other medicinal infusions. It must be enriched by foods tender and moist that melt in the mouth; foods prepared from the flesh of the choicest creatures that roam the land, the seas and the air; foods seasoned with the finest blend of ginger root, black pepper, cayenne, cane-sugar and pomegranate seeds, and served. My guess is that this person's blood is like the elixir of life. I am eager therefore to taste this sweet and fragrant substance which is bound to satisfy not only my taste buds but nourish my body as well; by your gracious favour, of course, my lady.'

'Impossible,' replied Crawly, 'it is quite inconceivable that fiery-mouthed stingers such as you can be permitted to do so. Therefore, be gone; leave this couch; out. For it is rightly observed that:

> *He who has no sense of time and place,* (254)
> *and of what is right and proper;*
> *who does not know a thing beyond himself;*
> *who acts without due deliberation;*
> *he is a fool who reaps no reward.'*

Drone fell at her feet and begged and pleaded with Crawly to grant him this great favour. Being of an exceedingly obliging nature Crawly was almost persuaded to say, 'Yes, all right,' when she remembered something she had heard on a prior occasion. It was like this. The short tale of Muladeva, son of Karni and prince of confidence tricksters, was being related to the king while she lay snugly ensconced in a corner of the coverlet listening; at one point Muladeva was answering the question of the maiden Devadatta, in the following words:

> *'However angry, we must not spurn* (255)
> *one who has fallen at our feet;*
> *in so doing we scorn all three gods,*
> *Brahmā, Viṣṇu and Śiva.'*

That clinched the matter. Crawly assented to Drone's plea taking care to exhort him, 'But, mind you, don't you ever begin eating at the wrong time and in the wrong place, understand?' she said.

'And what, noble lady, is the right time and the right place?' asked Drone, adding, 'Being a newcomer, I am unfamiliar with the protocol of such matters.'

Crawly then advised him, 'Listen, when the king's body is overpowered by wine or fatigue, or by sound sleep, then, you may quietly bite him on his feet; that would be the proper place and the right time; is that clear?'

But alas, in the early hours of the night, the moment the king had dropped off to sleep, Drone who was a silly creature indeed and unaware of the proprieties and also terribly famished, bit the king on his back. The king was startled as if he had been burned by the fiery point of a meteor; as if he had been touched by a live firebrand; as if he had been stung by a scorpion; he jumped up and then sat down. He felt the sore spot on his back. Turning around the king shouted to his attendants, 'Hey there! fellows, come here, something has bitten me. Look diligently through every inch of this couch; fine-tooth-comb it until you find the insect that is hiding in my bed.'

Hearing the king's words, Drone, terrified, scampered into an interstice in the frame of the couch and disappeared. Meanwhile, the royal attendants who had entered followed the king's commands, hunted through the bed searching with the aid of a lamp. As fate would have it, they found Crawly clinging to the nap of the fabric. And she was killed promptly with all her family.

Wily concluded, 'Therefore I said, my lord, "To one whose character is not known to you . . . " and so on. There is something else too, my lord. Your Majesty has forsaken his trusted, hereditary servants; that is wrong. For as the story goes:

> *Whoever clasps strangers close to his heart*   (256)
> *forsaking those in his close counsels,*
> *will assuredly meet his death*
> *as foolish Fierce Yowl did.'*

'Oh! What story is that?' asked Tawny with some surprise. Then Wily began the tale of *The Blue Jackal.*

Once a jackal named Fierce Yowl[37] lived in a cave in the outskirts of a city. One day as he was hunting around for food, his throat pricked with hunger, he entered the city. At once the street dogs fell upon him snapping at his limbs and jabbing with their sharp, pointed teeth. Terrified out of his wits by the savage barking, Fierce Yowl ran here and there, reeling and stumbling in his desperate attempts to escape. Finally, he rushed into the house of an artisan, where he tumbled into a huge vat of indigo dye. The dogs ran away in the direction they had come from.

The poor jackal whose alloted span of life had not yet run its full course, clambered out of the vat with much difficulty and ran back to the forest on the outskirts of the city, where a crowd of animals of various kinds, who were roaming around in the vicinity, took one look at him dyed a brilliant indigo and fled, their eyes widening and quivering in terror; and they ran crying out, '*Ayo, ayo* . . . what weirdly-coloured animal is this that has come into our midst?' As they ran they talked among themselves, spreading the news. 'What kind of creature is this . . . ? It has never before been seen around here . . . . Where has he come from . . . nobody knows what his strength is . . . or how he will act and behave . . . . We had better flee this forest . . . for as the wise say:

> *When you do not know someone's strength,*   (257)
>   *or his lineage and conduct,*
>   *it is not wise to trust him—*
>   *and that is in your best interests.'*

Seeing all the animals fleeing from his sight, Fierce Yowl understood that they were afraid of him: he called out to them, 'Hey there, hey, you wild creatures; why are you all fleeing in such terror? The sovereign of the gods, noticing that the wild creatures of this forest have no sovereign of their own, annointed me, Fierce Yowl, to rule over you as your lord. Come back, come and live happily in the safety of the cage of my paws, strong as thunderbolts.'

Hearing his declaration, the whole concourse of wild creatures: lions, tigers, leopards, monkeys, gazelles, hares, jackals and the rest, came forward, bowed low and paid homage to Fierce Yowl; then they addressed him: 'Lord, prescribe to us our several duties.'

Fierce Yowl appointed the lion as his chief minister, and the tiger as chamberlain; the leopard he put in charge of the royal betel casket; made' the elephant the royal doorkeeper and the monkey he designated as bearer of the royal umbrella. But, of the jackals, who were his own kith and kin, he would have none. He seized them by the throat and threw them out.

Fierce Yowl enjoyed royal glory in this manner, while the other beasts led by the lion hunted and killed and brought him food which they laid at his feet. He too following the customary manner of princes, divided the food placed before him and distributed it to the members of his court. And so the days went by pleasantly, until one day as Fierce Yowl was sitting in state in the Hall of Audience a pack of jackals nearby started howling. As soon as he heard it, Fierce Yowl's body thrilled with delight; his eyes filled with tears of joy; and he too began howling in a shrill, high-pitched tone. The lion and other members of the court hearing it gasped in surprise and exclaimed, 'Good Heavens! This is but a jackal.' For an instant they stood dismayed, ashamed of themselves and looking down at the ground. They then started murmuring and muttering, 'Listen; we have been taken for a ride by this jackal; let's kill the scurvy fellow.'

Fierce Yowl heard this and in attempting to flee was caught by a tiger and torn to bits.

Wily concluded, 'And that is why I say, "whoever forsakes those trusted . . . " and so on, my lord.'

Tawny asked Wily, 'How then am I to recognize Lively as having designs on my life? And what would be his plan of attack?'

Wily's answer came pat, 'At all times, my lord, Lively comes into His Majesty's presence humbly, limbs all drooping. If today he approaches His Majesty differently, displaying some nervousness and a readiness to thrust with his horns, then His Majesty may conclude from his behaviour that he is a deep-dyed villain.'

Wily then got up and went to seek out Lively whom he approached with slow, hesitant steps, presenting himself as somewhat dispirited. Lively seeing him in this state asked courteously, 'Well, my friend, and how goes the world with you? You are in good spirits, I trust?'

Wily sighed, 'Ah! Good spirits? How can dependants be ever in good spirits? Think of it:

Their fortunes lie in another's power; (258)
tranquillity they never enjoy;
they live in fear of their very lives;
such is the fate of those who serve a king.

Sorrows begin even at birth, (259)
miseries endure after,
life led in the service of kings,
is alas, a succession of ills.

Five endure living death— (260)
so sage Vyāsa declares;
poor man, sick man, fool, exile, and he
who in perpetuity serves a king.

He eats, but he's not in sound health; (261)
he sleeps not, yet he's not awake;
he speaks, but not on his own ever:
Such is his life, who serves a king.

'It is a dog's life' — whoever says this, (262)
idly prates without knowing,
for a dog roams about at will,
a servant by order of the king.

Living celibate, sleeping on the ground; (263)
sparing in food—skin and bones—an ascetic's life,
with a difference!—born and bred of sin,
is the life of one who serves a king.

Stranger to his own convictions; (264)
following another's bent of mind;
selling his body of his own free will:
what happiness for one who serves a king?

The closer he gets in serving a king, (265)
closely observing his master's moods,

111

the more a man trembles, seized with dread.
A king is fire, both alike,
and different only in name;
a burning thing men from afar can stand,
but unendurable when close at hand.

What good is fine fragrance, (266)
what good too the purest pearl,
what good is sweetest candy,
if it is gained through servitude?

'In short, think of this:

Is it the right time? Is it the right place? (267)
Who are friends? What's the cost, and what the gain?
And what am I? And what my power and strength?
Time and again, one should ponder over these.'

Lively listening to these words had the strong sense that Wily had some deep purpose in his mind; so he asked, 'My friend, you seem to want to tell me something; what is it?' To which Wily, who was waiting for exactly this kind of opening, answered, 'Look, Your Honour is my good friend. Therefore, I ought to tell you what is for your good. The fact is, our Lord Tawny is angry with you. And this is what he said to me today, "I shall slay this Lively and feed him to the beasts of prey." Hearing that I fell prey to the deepest dejection. Now that I have told you of this it is up to you to take whatever steps you think are needed at this point.'

These ominous words of Wily fell on Lively like a thunderbolt; he became extremely dejected. As Wily's comments always sounded plausible, Lively was greatly troubled at heart. Seized by creeping fear, he observed, 'Sir, you do speak truly,

Women seek the love of rogues; (268)
kings often uphold the unworthy;
money follows the miser;
the rain-god sheds his power on mountain and sea.

'O misery! O lamentable misery! What is this calamity that has befallen me?

> With utmost diligence one serves one's king— (269)
> One serves. Is that something to be wondered at?
> But—that the person served turns out your foe?
> A most peculiar return this—to be wondered at.

'And further:

> If a person is angered for a specific cause, (270)
> remove the cause—for certain he'd then be appeased;
> but if he harbours hate without a cause?
> What hope then to appease this man?

> How can one not dread a villain's fierce hate, (271)
> manifest; like a deadly snake's venom,
> it constantly drips from his lips as words,
> vicious, beyond all human endurance.

> Many a time at nights, the silly wild goose (272)
> in search of beds of moon-lotuses is fooled,
> and nibbles in vain at star-reflections on the lake:
> even by day, still deluded, the poor fool
> casts a suspicious eye at white lilies
> mistaking them for stars, and will not nibble.
>> Once bitten, the world-wary, senses danger
>> even in sincerity and truth.

'O! What ill luck! Have I ever committed an offence against our Lord Tawny?'

Wily replied, 'My dearest friend, princes are always on the lookout for weaknesses in others that make them vulnerable; they take pleasure in injuring others for no good reason.'

Lively agreed, 'Yes, my friend; that seems to be so. It is indeed excellently said:

> Serpents haunt sandalwood trees; in pools (273)
> where lotuses blow, lurk crocodiles too;

113

rogues are out to destroy virtue;
there's no happiness unmixed with trouble.

No lotus grows on mountain peaks; (274)
no good can come out of scoundrels;
the virtuous do not suffer passion's unease;
If you sow barley, you do not harvest rice.

The best of men endowed with virtue (275)
whose rectitude remains unbroken
bear in mind only acts good and well done,
and forget offences and oversight.

'On the other hand, I have to regard what has happened as my own fault in that I chose to serve an insincere friend. For we hear that:

One should never follow an inopportune course, (276)
    or keep undesirable company,
or serve an insincere friend; see how
    the bird sleeping among lotuses
    was slain by a flying arrow.'

'O, really! And how did that happen?' asked Wily. And Lively began the tale of *The Owl and the Wild Goose*.

In a certain wooded region there was a very large lake in which lived a wild goose named Love Mad.[38] He had lived in that lake for a very long time playing and enjoying himself in many different ways. One day an owl made his appearance there, his death in the shape of an owl as it turned out.

Seeing the owl alight on the bank, Love Mad enquired: 'Sir, where have you come from? And here, to this desolate forest?'

'I have heard so much about your excellent qualities, Your Honour,' answered the owl, 'that I decided to come here to meet you. You must know that:

Dedicated to the quest of virtue, (277)

I have roamed the world entire,
Not finding one with virtues greater than yours,
I have now come to sit at your feet.

I need your friendship; and right now and here; (278)
with great reverence cultivate it I shall.
Even what is sullied gains purity
when it touches Gaṅgā's holy waters.

'Moreover:

What was mere shell became in Viṣṇu's hand, (279)
the divine conch celebrated.
Association with the virtuous,
whom does it not ennoble?'

After this address was delivered by the owl, the wild goose declared, 'So be it, my noble friend. Dwell here by this great lake in this pleasant forest as long as you wish and enjoy my company.'

And the days passed by with these two friends enjoying various pastimes together. One day, however, the owl said, 'My friend, I think I'd like to return to my own home in Lotus Woods. If you set store by our friendship, if you entertain any affection for me, pray visit me there and be my guest.' With these words the owl flew off to his native woods.

As time went by, one day the wild goose began to reflect thus: 'I have grown old living in this same spot; I know of no other place to go to. Why don't I go to the place where my dear friend, the owl, lives? I am sure to find different kinds of dainty foods there, to be nibbled and eaten; and various spots to sport in and enjoy myself.'

After these reflections, Love Mad went in search of the home of his friend, the owl. But at first he could not find his friend anywhere in the woods. Having conducted a minute and painstaking search, Love Mad finally discovered the owl, who being blind during daytime was holed up in a deep and dark hollow at the lake's edge. He addressed the owl, calling out courteously:

'Hallo, hallo there, my friend; come, come out at once. Here I am, Love Mad, your dear friend, the wild goose, come to visit you.'

The owl heard his friend's greetings and replied: 'Listen, I am not a creature of daylight. You and I can meet and converse only after sunset.'

Hearing this, Love Mad waited expectantly for many hours until finally he was able to meet the owl. After making the customary enquiries about their mutual good health and spirits and having exchanged news, the wild goose, exhausted by his long and wearying journey, fell asleep then and there.

Now, it happened that a group of merchants with their caravan of carts had set up camp beside that very same lotus lake. At dawn, the leader of the caravan rose from sleep and ordered the conch to be sounded to signal preparations for the caravan's departure. Immediately, the owl set up a loud and harsh screech and flew into his nest in the cleft at the lake's edge. But the wild goose stayed still asleep. The caravan leader who was disturbed hearing this ill-omened screech of the owl at the start of their journey, ordered an expert archer in his company who could aim by sound, to shoot. The archer strung his powerful bow, drew the bowstring fully even up to his ear, let fly an arrow that struck the wild goose who was sleeping near the owl's nest and killed him.

Lively concluded his tale with the comment: 'You see, that is why I said, "Inopportune course, undesirable company . . . " and so on.'

Lively then continued rather pensively: 'You know, at first, our master Tawny's speech was all honey . . . now . . . it turns out that his mind is seething with poison. It is always right that:

A man should shun the friend (280)
who slanders him behind his back
while flattering him to his face;
for he is a jar of poison with milk on top.

'Ah! How well I know this from experience:

Hands raised high greet you from afar; (281)
eyes misting with affection, he tenders half his own seat;

116

he clasps you close in a loving embrace;
tirelessly attentive in kind enquiries,
he makes pleasant talk—
O what wondrous skill in deceit and tricks!
Poison hidden deep within—all honey without—
What unprecedented dramatic art is this!
That a rank villain receives his training in!

All finely decked in fascinations: fine manners, (282)
extravagant courtesies, compliments, that's how it starts;
Midway it is all abloom—Ah!
With such marvellous phrases of praise, esteem—
except they bear no fruit—
then, at the end see how loathsome it all turns out,
dark, overgrown by calumny, disdain, dishonour—
How and why has this course been created! Alas!
The course of friendship with the lowborn, the ill-bred—
whose only goal is the flouting of the just Law!

'And mark this too:

He bows as prescribed; he rises in welcome; (283)
he waits upon you, the villain;
he is attentive to your every need,
makes a show of unswerving devotion,
hugs you in an excess of affection,
wins your heart with his sweetest speech,
extols all your excellent qualities,
but never does what rightly should be done.
He is always a villain.

'O misery! Lamentable misery! How could I have struck up a friendship with a lion! I, a grass-eater . . . he a devourer of raw flesh. How well it is observed:

Where wealth matches wealth and lineage is equal (284)
there marriage or friendship works well;

117

but not between the well-fed, prosperous
and the lean and down-and-out in the world.

Even as the flaming sun stands on the western mountain (285)
flinging despondent his final glory,
the thirsty honey-bee explores the heart of the lotus,
unmindful of imprisonment at sunset.
So too, the suitor, his eye on the fruit,
scarce reflects on the risks he runs.

Passing nonchalantly at some distance, (286)
the coveted honey-filled cups of fresh blue-lotuses,
not caring to drink from them;
flinging away from fragrant night-blooming jasmine buds
that exhale their native scents intoxicating;
damselflies weary themselves tasting the rut
trickling down the temples of tuskers.
     So too, the world passes by what is effortlessly gained
     to seek delight in the company of knaves.

Greedy for a new taste of honey-sweetness, (287)
bees clamour over droplets of rut gathering
continually on wild elephants' cheeks.
When hurled to the ground by the gusts of wind
from the beasts' flapping fan-ears, they remember then
the happy times, sporting within lotus-chalices.

'Perhaps . . . the fault really lies within the qualities themselves:

The branches of the great lords of the forest (288)
bend low from the wealth of fruit they bear;
the peacock's gait is slow and indolent
from the proudly-swelling plumage he trails;
the noble horse, pure-blooded, he races,
fleet as wind, yet he is led like a cow.
     In persons endowed with qualities most admirable,
     most often, those qualities themselves become their
                                                  worst foes.

Where Yamunā flows with deep-blue waters and   (289)
                sapphire-sparkles of glittering sands,
there, in those depths, lies submerged, the dark-blue snake,
                coiling mass glossy as collyrium.
Who would track him down there? Unless . . .
he is betrayed by gleams of brilliant star-gems clustered in the
                circlets of his hoods?

    By virtues raised to lofty heights,
    by those same virtues the noble fall.

Great monarchs are mostly averse to men of merit;   (290)
riches are commonly enamoured of knaves and fools;
Oh! How false a statement — that in merit lies a man's
                greatness!
When, as a rule, people think little of manliness.

Lordly lions confined in cages, cowed down, and skulking,   (291)
    with disconsolate mien;
noble elephants, whose brows by constant pricks of sharp
              goads are dented and rent;
cobras, listless, lulled into dull stupor by charms and
                potent incantations;
scholars down-and-out, dogged by misfortune;
heroic warriors abandoned by fortune:
Time sports with such beings,
swinging them back and forth as if they were playthings
    serving for his amusement.

The greedy honey bee, poor fool, forsakes   (292)
blossoming lotuses in pools free of perils,
and goes for the trickling rut of majestic tuskers,
not counting the risks of flattening blows of winnowing
                elephant-ears.
    It is in the nature of those in hot pursuit of something,
    not to pause and reflect upon the final outcome.

'I see now that by entering the sphere of power where base

villainy operates, I have placed my life at risk . . . totally. How excellently is it said that:

> *How many there are among the sharp-witted,*   (293)
> *who, corrupt, earn their living by fraud;*
> *who do good as well as ill, as in the tale*
> *of the camel and the crow and others.'*

'Really,' asked Wily, 'and how did that happen?' Then Lively began the tale of *The Camel, the Crow and Others.*

Once upon a time, there lived in a certain city, a rich merchant, named Seafarer.[39] He set out in a certain direction, leading a caravan of a hundred camels, each laden with textiles of great value. One of his camels, named Disdain, buckled under the heavy load and powerless, with all his limbs drooping, fell down. The merchant seeing that he could not possibly break journey and camp in the forest full of dangers, had Disdain's load distributed among the other camels and continued on his way, abandoning poor Disdain.

When the caravan had departed, Disdain slowly got up and hobbling around began to crop the tips of the lush foliage. Thus, in a very few days, he regained his strength.

In the same forest there lived a lion named Lusty,[40] with a panther, a crow and a jackal as his attendants. As Lusty was roaming in the forest accompanied by his attendants, he came upon the camel who had been abandoned by the merchants. Seeing this extraordinary creature, never seen before, who was rather comical in appearance, the lion observed, 'Look, here is a strange animal that has entered our forest. Ask him who he is.'

The crow at once went up to Disdain and having enquired and ascertained the facts, informed his master: 'This is known in the world as a camel.'

Lusty then called out to Disdain: 'Hey there! How did you come here?' Thus addressed, Disdain told the whole story in all its details, of how he had been abandoned there in the forest. Taking pity on the camel and wishing to help him, Lusty offered Disdain his protection.

As the days passed, it happened one day that Lusty who had been in a fight with a bull-elephant and was severely gored by his enemy's tusks, had to keep to his lair in the cave. Five or six days passed; the lion and his attendants were in perishing distress for want of food. Noticing that his retinue was languishing, famished, Lusty addressed them: 'Being injured badly, I am unable to hunt and forage, and provide you with food as I used to. So, you fellows had better forage for yourselves somehow and manage.' To this the lion's attendants replied, 'While Your Lordship is in this condition, why should we attempt to sustain our lives?'

Pleased, the lion observed, 'Well said, fellows; you exhibit the proper devotion and conduct expected of attendants. Since I am in this disabled condition, pray go out and bring me some food.' They remained silent. But their faces showed quite plainly what was going on in their minds.

'Come, come,' admonished the lion, 'don't hang back and look so shamefaced. Go, round up some animal or other and bring it to me. Even in the state that I am, I shall slay it and make food for all of you and for myself.'

So the three of them started roaming the woods looking for prey. But when they were unable to rustle up any creature, the crow and the jackal started consulting with each other. The jackal spoke first, 'Friend Crow,' he said, 'Why are we wandering in the forest in this manner, when we see before us, Disdain, who trusts our master . . . ? Why not kill him so that our lives can be sustained?'

'A good suggestion, undoubtedly,' answered the crow, 'except for one thing . . . he cannot be killed because our lord has taken Disdain under his protection.'

'Ah! Yes, that is true,' replied the jackal, 'Let me talk to our lord and see if I can put the idea of despatching Disdain into his mind. You wait right here, while I run home and return soon with our master's orders.'

121

So saying, the jackal hastened to Lusty's lair and presenting himself to the lion began, 'My lord, we have roamed over the whole forest; we have now reached the point where hunger is so overpowering that we can hardly take one further step. Not only that, Your Lordship too is in a weakened condition and needs a wholesome diet. That being the case, if Your Lordship orders, a wholesome diet can be furnished today by Disdain's flesh.'

The lion was furious when he heard these cruel words; he exclaimed angrily, 'Shame! Shame upon you! Vilest of sinners! You say that again and I'll strike you dead instantly. When I have taken Disdain under my protection and given him sanctuary, how can I slay him myself? As the proverb goes:

No gift of cows, no gift of land, (294)
nor any gift of food holds pre-eminence;
of all the gifts in the world, say the wise,
the foremost is the gift of safety of life.'

The jackal listened attentively and responded thus, 'My lord, if having guaranteed Disdain the safety of his life, Your Lordship slays him, I grant that Your Lordship will certainly incur blame. But on the other hand, if Disdain out of devotion and of his own accord, lays his life at your feet, then no blame can attach to His Lordship. If he himself freely commits himself to slaughter, then he may be slain. Otherwise . . . one of us has to offer himself as Your Lordship's food, the reason being that His Lordship is in great need of a wholesome diet, so that his condition may not take a turn for the worse on account of the inroads that extreme hunger can make. And if that were to happen what do we have to live for? If we cannot offer our lives in the service of our lord, what use are we? If something undesirable happens to our lord, what is left to us but to follow him and enter the funeral pyre with him? For it is said:

At all times and at all costs (295)
the chief of the clan must be protected.
If he falls the clan is lost;
the wheel cannot turn if the nave does not hold.'

Lusty heeded what his retainer, the jackal, advised and said, 'All right; if this is so, then do what is best.'

No sooner had the jackal heard these words than he hastened to the others and addressed them, 'Alas! Our master's condition is extreme; the breath is even now in his nostrils about to fly away. Once he is gone, who is there in the forest to be our protector? When through privation, he is at the point of starting his journey to the other world, we should now go and offer our bodies to him. By so doing we shall free ourselves of the debt we owe our lord for his graciousness to us. For it is said:

> As long as there is life in him (296)
> a servant who simply looks on
> while his master's life is endangered,
> will surely find himself in hell.'

Then they all went, their eyes brimming with tears, bowed low to Lusty and sat around him.

Lusty glanced around and asked, 'Hey, fellows, did you catch something or see anything?'

The crow replied, 'Lord, we have tramped the whole forest; but we have found no prey or seen any. So, let our lord make his meal off me today to sustain his life. For our lord my body will serve to sustain his life for one day; for me it will be the means to attain the celestial world.[41] For it is said:

> The man who in a spirit of devotion (297)
> offers his life for his master's life
> will be freed from old age and death
> and attain Final Beatitude.'

The jackal who had been listening now interjected, 'You, sir, have such a tiny body that it will hardly serve the purpose of sustaining our master's life. There is also another objection here; for it is stated:

> Meagre is the flesh of crows, lacking (298)
> nourishment; and so are leavings.

123

> *Where no satisfaction is found,*
> *why dine on such things?*

'You have shown proof of your devotion to our master, sir; thereby you have won a reputation for virtuous conduct in both worlds. Now step aside so that I may address our lord.'

The crow stepped to one side. The jackal bowing low with respect, spoke, 'My lord, pray grant me the favour of using my body to sustain your life today so that I may inherit both worlds. For it is clearly stated:

> *Servants' lives are with their masters pledged*   (299)
> *in return for the wealth they earn by serving:*
> *if for some reason their lives are forfeit,*
> *the master is not guilty of sinning.'*

The leopard who had been listening to the jackal's words, now made his pitch, 'Oho! sir, you have spoken wisely, sir, yes, hm. But isn't your body also not . . . rather . . . insignificant? Besides, you cannot serve as food for our lord, because you belong to the same family of creatures . . . meaning those who have claws for weapons. Therefore your flesh is taboo. For it is wisely said:

> *As the breath of life struggles in the throat*   (300)
> *even then the wise refrain from forbidden food*
> *—and what a trifling mouthful too at that—*
> *for fear of losing both the worlds.*

'You have given ample proof, sir, of your devotion as a servant; there is excellent wisdom in the saying:

> *Men of noble families remain the same,*   (301)
> *first and last and at all times in-between;*
> *for this very reason, monarchs*
> *gather round themselves such a band of men.*

'So, make way, sir, move on so that I may also win the favour of our lord.'

As the jackal moved out of the way, the leopard bowed low in reverence and spoke, 'Lord, this day, let your life's journey be renewed by my life. Make my fame spread far and wide on this earth. Have no hesitation, my lord for it is truly observed:

> *Servants who remain in all matters*   (302)
> *ever-faithful to their masters,*
> *will attain everlasting life in the World of Light*
> *and imperishable glory on earth.'*

The camel, Disdain, having heard all this thought to himself: 'Why, these fellows have expressed their devotion in such fine phrases; and yet, our lord has not struck down a single one of them. Therefore, I too shall declare mine as befits the occasion. These fellows, all three of them, are sure to dismiss my offer.' Having concluded that this is what would happen, he spoke strongly, 'Aha! Admirably spoken, sir. But, you, sir, are also armed with claws. Then, how can our master eat you, sir? For it is rightly said:

> *He who even imagines wrongs*   (303)
> *that could be done to one's own kind,*
> *possesses neither world; and further,*
> *he is degraded into a foul worm.*

'So, make way while I ask for our lord's favour.' As the leopard moved away, poor Disdain stood before Lusty and bowing with respect, spoke, 'Lord, these creatures are not fit food for Your Lordship. Let Your Lordship be sustained by my body, so that I may possess both worlds: for it is wisely observed:

> *No ascetic, no doer of sacrifice,*   (304)
>   *can ever reach that high station*
> *that servitors who give up their life*
>   *to save their master's, attain.'*

At a sign from the lion who had been addressed in this manner by Disdain, the leopard and the jackal fell upon the poor camel and tore his entrails out, while the crow pecked out his eyes. The unfortunate camel, Disdain, breathed his last, and was devoured greedily by all four creatures who were ravenously hungry.

'Which is why I say to you, "Many are the sharp-witted who are mean-spirited . . . " and so on,' said Lively.

After he had retailed this short tale, Lively addressed the jackal, Wily, once again: 'Ah! My friend, this King Tawny with his shabby retinue . . . he is not good to those who take refuge with him. Better a vulture for a king who has wild geese for his retinue, than a wild goose for king who has vultures for his retinue. For it is out of the counsel of a retinue of vultures that many evils spring up for their master; evils sufficient to bring about his downfall. Far better to choose the former of the two kings. For a king who is duped by evil counsel becomes incapable of wise deliberation. And, don't we also hear the following:

> *That jackal by your side, and that crow over there,* (305)
> *sharp-beaked — your retinue — I see*
> *are not exactly reassuring:*
> *therefore, I have climbed up this tree.'*

Wily pricked up his ears: 'O really! And how was that?' he asked. And Lively began the tale of *The Lion and the Chariot-maker*.

In a certain city there lived a chariot-maker named Devagupta.[42] It was his daily routine to carry a packed lunch and, accompanied by his wife, to go to the forest to fell huge logs of rosewood. Now in that forest dwelt a lion, named Spotless,[43] who had for his attendants a jackal and a crow, both rabid flesh-eaters.

One day the lion while roaming alone in the forest encountered the chariot-maker. Seeing that lion of terrifying aspect, the chariot-maker considered himself as good as dead; or, perhaps he possessed great presence of mind which prompted him to think it best to face a powerful foe with firmness. Whatever the reason, he advanced boldly towards the lion and facing him, bowed low and said, 'Come, come, my friend; today, I am afraid you have to eat my lunch which your brother's[44] wife has prepared with care and brought; so here . . . .' And he proffered his own lunch to the lion.

The lion made a courteous reply. 'My friend, my life cannot be sustained by boiled rice and vegetables, for I am an eater of flesh. But, I shall certainly have a taste of your food, because I have taken a liking to you. What kind of special dishes have you there?'

Hearing the lion speak to him thus mildly, the chariot-maker began to gratify the taste buds of the lion with all sorts of special eatables: melting-in-the-mouth sweetmeats, and candies and cookies all made of sugar and spice, butter and nuts and raisins. The lion was highly gratified; out of gratitude he offered his host protection, and granted him safe, unhindered right of movement in the forest.

The chariot-maker then spoke courteously to the lion, 'Dear friend, now you must come and meet me everyday; but, mind you, always come alone. Don't ever bring anyone with you to meet me.'

Days passed in this manner as the two friends spent time together in affection. The lion, who received such hospitality and was provided everyday with different kinds of delicious food, soon gave up hunting. Now the two hangers-on, the crow and the jackal, who lived off the good fortune of others, being tormented by fierce pangs of hunger, respectfully asked the lion one day: 'Lord, tell us where you go everyday, and why you return from wherever you go in a very happy mood.'

To this the lion replied, 'O, nowhere in particular.' But the two parasites would not give up. They asked him the same question repeatedly, and with the greatest deference.

Finally the lion answered, 'I have a friend here in this forest, a chariot-maker who meets me everyday. His wife makes the most delicious dishes, which I eat with the greatest enjoyment.' The two parasites at once remarked, 'Well then, let us go there and kill this chariot-maker; his flesh dripping red blood will last

us for a long time and we shall wax plump on it.' But when the
lion heard these terrible words, he reprimanded them, 'Look
here, fellows,' he said sharply, 'I have assured the man of protection and guaranteed the safety of his life. How can you even
consider the possibility of perpetrating such a wrongful deed on
his person! But I tell you what. I shall get some delicious tidbits
for you both from him; what do you say?' They agreed to this,
and all three set out to meet the chariot-maker.

When Devagupta saw the lion at a distance coming towards
him, followed by his evil-minded attendants, he reflected, 'Oho!
This does not look good; for me it is a most unpropitious turn of
events.' And holding his wife close, he quickly climbed a great,
big tree.

The lion came close and enquired of the chariot-maker, 'My
friend, why did you climb into this tree as soon as you saw me
coming? Don't you know me, Spotless, the lion and your dear
friend, the very same? Do not be afraid.'

But the chariot-maker remained in the tree and replied,
'"That jackal by your side . . . " and so on, as I have already
quoted to you: which is why I repeat to you, Sir Wily, "A king
who keeps scurvy retainers by his side is no good to those who
take refuge with him,"' concluded Lively.

Having recounted this little tale, Lively once again remarked
to Wily, 'This king, Tawny, has been set up against me by
somebody. Besides:

Even firm mountainsides are diminished (306)
as waters softly flowing wear them down.
How easy then for those expert in intrigues,
softly whispering slander, to wear down pliant minds.

'In these circumstances what course is opportune now? What
course, indeed, but to fight. For it is well stated:

The Eternal Worlds of Light that mortals (307)
  desirous of everlasting bliss seek and gain
through penance, munificent charities,
and a host of ritual sacrifices,

> are those worlds heroes enter the moment
> they abandon their lives on the battlefield.

'And again:

> Dead, they gain the Worlds of Light,   (308)
>   victorious, happiness in life;
> both these courses worthy of heroes,
>   are bringers of great good fortune.

'And once more:

> Maidens decked in precious gems and gold,   (309)
>   elephant, horses and royal wealth,
> the throne complete with jewelled fans
>   and umbrella brilliant as the full moon:
> these are not for men who flee the battle
> and run to hide behind their mothers' skirts.'

Hearing such a brave speech from Lively, the jackal Wily began to worry, thinking, 'This fellow has sharp horns and a strong, well-nourished frame. It might turn out that through fate's decree, Lively might strike down our lord. That would not do at all. It is rightly said that:

> In battle, victory is uncertain   (310)
>   even for mighty warriors.
> Better try the three expedients[45] first:
>   to fight is the shrewd man's last resort.

'My best bet, therefore, is to turn Lively's mind away from thoughts of war.' So, Wily accosted his friend, 'My dear friend, *this* is not a good idea, because:

> Whoever adopts an adversarial stance   (311)
> before ascertaining the enemy's strength
>   runs the risk of defeat, like the Ocean
>   Who pitted himself against the lapwing.'

129

'What? enquired Lively sceptically, 'and how did *that* happen?' And Wily then began the tale of *The Lapwing who defied the Ocean*.

By the shores of the great ocean that teemed with an abundance of marine creatures: whales, dolphins and porpoises, sharks and great turtles, pearl oysters, shellfish and many other creatures, there lived a lapwing with his wife. He was named Long Legs[46] and she, Chaste.[47]

During the mating season, Chaste, who was heavy with eggs requested her husband, 'My lord, find a suitable spot where I can lay my eggs.' And Long Legs remarked, 'Why, here is a favourable spot that we have inherited from our forefathers, and it promises increase. Lay your eggs right here,' to which she replied, 'Oh, no, no, don't even talk of this spot, for it is too close to the ocean. Sometimes at high tide, the crested, frothing waves advance far inland, and my children might be washed away.'

'Gracious lady,' replied the lapwing, 'the Ocean knows me well; he knows Long Legs. And never will the great Ocean dare entertain hostile intentions towards me. Why, have you not heard the saying:

> Who dares to snatch from the cobra's hood   (312)
> the gem that burns brilliantly intense?
> Who dares to kindle the wrath of one unapproachable,
> who, by a mere look can strike a man down?

> However tormented by summer's heat   (313)
> in a desolate, treeless wilderness,
> who will ever seek the shade cast by the frame
> of a tusker inflamed with excitement?[48]

> When dawn's frosty breezes blow   (314)
>   mixed with tiny flakes of snow,
> what man with a sense of good and ill
>   with water would stave off the chill?

> *What man eager to visit Death's abode* (315)
>   *would ever think of awakening a lion*
> *who, Death's very image, lies sleeping sound,*
>   *weary from exertion splitting open*
>   *the globed front of spring-fevered elephants?*

> *Who will walk, fearless, into Yama's[49] palace* (316)
> *and, in his own words, command the Destroyer:[50]*
>   *'Here I am, take my life,*
>   *If in you such power rests.'*

> *What son of man, dull-witted, will enter* (317)
> *of his own free will, that Fire,[51] blazing smokeless*
>   *continually, terrible to behold,*
>   *and besieging the skies with hundreds of flames.'*

But even as he spoke, Chaste, who knew full well the truth about her husband's prowess, laughed loudly and said, 'Ha-ha! Fine words, indeed; and there's more where they come from:

> *What use are all these high-flying vaunts of yours?* (318)
> *O King of Birds! You will be the world's laughing stock.*
>   *What a marvel would it be if the hare*
>   *were to void turd the size of elephant dung!*

'How can you not fail to see your own strength and weakness; for it is well said:

> *Self-examination comes hard;* (319)
> *from not knowing how to, or lack*
>   *of discernment in carrying it out.*
> *But whoever has this knowledge,*
>   *never sinks under Misery's blows.*

> *The purpose will be served by this plan—* (320)
>   *the power to make it so, is mine—*

knowing this, whoever sets out and acts
is sure to find his plans bear fruit.

One who heeds not words of advice   (321)
from friends who care about his welfare,
will be destroyed like the turtle
who foolishly let go of the stick.'

The lapwing looked at his wife quizzically and asked, 'How ever did that happen?' And Chaste began the tale of *The Turtle and the Geese.*

In a certain lake there lived a turtle named Shell Neck who had as his friends, two geese, named Slender and Stocky. In the course of time, there befell a twelve-year drought, which started the two geese reflecting seriously on the situation.

'This lake has little water now; we should leave and seek another expanse of water. However, we should first make our farewells to our dear and long-time friend, Shell Neck.'

So when they went up to him to say farewell, Shell Neck enquired earnestly, 'Why are you bidding me farewell, friends? I am also a water-dweller. From the paucity of water and from the grief of separation from you, it will not be too long before I myself will perish. Therefore, if you have any affection at all for me, you ought to endeavour to save me from the jaws of death. Further, as the water in the lake shrinks to the bottom, all that you suffer is a scarcity of food; whereas, to me it is immediate death. You ought to reflect and consider whether the loss of food or the loss of life is the more grievous loss.'

The two geese pleaded in reply: 'Look, we are unable to take you along with us because you are a wingless aquatic creature.'

The turtle made prompt answer: 'I think there is a way to manage it. Bring a piece of wood that will serve as a good stick.'

When the geese had brought a piece of wood shaped like a stick, the turtle gripped it firmly in the middle with his teeth and told the geese, 'Now, take hold of this stick firmly in your bills,

one at each end . . . yes, like that . . . and fly up into the sky;
cruise along the aerial pathway, nice and easy, on an even flight,
until you reach another suitable expanse of water.'

As the geese followed his instructions, they took care to warn
him, 'Listen, this may look like a fine plan but it bears the distinct
marks of danger; for if you indulge in the slightest attempts at
conversation, you will let go of your grip on this stick, and falling
from a great height, you will be shattered.'

'Yes, of course,' the turtle rejoined. 'From this moment I have
taken a vow of silence which will last right through our aerial
journey.'

So, the plan was carried out. But as the two geese were
transporting the turtle with great difficulty, on their way from the
lake they passed over the nearby city. People began to look up at
this strange sight and talk among themselves: 'What on earth is
this cart-like object that those birds are carrying, flying through
the air?' A confused hubbub, a hum of voices of the crowd
gathered below rose up to the skies.

Hearing this, the turtle, whose hour of death was drawing
near, rashly opened his mouth to ask, 'What are these people
babbling?'

No sooner were those words out than the stupid turtle
slipped off the support on which he depended and fell crashing
to the ground. Immediately, those among the crowd who craved
meat, cut him up into pieces with sharp knives.

'Which is why I told you before, "of friends who are
well-wishers . . . " and so on,' commented Chaste; and then she
continued:

> *'Forethought and Readywit prospered*   (322)
> *while, What-will-be-will-be, perished.'*

Her husband, the lapwing, at once queried, 'And how did
this happen?' And Chaste began the tale of *The Three Fishes*.

In a certain vast lake there lived three very large fishes, whose
names were Forethought, Readywit and What-will-be-will-be.

One morning, Forethought heard some folks and some fishermen who were walking along the edge of the lake and talking among themselves frequently, 'See, this lake is abundantly stocked with fish; let us go fishing tomorrow.'

Hearing that, Forethought began to reflect. 'Hey! This is not a good prospect to contemplate, I'm afraid. Tomorrow or the day after, these people are sure to come here. I had better take Readywit and What-will-be-will-be and resort to some other large lake where the waters are trouble-free.' So, Forethought called out to the other two fishes and put the question to them.

Whereupon, Readywit replied, 'Having lived for such a long time in this lake, I am loath to abandon it all of a sudden. If the fishermen all assemble here, then, I shall somehow or other look after myself by means of a suitable plan which I am sure I can think up on the spur of the moment.'

What-will-be-will-be, whose death was definitely on the cards, now spoke, 'There are so many other broad lakes elsewhere too; who knows if these fishermen will come to fish here or not. It is not fitting that a person should abandon his native lake on mere hearsay. For as the proverb says:

Aims undertaken by serpents and knaves (323)
and those who live by exploiting chinks
in others' armour never succeed:
*   And so the world turns.*

'Therefore, my decision is not to go.'

So, recognizing that his two friends had their minds firmly made up to stay in that lake, Forethought went off to another large pool.

The very next day, after Forethought had gone, came the fishermen accompanied by servants. They stationed themselves in the middle of the lake, cast their nets wide, and caught all the fish without leaving even one behind. In this predicament, Readywit feigned death as he lay within the net; and the men, thinking, 'Oh! This huge fish seems to be already dead,' drew him out and placed him on the bank. Whereupon, in a trice,

Readywit wriggled his way back into the water. As for our poor What-will-be-will-be, he stuck his nose into the meshes of the net, and as he struggled and thrashed around trying to escape, the men pounded him repeatedly with their clubs, tearing his body to pieces until he gave up the ghost.

'Which is why I told you, "Forethought and Readywit prospered . . . " and so on,' concluded Chaste.

'What! My gracious lady, do you really think I am just another What-will-be-will-be?' asked Long Legs, rather put out.

> *'There is much difference to be seen*   (324)
> *between things: horses, elephants,*
> *iron, wood, stone, cloth, water,*
> *man, woman: all differently made.*

'You should not be afraid. While my arms protect you, who has the power to bring about your discomfiture?'

So, when Chaste had laid her eggs on the strand, the Ocean, who had been listening to the previous conversation of the lapwing pair, now thought to himself: 'Oho! Well, well; if there isn't sound sense in the saying:

> *Fearing that the sky might fall down,*   (325)
> *the lapwing rests with feet stretched up.*
> *Who in the world is not conceited*
> *o'er the image he creates of himself!*

'I shall put this bird's power to the test; let's see.'

So, the next day, when the pair of lapwings had gone foraging, the Ocean stretched out his foam-tipped wave-hands to their fullest and eagerly seized the eggs. When the hen-lapwing returned to find her nest empty, she reproached her husband, 'See what has happened to unfortunate me; the Ocean has robbed me of my eggs. I told you more than once that we should move and live elsewhere. But you, feeble-minded like What-will-be-will-be, refused to listen. Consumed by grief at the loss of my offspring, I shall enter the fire, now. This is my firm decision.'

To this, Long Legs replied, 'Oh! My gracious lady, just wait till you witness my power; see how I dry up this huge, ruffianly concourse of waters with my beak.' And his wife remonstrated with him, 'O, my dear lord, how can you talk like this—do battle with the mighty Ocean? What does the proverb say:

> *He who through folly, sets out impetuous* (326)
> *to face a foe without judging rightly*
> *the other's power and his own, will perish*
> *like the moth that flies headlong into the fire.'*

'O, my darling,' spoke Long Legs soothingly, 'don't, don't talk like this. See how—

> *Sunbeams fall over earth-supporting mountains* (327)
> *even though the sun is young, newly risen.*
> *What does age count in living things*
> *that are imbued with glorious might?*

'With this beak, I shall empty all the water of the Ocean, right to the last drop. I'll dry up this vast store of waters and turn it into dry land.'

'Oh! My beloved,' cried Chaste, 'with this beak of yours which can contain only a drop at a time? How will you dry up this vast flood of water, into which the great rivers Gangā and Sindhū, bearing with them the waters of nine times nine hundred tributaries, fall uninterruptedly? Think; why indulge in such vainglorious talk that strains even credulity?'

To this, Long Legs' confident reply was:

> *'Self-confidence is Fortune's base;* (328)
> *and my bill, it is strong as iron;*
> *toiling, long days and nights—*
> *Why will the Ocean not run dry?*

'For:

> *Without courage and manly execution* (329)

136

> *highest achievement is beyond one's reach;*
> *Why, the Sun Himself first mounts the scales*[52]
> *before he triumphs over the mass of rain clouds.'*

And Chaste answered reluctantly, 'If you feel that you must contend with the Ocean, at least call all the other birds to aid you and make it a joint enterprise. For there is great wisdom in the saying:

> *A host, though each member in it is weak,*   (330)
>   *working united brings victory to pass.*
> *Of simple straw, a rope is woven,*
>   *yet, with it an elephant is bound.*

'And so it was, that:

> *Sparrow and woodpecker*   (331)
> *gnat and frog, banded together,*
> *all with a single end in view—*
> *driving the tusker to his doom.'*

Long Legs enquired, 'And was this possible?' And Chaste began the tale of *The Sparrow and the Tusker*.

In the very densest part of a forest, a pair of sparrows lived in a nest that they had built in the branches of a great tamāla tree. In due course they were blessed with a family.

One day, a wild tusker in the grip of spring fever, being greatly tormented by the heat, resorted to the tamāla tree seeking shade. Blind with spring-fever excitement, he happened to thrust at the very branch in which the sparrows had their nest with the tip of his trunk, breaking it. As the branch broke and fell off, the sparrow-eggs were smashed, though the parent-birds themselves, who were destined to live some more years, somehow escaped death. The hen-sparrow, desolated by the death of her offspring, began to lament piteously.

137

Meanwhile, her best friend, a woodpecker, hearing her lamentations and moved by her grief, flew down to her and said, 'Dearest friend, what use is all this vain lamentation? There is profound wisdom in these sayings:

> *The wise do not sorrow*   (332)
> *for what is dead, or lost, or past.*
> *Between the wise and the fools,*
> *just this is the difference.*

'Again:

> *Let no life be mourned here on earth:*   (333)
>   *he is a fool who mourns for them,*
>   *pursuing vanity upon vanity:*
>   *for grief brings only more grief.*

'Furthermore:

> *Slimy, sluggish tears shed by kith and kin—*   (334)
>   *that is the sole lot of departed souls.*
> *So, let there be no wakes and wailing:*
>   *let last rites be done as best as can be.'*

To this Sparrow retorted, 'All very true, I grant you; but what of it? The fact is that this rogue elephant, maddened by spring fever, has destroyed all my children. So, if you are a real friend to me, then you ought to think of some plan to destroy this murderous beast. If that were done, at least the sorrow born of the loss of my children might be alleviated. For it is wisely observed:

> *Befriended by one in a time of distress,*   (335)
> *scoffed at by another in misfortune,*
> *by doing unto them what they did to you,*
> *a person, I think, gets a new lease of life.'*

Woodpecker responded saying, 'Yes, true. Your Ladyship has spoken truly; for, as the proverb says:

> *He is a true friend who stands by you in bad times* (336)
> *even if he be of another race.*
> *The whole world is your best friend in happy times:*
> *such is the way of the world.*

'And it is also heard:

> *He is a true friend who when times are bad is there for* (337)
> *you;*
> *he is a father who feeds and protects you;*
> *he is a friend too in whom you place your trust;*
> *she is a wife in whom you find repose.*

'Now watch what my wit can devise. I have another dear friend, a gnat by the name of Lute Hum.[53] Let me go and fetch her; with her help we are bound to compass the death of this wicked rogue-elephant.'

And Woodpecker took Sparrow along with her to her good friend, the gnat, whom she addressed courteously. 'Gracious lady,' she said, 'here is my dear friend, Sparrow, who has been made desolate by a villainous elephant who smashed all her dearly-cherished eggs. We have to devise a plan to take vengeance on this fellow; and I fervently hope that you will help us.'

'Of course,' replied the gnat, 'Dear Lady, what other answer can there be? But listen, I have another very dear friend, a frog named Cloud Messenger.[54] Let us call upon him for assistance and together we are bound to come up with a good plan; for it is said that:

> *Plans well-devised by friends shrewd and learned* (338)
> *with expert knowledge of texts on statecraft,*
> *of virtuous conduct who are well-wishers*
> *ready to help, will never come to naught.'*

So the three friends set out to meet Cloud Messenger and

when they had found him they related the whole story. Having listened carefully, Cloud Messenger gave a snort and remarked, 'Ah! This fellow . . . this miserable elephant . . . what is he when faced by a grand coalition of furiously angry personages . . . hm . . . ? Nothing. So, this is what we shall do. Lady Gnat, you go first to this passion-drunk creature and hum sweetly in his ear. In the state of fevered excitement that he is in, your music will soothe him so well that he will close his eyes in pleasure. And then, Lady Woodpecker go to him and peck his eyes out; while I . . . I shall sit on the edge of a great, yawning hollow and begin croaking. When he hears my voice, the thirst-tormented elephant will move in my direction in the hope of finding a pool of water close by. Once there, he will slip and fall into the hollow and attain the fivefold state.'[55]

The plan was then carried out to the last detail. The spring-fever-struck tusker closed his eyes from sheer pleasure at the song of the gnat and then, blinded by Woodpecker he wandered around until at noon, grievously tormented by growing thirst, he followed the sound of the frog's croaking, reached the edge of the deep hollow, fell in and died.

'Which is why I say to you, "The sparrow with the woodpecker . . . " and the rest of it,' concluded Chaste, the lapwing's wife.

Long Legs, the lapwing, then solemnly declared, 'So be it: with the help of an assemblage of my friends, I shall dry up this Ocean.'

Having come to this decision, Long Legs summoned all the birds and when they had gathered there, he related the whole sorry tale: the abduction of his children; the bitter sorrow this loss had brought him and his wife; her desire for restitution. All the birds sharing his grief started beating the waves with their wings hoping to alleviate Long Legs' sorrow.

After this had been going on for a while, one of the birds observed, 'Look, this is no way to accomplish our fondest desire. Instead, why don't we fill up Ocean himself with sticks and stones and clods of earth?'

No sooner were the words out of the speaker's mouth than all the birds began the task of filling the ocean with piles of sticks and stones and crumbling clods, carrying as much as the hollows of their bills would contain.

After some time one of the birds remarked, 'Listen, whichever way you look at it, it is quite plain that we are simply not equal to a contest with the Ocean. So, allow me to make a timely suggestion. There is an ancient wild goose who lives in a banyan tree. He is the one person who can give us counsel that is both sage and practical. Let us go and consult him; for as the story goes:

> *The captive flock of wild geese in the woods* (339)
> *by the plan of the ancient goose were saved.*
> *The ancient are those with experience ripe;*
> *listen to their words; they deserve a hearing.'*

All the birds asked at once, 'How was that possible?' And the wise bird began the tale of *The Ancient Wild Goose and the Fowler*.

In a certain wooded region there flourished a banyan tree with massive branches. In it lived a flock of wild geese. Once there sprang up a vine of the species known as kosāmbi at the base of that tree. Noticing the appearance of this vine, the ancient wild goose remarked, 'Look, here is a vine climbing up this banyan tree which in time will pose a threat to us. For, sometime or other, someone may climb up using this vine as a support and harm us. Therefore, while this vine is still slender and easily broken, it should be destroyed.' But the other birds disregarded his sage counsel and neglected to destroy the vine.

In the course of time, the vine grew and spread on all sides to encircle the whole tree. One day, while the geese were all out foraging, along came a fowler; he climbed up the tree by means of the thick, spreading vine and seeing the birds' nests, placed snares around them and went home.

Late in the evening, all the wild geese returned, having foraged and sported all day; and they were all caught in the snares. Then the ancient wild goose chided them, 'See, what has happened; disaster has struck: we are all caught in the snares; and all because you fellows disregarded my advice. And now we shall all perish.'

The birds then pleaded, 'What has happened has happened; now what do we do, O noble one?'

And the ancient, wise bird counselled, 'If you are all prepared to follow my advice, there is a way out. When you see the fowler returning, all of you had better be absolutely still and play dead. Thinking, "These birds are quite dead," the fowler will throw you all to the ground, one by one. When every one of us has been thrown down and the fowler begins to climb down the tree, then we should all rise simultaneously and fly away.'

At daybreak the next day, the fowler arrived, looked over the birds and saw that they were pretty well gone. With complete confidence, he disentangled the birds, one after the other and threw them to the ground. Then observing that the man was about to climb down, all the birds, following the counsel of the ancient, wise wild goose, rose up simultaneously and flew off.

'And this is why I quoted the saying about heeding the words of those old in experience,' concluded the speaker.

At the end of the tale, all the birds headed for the banyan tree where the ancient wild goose had his home and related to him the sad story of the abduction of the lapwing chicks.

The ancient bird listened and then spoke, 'As you all know, Garuḍa is King of all Birds. In the circumstances the most suitable course of action is this: that all of you should raise your voices in unison in wails of lamentation and cry out to Garuḍa to stir his deepest feelings, so that he will be moved to redress your grievance.'

Having settled on this plan, the birds sought Garuḍa's presence, who at the time was on the point of being summoned by the Blessed Lord Viṣṇu in connection with matters relating to the imminent War of Gods and Titans. Arriving at that very moment, the birds reported to their lord, the King of Birds, the sorrow of the loss and separation brought about by the Ocean's infamous act of carrying away the lapwing chicks. 'Lord,' they cried out, 'even as you dwell in glorious splendour, we, who live solely by what we can procure with our bills and are as a result afflicted by a weakness[56] in foraging, have been injured and humiliated by the Ocean who has carried away our young. As the proverb rightly points out:

> *To eat quietly out of sight is indeed*   (340)
>   *best, especially for the weak and needy.*
> *The lone ram with never a clue how to feed*
>   *was by the lion despatched as you will see.'*

'Oh?' exclaimed Garuḍa, 'and how did that happen?' The ancient bird then began the tale of *The Lion and the Lone Ram*.

In a densely-wooded region, there was a ram who had been separated from his flock. Stocky in frame, shaggy and long-horned, possessing a tough and strong body, he roamed the forest at will. Now, it happened at one time that a lion surrounded by his retinue of all species of animals, passed that way and saw him. Taking one look at the ram, a weird creature the like of which he had never set eyes on before, the lion grew afraid, his heart pounding with anxious thoughts that made his entire frame shake and tremble unceasingly while every hair on it bristled with apprehension, 'He must be stronger than I am,' he reflected, 'otherwise how could he roam here without a care in the world.' With such thoughts making him uneasy, the lion quietly inched away.

Next day, the lion again came across the ram who was now happily cropping the grass. 'What! Is this fellow then a grass-eater! Well, well, in that case his strength can only be in proportion to his diet,' said the lion to himself. And with a sudden, swift spring he killed the poor ram.

'Therefore, I say to you once more, "To eat quietly out of sight . . ." and the rest of it.'

As the ancient wild goose was concluding his tale, Lord Viṣṇu's messenger appeared on the scene and addressed Garuḍa,

'Oh! Divine Bird! Our Lord, Nārāyaṇa,[57] commands you to go at once to Amarāvatī;[58] make haste.'

Garuḍa answered the messenger with hurt pride, 'Oh messenger! What does our Lord want with an unworthy servant like myself!'

To this the messenger replied, 'Has the Lord ever spoken harshly to you? Why then do you display such pride against the Blessed One?'

Garuḍa replied, 'The Ocean, the resting place of the Blessed One has carried away the eggs of the lapwing, who is my servant. If I cannot chastise this wrongdoer, then I am not the servant of the Lord. Pray go and tell this to our Lord.'

Lord Viṣṇu, understanding from the messenger's words that the Winged One was hurt and feigning anger, reflected, 'Ah! Vinatā's son seems to be in a dreadful temper. I think I had better go myself, address him in person and bring him here with all honours. For, as the proverb rightly points out:

An able, loyal and high-born servant   (341)
    is never to be treated with disrespect
but cherished with affection as a son
    by a man wishing his fortunes to prosper.

A master though highly pleased with his servants   (342)
    may bestow on them nothing but high honour;
but servants setting on honour such high value
    will sacrifice even their lives for their master.'

Having arrived at this conclusion, Lord Viṣṇu quickly set out to visit Garuḍa, who, seeing that the Lord had come to his house looked down modestly at the ground and spoke, 'Supreme Lord! See what the Ocean has done from arrogance that you have made his depths your own dwelling place; he has deeply humiliated me by carrying away my servant's eggs, the lapwing's offspring. Out of deference to the Supreme Lord I have refrained from taking strong action; otherwise, I would have reduced this flood of waters to dry land this very day. For it is wisely observed:

Rather than perform a deed that makes him   (343)
fall low in the world's estimation,
or cause displeasure in his master's mind,
an estimable servant would choose death.'

Hearing these words the Supreme Lord declared, 'O, son of Vinatā! How truly you have spoken. In the same way:

The master who will not from his service   (344)
    dismiss a servant proven base and cruel,
is himself deserving of punishment harsh;
    that is the rule without exception.

'So, come with me; let us recover the eggs and pacify the lapwing and then proceed to Amarāvatī to look after the business of the immortals.' To this Garuḍa assented. The Supreme Lord then having reprimanded the Ocean, fitted a fire-arrow to his bow and spoke, 'Hear me, you evil-hearted one; return his eggs to the lapwing; otherwise I shall reduce you to dry land.'

On hearing these words, the Ocean with his whole retinue, trembling with fear, took up the eggs and as ordered by the Lord restored them to the parent lapwing.

'Therefore, I say this to you, "Without knowing your enemy's strength . . ." and so on,' concluded Wily.

Now Lively, the bull, who had caught the drift of the jackal's argument, asked him, 'Dear friend Wily, now tell me, what would be Tawny's mode of attack?'

To this, Wily, the jackal, replied, 'Normally, as you know, it is Tawny's practice to lie at ease on some flat rock, with all his limbs totally relaxed. However, if today you see him prick-eared, tail tensely drawn in, all four paws held close together tightly and looking straight ahead, watching you warily even from a distance, then you had better understand that Tawny harbours treachery in his mind.'

Having said all this, Wily left to visit Wary, who enquired at once, 'And what exactly has Your Honour accomplished?'

'Ah!' replied Wily, 'I have succeeded in sowing dissension between the parties.'

'Really! And is that a fact?' enquired Wary.

'Sure, it is,' answered Wily, 'and Your Honour will know it from the outcome.'

'Oh! I guess that is nothing to be surprised at, for is it not said:

As waters full-flowing crack and split mountains (345)
Earth-supporting, firm-built of close-packed rocks,
so too well-devised dissensions will not fail
to undermine even the most steadfast minds.'

Wily agreed, 'Yes; and having sown dissension a person ought to derive every advantage he can from it. For it is said:

Having studied deeply (346)
every text on policy,
grasped the essential meaning
in its entirety,
but to his advantage not turning
all that vast learning—
what use are texts so demanding.'

And Wary replied, 'Ah, but in truth personal advantage amounts to little; for:

Worms, ashes, dung; such is the body's final state— (347)
to pamper this body by another's pain—
Ah! What sort of statecraft do you call this.'

Wily promptly retorted, 'O, sir, you are totally ignorant of the ways of statecraft which by its very nature is crooked; yet it forms the firm base for the livelihood of the whole breed of politicians. For that very reason, it is shrewdly advised:

Steel your heart till it becomes hard and ruthless, (348)
let your tongue be sweet as sugar-cane juice;

146

brushing aside indecisions and doubts,
slay him at whose hands you suffered before.

'And one thing more; this bull Lively, though dead will still come in handy for our nourishment. For:

The shrewd person who accomplishes both (349)
the ruin of another and his own good,
keeps his counsel, gives no hint of his aims,
as Sly, the jackal did, deep in the woods.'

'Oh! And how did that happen?' remarked Wary. Then Wily began the tale of *The Jackal who outwitted the Lion.*

In a certain densely-wooded region there lived a lion named Thunderbolt Fang with his three ministers, a hyena, a jackal and a camel, named Carrion Hog,[59] Sly and Spike Ear respectively. At one time Thunderbolt Fang who had got into a furious fight with a rutting elephant and been sorely wounded with his body all rent by the pointed tusks of his enemy, retreated into his lair and remained there in total seclusion. After enduring seven days of bitter fasting, when his frame had become all emaciated, he looked around and saw that his ministers were pale with hunger. He ordered them, 'Look, fellows, go out into the woods and round up some prey or other, bring it here and even though I am in this disabled condition, I shall kill it and provide food for you.'

Receiving their master's orders, the three ministers began roaming the woods searching for prey but found nothing. Then Sly started thinking: 'If only Spike Ear were to be killed we should all have our bellyful of food for several days. But, out of friendship for him, our master will not kill him. However, I daresay by using my wit I can put the idea of slaying him into our master's mind. For surely:

There is nothing inviolable in this world, (350)
or unobtainable or improper,

147

if people are shrewd enough to make a try:
And that's what I shall now set out to do.'

Having reflected upon the matter, Sly trotted up to Spike Ear and said, 'Hey there! Friend Spike Ear; listen; lacking wholesome food our master is sorely distressed by hunger. If he should die then our deaths will soon follow; that's for sure. Therefore, I lay this proposition before you; by carrying it out you will benefit yourself and our master as well.'

'O, dear friend,' responded Spike Ear, 'tell me what it is; tell me quickly so that I may do as you say without the least hesitation. Besides, by serving one's master, a person earns the same merit that is gained by the performance of a hundred good deeds.'

Then Sly outlined his plan: 'Listen, dear friend, supposing you offer your body, but, at a hundred per cent interest; what *you* get back is your body twofold; and our master . . . *he* too will have his life prolonged.'

Spike Ear, having listened to this proposal, replied, 'Dear friend, Sly, if this is at all possible, why then, I am no loser. So, let our master be informed accordingly. But, the Ruler of Righteousness[60] ought to be entreated to guarantee this pact.'

Having decided thus all three approached the lion and Sly began, 'Lord, we have not found any prey and the glorious Sun is at the point of setting.' Hearing this the lion grew deeply dejected. Then Sly continued, 'Lord, our friend, Spike Ear, here, has however something to convey to His Lordship: that he is ready to offer his own body if the God of Death were to stand surety that in return, he, Spike Ear, would get his body back twofold.'

'O, what a beautiful offer, my friend,' observed the lion, 'and now, let this be done forthwith.'

On the basis of this pact, poor Spike Ear, felled and slain by a blow of the lion's paw was disembowelled by the hyena and jackal.

Sly began to think once more, 'Now, how shall I manage it so that I may have all this food to myself.' With this thought in mind, he addressed the lion whose limbs were blood-spattered, 'Let His Lordship go down to the river and wash himself and offer prayers to the divinities while I stay here with Carrion Hog to stand guard over the food.'

The lion gave heed to Sly's words and started for the river. As soon as he had gone, Sly told the hyena, 'Hey! Friend Carrion Hog, you do look famished; why don't you eat a little of this camel-meat before our lord returns from the river. Go on; I shall speak up for you before the master and exonerate you from improper behaviour.'[61]

Grateful, Carrion Hog took a bite of the dead camel. Hardly had he tasted it when Sly cried out, 'Hey, Carrion Hog, look out; the master is on his way, quick, run away.'

As the hyena was about to make himself scarce, the lion returned and noticed that the camel's heart was missing. 'What's this?' he roared in anger. 'Who has dared to turn this camel-meat into leavings?[62] I shall kill him straight away.' Threatened in this manner, Carrion Hog looked at Sly's face as if to say, 'For God's sake, say something to calm him down.' But Sly only laughed and taunted the hyena, 'O, sir, come now, you ate the camel's heart all by yourself and now you look at my face . . . .'

At these words, Carrion Hog, fearing for his life fled as fast as he could to another region. The lion went in hot pursuit of him for some distance and then stopped, thinking: 'O, no, he too is a claw-armed[63] creature; I cannot kill him,' and turned back.

In the meantime, as Sly's lucky stars would have it, a great camel caravan was headed that way, heavy-laden with merchandise, and announced by a tremendous jingling of bells tied round the necks of the beasts. Hearing that mighty sound of bells even from the distance, the lion ordered the jackal, 'My good Sly, go and find out what this dreadful sound is.'

Sly dutifully ran a little way inside the forest and almost immediately darted back crying out in great excitement, 'Run, master, run; that is if you *can* run.'

Exasperated, Thunderbolt Fang asked, 'Look here, my good fellow, why are you making me so nervous? Tell me what it is that you saw.'

149

'Oh, my lord,' replied Sly, 'It is the God of Death who is approaching in great rage against you for having brought about the untimely death of his own dear camel, and that too after making him stand surety for the safety of the poor beast's life. "I'll see that this wretch pays a thousandfold for having harmed my very own camel"—that is what the god is saying,' submitted Sly. 'And now the god comes leading a great herd of camels, further determined to make full enquiries about poor Spike Ear's forefathers. He is coming here towards us, my lord; he is close at hand.'

The lion becoming frightened by this news, abandoned the dead camel and in mortal fear of his life took to his heels and disappeared from sight.

Sly, pleased, consumed the camel's flesh bit by bit over a very, very long time.

'Which is why I way to you, Sir Wary, that a shrewd person while inflicting injury on another does himself a favour,' and Wily concluded his tale.

In the meantime, after Wily had left him, poor Lively being plunged into anxious thought, reflected: 'Whatever shall I do now? Suppose I decide to go elsewhere, it is quite likely that I might encounter some other savage creature who would kill me; for, this is a wild and inhospitable forest indeed . . . not to mention that with the master so angry with me, I could not even leave this place. For as we heard the wise say:

> *Once a man, thoughtless, commits an error* (351)
> *never again can he feel safe*
> *however far he flees;*
> *for the shrewd and conniving have long arms*
> *that stretch far enough to drag the poor man back.*

'And as things are at present, I think it is best to seek out the lion and throw myself at his mercy. Who knows, that looking upon me as a suppliant, he might even spare my life.'

Having settled his thoughts as best as he could, Lively proceeded very slowly towards Tawny's presence, deeply troubled in spirit. He saw Tawny displaying precisely the stance and demeanour that Wily had led him to expect. Sitting down at some distance he sadly reflected: 'Alas! This contrary nature of princes; how wisely have the sages commented:

> *A house full of hidden serpents crawling;* (352)
> *a forest with beasts of prey swarming;*[64]
> *a pool of crocodiles lurking*
> *beneath clusters of lotuses*
>   *in radiant beauty blowing . . .*
> *a place constantly debased by sneaking knaves*
>   *vicious, addicted to slandering;*
>   *such is the minds of princes . . .*
> *O, what tribulation for timid servants*
> *to penetrate there in fear and trembling.'*

Now, Tawny, who on his part had been narrowly watching Lively, noted that the stance and demeanour of the bull was exactly as had been described to him by Wily; and he suddenly leaped on the bull. With his body rent and bloodied by the cutting edge of the lion's thunderbolt claws, Lively rose and charged, goring Tawny's belly with the sharp points of his horns. Then, disengaging himself from his foe, he stood at bay, ready to charge again and gore the lion.

Wary, watching this bloody drama at a distance, saw the two, Tawny and Lively, stand facing each other with murderous intent. They looked like two palāśa[65] trees in full bloom. Turning to his friend Wily, he spoke bitterly, chiding the latter: 'Oh! You, miserable dunderhead! Is this well what you have done? Causing such enmity between these two who were friends? By your actions, sir, you have brought disorder and confusion into this whole forest-domain. You have further clearly demonstrated your ignorance of statecraft. For as it has been wisely observed:

> *Resorting to conciliation*[66] (353)
> *as sole expedient of policy*
> *men well-versed in diplomacy*
> *calm with gentle touch a situation*
> *whose ends have else to be compassed*

by arduous efforts undertaken
in the hazardous course served
by the expedient of violence:[67]
    these alone are true ministers.
While those hell-bent on violence,
driven by desire for paltry gains
unlawful, and lacking pith, plan actions
impolitic, that leave the fortunes
of the monarch hanging in the balance.

'Therefore, you bumbling fool:

To men who clearly discern right from wrong   (354)
    the expedient of conciliation
    stands first and foremost.
Lawful are ends wrought by conciliation;
    ends that defy frustration.

'Therefore, O, you misguided fool! You hanker after the post of minister; yet, you do not even know the word, "conciliation". You only think of one expedient, war. How vain and useless are all your fond imaginings! For it is sagely observed:

Beginning with peace, extending up to war:[68]   (355)
Thus, the Self-Existent enunciated
the guidelines of polity for princes: of these
war most reprehensible is best excluded.

The darkness that breeds in a foeman's heart   (356)
is only through conciliation destroyed:
not by the lustre-rays of a priceless gem,
not by the sun's heat, not by the fire's flames.

'And what's more:

Where conciliation promises success   (357)
    why resort to measures of war;
if candied sugar cures the bilious fit,
    why prescribe juice of bitter-gourd for it.

'Then again:

> *Conciliation, bribes, intrigue, these it's true* (358)
> *are the doors open for intelligence.*[69]
> *The fourth expedient, the noble speak of*
> *as that which displays masculine vigour.*[70]

'Besides:

> *Intelligence without manly vigour* (359)
> *may be rated as mere womanishness;*
> *while bravery exercised with unfairness*
> *is, doubt not, nothing but sheer brutishness.*

> *Lion, elephant or venomous snake,* (360)
> *Fire, water, air or blessed sun; in them*
> *we witness the might of the mightiest shown—*
> *barren might lacking a purposive plan.*

'Therefore, if from the overweening pride that comes of being a minister's son, you have exceeded your authority, it is only to court your own downfall. For it is a wise observation:

> *What is Knowledge,*[71] *if having won her* (361)
> *firm control over passions fails to follow,*
> *or rightful use of Intelligence lost;*
> *if with Righteousness, Knowledge does not dwell,*
> *if She leads not to Serenity or Fame;*
> *if to have Her is to simply bandy*
> *her name in this world—what use is She then?*

'Now, the texts on statecraft enunciate a fivefold counsel, as follows: an initial plan of action; organization of resources, men and material; a clear determination of time and place; counter-measures in case of reverses; and successful action. At this very moment, the master is in grave danger. So, you had better think of proper counter-measures if indeed you have the ability to do so. The test of a minister's political sagacity is his ability to cement friendships. But, you, O blockhead, you are incapable of doing that because you have a truly perverse nature. How aptly said then:

> *A scurvy knave is expert in ruining others' work* (362)
> *but he knows not how to make it prosper.*
> *The mole can cause the mulberry tree to fall;*
> *but to raise it again straight—that he cannot.*

'On the other hand the fault is really not yours; rather, it is the master's fault who paid close attention to the words of a silly fool like you. For how excellently is it observed:

> *Good counsel while it aims to cleanse the sluggish mind* (363)
> *fogged by fatuous conceit and other imperfections,*
> *only serves to inflame that mind and madden it*
> *as sight-awakening light only makes owls go blind.*

'And further:

> *Learning, they say, is the cure for conceit;* (364)
> *but where's the physician to cure the man*
> *that same learning maddens with gross conceit?*
> *When ambrosia itself poisons a man,*
> *where is the physic to heal him be found?'*

Seeing his master in a pitiable condition, Wary was plunged into despair. 'Alas! Alas!' he lamented, 'What calamity is this that has befallen our lord . . . all from listening to evil counsel! Oh! How wisely has it been said:

> *Monarchs who pursue counsels of base men* (365)
> *and stray from the path enjoined by sages*
> *enter that cage of evils thronged by rivals*
> *from which no door of deliverance can open.*

'Oh! You miserable fool! The whole world beats a path to the door of a master who has a retinue of merit and virtue, to seek his service. How then can our master ever gain that wealth of allies and retainers, all men of merit, when a mere beast like you who knows only to rend and tear and destroy, serves him as his minister? For, as the saying goes:

> *A monarch counselled by evil ministers* (366)
> *though himself virtuous attracts not that wealth;*
> *as a pool of sweet waters, pellucid,*
> *where monstrous crocodiles lurk, does not invite.*

'As for you, seeking your own advantage, in all probability you wish only to see our lord isolated, cut off from all other relations. You blockhead! Don't you see that:

> *A monarch shines most brilliant at the centre*[72] *of his court,* (367)
> *never isolated in lonely splendour.*
> *He must surely be an adversary*
> *who likes to see the king solitary.*

'Moreover:

> *In stern and harsh speech seek what is wholesome,* (368)
> *it is not as if it is all poison.*
> *In honey-sweet speech seek out treachery,*
> *it is not as if it is all ambrosia.*

'And if seeing another's good fortune makes you unhappy, that too is wrong. It is most unbefitting of you to act in the manner you have, to break a friendship that sprang up spontaneously. For:

> *Through treachery to gain friends,* (369)
> *through deceit moral ends,*
> *through others' afflictions their own affluence,*
> *to want learning without effort, woman through violence:*
> *men with such desires, it is clear,*
> *are devoid of good feeling and good sense.*

'Besides:

> *Wealth and prosperity flowing from the people* (370)
> *are a monarch's true might and majesty;*
> *what indeed would the mighty ocean be*
> *without waves rising crested with the gleam of gems!*

'And further, the man who receives high favours from his lord, should on that account show greater modesty and a sense of decorum to a higher degree; for it is aptly observed:

> *As the master bestows on his man* (371)
> *more and greater favours, the more discreet*
> *the servant's conduct should be;*
> *humbler his gait, the lower the profile he keeps.*

'But you, sir, you are a man of mean disposition; surely you are aware too of the saying:

> *The great and noble though greatly battered* (372)
> *stand firm, unfaltering;*
> *the mighty ocean is never sullied*
> *even as its shores are crumbling;*
> *the meanest, pettiest causes*
> *make shallow minds change and veer;*
> *the pliant grass is set a-trembling*
> *by lightest, gentlest breezes.*

'On the other hand, it is our lord who is entirely to blame. For, without proper scrutiny and due deliberation, he accepted the advice of one such as you, who are a minister in name only; who has no comprehension of the six royal qualities[73] and the four expedients[74] of *realpolitik*, all of which are essential for success in the attainment of the threefold goals of life.[75] Ah, what wisdom is contained in this statement:

> *If monarchs delight in consorting with retainers* (373)
> *whose bows are unstrung but whose tongues ever ply*

> *in wonderfully clever ways, and many,*
> *is it any surprise the enemy*
> *   consorts in delight with Royal Fortune?*

'Indeed, the moral is perfectly pointed out in the well-known tale;
as it has been said:

> *The naked monk he burned with fire;* (374)
> *he gained the king's special favour;*
> *he raised himself to high estate:*
> *he accomplished it all, did Minister Strong.'*

'Oh! Was that so? How?' exclaimed Wily. And Wary, the
jackal, then began the tale of *Strong and the Naked Mendicant.*

In the Kingdom of the Kosalas there flourished the city of
Ayodhyā, [76] where King Fine Chariot[77] ruled, upon whose footstool rays of lustre bursting from gem-studded diadems of innumerable vassal princes who kneeled to him, fell shimmering.
One day, one of the king's forest-rangers presented himself at
the court to convey a message. 'My lord,' he said bowing low,
'the forest-rulers are all becoming restless; one among them, the
forest king, Vindhyaka, needs to be taught a lesson; it is up to
His Majesty to take a decision.'

Then the king summoned one of his ministers, called
Strong,[78] and despatched him to subdue the rebel kings.

While Strong was away on his mission, a naked mendicant
entered the city at the close of summer. Such was his knowledge
of various matters—astrological predictions, prophecies, horo-
scopy, augury; the rising of zodiacal signs and division of each
sign, threefold, ninefold, twelvefold, thirtyfold; the gnomon and
its shadow, eclipses, ecliptic and ascendant; courses of celestial
bodies; their varied measurements, their correspondences with
elements of the body, their houses and influences on life and
thoughts—that in a few days, the fellow had the whole citizenry
eating out of his hand as if he had bought and owned it. Finally,

157

as the report of the mendicant's fame spread around by word of mouth, it reached the king's ears, who out of consuming curiosity ordered that he be brought to the palace. Having offered the mendicant a seat and all the courtesies, the king asked, 'Is the revered preceptor truly a reader of other men's thoughts?'

'His Majesty can be a judge of that by seeing the results,' answered the mendicant. And by involving the king in discourses of absorbing interest, the mendicant brought him to a fevered pitch of curiosity.

One day the mendicant failed to appear at the customary hour of discourse. Next day he entered the palace at the usual hour and announced, 'Oh! King! I have brought you happy tidings. Just this morning, I left this body of mine behind in my hut and assuming another body befitting the World of the Immortals, I went to the Realms of Light with the firm conviction that the Immortals were remembering me. Your Majesty, I have returned from that world just this moment. And while I was there, the Immortals exhorted me to make kind enquiries after Your Majesty's welfare on their behalf.'

The king was overpowered by great admiration, hearing these words of the mendicant. Lost in wonderment he cried, 'Holy Preceptor! Is this really possible? That Your Holiness can actually go to the Realms of Light?'

'Certainly, great king,' answered the mendicant, 'Why, I travel to the Realms of Light every day.'

Completely taken in by it all, the foolish king grew indifferent to the affairs of state, lost all interest in the life of the Inner Apartments[79] and became totally involved with the mendicant.

In the meantime, the minister, Strong, having made thorn-free the forest domains of the kingdom, returned to the capital and entered the royal presence. And what did he see but his royal master alone, disengaged from the council of ministers, closeted all by himself with a naked mendicant and engaged in animated discourse, his face glowing like a blossoming lotus, about some apparently marvellous event that seemed to have occurred.

After ascertaining the facts of the situation, Minister Strong approached the king, bowed low and greeted him with the words, 'Victory to our lord,[80] Beloved of Gods.'[81]

The king having made the customary, kind enquiries after his minister's health and well-being, asked, 'Does Your Honour know of this learned preceptor?' To which the minister replied, 'Know him, my lord; who does not know of one who is the progenitor and master of a whole school of learned preceptors? Further, the preceptor's journey to the Realms of Light is now common knowledge. Is that a fact, my lord?'

'Oh, yes,' responded the king warmly, 'What Your Honour has heard is true, beyond the shadow of a doubt.'

The naked mendicant now interposed to add, 'If the worthy minister is interested, he can see for himself.' So saying, he entered his hut, bolted the door and waited inside.

After a few minutes, Strong asked the king, 'How soon will the mendicant come out, my lord?'

'What makes you so impatient?' answered the king rather testily, 'No doubt when he has shed his earthly body and left it within his hut and assumed a celestial one in its place, the mendicant will come out.'

To this the minister replied, 'If that is indeed the case, my lord, let a pile of firewood be brought straight away so that I may set fire to this hut.'

'And why would you want to do that?' questioned the king.

'Because, my lord,' the minister retorted promptly, 'when his earthly body is consumed by fire, the mendicant would stand before Your Majesty in the very same body in which he journeys to the World of the Immortals. In this connection, we hear of a tale; let me relate it to you.' And the minister, Strong, began the tale of *The Maiden wedded to a Snake.*

In Rajagṛha,[82] there lived a Brāhmaṇa named Deva Śarma. His wife, being childless, wept bitterly everytime she saw the children of her neighbours, until one day the Brāhmaṇa spoke to comfort her, 'Do not distress yourself any further, dear wife: listen, dear lady, to what I have to say. While I was performing the sacrifices for obtaining offspring, I heard the voice of an invisible being speaking quite clearly and it declared, "Oh! Brāhmana, hear, you shall obtain a son surpassing all others in beauty of face and form, in virtue and good fortune."'

At her husband's words, the Brāhmana lady felt her heart swell with supreme joy. 'O, may that gracious utterance come true,' she repeated fervently.

The lady soon conceived and in due course, she was delivered—of a snake. When she saw the snake, disregarding the words of her friends who, one and all, advised her to abandon her offspring, the lady picked him up with tender affection and after bathing him, placed him in a large, clean chest, where she fed him on milk and butter and other fine foods so that in no time the snake grew to maturity.

Once, while watching the marriage festivities of the son of one of her neighbours, the Brāhmana lady turned to her husband with tears streaming down her face and said, 'I am convinced that you have nothing but utter contempt for me, for you make no attempt to arrange for the marriage of my darling boy.'

To this the Brāhmana's answer was, 'Oh! Noble lady; do you expect me to go down into the depths of the underworld and ask Vāsuki, King of Serpents, for the hand of his daughter? Foolish woman, who else do you think will offer his beloved daughter in marriage to a snake?'

As he spoke these words, the Brāhmana noticed the look of utter misery on his wife's face. Deeply disturbed by what he saw and out of affection for his wife, the Brāhmana packed a goodly store of provisions for the way and set out on a long journey.

Travelling some months in distant lands, Deva Śarma finally arrived at a place known as the City of Warbling Birds, located in some far-off land. There, in the house of a kinsman where he knew he could halt and ask for hospitality without feeling embarrassed, because relations between them were based on mutual respect and affection, he spent the night having received due hospitality: a pleasant bath, a fine dinner and other comforts.

Next morning when he had thanked his host and was ready

to depart, the latter enquired, 'Your Honour, what brought you to this place? And where do you plan to go next?'

In answer to these queries, Deva Śarma said, 'Your Honour, I set out from home in search of a young girl who would make a suitable bride for my son.'

Having gained this information, Deva Śarma's host immediately responded, 'Why, in that case, let me say that I have an extremely beautiful daughter; and I am yours to command. Accept my daughter, sir, as your son's bride.'

Accepting the offer, Deva Śarma took the maiden accompanied by her kinsfolk and returned home. No sooner had the townsfolk seen that maiden of exquisite loveliness—the loveliness of lustrous pearls—and blessed with innumerable graces, a girl of uncommon opulence of beauty, than their eyes dilated in wondering delight and they spoke to her kin as follows: 'How can anyone noble and high-souled, give in marriage this priceless gem of a maiden to a snake!'

Hearing such words, the girl's elderly relatives, with hearts wrenched by anxiety began to murmur: 'Let this maiden be removed far away from this boy who seems to be possessed by some baleful goblin.' Then the maiden cut in sharply with, 'Enough; no more of such derisive talk; pay heed to the text:

> *A monarch speaks but once;*   (375)
> *The sage and holy speak but once;*
> *a maid is given in marriage but once:*
> *these three things are done once and once only.*

'Besides:

> *An act with its inevitable end is twinned,*[83]   (376)
> *and what is prefigured must come into being;*
> *nothing can make it otherwise; the gods themselves*
> *had no way of altering poor Little Blossom's fate.'*

Then all those who were gathered there asked at once: 'And

who was this poor Little Blossom?' Thereupon the maiden began
the tale of *Death and Little Blossom*.

Indra, Lord of the Immortals, once had a parrot named Little
Blossom, a bird of exquisite beauty, like the beauty of lustrous
pearls, who was endowed with innumerable excellences and a
fine intellect and who wore lightly his prodigious learning in
scientific and sacred texts.

One day while sitting on the palm of great Indra's hand, the
parrot with his body thrilling with delight at the god's touch was
reciting various Vedic verses,[84] when he saw Yama, Lord of
Death, approaching at the appointed hour to pay his respects to
the great god. At once, Little Blossom moved aside. The whole
host of Immortals who were watching, asked the parrot, 'Why
has Your Honour moved aside upon beholding this personage?'
And the bird answered, 'This personage is indeed the one who
deprives all creatures that breathe, of their life's breath; is it not
right then to distance oneself from him?'

Hearing the parrot's words, all the gods eager to allay his
fears, requested Yama, thus, 'Lord, pray honour our words and
never ever deprive this parrot of his life.'

'Oh! I don't know about that,' replied Yama; 'such matters
are under the control of Time.'

The gods then took Little Blossom and sought the presence
of Time, and repeated their request. Thereupon, Time replied,
'This is a matter for Death; you had better speak to him.'

The Immortals did as instructed, but at the mere sight of
Death, the poor parrot dropped dead. Overwhelmed by grief at
Little Blossom's death, the whole host of Immortals repaired to
Yama's world and demanded, 'What is the meaning of this?'

And Yama explained, 'It was preordained that this bird
should die at the mere sight of Death.' Accepting these words,
the gods returned to their own world.

'Which is why I said before, "An act with its own inevitable
end is twinned . . . " and so on,' observed the maiden; and she
continued, 'Besides, my father should not incur the censure of

having made a false promise of his daughter in marriage.' And obtaining the permission of her kinsfolk who were attending on her, the maiden was wedded to the snake. Immediately, she began to wait upon her husband with devotion, offering him milk to drink and performing other services for him.

Once, at night, the snake slid out of his spacious chest that had been placed in the maiden's bed-chamber and climbed into her bed. At once she exclaimed, startled, 'Who is this in the form of a man?' And thinking him to be some stranger, she rose and with every limb trembling, went to the door, unlocked it and was about to dash out when she heard him say, 'Stay, gracious lady; I am your husband.' And to convince her, he re-entered the snake-form that he had shed and left within the chest and once again emerged from it to stand before her as a man. When the maiden saw him standing before her in a lofty diadem flashing with gems, and wearing gleaming earrings, armlets, bracelets and rings, she dropped down at his feet. They came together in an embrace and experienced the raptures of love.

The young man's father who had in the meantime risen very early saw how matters stood. Discovering the truth, he removed the snake-form lying within the chest and consigned it to the flames, telling himself, 'Let not my son ever again enter this snake-form.'

In the morning, the Brāhmana and his wife, their hearts bursting with supreme delight, introduced the marvellous young man lost in love of his beautiful bride to everyone gathered there as their very own son, extraordinary beyond all imaginings.

Having related this tale to the king as an illustration, Minister Strong then set fire to the hut where the naked mendicant crouched as in the womb.

'Which is why I say to you once more, "The naked mendicant, he burned . . . " and the rest of the verse.

'O, you miserable fool! It is men like Strong who are true ministers; not those such as you, ministers in mere name, who earn a living by making fraudulent claims of competence in the art of government, albeit they are totally ignorant of the knowledge of statecraft and its methods. By your evil conduct you have clearly demonstrated in every way, your inherited incapacity to be a true minister: for surely, your father before you must have been the same sort of person. For:

> *A father's ways the son surely emulates, we know,*   (377)
> *never on screw-pine[85] do cherry-plums[86] ever grow.*

'In men of learning with a natural reserve which they retain even with the passing of time, inner weaknesses are difficult of detection, unless, they themselves choose to put aside their impenetrable reserve to reveal hidden vulnerabilities. As it is said:

> *In joyous response to resonant rain clouds*   (378)
> *peacocks dance; more fools they to reveal plainly*
> *their secret places;[87] or who would see them*
> *however hard he tried to peer intently.*

'But what use is it offering good advice to someone so depraved as you. How excellently is it said:

> *No sword can bend an unbending tree*   (379)
>   *nor prevail against stone.*
> *as Needle-bill's good advice could not, upon one*
> *who took life easy and would not learn.'*

Wily asked eagerly, 'And how was that?' Then Wary began the tale of *The Tailor-bird and the Ape*.

In a certain wooded region there lived a troop of apes. One winter evening at dusk when the apes were extremely distressed they noticed a firefly. Believing it to be fire, they lifted it up with great care, covered it with dry grass and leaves and thrusting out their arms, started rubbing their arms and armpits, chests and bellies, all the while enjoying what they truly imagined to be the warmth of a fire.

One of these arboreal creatures in particular, being far too distressed by the cold, repeatedly blew hard on the firefly. Now a tailor-bird, who had been watching, flew down from her tree and admonished the ape, 'Friend, why do you go to all this trouble? This is not fire; it is a firefly.' Nor would he stop even after she had counselled him many a time not to do so. To cut the story short: when the bird came close to the ape and annoyed him intensely by screaming her advice right into his ear, he seized and dashed the poor bird against a rock. With her face and eyes, neck and head crushed to bits, the bird died.

'Which is why I said, "No sword can bend an unbending tree . . ." and the rest of it. Rather:

> *What avails instruction to those unfit?* (380)
> *It is like a lamp in a house that's lit*
> *within a jar with a lid on it.*

'You, my friend, are definitely the black sheep of the family. As the proverb points out:

> *The wise count four kinds of sons in this world;* (381)
> *'born' and 'equal-born', 'best-born' and 'worst-born'.*

> *The first has the qualities of the mother,* (382)
> *the second is the equal of his father,*
> *'best-born' surpasses all,*
> *'worst-born' is lowest of the low.*

'Another wise saying goes as follows:

> *By far-reaching wisdom, by wealth or power,* (383)
> *the son who carries the family fame*
> *gains for his mother a mother's true name.*

'And further:

> *Beauty that's the adornment of the moment—* (384)
> *indeed, where can you not find such beauty!*
> *But the beauty of great intellect—*
> *hard to find indeed are those whom it adorns.*

165

'Or again, see how excellent is the moral pointed out in:

> *The celebrated tale of* Fair Mind, Foul Mind,[88] (385)
> *wherein the son crafty, too clever by half,*
> *and father cleverly smoked out, both came unstuck.'*

In a certain city, there lived two friends named Fair Mind, and Foul Mind, both sons of merchants, who travelled to far-off lands in search of wealth. Now, by a stroke of his own good fortune, the one named Fair Mind, found a jar filled with a thousand dinars[89] which had been buried in the ground a long time ago by some holy man. Fair Mind thought, 'Now that we have been successful in our quest, why not return home.' He put the proposition to his friend Foul Mind, who concurred with it and they both started back home.

As they neared their native city, Fair Mind addressed his friend, 'Dear friend,' he said, 'half of this treasure is yours: so, here, take it, so that when we reach home we may cut a fine figure before friend and foe alike.'

Foul Mind however had other ideas in mind. Motivated by crooked intention and wishing to further his gains, he answered, 'Dear friend, so long as we hold this wealth in common the warm friendship we enjoy will remain intact. So let us each take out a hundred dinars and bury the rest in some safe spot before we go home. And the decrease or increase of our common wealth will then be the test of our virtue.'

Now Fair Mind, in the nobility of his nature, unaware of the hidden duplicity of his friend's intentions, readily agreed. Each then took out a portion of the treasure and after burying the rest in a secure spot under the ground, they entered the city.

Now Foul Mind, addicted as he was to the vice of squandering money and having his life overshadowed by an unlucky fate that made him vulnerable to temptation, quickly ran through the sum of money that he took as his initial portion. So, once again he approached his friend to dip into the buried wealth and he and Fair Mind each took another hundred dinars from it. But this too got spent within the year. As a result, Foul Mind was plunged into thought. 'Supposing I divide the treasure once more with Fair Mind and take out a hundred dinars what will then be left of the common hoard? A mere four hundred coins; and that would be a paltry sum, even if I decide to steal it all at one go. Therefore, it is better, I think, to steal the whole lot—all the six hundred coins that remain buried.'

Having decided that this was his best plan, Foul Mind went one day, alone, to the spot where the treasure was buried, dug it up, took it all out, covered up the hole and smoothed the spot over.

A month had barely passed when Foul Mind decided to approach his friend and broach the subject of the remainder of the buried treasure. 'Ah! My friend,' he began, 'let us now divide the remaining dinars equally between us.'

Foul Mind went along with his friend to the spot where they had buried the treasure and began to dig. As he continued digging and failed to find the treasure, the impudent fellow first beat his head with the now empty jar and then said, 'Where, O, where is this Prime Mover of the Universe.[90] Surely Fair Mind, it is you who have taken it. Now, hand over half of it to me, or I shall take you to the palace for justice.'

Then Fair Mind retorted, 'You double-dyed villain! How dare you speak like this. I am aptly named Fair Mind; and I would not dream of committing an act of theft. How well it is said:

> *The fair-minded man looks on other men's wives*   (386)
> *as mothers; others' wealth as so much trash;*
> *and all that lives as his very own life.'*

In hot dispute they went straight to the king's court and related the whole story of the theft to the judges who, after listening to the facts of the case pronounced that each one undertake a trial by ordeal; at which Foul Mind exclaimed, 'O, no, this is not a fair judgement; for it is said:

> *Documents are prime evidence in disputes,*   (387)
> *lacking which eyewitnesses are produced;*

167

> *where eyewitnesses cannot be found, there,*
> *ordeals are in order, jurists declare.*

'And in this matter, Your Honours, I have a divinity of the woodland to bear witness to the truth of my statement. She will declare to Your Honours which one of us is honest and which is not.'

To this the judges assented, saying, 'You have spoken rightly, sir; for it is stated:

> *When even a man base-born may be produced*   (388)
> *as proper witness in any dispute*
> *there an ordeal is deemed inappropriate:*
> *what to say of a woodland-goddess for witness!*

'We too on our part are consumed by curiosity in this matter. So, early in the morning, we require both of you to go with us to that particular spot in the woods to hear the divinity testify.' Having obtained a security from each of the two parties to the dispute, the judges dismissed them.

When Foul Mind reached home he pleaded with his father, saying, 'Dear father, the gold coins are in my possession; but retaining possession of them depends entirely on your testimony. I shall take you tonight to the place in the woods where I dug up these coins, and hide you out of sight in a hollow of the mimosa tree growing close by. When the judges arrive at that place in the morning, pray bear witness to the truth of the statement I made to them.'

And the father remonstrated with Foul Mind, saying, 'O, my son, we shall both be lost, for this is not a good scheme. As the proverb states wisely:

> *A shrewd, sagacious man should think with care*   (398)
> *of expedients and the evils thereof.*
> *Even as the foolish heron was looking on,*
> *the mongoose dined off the flock of herons.'*

'O, really!' exclaimed Foul Mind, 'How did that happen?'
And the father then began the tale of *The Foolish Heron*.

In a certain woodland region there grew a banyan tree that was
home to a flock of herons. In a hollow of its trunk lived a black
serpent who made a regular practice of eating up the heron chicks
before they sprouted wings. After a while, one of the herons,
desolate at seeing his offspring destroyed by the serpent,
repaired to the lakeshore and stood there downcast, weeping a
flood of tears. Seeing him in such a state, a crab came up and
asked the heron, 'Uncle, what makes you weep so bitterly today?'
And the heron answered, 'O, my friend, what am I to do? I am
such an ill-fated person; for my children and the children of my
kinsfolk are being regularly eaten up by a serpent that lives in the
hollow of yonder banyan tree. Therefore, with sorrow piled on
sorrow, what can I do but weep. Now tell me, is there some way
of destroying this serpent?'

Listening to the heron's words, the crab reflected, 'Ah! This
fellow is the natural enemy of my race. Therefore let me give him
a piece of advice that sounds good but is in fact harmful, so that
the rest of the herons will also perish. For it is rightly observed:

> *Make your speech butter-smooth;* (390)
> *make your heart pitiless;*
> *and so convince your foe*
> *that with all his kin he perishes.'*

The crab now addressed the heron, 'Listen, Uncle, if this is
the problem, then what you should do is to strew bits of fish all
the way from the mongoose burrow out there right up to the
hollow where the serpent lives, so that the mongoose following
the trail will find the vicious serpent, and kill him.'

The heron did as instructed and the mongoose following the
trail of fish-pieces killed the serpent; and he also ate one by one,
at his leisure, all the herons that had made the banyan tree their
home.

'Which is why I say to you, "A proper expedient should be devised . . ." and so on and so forth,' concluded the father.

However, not paying the slightest heed to the paternal warning, Foul Mind hid his father out of sight in the hollow of the mimosa tree at night.

Next day, at the crack of dawn, Foul Mind had his bath, put on fresh clothes and with Fair Mind leading the way, accompanied the judges to the mimosa tree. Standing under it he called out in a loud and clear voice:

'Sun and Moon, Fire and Wind, Heaven and Earth!   (391)
The Waters, Death and the Self! Day and Night,
and both the Twilights! You all watch the round
of Man's Existence and see if it is right.

'O, holy divinity of the woods! Which of us two is the thief; declare it.'

Then, Foul Mind's father, hidden in the mimosa tree-hollow spoke out loud, 'All of you out there! Listen; it was Fair Mind who stole the gold.'

Now, while the king's officers of justice all stared with eyes widening in astonishment and searched their minds for the appropriate punishment laid down in the law which could be inflicted on poor Fair Mind for stealing the treasure, he slipped out to gather materials that would catch fire quickly. Covering the hollow with these, Fair Mind set the heap alight.

As the fire burned strong, Foul Mind's father came rushing out of the mimosa tree-hollow uttering piteous wails, his body half-burnt, his vision smoke-blurred. And everyone gathered there turned to Fair Mind and burst out with, 'Oh! Great Gods! What is the meaning of this, sir?' To which Fair Mind coolly replied, 'It is all Foul Mind's doing, sirs.'

Immediately, the officers of justice seized Foul Mind and hanged him straight away on a branch of the mimosa tree; and highly commending Fair Mind, they bestowed on him many royal favours and gifts, to his heart's content.

'Which is why I said to you, friend Wily: "Fair Mind, Foul Mind . . . " and the rest of it,' concluded Wary.

Having told his tale, the jackal, Wary, continued, 'Alas! Alas! You miserable fool! By being too smart in the policy you followed, you have burned your own family. As it is wisely stated in the proverb:

> *In salty oceans rivers have their end;* (392)
> *in women's feuds kinship bonds break and end;*
> *in gossip of backbiters secrets do end;*
> *in wicked-minded sons do families end.*

'Moreover, who can trust a person who speaks on both sides of his mouth;[91] and this saying too is full of wisdom:

> *Double-tongue mental anguish arouses;* (393)
> *villain's mouth or serpent's implacable,*
> *cruel beyond all endurance it only*
> *serves to heap injuries upon injury.*

'What's more, seeing your conduct I am beginning to fear for my own person; for which reason, I say:

> *Never should you put your trust in villains;* (394)
> *Oh! How well have I understood their ways:*
> *wait upon a snake for ever so long,*
> *he will always bite the hand that feeds him.*

'And further:

> *Fire that's kindled even in sandalwood* (395)
> *will still spring up to burn;*
> *a villain always remains a villain,*
> *though to noblest family he belongs.*

'After all, consider, such is the very nature of villainy; as the proverb points out:

> *Expert in recounting the vices of others,* (396)
> *devoted to praise of his own virtues,*

171

> *skilled in engineering everyone's ruin,*
> *the villain—wills his own retribution.*

> *And the tongue that wags within the hollow* (397)
> *of the human face retailing others' vices*
> *and does not at once split a hundred times over,*
> *must in truth be fashioned of adamant.*

> *May no harm befall those lions among men*[92] (398)
> *ever-devoted to the good of others,*
> *whose own tongues observe the vow of silence*
> *when other tongues prate about others' vices.*

'Therefore it is wise to form friendships after careful scrutiny. As the saying goes:

> *Seek out one resourceful and also straight;* (399)
> *scrutinize one resourceful but a rogue;*
> *pity him who is straight but a big fool,*
> *and shun him who is both rogue and fool.*

'The point however is: you have striven hard to bring about the destruction of not only your own family but also the destruction of our lord and master. Since you have chosen to reduce our lord even to this pitiable condition, what it means is that you don't care a straw for anyone but yourself. And, the tale makes this point well:

> *Where mice may eat up an iron balance* (400)
> *solid, of a thousand weights,*
> *there, a hawk too may carry off an elephant;*
> *small wonder then if it carries off a boy!'*

'Oh?' asked Wily, the jackal, 'What was that all about?' And Wary began the tale of *The Preposterous Lie.*

In a certain settlement there lived the son of a merchant, named

Nāduka, who having lost all his wealth determined to go to another land. For:

> *A man who has lost all his fortune but dwells* (401)
> *still in the land or place where once he enjoyed*
> *all pleasures by virtue of his own power,*
> *is indeed the most despicable of men.*

And further:

> *Where a man once strutted proud and for long* (402)
> *in flashy play, and now in that same place*
> *creeps miserable, poor, he is reviled*
> *shamelessly by gossipping neighbours.*

In his house lay a balance made of a thousand kilos of iron which he had inherited from his ancestors. This Nāduka left as a pledge[93] with Lakṣmaṇa, President of the Guild, and then went off on his travels to distant lands. Having travelled for a long time in many lands, wherever his business took him, Nāduka finally returned to his native place and proceeded to the house of the guild-president, Lakṣmaṇa. 'Friend, Lakṣmaṇa,' he said, 'please return the balance that I pledged with you.' To this the merchant Lakṣmaṇa replied, 'Ah! Friend Nāduka, your balance has been eaten up by mice.'

Hearing these words, Nāduka replied, 'Oh! Well, friend Lakṣmaṇa, if the balance has been eaten by mice, that is surely no fault of yours; such is life; nothing in this world is permanent. However, I am planning to go down to the river for my bath. Kindly send your son whom you have named Golden god with me to carry the necessary articles for my bath.'

The merchant Lakṣmaṇa, who was somewhat conscience-stricken over the theft he had committed, summoned Golden god and said to him; 'My dear boy, this is Nāduka, like an elder brother to you and he is going to the river for a bath. So, do go with him and carry whatever articles are needed for his bath.'

Alas! Alas! how much wisdom is found in the saying:

None does another person a good deed (403)
out of pure loving-kindness;
only out of fear or greed,
or motivated by some personal need.

And again it is said:

Where excess of solicitude is shown (404)
for no special rhyme or reason known,
there, some suspicion should be entertained:
your safety is then assured in the end.

Then Lakṣmaṇa's son picked up the articles for a bath and went along happily with Nāduka who, after finishing his bath in the river, seized the boy and pushed him into a cave nearby. He then blocked the entrance to the cave with a great big boulder and returned to Lakṣmaṇa's house. Whereupon Lakṣmaṇa asked, 'Hey there, friend Nāduka; tell me; where is my son, Golden god, who accompanied you to the river?'

'O, your son?' replied Nāduka, 'A hawk carried him off from the river-bank.'

'What?' retorted Lakṣmaṇa, 'A hawk carried off a big boy like Golden god? Impossible.'

'But it is possible for mice to eat up a balance made of solid iron, is it?' retorted Nāduka, 'Look, friend Lakṣmaṇa, return me my iron balance, if you want your son back.'

Hotly disputing in this manner, the two of them went to the palace gates, where Lakṣmaṇa started crying out loud in piercing tones, 'Help! Help! A dastardly deed has been committed; Nāduka here has kidnapped my son, Golden god . . . . '

The officers of justice came out and ordered Nāduka, saying, 'Hey! Sir, you had better return Lakṣmaṇa's son to him, immediately.'

'What can I do, Your Honours?' pleaded Nāduka, 'Before my very eyes, the hawk carried off the boy.'

'Come, come, Nāduka, you are not telling the truth,'

retorted the judges, 'Is it possible for a hawk to lift up and carry off a fifteen-year-old boy?'

Then Nāduka laughed and spoke out boldly. 'Let Your Honours listen to my words:

> *Where mice may eat up an iron balance,* (405)
>   *solid, of a thousand weights,*
> *there, a hawk too may carry off an elephant;*
>   *small wonder then if it carries off a boy!'*

The judges asked eagerly, 'What do you mean, Nāduka?' Nāduka at once told them the whole story of his balance. They listened and then laughing, ordered that the one should have his balance restored and the other his son.

'Which is why I quoted the verse to you, "Where mice may eat up an iron balance . . ." and the rest of it,' concluded the jackal, Wary.

And he continued admonishing Wily. 'You blockhead! You have done what you did because you could not bear to see Lord Tawny's favour bestowed so freely on Lively. What's more, there is much wisdom in the proverb:

> *Rascals revile men of noble birth;* (406)
> *rejected suitors sneer at lovers women adore;*
> *cowards condemn men of shining courage,*
>   *and misers munificent donors;*
>   *the destitute despise the prosperous,*
>   *and the crooked the upright;*
> *those with deformities cursed ridicule*
>   *men with great beauty blest;*
> *fools censure men proficient in diverse fields:*
>   *this is the rule of the world!*

'Also:

> *The wise are hated by the ignorant,* (407)
> *the immensely wealthy by the indigent;*

175

the pious of strict vows by men of sinful ways;
chaste wives by women of easy virtue.

'Or else, consider:

> *All beings follow the bent of their natures;*   (408)
> *men of discernment even, they only act*
> *as their own nature directs them to do:*
> *this being so, what can chastisement effect?*

'The person who grasps what is said once, only he can be instructed properly; whereas you are like a stone, mindless, inert. Why try to instruct you? And further, you fool, even associating with you is not right. From close contact with you, Wily, who knows what misfortune might not come upon me. How wisely is it observed:

> *Merely to live beside a blockhead*   (409)
> *in country, village, city or homestead,*
> *even if one has no dealings with him,*
> *is simply a way of inviting misfortune.*

> *Better plunge in the ocean or blazing fire,*   (410)
>   *in deepest pit or underworld abyss,*
> *than keep company with a wretched fool*
>   *who has parted company with his judgement.*

> *As breezes wandering over many lands*   (411)
>   *come laden with odours foul or fragrant*
> *so do men consorting with good or bad*
>   *have virtues or vices clinging to them.*

'And this tale contains the wisdom that teaches a lesson:

> *Two birds were we, I and he,*   (412)
> *with selfsame mother, with selfsame father,*
> *Well brought up by hermits was I,*
> *and he by eaters of cattle flesh.*

176

He hears the speech of beef-eaters, O, King! (413)
I of hermits continually,
Association fosters vice or virtue;
and this Your Honour has seen for yourself.'

'And was that so?' quizzed Wily, the jackal. Then Wary
began the tale of *The Twin Parrots*.

In a certain part of a mountainous region, a hen-parrot gave birth
to two chicks. Once, while she had left the nest to go foraging, a
fowler trapped her two sons. However, one of them, watched
over by a kind fate, got away, while the other was kept in a cage
by the fowler who trained him to speak. The chick who got away
was found by a wandering hermit who picked him up, took him
to the hermitage and tended him with care.

As time went by in this manner, one day, a king whose horse
had bolted with him thus separating him from his army, came
galloping into that wooded region where the band of fowlers
lived. No sooner had the fowler's parrot in the cage seen the king
approaching on horseback than he started twittering
melodiously, 'Come, come, O my masters; here comes some
fellow riding a horse; quick, seize him, bind him; kill him, kill
him.'

As soon as the king heard this parrot-talk, he spurred his
horse on and sped away. He rode on and on until he approached
another forest, distant, where he saw a hermitage in which a
company of hermits resided. There too, a parrot in a cage seeing
the king, addressed him affably, twittering: 'Come, O, King;
come and rest yourself here. Taste our cool waters and our sweet
fruit.' Then he turned and called out, 'Hey there! O, holy hermits!
Honour this guest who has come to our hermitage; welcome him
with the guest-offering,[94] here under the cool shade of this tree.'

Listening to the words of welcome spoken by this parrot, the
king was lost in amazement. His eyes widening with wonder, he
reflected, 'How strange all this is!' Then he questioned the parrot,

177

'Sir, I am amazed, for, a while ago, a great distance from this place, I saw another parrot in another forest who looked exactly like you: except that he displayed a cruel nature. He kept repeating, "Seize him, bind him, kill him, kill him."

When the virtuous parrot heard what the king said, he narrated all the events of his life in detail.

'Therefore I say to you, Sir Wily, "Association fosters vice or virtue . . . " and so on. And let me add, Sir Wily, that even casual acquaintance with you is not salutary. As the moral in the tale clearly says:

> *Better a wise, learned man for a foe,*   (414)
> *than an ignorant blockhead for a friend,*
> *The robber for his victims gave his life;*
> *the monkey killed the king.'*

'Oh! Sir Wary, tell me, tell me how that happened,' exclaimed Wily. Then Wary, the jackal, began the tales of *The Three Friends and the Noble Robber* and *Faithful but Foolish*.

There was a certain prince who had formed close friendships with a merchant's son and the son of a scholar. Everyday the three friends went out together to the public square, to the pleasure gardens and recreation-grounds, to enjoy themselves in various sports and amusements; and in amorous pastimes. The prince was averse to the science and practice of archery, to elephant and horse-riding and to other kingly sports such as hunting and chariot-racing.

One day when his royal father had roundly reprimanded him for not displaying any aptitude for or interest in princely pursuits, the prince opened his heart to his two friends, conveying to them his bitterness at the deep hurt to his self-esteem. They too responded in kind, saying, 'Our fathers also berate us in like manner for not showing any interest in the pursuit of our family professions; not a day goes by without their confronting us with the same charges, babbling on and on incoherently. But up to now we have paid scant attention to their complaints, happy and secure in our friendship with you, sir. But now, seeing you in the same plight, hurting from a similar grievance, we are even more miserable than before.'

Then the prince spoke with determination, 'Having been humiliated thus it is wholly unbefitting for us to remain here. Therefore let us three depart sharing a common resentment, and go elsewhere. For:

> *Courage and resoluteness, character and strength,*   (415)
> *virtue and knowledge; of self-respecting men*
> *such qualities are tested and known from results,*
> *when fired by pride they abandon their native lands.'*

Having determined on this, the question of which place was best to travel to was next on their minds. The merchant's son then made a suggestion, 'Since it is undeniable that no success that one wishes for is possible without wealth, I think we should set out towards Mount Ascension, where we may find gems that would provide us the means to enjoy all imaginable pleasures.'

Agreeing to this as a most suitable course to pursue, the three friends set out for Mount Ascension, where by a stroke of good luck, they each found a priceless gem. Now they began to deliberate. 'How shall we protect these gems while travelling by this forest-track which is beset by innumerable dangers,' they asked each other as they conferred amongst themselves.

Then the scholar's son came up with an idea, 'Look,' he exclaimed, 'here I am, a scholar's son, and a good plan has come into my mind; this is it; let each one of us swallow his gem so that being inside our stomachs it will be safe from other merchants, highway robbers and other such persons.'

Deciding on this as an excellent plan, at dinner-time, each placed his gem in a mouthful of food and swallowed it.

While this was happening a fellow who was resting on the mountain slope without being seen, witnessed it all.

'Just see my luck,' he reflected, 'here I have been wandering around so many days tramping up and down Mount Ascension searching for gems; but being ill-starred I found nothing.

Therefore, let me follow these men; sometime or other they will lie down tired out and fall asleep; and then, I shall rip open their bellies and possess myself of all three gems.' Having determined to carry out his plan, the stranger came down the mountain and started following the three friends as they continued on their journey.

Soon he started talking to them, thus, 'Hey there! Hey! Worthy gentlemen! I simply cannot think of passing through this terrifying forest all by myself to get to my native land. So, pray allow me to join you and travel in your company.'

Out of friendly feeling, the three friends readily agreed; all four of them journeyed on together. Soon they came to an impenetrable part of the hills, where a settlement of Bhils came into view, hugging the curve of the track. As the travellers passed by on the outskirts of this settlement, one old bird which was part of the aviary of many different species of birds that the Bhil chieftain kept as pets out of interest, began calling from its cage.

Now the Bhil chieftain was conversant with the language of birds; he comprehended the messages conveyed by their calls and songs. Understanding perfectly the meaning of the old bird's song, he was transported with delight; calling to his attendants, he spoke to them: 'Listen fellows: listen to what this bird is saying; it says, "Hey! there are priceless gems in the possession of the travellers who are this very minute going along on the forest trail that passes by our settlement. Seize them; seize them." So, fellows, do as the bird says; go, stop them and bring them before me.'

When his men had followed his orders and brought the travellers before him, the Bhil chieftain himself made a thorough search of the four travellers. He even stripped them and took everything they had; but he found no gems. When the travellers resumed their journey having been released with nothing but a loin-cloth on their person, the same bird again began to sing, saying the same thing again. Listening carefully to the bird's song, once again the Bhil chieftain had the travellers seized and brought back. Once again, he undertook a most particular and minute inspection of the persons of the travellers; finding nothing he let them go.

As the travellers were again about to continue their journey, the same bird began to sing again, expatiating on the same theme in loud, shrill tones. Once again the Bhil chieftain ordered his men to bring the departing travellers back into his presence and questioned them, 'Listen, fellows, I have tested this bird time and again; never have I heard him utter a falsehood. Now, the bird says repeatedly that you have gems in your possession. So, where are they?'

The travellers answered, 'Your Honour, if we do have gems in our possession, as your bird alleges, how is it that even after the thorough search that you worthy gentlemen have subjected us to, you have not found them?'

The Bhil chieftain retorted, 'If this bird says so and repeats what he says you must have the gems; it must be that they are inside your bellies. It is now near sunset; but at dawn tomorrow, I shall without fail cut open your bellies; and find the gems I shall.'

Having made his decision, the chieftain had all four travellers thrown into a dungeon underground.

Then the robber among them began to reflect deeply, 'There is not the slightest doubt that in the morning, when this Bhil chieftain cuts open the bellies of these three men and discovers the gems hidden inside, evil-hearted man that he is and excessively greedy, he is bound to rip open my belly too. So whichever way you look at it, my death is certain. In the circumstances what ought I to do? As has been wisely observed:

At the moment of death of noble souls, (416)
if their last breath, inexorably transient,
serves to render some kindly aid to others,
that death fulfils itself in deathlessness.

'Therefore, it is most fitting that I offer my own life to preserve the lives of these men, and consequently, bare my own belly first to the knife. Because, in the event that this evil-hearted man finds

181

right at the beginning that the minutest and most thorough search of my ripped-open belly reveals nothing and his surmises about the existence of gems are, as a result, dispelled, he may of his own accord, merciless though he is, desist from cutting open the bellies of the others out of some trace of compassion. Were I to do this, by bestowing the gift of life and of wealth on these men, I shall surely gain the glory consequent upon a generous deed, in this world and in the next, as well as the cleansing of all my sins in this birth. Though this opportunity has presented itself unsought as it were, this, I think, is the right kind of death—the death of one wise and noble.'

The robber passed the night thinking such thoughts. At daybreak when the Bhil chieftain got ready to rip open the bellies of the travellers, the robber folded his hands in respect and humbly pleaded, 'O, sir! I simply cannot bear to see the bellies of my brothers here ripped open before my very eyes. Therefore, be gracious, sir, and let my own belly be ripped open first.'

Thereupon, the Bhil chieftain mercifully consented to do so and had the robber's belly slit open; but even after he had looked in and scrutinized the insides with great care and thoroughness, he found no gem; nothing whatsoever. Then he began to bewail his action, 'Oh! Woe! Woe is me!' he lamented, 'What have I done! Going entirely on what I thought was my understanding of a bird's song, and obsessed by cruel greed, I have done a dastardly deed. I guess I shan't discover gems in the bellies of the other three travellers any more than I did in this man's!' So, the three friends, set free without a scratch on their bodies hastened to cross the forest with the utmost speed and soon reached another kingdom.

'Therefore, I tell you again, "The robber died for his victims; it is better to have noble men for foes."'

When they reached this other kingdom, the priceless gems were sold by the merchant's son who brought the money and laid it at the feet of the prince. The prince appointed the scholar's son his chief minister and thinking to wrest from the reigning monarch, the sovereignty of the kingdom to which they had come, he put the merchant's son in charge of the treasury. Next, the prince assembled a great army of picked elephants, horses and infantry by offering twice the usual pay and emoluments; and with the help of his chief minister who was fully conversant with the six measures[95] of foreign policy, he started hostilities, killed the reigning monarch and seized the kingdom. Thus the prince became the monarch of that kingdom. Entrusting the heavy burden of care of administering the body politic to his minister, the prince, now king, remained free of all cares, passing his time in the enjoyment of all the luxuries and pleasures in elegant ease.

At one time, as the king was dallying with his queens in the Inner Apartments, he took a fancy to a monkey that often visited the stables close by. Making it a pet, he kept the creature always by his side; for, as we know, kings naturally love to keep as pets, parrots and partridges, ringdoves, rams, monkeys and other creatures.

In the course of time, the monkey, thriving on the variety of dainty foods the king fed him upon, grew to be a hefty fellow. And he also became an object of great respect to the entire court. The king out of tenderness for the creature, as if it were his own offspring, developed such confidence in the monkey that he actually made it his personal sword-bearer.

Adjoining the palace was a pleasure-grove beautifully laid out with copses formed of many different kinds of trees. It was springtime. The king looked out at the charming sight that the grove presented, as if it were celebrating the glory of the God of Love: swarms of black bees humming rapturously; innumerable flowers shedding their fragrances around. In a passion of love, the king entered the grove in the company of his consort, the chief queen, instructing all his attendants to remain at the gate.

After a while having wandered in eager delight all over that beautiful grove and enjoyed its beauties, the king grew tired. Addressing the pet monkey, he charged it saying, 'Look fellow, I shall spend a little time sleeping here in this flowery bower. You'd better take good care to see that no one drops in here all of a sudden and disturbs my sleep.' Thus having instructed the monkey, the king fell fast asleep.

In a little while, a bee flew in, drawn by the fragrance of flowers and of musk and other perfumes used by the king, and settled on his head.

Seeing the bee settled comfortably on the royal head, the monkey was perturbed; it thought in raging fury, 'What! How dare this mean little creature try to bite my king, right before my eyes!' It began to ward off the bee trying to drive it away. But in spite of all its efforts, the bee repeatedly approached the king, hovering over his head. In a blind rage, the monkey now drew the royal sword and fetched a blow at the offending bee; that blow split the king's head in two. The queen sleeping beside him, now started up in terror; seeing that good-for-nothing creature, sword in hand, she started screaming, 'You! You blockhead of a monkey! What's this that you've done! When the king put such implicit trust in you, how could you do such a thing?' The poor monkey explained what had happened. But everyone gathered there, screaming in rage at the monkey and hurling imprecations at it; they all ostracized him after that.

'Now you see why the proverb says, "Never make friends with a fool; the monkey killed the king." And, for this reason, I repeat this verse to you, friend Wily:

> *Better a wise, learned man for a foe*   (417)
> *than an ignorant blockhead for a friend.*
> > *The robber for his victims gave his life;*
> > *the monkey killed the king.'*

And Wary, the jackal, continued:

> *'Skilled in nothing but slander,*   (418)
> *of warm affection the destroyer;*
> *with one like you making the decision,*
> *nothing right or good can ever be done.*

'And further:

> *A virtuous man will never perform*   (419)
> *an act the world will be quick to blame.*

184

> *In direst straits he will do no harm*
> *by doing that which will stain his fame.*

'Also:

> *By sense of family-honour imbued,*   (420)
> *a wise man though placed in direst straits*
> *does not swerve from the path of rectitude.*
>   *Eaten, then dropped by a peacock, a shell*
>   *is not robbed of its whiteness, natural.*

'As it is taught:

> *Wrongdoing will always remain wrongful;*   (421)
> *a wise man will not direct his mind towards it.*
> *However tormented by thirst one is,*
> *none drinks the water of puddles*
> *that lie on well-trodden highways.*

'Moreover:

> *Do only that which it is right to do:*   (422)
> *even as the breath struggles in the throat.*
> *What is not right, do not attempt to do;*
> *even as the breath struggles in the throat.'*

Thus admonished by Wary, whose words were spoken in accordance with the precepts of moral wisdom, Wily, the jackal whose mind worked in crooked ways, quietly slunk away, because these words were sheer poison to him.

At this point, both Tawny and Lively, whose minds were blinded by rage, renewed the battle in which Tawny killed Lively, after which his rage subsided. Then, recollecting past affection, his eyes filled with tears of pity. As he wiped them off with a blood-drenched paw, Tawny, overwhelmed by remorse, lamented, 'Ha! Ha! O misery! What a dastardly crime! Lively, who was my second self, lies here slain, and by me; in slaying him I have only hurt myself. How wisely it has been said:

Parts of a kingdom may be lost, (423)
or a retainer rich in worth;
the discerning man rues the latter;

> *for loss of retainers is death to monarchs.*
> *Lands once lost may be easily regained,*
> *but retainers of worth are not readily obtained.'*

Seeing Tawny shaken, overcome by irresolution and lack of confidence, Wily, the jackal, ever self-confident to the point of audacity, drew near him, slowly, by degrees.

'Ah! My lord,' Wily expostulated with the lion, 'Where's the propriety or logic in this? Your Lordship has slain your rival, yet I witness such lack of firmness—of confidence! As it has been wisely observed:

A tender-hearted king, (424)
a gluttonous Brāhmana,
an evil-minded companion,
a self-willed wife, fancy-free,
> *a menial quite contrary,*
a man in authority negligent:
throw them all out, out of sight,
if they don't do what is right.

If a father or brother, a son or friend, (425)
is intent on practising on your life,
> *he doubtless deserves to be slain,*
if you wish to survive and prosper.

Go where you find happiness (426)
> *even if it's far to go;*
seek to learn from one learned
even if he's only a child;
give your own body to a suppliant;
cut off your arm if it turns malignant.

'As for the morality of princes, it has nothing in common with that of ordinary men. As it has been wisely said:

> *A state cannot be governed in accordance* (427)
> *with the nature and norms of the common man.*
> *What are vices in ordinary men*
> *those very vices are virtues in kings.*

'And further:

> *The policy of princes is protean,* (428)
> *assumes many forms like a courtesan!*
> *by turns true or false; now harsh, now sweet-spoken;*
> *cruel, but compassionate too; at once*
> *avaricious and munificent;*
> *amasser of great wealth and opulence,*
> *yet, a perpetual prodigal, extravagant.'*

Seeing that Wily had not come back, Wary now sought him out and found him sitting close to Lord Tawny. And Wary began exhorting him, 'As for you, sir, you don't have a clue to what statesmanship really is. Since dissension is the cause of destruction of two people who have enjoyed mutual affection, it is not a policy that good ministers ought to pursue. Nor is it an example of statesmanship to raise doubts and suspicions in the master's mind and place him in jeopardy by advocating war, when all the other policy expedients exist and are available: such as conciliation, winning over the rival by generous gifts, or by attempts to change the situation. As the proverb says:

> *The fortunes of the God of Wealth*[96] (429)
> *and Wielder of the Thunderbolt*[97] *as well,*
> *of Gods of Winds and Waters too*
> *were foiled and crushed by petty strife;*
> *no one ever comes out victorious every time.*

> *Those who discard statesmanship command war;* (430)
> *those lacking insight strive to start a war;*
> *but sages commend statesmanship in their texts;*
> *texts state the policies and their employment.*

'Therefore, it is important that ministers refrain from advocating war as a policy to their masters. As it has been wisely stated:

> *Where men of integrity, accomplished,*   (431)
> *engaged in fostering their master's interests*
> *and plotting the ruin of his opponents,*
> *choose to dwell in palaces, free from greed,*
> *those kings will never be subdued by foes.*

'Therefore:

> *Always give wholesome if bitter advice:*   (432)
> *dangers loom when royal servitors*
> *constantly speak only what is nice.*

'Moreover:

> *Asked or unasked by their royal master,*   (433)
> *if ministers proclaim what is pleasing*
> *but harmful to the interest of the king,*
> *they'll cause Royal Fortune to waste away.*

'And further, the master on his part should make it a point to consult every single one of his ministers; having solicited their several opinions, the king should then deliberate over the counsel offered by each and decide for himself what is to his advantage and what is not. For sometimes it happens that a fact once established, appears in a different light due to some confusion of mind.[98] As the adage points out:

> *The sky looks like the flat roof of a house;*   (434)
>   *the firefly glows like flame;*
> *but the sky's vault has no roof as we know;*
>   *the firefly is not fire.*

'Also:

> *What is false appears to be true;*   (435)
> *what is true seems untrue;*

things are perceived in various ways;
they should be looked at with care, in any case.

'Therefore, it is not right that the master should implicitly rely on whatever a retainer who has strayed from the course of statesmanship has to say; for the reason, that a crafty retainer keeping his own advancement in the forefront, pulls the wool over his master's eyes by presenting him with incredibly artful arguments; facts as they are not. The master should undertake an action only after deep deliberation: as the proverb puts it:

One who weighs a plan deliberated upon   (436)
several times by trusted friends; and himself
reflects upon, applying the Law's dictates
with discerning mind, then carries it out,
he truly is a man of judgement; only he
is the fit and chosen resort for Fortune, and for Fame.

'Therefore, the master should not turn into a person whose mind retreats before the persuasive speech of others. Accurately understanding other men from every angle, he should carefully consider the advantages and disadvantages, the ultimate consequences, of their counsel. Master of his own thinking and decisions, uninfluenced by other pressures, the master should be fully cognizant in his own mind of every single aspect of his responsibilities and functions.'

So ends Book One known as the *Estrangement of Friends*. Of which the opening verse runs thus:

Oh! What a beautiful friendship it was!   (437)
    of noble bull and lion majestic—
In the deep, dark woods it waxed and grew strong,
    then—along came a jackal treacherous;
    consumed by greed, he hacked it down.
        And—Alas! It died.

BOOK II

Winning of Friends

And now begins the second book known as the *Winning of Friends*, whose opening verse runs thus:

> *Lacking resources, destitute of wealth,* (1)
> *wise men possessed of knowledge and insight,*
> *are quick to accomplish their desired aims,*
> *as* the crow and mole, the deer and tortoise *did.*

'Oh! How was that?' asked the princes eagerly. And Viṣṇu Śarma began the tale.

In the southern land flourished the city known as Pramadāropya. Not too far away grew a lofty banyan tree with mighty trunk and branches providing a home for all creatures. As it has been said:

> *Deer recline in its shade;* (2)
> *birds in multitudes gather to roost*
> *darkening its dark-green canopy of leaves;*
> *troops of monkeys cling to the trunk;*
> *while hollows hum with insect-throngs,*
> *flowers are boldly kissed by honey-bees;*
> *O! What happiness its every limb showers*
> *on assemblages of various creatures;*
> > *Such a tree deserves all praise,*
> > *others only burden the Earth.*

A crow named Lightwing,[1] had his home in that tree. One day as he was about to fly towards the city in search of food, he saw a fowler approaching the tree with every intention of snaring birds; for he carried a net and a club in his hands and hunting dogs followed at his heels. He was a man of fierce appearance with splayed hands and feet, bloodshot eyes, bulging genitals; thickset, with a very rough, gnarled frame and swarthy complexion; his hair was knotted in a bunch on top of his head. Why describe him at great length? Suffice it to say that he appeared a second god of destruction, noose in hand; the very incarnation of evil and the soul of unrighteousness; prime instructor in crime and bosom friend of Death.

On seeing him, Lightwing was alarmed and started reflecting nervously, 'Oho! What crime is this fellow planning to commit now? To cause *me* mortal harm? Or, alas, has he some other purpose in mind?' With a burning desire to find out, he kept close behind the fowler.

Soon, the fowler picked a spot, spread his net out, scattered some grain and hid not too far away. The birds that lived there checked by Lightwing's warning looked askance at the grain as if it were deadly poison and remained quiet.

At this juncture, Sheenneck,[2] King of Doves, surrounded by hundreds of dove-retainers, who had been flying around in search of food, saw the scattered grain from far away. In spite of Lightwing's strong dissuasions, greedy-tongued Sheenneck, alighted on that large net to peck. The moment he settled on the robber's net, he, with his whole retinue, was caught in its meshes. Nor was it any fault of his; it happened because of an adverse fate. As it is wisely observed:

> *How did Rāvaṇa fail to consider* (3)
> *how wrong it was to steal another's wife!*
> *How too was Rāma unable to see*
> *that a golden deer could never be!*
> *And how did Yudhiṣṭhira as well fall prey*
> *playing a game of dice, to calamity!*
> *As a rule, in the face of adversity*
> *that causes men's minds to whirl in a daze*
> *the intelligence loses its clarity.*

Further:

> *Fettered fast by doom's deadly coils,* (4)

the feeling heart fate-burdened,
the judgement of even the great
goes with twisted, crooked gait.

Now the fowler seeing things turn out so well darted out in great glee with his club held high over his head. Sheenneck though deeply distressed by the calamity that had befallen him and his whole retinue and seeing the fowler advancing, yet with great presence of mind, reassured his followers, saying, 'Have no fear, friends, have no fear; for:

Though caught in the throes of calamities (5)
if a person's wits do not forsake him,
he will safely cross to the far shore
and enjoy supreme happiness and more.

'We now have to be of one mind; all of us acting together have to carry away this net. If we err in this by not acting in unison, we shall never be able to carry it off. In the absence of a concerted effort, death will be the certain outcome. As it is wisely said:

Single-bellied, double-throated (6)
the poor Bharunda birds perished
  eating one thing and another:
  So too will the disunited.'

'O! How did that happen,' clamoured the doves. And Sheenneck then began the tale of *Bharunda Birds.*

'Beside a certain lake, there lived a species of birds known as Bharunda. They each had two necks but only one stomach. Now, one day, one of these birds, was rambling around happily when one of his necks chanced upon some ambrosia spilt somewhere there; whereupon his other neck pleaded, 'Give me half of that.' When the first neck refused outright, the second neck, mad with rage began searching for poison and finding some, ingested it. As the bird had only one stomach it dropped dead.

'Which is why I said to you before, "Single-bellied, double-throated . . . " and the rest of it. To have a common purpose is to be successful,' concluded Sheenneck.

Paying heed to this piece of advice, the doves impelled by the strong urge to survive and live, now took hold of the net all together and soared into the sky, high up in an instant, no more than it takes an arrow to shoot upwards out of sight. Then, holding the net aloft as if it were a canopy, the birds travelled on, free from fear.

The fowler, on his part, seeing his net carried away by the flock of doves, gazed at the sight with upturned face, lost in astonishment, thinking, 'Ha! How strange! Never have I witnessed anything like this before!' And he recited this verse:

'So long as these birds amongst themselves agree,   (7)
they might succeed in carrying my net away:
but once they quarrel and start to disagree,
there's not the slightest doubt they'll become my prey.'

Convinced of this the fowler started to follow the birds. Sheenneck, noticing that cruel fellow pursuing him and his flock, and realizing quite clearly what the man was upto, remained calm and collected. In an unhurried manner, he led his flock over regions uneven and rugged with hills and shrubs and trees where the going was rough.

Now, Lightwing, the crow, who was watching it all wondering at both Sheenneck's circumspect behaviour and at the fowler's foolish attempts to follow the birds, gave up all thought of foraging and filled with consuming curiosity, began flying behind the flock of doves, frequently looking up and down as he flew, at the birds above and the fowler below. As he followed the doves, Lightwing thought to himself, 'What will happen next? What will this noble soul do now? And what will that perfidious villain think of next?'

In the meantime, the fowler, following the birds on foot, realized that the flight of doves was safe from him on account of the difficulties of the terrain. Losing hope, he turned back, disappointed, muttering to himself:

'What is not to be can never be, (8)
what will be comes effortlessly;
what one is not destined to have is lost
even as it lies on the palm of one's hand.'

'And further:

If fates be adverse, even wealth that comes, (9)
flies away: and it takes something more as it goes.
This is the way Kubera's treasures behave!

'To say nothing of not netting any birds for food, that net which was the mainstay for the support of the family, that too is lost.'

When Sheenneck saw that the fowler was turning back having lost hope, he addressed his flock. 'Well, friends, now we may all go on our way in peace, without fear: for it looks as if that villainous fowler has gone back. Our best bet now is to travel to the city known as Pramadāropya. Because, in the north-eastern quarter of the city lives my dear friend, Goldy, the mole. He will sever our bonds in a trice; so skilful is he that in no time he will release us from our distress.'

Eager to get hold of Goldy,[3] the mole, and have him help them out, the birds followed Sheenneck's advice. Soon, they reached Goldy's fortress-den and alighted near its entrance.

And there it was:

To guard against impending dangers, the mole, (10)
in moral and political wisdom
expert, built his burrow of hundred mouths;
a fortress to live within safe and sound.

In the circumstances, alarmed at the sound of birds alighting, Goldy with timorous heart, took one small step no bigger than a cat's paw, along the path leading out of his fortress-den and stood peering out, wondering, 'What on earth is happening?'

Sheenneck, however, took his stand at the entrance to the burrow and spoke as follows, 'Ah! Dear friend Goldy, come out quickly; come and see the plight I am in.'

Goldy listened carefully to these words but remaining within his fortress called out, 'Friend, who may you be? What brings you here? And what sort of trouble are you in? Tell me.' To which Sheenneck answered, 'Why, I am your old friend, Sheenneck, Lord of Doves; so pray, come out quickly.'

Shivers of joy coursed through Goldy's little frame when he heard these words; his heart trilled with delight and he hurried out of his den saying,

> *'To the home of the self-disciplined,*   (11)
> *friends full of affection come daily,*
> *bringing delight to the householder's eyes.'*

Taking one good look at Sheenneck who with his whole retinue was caught in the meshes of the fowler's net, Goldy enquired sadly. 'Ah! My friend, what is this? How did all this happen? Tell me.'

'Where's the need to ask me, my friend, when you know it all quite well,' replied Sheenneck. 'As the saying goes:

> *What and wherefore? How and when?*   (12)
> *Because of? By whom and where? —*
> *And one's action? Was it well or ill?*
>   *That and for that reason, then,*
>   *and thus, by him, therefore, there—*
>   *So it comes: it is all the Will of Fate.*

'And again:

> *With glances brilliant*   (13)
> *as blue-lotuses unfurling,*
> *the peacock looks at the world*
> *out of his thousand eyes, indeed:*
>   *But when Death yawning wide*
>   *stares him in the face, poor bird,*
>   *like one born blind*
>   *he sinks down dispirited.*

From a hundred yojanas[4] and twenty-five   (14)
how an eagle descries a piece of flesh!
But he too, when Fate wills it to be so,
fails to see the deadly snare near his feet.

'Then again:

I see Sun and Moon afflicted by eclipses;   (15)
elephant, snake, bird, imprisoned in cages;
the intelligent and thoughtful sunk in penury:
And my creed is: Alas! all-powerful is Destiny.

'What's more:

Even birds that soar secure in the sky meet with calamities,   (16)
while fishes are netted by skilled men who scour the
                                    fathomless seas.
Why speak of wrong policy or of virtuous conduct, here,
                                    in this world?
What avails position, what advantage?
     It is Time who inevitably stretches forth
     a calamitous arm that arrests even at a distance.'

As Goldy started to gnaw through Sheenneck's bonds who
was lamenting after this fashion, the Lord of Doves stopped him
to say, 'No, no, my friend; this is wrong: not my bonds first; the
bonds of my flock should be cut first.'

Goldy took umbrage at this and reproved his friend, 'Your
Honour has not spoken well, nor out of decorum, sir. For
servants come after the master.'

To this Sheenneck's reply was, 'O, no, don't speak like this,
dear friend; these poor fellows, all of them, abandoned others to
attach themselves to me. How can I not show them this modicum
of honour? As the wise saying points out:

When a monarch heaps honours on retainers   (17)
constantly and far beyond their due,

they, replete with happiness do not forsake him
even if he lacks resources; not even then.

'And then:

> *Trust is at the root of honour and success;* (18)
> *by that a tusker becomes lord of the herd.*
> *Though sovereignty over beasts is the lion's,*
> *yet deer do not wait upon him.*

'Besides, after gnawing through my bonds you might get a tooth ache; or that evil-minded fowler might come upon us here. In that case I shall be doomed to perdition. As the saying teaches:

> *The king who watches his retainers,* (19)
> *all men of virtuous conduct*
> *sunk in misery,*
> *and yet remains at ease, unaffected,*
> *sinks down in this world and in the other—*
> *doomed.'*

Goldy listened and then responded saying, 'Ah! My friend, I know well what your duties as a ruler are. I said what I did only to test you. And now I shall gnaw through everyone's bonds. And in no time will have your whole retinue around you. As the proverb observes pertinently:

> *The Protector of the Earth who at all times* (20)
> *displays compassion for his retainers,*
> *and duly shares with them, is worthy to be*
> *no less than the Triple-World's Protector.'*

After making these wise observations, Godly cut the bonds of all the birds and said to Sheenneck, 'Dear friend, now you are free and can return to your own residence.' Accompanied by his retinue the King of Doves went home. Mark you, there is much wisdom in the saying:

> *A job however difficult to do* (21)

may be carried through with the aid of friends;
therefore, a person ought to find friends, and
finding, regard them as his good fortune.

Lightwing, the crow, who had witnessed the whole matter of Sheenneck's capture and subsequent release, reflected in astonishment. 'See, how admirable it all is! The intelligence of this mole, Goldy! His skill! And this whole idea of his fortress! It'd be wise indeed on my part to strike up a friendship with Goldy. Granted that I, who am rather capricious of nature, never place my trust in anyone; granted too that I cannot be easily fooled by anyone: still, I should have a trusted friend. As it has been wisely observed:

Though self-sufficient, a person should still (22)
have friends if he desires to raise his standing.
The ocean ever full yet waits eager
for the waters bright Svāti's[5] bounty brings.

Having arrived at this conclusion, the crow flew down from the tree and stationing himself at the entrance to the mole's burrow, called out to him by the name he had previously heard, 'O, friend, Goldy; pray come out.'

At this Goldy reflected, a bit uncertain, 'Is this one of the doves still somewhat entangled in the cords of the net, standing at my door and calling for help?' And he enquired, 'Sir? Who are you?'

'I am the crow named Lightwing,' came the reply. At once Goldy scurried off to a far corner of his den and called out, 'Begone, sir; leave this neighbourhood.'

'I have come to you, sir, on some grave business; so kindly grant me an interview,' replied Lightwing.

'I see no particular need to make your acquaintance, sir,' replied the mole.

'Listen to me; having witnessed the release of Lord Sheenneck from his bonds through your exertions, I feel great confidence in you, Sir Mole. And, if sometime I get similarly caught, my deliverance too could be effected through your kind exertions,' explained Lightwing.

To this Goldy retorted, 'Sir, you are the eater; I am the food. What kind of friendship can exist between us? You know the saying:

> *One who is fool enough to make friends* (23)
> *with a person not his equal,*
> *be he inferior or superior,*
> *merely becomes the world's butt of ridicule.*

'So make yourself scarce.'

The crow however remonstrated with the mole. 'Look, sir, here I am, standing at your fortress-gates. If you will not be my friend, I shall go on a hunger-strike.'

'For god's sake, man,' retorted Goldy, 'how can I build a friendship with you who are my enemy. For is it not said:

> *Never form an alliance with a foe;* (24)
> *even an alliance well-contracted, approved.*
>   *Water though boiling hot*
>   *will do no less than put the fire out.'*

To this, the crow promptly replied, 'Listen, Your Honour has not even set eyes on me; where's the question of enmity? Why speak in a manner so unbecoming?'

Goldy retorted, 'Look here; enmity is of two kinds; one that is natural and the other, incidental. You are the natural enemy of us moles. The point is:

> *You may speedily end bad blood* (25)
>   *by making due amends.*
> *But enmity in Nature only ends*
>   *with the spilling of blood.'*

'Ah, well, if that is so, I wish to learn what the distinctive quality of each of the two kinds of enmity is,' said the crow.

'Well, it's like this,' the mole replied, 'the enmity that is incidental springs from some cause. And if and when proper remedial measures are adopted, it ceases to operate. But the other kind of enmity which is inborn, will always exist: for instance, the enmity between snake and mongoose; grass-eating animals and those armed with claws; dogs and cats; fire and water; Gods and Titans; rival wives; lions and elephants; hunter and deer; crows and owls; scholars and dunces; the chaste wife and the harlot; saints and sinners: between these there is perpetual enmity. It is not as if anyone is killed by anyone else all the time; yet they all strive to fight the other to death.'

Now the crow demurred, 'There is no reason, no cause for this kind of thing, you know. And, now, sir, pray listen to my words.

> *A person seeks friendship for a reason;* (26)
>   *with reason a person incurs enmity.*
> *So, is it not reasonable for a person*
>   *to seek amity rather than enmity.'*

In reply all Goldy had to say was this, 'O, come, come, what sort of fraternization can there be between you and me? Just listen to me while I expound the essence of ethics to you.

> *Once a friend is faithless* (27)
> *to trust him once again*
> *is to court death, no less,*
> *as the mule who conceived, did.*

> *A lion deprived of his precious life, Pāṇini* (28)
>   *the Father of Grammar;*
> *an elephant suddenly struck and killed Jaimini,*
>   *the sage, Mimamsa's[6] author;*
> *Piṅgala,[7] treasure-house of knowledge of metres was slain*
>   *on the seashore by a sea-monster:*
> *to brutes caught up in fury, their minds wrapped in*
>   *ignorance,*
>   *what meaning does excellence have?'*

'Perfectly true,' said the crow, 'but listen to this:

> We make friends with people because they help; (29)
> with birds and beasts for some special reason
> or other; with fools out of fear or greed:
> but with the good we make friends at first sight.

'Moreover:

> Alliance with villains is like earthen pots (30)
> easily broken, difficult to mend;
> alliance with the virtuous, like golden pots
> difficult to break, easy to mend.

'Besides:

> Starting from the tip, sugarcane juice (31)
> grows sweeter by degrees, node after node;
> so does friendship of the upright; the reverse
> is true in the case of those perverse.

'I am upright in all respects,' continued Lightwing; 'and further, I shall dispel your fears by binding myself with oaths.'

To this Goldy's reply was, 'Confidence in your oaths? I have none; as the proverb points out:

> Do not trust a foe though he binds himself (32)
>   with strongest oaths;
> having sworn incredible oaths, Indra
>   struck down Vṛtra.[8]

> Without first gaining the trust of their foes (33)
> the gods themselves cannot win against them.
> After instilling trust in Diti's[9] heart
> Indra, Lord of Gods, smote her unborn child.

> Let him find the smallest chink (34)
>   and the enemy slips right in;
>   then working slowly, surely,
>   he wreaks total ruin,

as water seeps in gradually
filling the raft till it sinks.

If relying on bountiful resources (35)
a man reposes full trust in a foe,
or in wives estranged who love him no more
he might as well bid goodbye to life.'

Having heard Goldy's sage observations, Lightwing found himself at a loss to reply; he began to reflect with great seriousness; 'Aha! How admirable is this fellow's firmness and depth of knowledge in matters of social and moral ethics! This and this alone is my overriding consideration for desiring his friendship.'

And he said:

'Wise men have declared this: (36)
comradeship is, when seven words are spoken
(or seven steps[10] *together taken).*
Friendship has been thrust upon you,
O, friend; so listen to my words.

'Grant me your friendship; otherwise I shall give up my life right here at this spot.'

Goldy, hearing this plea, thought to himself, 'This fellow is by no means unintelligent; that is plain from his talk. As the saying wisely puts it:

None lacking in polish speaks affably; (37)
none but a lover is fond of finery;
none ambition-free craves for authority;
none frank and open practises chicanery.

'So, I must certainly extend my friendship to him.'

Having resolved this in his mind, Goldy accosted the crow, 'Friend; you have gained my trust. I spoke the way I did because it was necessary to test your intelligence first. I now embrace you in affection.'[11]

Saying this the mole was about to step out when he stopped

halfway and stood there. Lightwing queried: 'Sir, is there still some reason in your mind to mistrust me, that you are hesitant to emerge from your fortress?'

'Oh, no,' answered the mole, 'I have no fear of you because now I know your mind. But by being so trusting I might sometime fall into the clutches of some friend or other of yours and meet my death.'

To this Lightwing replied,

'*Sacrificing a friend blessed with virtue* (38)
   to gain another is like planting fields
with coarse millet that overpowers and chokes the rice;
   something at all costs to be avoided.'

At these words Goldy hurried out; the two greeted each other warmly and stood for a few moments clasping each other. Then the crow said, 'Let Your Honour now go inside your mansion, while I go in search of food.'

With these words, Lightwing left Goldy's presence and flew into the dense woods nearby where he noticed a wild buffalo lying, killed by a tiger. He ate his fill of the animal's flesh and then pecking out a choice piece of meat crimson as fresh palāśa-flowers, flew back to Goldy's residence, and called out to his friend, 'Hey there! Come out, friend Goldy, come and enjoy this nice bit of meat that I have brought you.'

On his part, Goldy had already gathered with diligence a great heap of grains of rice and millet. 'Pray, eat and enjoy this grain that I have done my best to gather for you, my friend,' he said.

Each, highly gratified by the other's efforts, ate the other's food out of affection; this is truly the seed of friendship as the proverb puts it neatly:

Giving and receiving, (39)
each other's secrets sharing,
dining, entertaining:
these six are sure signs of affection.

> *Unless some act of kindness is done,* (40)
> *affection scarcely comes to anyone;*
> *the very gods grant their blessings*
> *when entreated with offerings.*
>
> *As long as a gift is in the offing* (41)
> *so long will affection be forthcoming;*
> *once the calf sees the udder dry*
> *he bids his mother goodbye.*

Why speak at length:

> *By unfailing affection closely knit* (42)
> *like claw and flesh hard to split,*
> *they celebrated, the crow and mole,*
> *a friendship absolute and sole.*

Thus, as time passed, the mole charmed by Lightwing's attentions grew so trusting that he would snuggle between the crow's wings and rest there.

Now, one day, Lightwing appeared with tears welling from his eyes and words made indistinct by his sobbing, to announce, 'O, my dear friend, Goldy, I am so sickened by this place that I intend going elsewhere.'

'Why, what's the reason, dearest friend, for your feeling so disgusted with this land?' asked Goldy anxiously.

And Lightwing explained, 'Listen, dear friend; such a terrible drought has struck this land that the citizenry, driven by hunger, don't even leave the most meagre of offerings of food for the birds. And that's not all. In house after house snares have been set to trap birds. It is only because the thread of my life has still to run some more that I myself have not as yet been caught in one of these traps. That is the situation. I am shedding tears because I have to go to another land.'

'If that is so, where are you planning to go; tell me that,' said Goldy.

Then Lightwing answered, 'In the far south, in the heart of

a dense forest, lies a great lake, where my bosom friend, a tortoise named Slowcoach lives, who is dearer to me than even you are. He will provide me with delicate bits of fish, easy on the stomach; and there, I shall pass my days happily in his company enjoying the delights of his conversation that is liberally spiced with pithy sayings. To tell you the truth, I simply cannot bear to see the kind of decimation of us birds that is going on here. There is wisdom in the saying:

> *How fortunate indeed are those* (43)
> *who do not have to see the ccuntry ravaged,*
> *the family ruined, a dear wife ravished*
> *or a friend on the edge of a precipice.'*

'In the circumstances,' said Goldy, 'I think I shall go with you, for I too have great sorrow.'

'Oh?' asked Lightwing solicitously, 'What kind of sorrow?'

To this Goldy's reply was, 'Ah, my friend; there is much to tell. After we get there I shall tell you everything.'

'But, listen,' interjected the crow, 'I travel by air and you move on the ground. How can Your Honour accompany me to that place where the lake is?'

Goldy answered, 'If the protection of my life is at all of any consequence, then Your Honour might let me ride on your back and carry me along, proceeding very gently.'

Hearing the mole's words, the crow was delighted, 'If that is how Your Honour feels, I am indeed blest; no one can be more fortunate than I. Then, that's settled; let us do it this way. I know all the eight kinds of flight of birds, *Sampāta*[12] and the rest and I shall transport you there in utmost comfort.'

'Eight kinds of flights?' asked Goldy curiously, 'I would love to know their names, dear friend.'

Lightwing readily assented and reeled out the names:

> *'You have the easy-even flight* (44)
> *the short, sharp-darting flight*
> *and the long, sustained cruising;*
> *then, the swooping-diving-down flying,*

the wide-sweeping-in-curves circling,
and the tortuous, zigzagging flight;
the last is known as the light-quick flight.'

After being enlightened on the subject of aerial flights, Goldy climbed on to the crow's back and settled himself. Lightwing then took off using the mode of the easy-even flight. Very gently he travelled and brought Goldy to the lake.

In the meantime, Slowcoach, who had been closely watching a crow approaching with a mole riding piggyback, wondered, 'Who on earth could this be?' And being a good judge of time and place, he quickly ducked into the water.

Lightwing now alighted on a tree growing beside the lake and having deposited Goldy in a little hollow, hopped on to a branch and cried out in sharp, high tones. 'Hey there! Slowcoach, come here; here I am, your friend Lightwing. After a long absence I have arrived here at the lake, and my heart is filled with longing to see you, dear friend. So, come quickly, embrace me; for it is aptly said:

Can sandal-paste blended with chill camphor (45)
or snowflakes delightfully cool, compare
with the refreshing touch of a friend's body?
They are not a sixteenth part of this delight.'

When he heard Lightwing call out to him, Slowcoach made a close inspection of the caller and recognizing his friend, quickly emerged from the water. His body quivered with delight, his eyes brimmed over with tears of joy as he said apologetically: 'I did not at first recognize you; do forgive this lapse on my part.' With these words, the tortoise embraced Lightwing who had flown down from the tree on to the ground.

Then the two friends after exchanging embraces sat down together at the base of the tree with their bodies still thrilling with happiness; and they began exchanging news, and recounting all the events that had happened in their lives over the long period of time that they had not seen each other.

Goldy now came down from the tree and having bowed to Slowcoach also sat close to them. Looking him over carefully, the tortoise asked Lightwing, 'Hey, friend, who is this mole? And why have you brought him here with such care letting him ride on your back, when he is your natural food?'

'This is Goldy,' replied Lightwing, 'this mole is my good friend; he is almost my second life. Why explain at great length:

> As the showers of the Rain-god,   (46)
>   as the stars in the sky,
> as particles of dust on the earth,
>   defy enumeration,
> so also the virtues of this noble soul
>   are beyond all reckoning;
> but disaffected with the world
>   he now seeks your presence.'

'And what may his reason be for turning away from wordly matters?' queried Slowcoach.

'I asked him that very same question, and his answer was that after arriving at this place, he would tell me all about it; but he has not said anything as yet. Friend Goldy, now that we are here won't you tell us the reason for your aversion from all wordly things?'

Then Goldy began the tale of *Goldy's Sorrows*.

In the southern land is the fair city known as Pramadāropya, not far from which is situated the shrine of the Great Lord.[13] In the neighbouring monastery lived a mendicant monk named Crumplyear,[14] who would visit the city on his daily rounds to receive alms.[15] During his rounds he would get his almsbowl filled with all kinds of goodies flavoured and stuffed with crystallized sugar, jaggery,[16] pomegranates, that were moist and deliciously-melting-in-the-mouth. Returning to the monastery, the monk would partake of just the amount prescribed by the rules of his order; the rest he would put away in the bowl which he would hang on an ivory peg in his cell, keeping it for the early morning meal of the attendants. I, with my family and friends, lived on this food; and so the days passed.

The monk noticed that however careful he was in hiding the food, I still got to it and had a good tuck in. Upset by this and out of fear of my inroads into his bowl he moved it from place to place and hung it higher each time. But I got at it easily enough and continued eating the food.

It happened one day that the monk got a visitor, named Broadbottom,[17] whom Crumplyear received with all the rites of hospitality extended to a guest, providing him with all the comforts needed to relieve his travel-fatigue.

That night lying side by side on the same pallet-bed the two friends began discoursing on religious themes.[18] Now Crumplyear, with moles and mice on his mind kept striking his almsbowl with a rotten old bamboo stick, while making irrelevant responses in an abstracted manner to Broadbottom's conversation. Soon the guest became nettled and burst out with, 'Ho-ho! Crumplyear, it is plain that your friendship for me has cooled off, for I can see that you do not care to converse with me with any zest. Therefore, although it is night now, I shall straight away depart from your monastery and go elsewhere. How true is the saying:

> *Come in, please enter, sir, do sit down,* (47)
> *here's a seat; long time no see; how come?*
> *What news? You look pulled down:*
> *trust all is well with you?*
> *Oh! How delighted I am to see you, sir—*
> *when dear friends greet arriving guests*
> *with such pleasant words,*
> *welcoming them with respect to their homes,*
> *it is only natural for friends to come always*
> *to those houses*
> *without fear of feeling ill at ease.*

'On the other hand:

211

> *Those who visit a house where the host* (48)
> *on arrival of a guest looks down, or*
> *in every other direction but his—*
> *what are they but oxen? Without horns?*

> *Where the host does not rise and come forward* (49)
> *to greet his guest, engage him in pleasant talk*
> *and converse with him on virtue and vice,*
> *should never set foot in that house.*

'Now, you, puffed up with pride at becoming Master of some small monastery have thought fit to abandon an old friendship; what you don't understand is, that under the semblance of presiding over a monastery, what you have in fact earned is a place in Hell. As the proverb wisely states:

> *If you have a mind to go to Hell,* (50)
>   *act as a family-priest*
>   *for just one year:*
> *Or better still become the Master*
>   *of a monastery*
>   *for three days only.*

'Therefore, you miserable fool! That you should feel so proud when in truth you are to be really pitied . . . !'

At these words Crumplyear trembled in fear, 'Oh! No, Your Reverence, please do not say such things; truly, I have no other friend but yourself. Pray hear the real reason for what you perceive as a certain coldness on my part in our conversation. You see, sir, there is a wicked mole around here who jumps high up and climbs into my almsbowl, however high I hang it, and he eats up the leavings, so that the attendants not receiving their share fail to clean and tidy up the cell. It is only to frighten this mole off that I repeatedly strike the almsbowl with this bamboo stick. Believe me, there is no other reason. And one thing more; the surprising thing about this evil creature is, he is so nimble in jumping that he puts to shame cats, monkeys and other such creatures.'

'Have you any idea where this mole has his hole?' asked Broadbottom.

'Oh, no, sir, I don't,' answered Crumplyear.

'It is quite certain that the mouth of this hole has to be right on top of his store; it is the hot vapours arising from his store that makes this creature jump so spiritedly, no doubt about that. For the old adage says:

> *When the mere warmth of wealth is sufficient* (51)
> *to enhance the spirit and rouse energy,*
> *how much would its enjoyment be*
> *specially when sharing is a part of it!*

'Moreover:

> *If Mother Śāndilee[19] sells hulled sesame* (52)
> *for unhulled seeds, it's not by chance, believe me!*
> *There has to be some good reason for it.'*

Crumplyear asked with some curiosity, 'Pray, Your Reverence, how did that happen?' Then Reverend Broadbottom began the tale of *Mother Śāndilee.*

Some time back, once, I earnestly requested a certain Brāhmana living in a certain settlement for a place to serve as a retreat[20] which he readily agreed to. I lived there performing all the rites of worship to divinities as ordained. One day it happened that very early in the morning I was listening attentively to a conversation between the Brāhmana and his wife.

The Brāhmana was saying, 'Lady, the winter solstice falls tomorrow at dawn; it is a profitable time and I shall sally forth to another village in expectation of priestly largesse. You too should feed some Brāhmana tomorrow as part of the worship of the sun—according to our means of course.' At this the Brāhmana's wife burst out, reviling him with harsh words, 'Who do you think

can be fed in the home of a poverty-stricken Brāhmana like you?
Are you not embarrassed talking this way? Besides:

> *Since the day you first took my hand in yours*   (53)
> *I have not enjoyed the least happiness;*
> *fine, flavourful food have I not tasted;*
> *what to speak of ornaments and the like.'*

Listening to her harsh words, the Brāhmana, somewhat
cowed spoke very gently to her, 'Lady, it is not proper to say such
things; for there is great wisdom in the saying:

> *You may have only a morsel yourself,*   (54)
> *why not give half of it to a suppliant?*
> *Who gains prosperity sufficient,*
> *and when, to satisfy his heart's desires?*

'Moreover:

> *The poor man can only offer his mite,*   (55)
> *but the reward he reaps, the Vedas say,*
> *is just the same as that which great lords gain*
> *from the munificent gifts they dispense.*

> *What does the raincloud give but water,*   (56)
>   *yet the whole world dearly loves him;*
>   *while with outstretched ray-hands*
>   *the sun continually stands;*
>   *yet who can bear to see him?*

'Aware of this truth, even the poorest of the poor ought to give
a little out of his little, to the right person, at the right time. There
is a saying about this:

> *A worthy recipient, great devotion;*   (57)
> *giving the right gift at the right moment;*
>   *(when these come together)*
> *what is given by a discerning person*
>   *always redounds to his Eternal Good.*

'While some others say this too:

> *Keep a tight rein on excessive desire,*[21]   (58)
> *but do not give up desire altogether.*
> *But one, by excessive desire obsessed*
> *soon grew a crest on the top of his head.'*

'O, really?' exclaimed the Brāhmana lady, 'And however did that happen?' And the Brāhmana began the tale of *The Greedy Jackal.*

In a certain country there lived a man of the Pulinda[22] tribe who set out one day in search of more sins to add to his stock.[23] As he walked along he encountered a wild boar who seemed the very image of the peak of the Great Sooty Mountain. Seeing the boar the hunter drew his bowstring right back to his ear as he recited this verse:

> *'He sees my bow and the fitted arrow,*   (59)
> *yet no signs of alarm does he show.*
> *As I watch his firm resolve I am sure*
> *it is Death that has directed him here.'*

The hunter then shot a sharp arrow into the animal who in turn charged in fury and tore open his entrails with the sharp point of his tusk that shone like the crescent-moon. The man dropped dead. Having killed the hunter, the wild boar convulsed with pain from the fatal arrow-wound and died.

At this juncture, a starving jackal whose death was imminent arrived at that place in the course of his wanderings here and there in search of food. When he saw a hunter and a boar both lying dead his joy knew no bounds as he reflected deeply: 'Ah! Fortune is in my favour for she has provided this unexpected feast for me; there is such wisdom in the saying:

> *The fruits of action good and bad*   (60)

215

done in a previous life still attend us
>   put in place by Fate,
without further effort on our part.

'And again:

Whosoever does an act good or bad   (61)
>   at any time or place
>   or at any age, reaps
its inevitable consequence.

'Now, I shall consume this food in such a way that it lasts for
many days to sustain my life. So, let me start with this nice clump
of muscle caught at the bow's curved end and eat it slowly
holding it between my paws:

Bit by bit, the wise enjoy,   (62)
the wealth they earn, slowly, very slowly,
as some precious elixir is savoured
drop by drop, not gulped unceremoniously.'

Having resolved how to do this, the jackal seized the meat
hanging from the bow's tip and started gnawing it. When the
ligament he was chewing on snapped, the tip of the arrow pierced
the roof of his mouth and came out through the centre of his skull
forming a crest on the top of his head. Writhing in violent pain
he fell dead.

'Therefore I say to you,' concluded the Brāhmana: "Do not
lust after anything . . . " and so on.' Once again he addressed his
wife. 'Lady, have you not heard of this?

For every living being, these five are fixed   (63)
>   while still in the womb:
length of life, fortune and knowledge, wealth,
>   and the precise moment of death.'

Thus instructed the lady said, 'Well, if this is so, then I shall
see what can be done. There is a bit of sesame seed in the house

which I can grind and make into little sesame cakes to feed a Brāhmana with.' Accepting her words her husband set out for the next village.

The lady then soaked the sesame seeds in hot water, cleaned and hulled them and laying them out in the sun to dry went about her household chores. While she was thus preoccupied a dog came along and pissed on the sesame seeds, noticing which the lady began to reflect sadly. 'Ah, dear me! See how tricky Fate can be when it has turned against you! It has contrived to make even this miserable bit of sesame seed unfit for human consumption. I think I had better take it around to some neighbour's house and see if I can exchange my hulled sesame for someone's unhulled seed. Any one should be happy to make such an exchange.'

So she placed the sesame in a winnowing-pan made of palm leaf and went from house to house crying her wares, 'Ho there! Hi there! Who'll take hulled sesame for unhulled . . . .' Hawking her hulled sesame seeds the Brāhmana lady soon entered the house where I had entered at that moment seeking alms, and made her offer—hulled for unhulled sesame. The lady of the house was delighted at such a bargain and exchanged her unhulled sesame for the caller's hulled seed.

As the transaction was completed the man of the house came home and exclaimed, 'My dear; what is this?' To which his wife replied, 'Look I have got sesame cheap.'

The husband thought over this for a moment and then asked, 'And whose sesame seed was this?' To which his son, Kamandaki, replied promptly, 'Mother Śāndilee's.'

'Ah,' replied the man, 'Mother Śāndilee's is it? O, my dear, she is a sharp person, extremely clever at driving a bargain. You had better throw this sesame out; for Mother Śāndilee is not one to barter hulled sesame for unhulled without some good reason to do so.'

'Therefore,' continued Broadbottom, 'it is certain that the warmth exuded by his stockpile is what gives this mole his ability to jump as he does.' And the visitor asked his friend again: 'Have you any idea, friend Crumplyear, as to how this mole tackles his job?'

'Oh, yes, Your Reverence; I do know that; this chap never comes by himself, but always with his whole clan,' said Crumplyear.

'I see,' said Reverend Broadbottom, 'now tell me, do you have something in the way of a digging instrument around here.'

'Indeed, I do, sir,' answered Crumplyear, 'here, I have a pickaxe of solid iron.'

Reverend Broadbottom then said, 'Good: you had better wake up at the first streak of dawn, when I get up, so that we can both follow the trail of pawmarks still fresh on the ground.'

When I heard these words of that evil-hearted person, that fell on me like a thunderbolt, I began to reflect anxiously, 'Oh, God! I am done for; for this man's words sound purposive; for once he locates my hoard, it is very easy to know the whereabouts of my fortress; and that is his aim, it is quite plain. As the wise proverb puts it:

> *A wise person takes a man's true measure* (64)
>   *at one shrewd glance,*
> *as an expert jeweller gauges the true weight*
>   *of metal by simply holding it on his palm.*

'And again:

> *It is the first stir of desire that points* (65)
>   *ahead of time to the coming event—*
>   *reward for good or evil done in former lives.*
> *As yet he has not grown the gorgeous train*
> *that marks his kind; but watching his mincing steps*
> *as he walks backwards[24] from the lake, you say,*
>   *Ah! There goes a peacock chick.'*

Terrified, I therefore abandoned the road to the fortress and with my dependants started on another path. But there right in front was an enormous cat, who seeing a whole pack of moles facing him, hurtled right into our midst. The moles that survived the slaughter, reproaching me for leading them on a dangerous path, ran for safety into our selfsame fortress, drenching the ground with their blood as they ran. O, what wisdom is in the verse!

> *Bursting his bonds, flinging aside the trap;* (66)
> *tearing asunder the net that held him fast,*
> *fleeing far from woods encircled by twisting fires*
> *with crested flames angrily bristling;*
> *leaping and bounding with incredible swiftness*
> *out of reach of the arrows of hunters,*
> *the stag raced only to tumble into a well.*
>   *Alas! What can manly effort avail*
>   *when the fates themselves prove hostile!*

Alone, I went elsewhere while the others, poor fools, rushed into the old fortress. The visiting monk noticing the drops of blood on the ground, followed the trail to the fortress and fell to digging with the pickaxe; and soon he came upon the hoard over which I had my residence and the warm odours of which had always guided me back to the fortress. Delighted he turned to his friend and remarked, 'So now, Crumplyear, you can sleep in peace. It is exactly as I said; it is the warm odours of this hoard that enabled the rascally mole to disturb your sleep.' With those words they both cleaned out my hoard and taking it with them set out towards the monastery.

As I returned to that spot I could scarcely endure the unlovely sight it presented; it made my blood curdle. I fell into anxious thought, 'Alas! Alas! What shall I do now?' I asked myself; 'Where can I go? How can I find any peace of mind?' I spent the day with great difficulty in anxious thought. Then when the thousand-rayed god had gone to his rest, I gathered my clan and though dejected and lacking enthusiasm, went back to the monastery.

On hearing the patter of the pack, Crumplyear began striking the almsbowl again and again with his old, frayed, bamboo stick. Seeing this, his guest remonstrated, saying, 'What is this, my friend, you don't seem to be able to go to sleep peacefully?'

To this Crumplyear replied, 'Your Reverence, it is that

scoundrel of a mole; I am sure he has returned with all his
dependants. I do this out of fear of him.'

The guest replied laughing, 'Have no fear, my friend. The
fellow's energy which enabled him to jump high is gone with his
wealth. This is true of all living beings. As the proverb rightly
points out:

The man who is always full of energy, (67)
    who overcomes others easily,
who in his speech is scornful and haughty,
    is what he is, owing to the power born of wealth.'

Hearing these words I was possessed by such anger that I
gathered all my strength and made a desperate leap towards the
almsbowl—only to miss and fall down on the floor. Seeing me
humiliated, my enemy chuckled and told Crumplyear, 'Look,
look, my friend: what fun! Splendid! How true to say:

Every man becomes powerful through wealth; (68)
and a scholar to boot if he has wealth;
just look at this mole who has lost his wealth—
now a plain mole like any other of his kind.

'And there is wisdom in the proverb:

Like a serpent deprived of his fang, (69)
like an elephant not in rut,
so is a man lacking wealth,
    man only in name.'

These words only made me reflect ruefully, 'Alas! What my
enemy says is so true; for today I have not the power to jump
even a finger's breadth. Ha! What is a fellow's life worth when
he has no wealth. Shame, shame upon such a life! As the saying
wisely points out:

With men of dim intelligence, (70)
    and lacking wealth to boot,

all undertakings fail and get lost
as little streams in summer do.

Barren[25] barleycorn, seed of wild sesame, (71)
and men lacking wealth own only a name;
without substance, they produce no fruit.

Your beggar may be an excellent man, (72)
but his other qualities fail to shine.
For as the sun illumines all living things
so wealth makes all virtues shine bright.

Those born poor into this world suffer less (73)
than those who accustomed to happiness
having possessed wealth, lose it all.

Beggar's desires mount higher and higher (74)
only to fall back into their hearts,
unprofitable[26] like the breasts of widowed women.

Encompassed by Poverty's dark night, (75)
however hard they try they scarcely see
the sun shining in splendour in the day,
manifest clearly before their very eyes.

Thus bewailing my sorry lot and enduring the mortification of seeing my precious hoard used as a pillow, I retreated towards my fortress at dawn, a failure; I had lost all zest for life. My retainers went around prattling in private, 'Alas! This fellow has no longer the power to fill our bellies. By riding on his coat-tails we get nothing but misery—encounters with cats and the like. So what is the use of rendering him obeisance? As the proverb expresses it succinctly:

A master from whose presence no bounties flow, (76)
and only miseries come flooding—
It is best not to touch him with a bargepole,
is it not? Specially for those who live by arms?'

Such words as these I heard as I entered the fortress; and not one from among my entourage cared to enter the fortress with me; and all because I was penniless. So I began to brood over it all. 'Ha! A plague upon this poverty,' I told myself. 'Alas! How true is the saying:

> *When a man is penniless, his kinsmen* (77)
> *find no time to give him the time of day;*
> > *his pride takes a beating;*
> *his moon of good conduct wanes, vanishes,*
> > *leaving no trace;*
> *in cold indifference his friends turn away;*
> > *misfortunes swell and burgeon;*
> *soon, others' misdeeds are imputed to him.*

> *Oppressed by waning fortunes,* (78)
> > *struck down by cruel Time,[27]*
> *a man sees his friends even become foes,*
> > *while long-standing affection turns cold.*

'And again:

> *Empty is a childless home;* (79)
> *empty the heart that lacks a true friend;*
> *empty the horizons to a fool;*
> *all, all is emptiness to the poor.*

'Then again:

> *Senses unimpaired; speech the very same;* (80)
> *mind still keen; he answers to his name;*
> *the very same man, yes, and yet,*
> *in a trice, he has become another.*
> *How strange! Is it because*
> *he and his wealth are now separated?*

'On the other hand what do such fellows as we have to do with such things as wealth? Fellows whose lives bear this sort of final fruit? For one who has lost his fortune as I have, the best course now is to live in a forest-retreat.[28]

> *Resort to a life imbued with surpassing honour;* (81)
> *never rest content with a life of dishonour;*
> *If riding with gods in a celestial car*
> *means eating humble pie—perish the thought!*

> *Men whose heads are held high in honour* (82)
> *should choose adversity*
> *that follows them every step of the way,*
> *rather than expansive prosperity*
> *smeared all over with the slime of dishonour.*

And I continued my reflections on this theme: 'Ah! Beggary is as terrible as death:

> *Even the life of a tree* (83)
> *that stands in a salt-flat,*
> *twisted, worm-eaten*
> *burned black by forest-fires*
> *is more blest*
> *than the life of a beggar.*

'Besides:

> *Ah! Beggary! To high-minded man, what is it* (84)
> *but a sanctuary for misfortunes!*
> *An admirable hoard of fears,*
> *ground of fancies and false notions!*
> *An asylum for adversity; meanness incarnate;*
> *ravisher of wise and holy thoughts,*
> *destroyer of the proud spirit;*
> *a pitiable state synonymous with Death!*
> *I cannot see how it is different from Hell.*

'And further:

> *A man without means feels shame:* (85)

covered by shame of spirit he is stripped;
dispirited he is easily humbled;
humbled, he falls into a depression;
depressed, a sadness comes over him;
sad, his intelligence is dimmed;
a weak intelligence leads to wasting;
Alas! Poverty is at the root of all evils.

'On the other hand, it is:

Far better to thrust your hands into the jaws   (86)
    of a snake hissing in fury:
far better too to swallow deadly poison
    and sleep in the house of Death;
far, far better it is to fall down the slopes
    of the Hoary Mountain[29]
and be dashed into a hundred pieces
rather than revel in riches got from rogues.

'And further:

It is better for the penniless   (87)
to offer their lives up to the flames
than cringe for help before the niggard
who has brushed aside the duty to help others.

It is better to roam with wild beasts   (88)
    over mountains and gorges
than importune in an abject voice: 'Give',
    a mean, despicable word.

'Under such circumstances, what possible course can I adopt to
sustain my life? Thievery? But that is most pernicious because it
involves appropriating the property of others; and on principle:

It is better to be struck dumb forever   (89)
    than utter a lie;

> *it is better to be a eunuch*
>> *than approach another's wife;*
> *it is better to lose your life*
>> *than mouth spiteful words;*
> *it is better to subsist on alms*[30]
>> *than lust after the wealth of others.*

'In that case, should I live on charity? That too is a dreadful prospect, my friends; quite dreadful: for what is it but a second gateway to death? As the saying goes:

> *A sick man, a long-time vagrant,*　　　　　　　　(90)
> *an eater-of-crumbs-off-another's-table,*
> *one who sleeps on the doorsteps of strangers:*
>> *for these, life is death;*
>> *for these, death is best.*

'Therefore, looking at the matter from all sides, the only thing left for me to do is to recover my wealth that was carried away by Broadbottom; for surely I did see my treasure-chest put to the use of a pillow by those two evil-hearted men. Even if I die in the attempt it is preferable to this; for:

> *Even his ancestors will not accept*　　　　　　　(91)
> *the holy water offered ritually*
> *by the coward who sees his treasure ravished,*
> *yet lives to endure the loss patiently.'*

Having decided upon this course of action, I slipped quietly at night into the monk's cell. Seeing him sound asleep I gnawed a hole in the bag that held my treasure. The monk woke up and hit me hard on the head with his frayed, old bamboo stick. For some reason or other I escaped death, perhaps because I still had some more years to live. What! Is this not so? That:

> *A man gets what he is destined to have;*　　　　　(92)
> *God Himself cannot violate this law.*

225

Therefore I do not grieve; I am not dismayed;
what is ours can never be another's.'

The crow and tortoise exclaimed, 'O, how is that?' And Goldy began the tale of *The man who received what was his.*

In a certain city there lived a merchant named Sāgaradatta[31] whose son once picked up a book which was on sale for a hundred rupees. In it was written just one line of a verse:

A man gets what he is destined to have.

Reading that Sāgaradatta asked his son, 'My dear boy, how much did you buy this book for?' And his son replied, 'For a hundred rupees, sir.'

'What?' expostulated the father. 'You inimitable blockhead! You went and paid a hundred rupees for a book in which just one line of a verse is written! With this kind of intelligence how will you ever acquire wealth? Leave my house this minute never to enter it again.' Thus severely reprimanding his son, Sāgaradatta threw him out of the house.

Bitterly humiliated by his father's words, the son left his home for some very remote land and landed up in a certain city where he took up residence. After some days a native of that city approached him and enquired, 'Sir, where have you come from? And what may your name be, sir?' And the young man answered, 'The-man-who-receives-his-desserts, sir.' When some other person asked him the same question, he gave the same reply, 'The-man-who-receives-his-desserts.' On every occasion that he was asked his name, he gave the same reply, so that soon he became known by this name, Mister Justdesserts.

Now, one day, Princess Moonlight[32] stood with her friend, looking out at the city. She was radiant, in the first flush of youth and beauty. A certain prince, uncommonly handsome and charming, happened, by one of those tricks of Fate, to be just at that spot at that very moment. The very instant the princess set eyes on him, she was struck by Love's flower-arrows. Turning to her friend, she cried, 'O, my dear friend, pray try your best to arrange for a meeting today with this person.' The friend hurried at once to the prince and said, 'I come to you from Princess Moonlight and she sends you this message : "From the moment I set eyes on you, I have been sick unto death for love of you; if you do not come quickly to me, I shall surely die."'

Hearing these words, the prince remarked, 'If there is this dire need for my presence, then tell me how I can enter the palace.'

'Listen,' said the friend, 'At night you will see a stout ladder of woven leather hanging from an upper balcony of the palace for you to climb.' 'Well,' replied the prince, 'If this is Your Ladyship's plan, I shall follow it accordingly.'

Having concluded the arrangement, the friend returned to the princess. When night fell the prince remained lost in thought. He said to himself:

> 'A preceptor's daughter, or a friend's wife,   (93)
> the wife of one's master or of one's man:
> A man who approaches any of these, it is said,
> is guilty of Brahmanicide.[33]

'And further:

> Action that brings dishonour,   (94)
> or leads to one's downfall,[34]
> or brings about the loss of one's wealth
> should never be undertaken.'

Having thought over the matter carefully, the prince decided not to meet the princess. In the meantime, Mister Justdesserts who was roaming around in the city at night noticed a ladder of woven leather hanging down the side of a fine, stucco mansion. And out of a mixture of curiosity and adventurousness he took hold of it and climbed up. On seeing him, the princess quite confident that he was the right man, received him with all the courtesies; offered him a luxurious bath, fine food and drink, finest garments and the like; after which she led him to her bed.

With her limbs thrilling with rapture from his touch, she whispered, 'Having fallen in love with you at first sight, I have given myself to you. Never shall I even think of another man as my husband. Now that you know this, why don't you converse with me?' But all the young man said in reply was:

'A man gets what he is destined to have.'

Hearing this, the princess whose heart almost stopped beating, quickly sent him packing down the ladder. The young man made his way to a ruined temple and went to sleep. After a while a policeman, who had an assignation at that temple with a woman of easy virtue, came and found a man fast asleep. Wishing to keep his secret safe, the policeman asked him, 'Who are you, sir?' And the man replied:

'The man who gets what he is destined to have.'

When he heard this, the policeman said, 'Look, this is a deserted temple; why don't you go and sleep in my bed.'

Reaching that place as directed, the young man by mistake entered the wrong room, where the policeman's daughter, named Miss Modesty, a big girl blessed with youth and beauty, lay waiting, having made a date with a certain man she was infatuated with. When she saw Mister Justdesserts walk in, she thought to herself, 'Ah! Here he is, my own beloved.' Failing to recognize the man in pitch darkness, she rose and married herself to him by Gandharva rites.[35] Then, lying in bed with him, her eyes and face radiant like blossoming lotuses, she whispered, 'How is it that even now you refrain from speaking freely with me?' And the man replied:

'A man gets what he is destined to have.'

Thoroughly nonplussed, she was plunged into thought; 'Alas! This is the kind of unripe fruit that one picks when one acts without due deliberation.' She pondered ruefully over what she had done, then having reprimanded him more from sorrow than anger, she sent him out of the house.

As Mister Justdesserts went down the main street, a marriage procession was entering the city to the sound of splendid music, and headed by a bridegroom named Fineglory, a man from another city. Mister Justdesserts decided to join this procession.

Since the auspicious moment was fast approaching, the bride, daughter of a rich merchant, who was president of the guild, was waiting at the gateway of her father's mansion on the Royal Highway. Dressed in her ritually-sanctified wedding clothes, with the sacred marriage-thread already wound round her wrist, she stood on a beautifully decorated dais.

At that moment, an elephant in rut was rampaging, maddened, having killed its rider; and it was creating no end of confusion as people ran here and there, terrified. And worse, the animal was headed in the direction of the marriage procession. One glimpse of the fierce animal and the whole entourage of the bridegroom, and the bridegroom too, fled towards the far horizon.

In this crisis, Mister Justdesserts noticed the bride, left all alone; her eyes were trembling in wild terror. 'Do not be afraid; I shall protect you,' he said in a resolute and reassuring tone. Then putting his right arm[36] round the bride, he addressed the elephant with admirable boldness, severely taking it to task for its misdemeanour. And strangely enough, as Fate would have it, the animal actually retreated and left the place.

In the meantime, seeing the coast clear, the bridegroom, Fineglory, with his entourage of relatives and friends arrived well past the auspicious time set for the wedding. And what does he see but his bride-to-be held by another man. He looked around and noticing the bride's father, remarked sharply, 'Hey! Father-in-law, sir! What is this that you have done? It is hardly right that you should promise me your daughter in marriage, and then give her to this man.'

'I was also frightened by the elephant, Sir Fineglory, and fled in fear; I have just this minute returned with the rest of you; and

I haven't a clue as to what happened in the interval,' answered the bride's father, and then began to question his daughter. 'My darling, it is not a nice thing that you have done. So now, tell me what happened.'

And the girl replied, 'Dear Father, this man came to my rescue when my very life was in danger. So, no other man will ever hold my hand; not as long as I live.'

By the time these events had become common knowledge the night was over. As dawn broke a great crowd had gathered at the merchant's house. Hearing this story that was on everybody's lips, Princess Moonlight arrived there. Learning of these events that had spread by word of mouth, the policeman's daughter also came there. Not only that: the king himself, informed of the great concourse milling at the gates of the merchant's mansion, arrived and spoke to Mister Justdesserts, 'Now, look, sir, speak freely; tell me everything as it happened.' To this Mister Justdesserts' only reply was:

'*A man gets what he is destined to have.*'

The princess now remembered him and added a line:

'*God Himself cannot violate this law.*'

Then the policeman's daughter spoke yet another line:

'*Therefore, I grieve not; I am not dismayed.*'

Having listened to it all, the merchant's daughter added a line that completed the verse:

'*What is ours can never be another's.*'

After promising immunity to everyone concerned, the king arrived at the whole truth by piecing together the separate narratives of the events provided by each one of the persons involved. Finally, the king accorded great honours to Mister Justdesserts, giving him his daughter in marriage, with a grant of a thousand villages. Then a thought struck the king. Remembering that he was without a son and heir, he had Justdesserts anointed and appointed as the crown prince.

Justdesserts lived happily ever after in the company of his whole family, enjoying all comforts and pleasures that life has to offer.

'Now you see why I said to you: "A man gets what he is destined to have . . . " and the rest of it,' said Goldy, concluding the tale. Again Goldy continued: 'So, I reflected upon this carefully and was relieved of my obsession with the treasure that I had lost. What wisdom is contained in the following verse:

> One sees with Wisdom, not with the eye; (95)
> conduct, not birth, is the mark of breeding;
> contentment is prosperity;
> turning away from wrong is true learning.

'Similarly:

> All prosperities are his (96)
> whose spirit is contented;
> to the sandal-shod foot
> the Earth is covered with skins.

> A hundred leagues is not far (97)
> to one driven by Desire.
> The contented man disregards Wealth
> even if it lies within his grasp.

> O, dread goddess, Desire!³⁷ (98)
>   I humbly bow to you,
>   O, Wrecker of Fortitude!
> Even Viṣṇu, Lord of the Triple World,
>   was made a dwarf³⁸ by you.

> Nothing is beyond your power to do, (99)
>   Divine Consort of Dishonour!

For you offer a taste of yourself
    to the most high-minded men, O, Desire!

I have borne what no one should have to bear: (100)
I have spoken words most distasteful to hear;
I have waited at the doorsteps of strangers:
    Now pray desist; be at peace, Goddess Desire!

Of foul stinking water I have drunk;   (101)
of clumps of mown grass I have made my bed;
grievous parting from my beloved I have endured;
with pain rising from deep down in my loins
I have cringed and spoken humbly to strangers;
Footweary I have trudged and even crossed the seas;
a half-skull-bowl[39] *I have carried around:*
Is there anything else you'd have me do, O, Desire.
Then, for God's sake command me quickly
    and be done with me.

A poor man's statement carries little weight   (102)
    though Logic and Authority[40]
    shape its truth and clarity;
while words of the wealthy, harsh,
lacking merit and meaning
always command a respectful hearing.

Albeit baseborn a man with wealth   (103)
is by the world most highly honoured;
while a poor man of noble lineage,
moon-bright, is spurned and scorned.

Wealth makes sprightly youths   (104)
of men old and decrepit; lacking wealth
those in the very flush of youth are viewed
as already decrepit and old.

Since friend and brother, wife and son   (105)
desert the man whose wealth is gone
to return when he is wealthy again,
    it seems only wealth is next of kin.

Having reflected in this manner as I went back home, Lightwing here came to me the moment I entered my residence, and mentioned the journey he intended making to this place. Therefore, I have accompanied him to visit Your Honour. Thus, I have related the causes of my depression to Your Honours. Indeed, it is truly observed:

> *Deer, snake and elephant,*   (106)
> *gods, demons and humans,*
> *all have their meal before it is noon;*
>   *such is the way here in the three worlds.*[41]

> *When the hour comes around and hunger calls,*   (107)
>   *World-conquering monarch, or humble slave*
>   *eking his life out in misery,*
>   *must have his little bowl of rice.*

> *If this is the way of the world what man sensible*   (108)
> *would do deeds most reprehensible,*
> *deeds whose outcome is sure to land him*
>   *in a state most odious and wicked?'*

Slowcoach having listened to Goldy's story of his life, now began offering him consolation: 'Ah! My friend,' he began, 'you must not lose heart because you have been forced by circumstances to abandon your native land. Wise as you are, why do you allow yourself to become so disoriented? Consider:

> *Possessing mere book-learning men remain fools;*   (109)
> *the man who acts using his knowledge, he is wise;*
> *however carefully selected*
> *no drug can cure the sick*
> *by mere mention of its name.*

> *Lives there a man of mettle, resolute,*   (110)
> *skilled, who thinks: 'This is my native land*
>   *and that is alien.'*
> *The land he resorts to he makes his own*
>   *by the valour of his arms alone.*

> *Whichever forest the lion plunges into, armed*
> *with striking force of tooth and claw and tail,*
> *it is there he slakes his retainers' thirst*
> *with blood of lords of elephants he slays.*

'Therefore, dear friend, we should always strive with energy.
Where can wealth or pleasures find a home? Mark:

> *As frogs seek wells,* (111)
> *as birds a brimming-lake,*
> *so too wealth and allies*
> *resort to a man with enterprise.*

'Besides:

> *Fortune of her own accord seeks as home* (112)
> *a man of mettle, brave, prompt in action,*
> *expert in policy-expedients,*
> *firm in friendships, unhampered by misfortunes;*
> *imbued with a keen sense of gratitude.*

'Looked at another way:

> *If Fortune fights shy of a man, brave, wise,* (113)
> *discreet, diligent, full of enterprise;*
> *who is not mean, wayward, disloyal*
> *or given to despair, then, she is the loser.*

> *As a young woman proud of her beauty,* (114)
> *heartily loathes an old husband's caresses,*
> *so too, Fortune loathes the lazy man who flounders*
> *   irresolute, trusting in Fate implicitly.*

> *Learning can do little to help him* (115)
> *who shies away from strenuous effort.*
> *Will a lamp placed right on a blind man's palm*
> *   help in recovering a thing lost?*

> *Donors may become beggars* (116)
> *and beggars may be choosers;*

234

slayers may by the weak be slain;
and all through sheer misadventure.[42]

'Your Honour ought not to take the following maxim to heart:

Teeth, hair, claws, men, when out of place (117)
    do not shine to best advantage:

'And from it draw the conclusion that is a coward's conclusion :

No one should abandon his native place.

'To a man of mettle, there is not the slightest distinction between his own and a foreign land. As the saying goes:

Warriors and scholars (118)
and beautiful young women
make a home for themselves
    wherever they go.

The man who mounts an enterprise (119)
    with skill and expertise
is always a master of wealth.
But even so keen an intellect as Bṛhaspati's[43]
    yoked to a listless enterprise,
    fails; and that is certain.

'The fact that Your Honour lacks resources at this point in time does not however, make you an ordinary person; for you are richly endowed with intellect and spirit. For as we all know:

The man of mettle though he has no wealth (120)
still touches the topmost peak of high esteem;
while the scurvy knave surrounded by riches
sinks to the lowliest of places.
No golden-collared dog gains the glory,
opulent, of inborn leonine majesty
that springs from fine innate qualities.

235

A man, compacted of courage and spirit, (121)
of perseverance and indomitable will,
who views with the same indifferent eye,
the great ocean and the pitiful puddle,[44]
The Lord of the Mountains[45] and the tip of an anthill—
Fortune gladly resorts to such a man,
not to someone craven and woebegone.

'And further:

When enterprise is a man's second nature, (122)
  Mount Meru is not too lofty,
  The Abyss not too low,
nor the great ocean impassable.

'On the other hand:

Why grow proud from possessing wealth? (123)
  why sink into despair
  when your greatness vanishes?
  Man's rise and fall
  is like that of a ball
  bounced by the hand.

'In all respects, youth and wealth are unstable as water bubbles; for:

Shadows of passing clouds, (124)
friendship of rogues,
new grain, young women,
youth and riches—
Oh! How fleeting the enjoyment of these!

'Therefore, the intelligent man takes charge of wealth that easily slips through one's fingers and makes it yield fruit, either by giving it away or enjoying it himself; as is wisely observed:

Obtained by a hundred painful efforts, (125)
even dearer than one's own life,

236

riches have but one right way to follow;
    any other is the wrong course.

'Moreover:

> *He who does not enjoy his wealth*   (126)
> *or gives it away is not its true owner.*
> *The jewel in your home, your daughter,*
> *waits for another; for she is his.*[46]

> *The miser hoards his riches for others;*   (127)
> *some gather honey with great effort,*
> *for others to taste with delight.*

'In every case, it is Fate that decides all; as is well stated:

> *In battle, at the critical moment of attack,*   (128)
>   *or in one's home;*
> *in a blazing fire, in a yawning mountain chasm,*
>   *or in the fathomless ocean;*
> *even as one lives in the midst of snarling serpents*
>   *with wide-gaping jaws,*
>   *what-is-not-to-be will not be,*
>   *what-is-to-be will never be lost.*

'Your Honour is at this moment in good health and excellent spirits, in themselves priceless benefits. As the proverb expresses it aptly :

> *The Lord of the Seven Continents*[47]   (129)
>   *beset by creeping greed*
> *is but a beggar; but the man who lives content*
>   *is Lord of the Universe.*

'Besides:

> *No treasure equals giving to others;*   (130)
> *Is there any wealth equal to content?*

Where is the jewel to compare with good conduct?
No gain on earth compares with health.

'Nor should you worry as to how to live without wealth; for wealth is perishable; manliness is lasting. As it is wisely pointed out:

All of a sudden (131)
a noble man may fall;
        but his fall,
        like that of a ball,
        is upspringing.
But the coward who falls
        stays fallen—
call it the flattened-out fall
        of a lump of clay.

'But why speak at length; here is the crux of the matter; listen. Some are born to enjoy the pleasures that wealth buys, while others remain merely the watchdogs that guard it. How well the point is made in this verse:

A man might not enjoy the wealth he earns (132)
        unless Fate has dealt him a share in it.
Little Simple, the great forest entered
        only to become quite, quite bewildered.'

'Oh! How was that?' asked Goldy; and Slowcoach began the tale of *Little Simple, the weaver.*

In a certain settlement there lived a weaver named Little Simple. All the time he was busy weaving, creating many different designs of cloth and dyed in rich shades, all eminently suited to be made into garments for princes and noble persons. But somehow, he was simply not able to get together the smallest bit of wealth over and above what was necessary to buy the bare essentials—food, clothing, shelter. While others in his trade, weavers of coarse cloth, were rolling in wealth.

'Dearest,' he said to his wife observing their affluence. 'Just look at these fellows; they weave the coarsest cloth and yet they rake in pots of money. This place does not offer me a decent living; so I intend moving elsewhere.'

To which his wife replied, 'Oh! Come, come, dear lord, it is not true to say that wealth may be gained by going to other places. For the saying is, as you know:

> *What is not to be can never be;* (133)
> *what is to be comes effortlessly;*
> *what lies right on the palm of your hand*
> *is lost if you are not destined for it.*

'Moreover:

> *As a calf can find his mother* (134)
> *among a thousand cows,*
> *so, a deed done in a previous birth*
> *closely follows the doer in this.*

'Besides:

> *As sun and shade are ever interwoven* (135)
> *so, Doer and Deed cling to each other.*

'So you had better stay right here and carry on your business.'

'Oh! My dearest wife,' replied Little Simple, 'What you say is simply not right. Nothing bears fruit without persistent effort. As it has been aptly said:

> *You cannot clap with a single hand;* (136)
> *deeds don't bear fruit without perseverance.*

'And again:

> *I grant you, food is right there at mealtime* (137)
> *by the grace of Fortune.*

But for God's sake, how do you eat it
without raising your hand to your mouth?

'Besides:

Perseverance, not wishes, gets work done;   (138)
deer do not walk into the mouth of a sleeping lion.

'Moreover:

A man may perform as best as he can   (139)
yet, success eludes his reach;
the man is not to blame,[48] though;
Fate muzzles his manliness.

'It is imperative therefore, that I try my luck elsewhere.'

With these words Little Simple set out for Prosperityville[49] where he lived and worked three whole years until he had earned three hundred gold pieces; and then he decided it was time to come home again.

Halfway, as he was travelling through a great forest, the glorious Sun lay down to rest. Fearful for his safety, Little Simple climbed up a stout branch of a banyan tree and fell asleep. In his dreams he heard two men, wrathful, with bloodshot eyes, railing at each other. And one was saying, 'Hey, you there! Doer! Many a time have you prevented this fellow, Little Simple from acquiring any income over and above what is needed to buy the bare essentials of food and clothing because he is not destined for anything more. You have never at any time given this man anything. Then why is it that now Your Honour has chosen to freely grant him these three hundred gold pieces?' To which the other replied, 'Hey! You! Deed! I am under an obligation to give a person who exerts himself the return proportionate to his exertion. The final outcome,[50] however, is in *your* hands. So, *you* deprive him of it.'

Little Simple woke up at this point and looked for his bag of gold; it was empty. And he began to think, 'Alas! Alas! All this wealth that I earned with so much trouble, is all gone, in a flash.

240

Now, with all that labour gone to waste and nothing to show for it, how can I possibly show my face to my wife and friends?' So he decided to return to Prosperityville and work some more. And in just one year he earned five hundred gold pieces. Taking it he set out for home, following another route.

As the sun went down, he found himself at the foot of that very same banyan tree. 'Oh! My god! What is this? What is this goddam Fate up to? For this same demonic banyan tree confronts me once again.' He reflected thus. Then he saw those two same figures that he had seen before; and one spoke to the other saying. 'Doer! What do you mean by bestowing five hundred gold pieces on this fellow, Little Simple? Don't you know, sir, that he is not destined to receive anything over and above what is needed to provide him with food and clothing?'

The other responded, 'O, Deed! I am obligated to give to those who perservere in their exertions. But the final outcome is in your hands, Your Honour.'

As soon as he heard these words; Little Simple hastily looked into his bag. It was empty. Plunged into the depths of despair, he reflected, 'Alas! Alas! What use is my life without wealth? It is better that I hang myself right here from this banyan tree.'

Having made his decision, poor Little Simple wove some sacred grass[51] into a rope and having made a noose at one end, put it round his neck, climbed the branch, fastened the rope to it and was about to let himself drop when one of the figures appeared in the sky to say, 'No, no, dear friend, Little Simple; don't do it; it is a rash act indeed. I am the one who takes away your wealth, because I cannot suffer you to have even a cowrie[52] over and above what you need for food and clothing. So, go home, my friend. But your meeting with me should have something in it for you and not remain unfruitful. So ask me for a boon, whatever you wish, to your heart's desire.'

Little Simple replied, 'In that case, give me enormous wealth.'

The figure asked, 'Friend, what will you do with wealth that you can neither enjoy yourself or give away to others, since your portion does not include even a moiety above and beyond what is needed for food and clothing?'

'Even so,' replied Little Simple, 'even if I derive no benefit from the wealth, let me have it. For it is wisely said:

A man of substance (140)
though base-born or ill-favoured
is yet served by those who have to depend
on the charity of the good.

'Let me point out something else; as the story goes:

I have closely watched them, my dear, (141)
 now, for the five-and-tenth year.
They look floppy, yet they are firm;
they may fall off, or they may hang on.'

And the figure exclaimed, 'Oh! How was that?' And Little Simple began the tale of *Hangballs and the Vixen*.

In a certain settlement there lived, carefree, a stud-bull named Hangballs,[53] who from an excess of virility abandoned the herd and became a forest-dweller. He tore up the riverbanks with his horns and browsed as his fancy took him on the emerald-green tips of lush grass.

In that very same forest there lived a jackal named Allure.[54] One day as he was lying at ease on a sandbar by the river's edge with his wife, Hangballs came sauntering along and went down to the river for a drink of water by that same sandbar.

The jackal's wife noticed the bull's pendulous testicles; turning to her husband, she said, 'Dear lord, do you see those two fleshy lumps hanging from that bull. Any minute now they will fall off; or in a couple of hours, perhaps. So, I think you should keep close to that fellow and follow him.'

The jackal replied, 'Sweetheart, we do not know if those lumps will fall off or not. So why send me off on a wild-goose chase? I had rather stay with you here and dine off field-mice that come down to the river to drink. You know they come this way. And if I should trudge behind that bull who knows if someone else would not come and usurp my place here. So I had better not do as you say. For there is wisdom in the saying:

> *Better hang on to something certain* (142)
> *than chase after the uncertain,*
> *what was once certain may be in some doubt;*
> *the uncertain remains just that—uncertain.'*

To this the vixen replied, 'Hm . . . what a coward you are! Always content with a trifle. Hm . . . Not the right attitude, I say: especially for a man—who should be up and about, always. For it is said:

> *Where valour is united with wise policy* (143)
> *and slackness notable by its absence;*
> *when plans are supported by energy,*
> *there, absolute Fortune dwells with assurance.*

> *Weighing the fact that Fate is not absolute,* (144)
> *a man ought to press on with diligence,*
> > *How can sesame-oil be extracted*
> > *unless you press the sesame-seed.*

'And mind you, what you say about these lumps—perhaps they may drop, perhaps not—that is not right either. Surely, you have heard this:

> *Loftiness of rank is not what counts;* (145)
> *men of firm resolve are worthy of praise.*
> *Who dares say of the crested cuckoo bird,*[55]
> *'Oh! What a pitiful little creature'*
> *Great Indra Himself serves as his water-carrier.*[56]

'Besides, my lord, I am truly sick and tired of mouse-flesh: furthermore, these two lumps of flesh are on the point of falling. So, it is imperative that you do not act contrary to my wishes.'

And the poor jackal obeyed her and leaving that spot where

field-mice were an easy catch, he started following Hangballs. O!
What wisdom do we find in the saying:

> *Only as long as a man is not controlled*   (146)
>   *against his will by the sharp goad*
> *of a woman's words wounding his ear*[57]
>   *will he remain his own master in all that he does.*

> *Driven by the words of a woman*   (147)
> *a man believes wrongs to be right;*
> *thinks the hard way easy to go;*
> *and eats what is unfit to eat.*

And so the jackal spent long years wandering with his wife,
following the bull. However, the bull's balls did not fall. Finally,
in the fifteenth year, through sheer despair, he said to his wife:

> *'I have closely watched them, my dear,*   (148)
>   *now, for the five-and-tenth year.*
> *They look floppy; yet they are firm:*
>   *they may fall off; or they may hang on.*

'They will not fall off in the future either. So let us go back and
follow the mouse-trail.'

'And that is why I say, "They look floppy: yet they are
firm . . . " and the rest of it. The fact is that a man of wealth
becomes an object of desire. So bestow an immense fortune on
me.'

The figure then replied, 'Well, if that is how you feel, then
return to Prosperityville. There you will find two men, Closefist
and Openhand, both sons of merchants. Closely watch the
conduct of these two; then ask for the nature of one or the other,
whichever appeals to you.' With these words, the figure vanished
into thin air. Lost in wonder, Little Simple returned once again
to Prosperityville.

At sunset, Little Simple, asking around for the location of the
residence of Closefist and having found it with some difficulty,
finally arrived there, dog-tired. In spite of harsh denials of entry

by the wife, children and others, he persisted in getting into the courtyard and sat down. At dinner-time some food was ungraciously thrust in front of him, which he ate and then lay down to sleep.

At midnight whom did he see but those same two figures who were consulting with each other; and one was saying to the other, 'Look, friend Doer, what are you up to now, putting Closefist to the needless expense of a meal for this fellow—Little Simple? I don't think that is right.'

The second figure responded, saying, 'Ah! My friend, Deed, how am I to blame? I am obliged to allot the getting and the spending. However, the final outcome is in your hands.'

Little Simple, poor fellow, was now wide awake. The next morning he had to fast because Closefist was suffering from a stomach ailment for the second day running. So he left that house and proceeded to the residence of Openhand, who received him cordially, showed him great courtesy providing good food and fine clothes and a comfortable bed to sleep in right within his house.

Again at midnight, Little Simple saw those two figures arguing with each other. And the first said, 'Hey there! Friend Doer, you see what expense you are putting Openhand to in entertaining this fellow, Little Simple? How will he repay his debt? For he has drawn everything out of the Guild-members' Fund.'

To this, the second figure replied, 'My friend, Deed, I have to carry out my obligations; you look after the consequences.'

Early the next morning, an officer of the king arrived at Openhand's residence carrying a large sum of money as a gift from the king which he offered to Openhand. Watching this, Little Simple thought, 'This fellow, Openhand, though he does not have a single coin in the Fund is a far better person than that crabby old Closefist. Listen to the apt saying:

> *The Sacred Fire kindled in the home*   (149)
>   *is the fruit of the Vedas.*
> *The practice of Virtue is the fruit of learning,*

> love and offspring the fruit the wife brings;
> Charity and the enjoyment of life
> are the fruits of Wealth.

'Therefore, Blessed Creator, make one into me who gives to others, and enjoys life as well. I see no good in watching over wealth.'

The Creator listened to his prayer and granted him his wish.

'So, I repeat, my friend, "A man might not enjoy the wealth he earns . . . ."' concluded Slowcoach.

'Therefore, my dear friend, Goldy,' continued Slowcoach, 'Realizing these truths, don't ever fall into despair over the matter of wealth. You know what is said:

> When times are good, noble hearts   (150)
> are tender as lotus blossoms.
> When times are bad they become hard
> as the solid rock of the Great Mountain.[58]

'And think of this:

> What effort does he make?   (151)
> He is even lost in sleep; yet,
> if it is his destined[59] portion
> Wealth comes; he enjoys it—
> While others in endless effort struggle.
> If it is not to be, it will never be.
> What is to be will never perish.

'Then:

> Why plunge into endless thought?   (152)
> Why with despair plague the heart?
> Whatever is written on your page[60]
> in the Book of Life comes to pass.

'Furthermore:

> No sooner has Fate's command rung out   (153)

246

'Bring it, at once'—it is done.
From some far island or mid-ocean,
or from the farthest horizon,
there, facing you stands the wish realized.

'Besides:

It joins together what is divided; (154)
what is firmly joined it breaks apart.
It is Destiny that makes events happen;
*   events beyond a man's imaginings.*

Sorrows come all unwished for (155)
to all that lives in this world;
so too happiness, I guess, sometimes:
*   so why droop in despair?*

'Yet again:

With a mind pregnant with learning (156)
a man of courage strives to succeed one way.
But his former deeds like a master come
and dispose of his endeavours another way.

He who made swans snow-white (157)
*   and parrots a bright green;*
who painted peacocks in brilliant hues,
*   He will set in order our daily round.*

Rolled into a lump within a basket. (158)
*   his senses numbed with hunger,*
*   a serpent lay emaciated.*
A mole dropped right into his hungry jaws at night,
*   tumbling through the hole it gnawed to get inside.*
Slithering quickly out by that selfsame path,
*   replete, revived by that tasty meat,*
*   the serpent beat a hasty retreat.*

'Aware of this, you ought to think of what is best; therefore, it is wisely observed:

> Let some little rite be performed each day (159)
>   with a tranquil mind:
> a vow, a fast, an act of self-restraint.
> Though all forms of life energetically strive,
> Fate constantly chips away at their spirit.

'So, consider this; contentment is your best bet:

> The tranquil mind happily drinks (160)
> out of Contentment's ambrosial cup.
> Where can those who run back and forth,
> mad after wealth, find such happiness?

'And besides:

> No penance equals patience; (161)
> no joy equals contentment;
> no giving is like friendship;
> no virtue equals compassion.

'But why go on expatiating at random? Think of this place as your home, Your Honour; and free from all anxieties, with a new look on life, pray, spend your time with me here in happiness.'

Hearing Slowcoach speak such words of wisdom in accordance with the true meaning of many texts, Lightwing's face shone with delight as he spoke with a full heart. 'O, dear friend Slowcoach; you are a person whose fine qualities deserve to be emulated. That you have conferred this kindness on Goldy makes my heart dance with excess of joy. It is aptly said:

> Those who enjoy happy times, (162)
>   friends with dear friends,
>   lovers with their beloved,
>   joyful with the joyous,
> only they fully taste Pleasure's quintessence,

and live life to the fullest;
> *they are the salt of the earth.*

'Moreover:

> *Those who will not see that Fortune* (163)
> > *by her spontaneous embrace*
> *becomes an adornment of friends,*
> > *because Greed has ravaged their hearts,*
> *are in truth poor, though they possess wealth;*
> > *they toil in vain; they are merely alive.*

'It is Your Honour who by offering salutary advice has pulled this unfortunate person out of the sea of despair in which he was drowning. How aptly observed:

> *The good forever aid the good* (164)
> > *in overcoming distress.*
> *Only elephants yoked to elephants*
> > *get them out of the mire.*

'And then again:

> *One person above all deserves high praise* (165)
> > *in this mortal world of ours:*
> *he who carries out to the last particle*
> > *the dictates of virtuous conduct:*
> *from whom no suppliant turns away,*
> > *no seeker of sanctuary leaves*
> *disappointed, his hopes shattered.*

'There is true wisdom contained in the saying:

> *What use is that manliness that fails* (166)
> > *to succour the distressed?*
> *Or that wealth that is not at hand*
> > *to come to the suppliant's help?*
> *What good indeed is the kind of deed done*

without the good of others in mind?
What good is that life
that is an enemy to Fame?'

As they were talking back and forth in this manner, a deer named Speckle[61] ran in, panting with thirst, trembling from fear of the hunter's arrows. As soon as the deer stopped there, the crow, Lightwing, flew up into a tree: Goldy, the mole, went scuttling into a clamp of reeds; while Slowcoach dived for safety into the water. Speckle stood still on the banks of the lake, greatly alarmed for the safety of his life.

Then, Lightwing flew up and having looked carefully around the terrain for a distance of a league, settled again on the tree and called out to the tortoise: 'Friend Slowcoach, come out, come out. There is nothing around here which would pose a threat to you. I have inspected the forest carefully. There is only this deer that has run here to the lake for a drink of water.'

As he said this, all three friends gathered there. Slowcoach spoke affectionately to the deer, treating him as a guest should be treated, 'Friend, have a drink of water, and a dip in the lake. The water here is cool and of excellent quality,' he said.

As he accepted the kind invitation, Speckle thought to himself, 'I feel not the slightest fear in the presence of these fellows. Why? Because, a tortoise is in his element only in water; and as for the crow and mole, they live only on dead creatures. Therefore, I think I shall become one of their company.' And so he joined them.

Slowcoach then duly welcomed Speckle and prefacing his words with all the courtesies offered to a guest, said, 'I trust everything goes well with Your Honour. Now, pray tell us what has brought you here, into this deep, dark forest.'

Speckle answered, 'I have grown weary of the life that I have been leading; roaming around for pleasure and lacking commitment. Hemmed in by hunters on horseback and chased from pillar to post by hunting dogs, I put on a tremendous spurt of speed; and having left all my pursuers far behind I came bounding here to this lake for a drink of water. Now, I would like very much to be friends with Your Honours.'

'You see, we are small, of slight build,' observed Slowcoach, 'it is not a good idea that Your Honour should strike up a friendship with us. For it is always advisable to make friends with those who can help you in times of need.'

Speckle's rejoinder to this comment was:

'Better to live in Hell, I say, with the wise and learned (167)
    than keep company with vile trash,
though these might roam in mansions bright,
    of the Lord of the Immortals.

'You say, sir, "We are small; we are of slight build," why do you make these self-deprecatory remarks? Of course I know that it is in the nature of those noble to speak of themselves this way. I still insist that I be accepted as a friend by Your Honours. You have heard the old saying:

Make friends with the powerful; (168)
and with the powerless too:
caught in toils in the woods, the herd of elephants
    were by tiny mice released.'

'Oh,' exclaimed Slowcoach, 'and how did that happen?' And Speckle began the tale of *The Mice that freed the Elephants.*

There was once a land where the people, their houses, as well as the places of worship had all fallen into decay. The mice who were old settlers in that land, occupied the chinks in the floors of mansions, with sons, grandsons, grandchildren born of daughters and the like. Successive generations of mice as they were born made their homes in that region. And they spent their days and nights in supreme comfort and happiness, enjoying themselves in a variety of activities: feasts and festivals, weddings, banquets and drink-parties, dramatic performances and the like. And so time passed.

One day, a bull-elephant, lord of a thousand elephants, came there surrounded by his herd, to drink at the lake of which he had heard much praise, that it was ever full. As he passed with his herd through Mouse Town, the mice that were in the way were trampled upon; faces, heads, necks, all crushed.

The mice that survived this disaster, now called a council of war. 'We are being slaughtered by these vicious elephants that come lumbering through our settlement,' they cried. 'And they are sure to come again. In the end there will not even be a few of us left to start a new generation. As it has been aptly said:

An elephant kills by a mere touch;   (169)
   a serpent if he only sniffs;
 a king has only to smile to kill;
   a knave by simply paying honour.

'Therefore, let us decide on an effective plan of action to cope with this crisis.'

When they had decided on a plan, a few of the mice went down to the lake, bowed to the Lord of Elephants and pleaded humbly, 'Lord: not far from here is our settlement inherited over a long period of time and coming down in orderly succession from our forefathers. Living there we have prospered and increased over generations of sons and grandsons. Your Honours passing through our settlement on your way to the lake to water have trampled upon and destroyed thousands of our community. If Your Honours do this once more, there will not be one mouse left, not even for seed. Therefore, if Your Honours feel the slightest compassion for us, we beseech you, pray follow some other path to the lake. Sirs, please bear in mind that even creatures of our size might be of some help sometime to Your Honours.'

The lord of the herd listened to their words and recognized that there was sound sense in what the mice said and agreed to their request. 'It shall be so; never otherwise,' he said.

As time passed, one day, a certain king ordered his elephant-keepers to go out and trap some elephants. They went into the forest, constructed a decoy water-tank in which the King of Elephants with his herd was trapped. After three days the trappers captured the elephant-king by means of a sturdy tackle of stout ropes, dragged him with his herd forcibly to the very forest where Mouse Town was located and bound them all to the strong trunks of great trees. When the trappers had left, the king-elephant reflected in sorrow, 'By what means can we be delivered from bondage? Who will come to our aid now?' Then remembering the little mice he thought to himself, 'Except these little fellows, I see no one who can effect our release.'

Then he ordered one of his attendants, a cow-elephant that had not walked into the trap with the others, and who knew the whereabouts of Mouse Town from previous talk among the elephants, to go and inform the mice of his grave predicament and that of his herd. No sooner had the mice heard the sad tidings than they gathered in thousands; and prompted by the desire to repay the favour done to them, came running to the spot where the Lord of Elephants stood bound with his herd. Seeing him in this state they began gnawing at once at the holding ropes. Then they clambered up the branches of the trees and gnawed away and broke the ropes that bound the animals to the trees. Soon, all were set free.

'Therefore, I told you, "Make friends with the strong, make friends with the weak . . . " and the rest of it,' concluded Speckle, the deer.

When Slowcoach had listened to it all, he observed, 'Well, my friend; let it be so; don't be afraid. This is your home. Live in it in a happy frame of mind, free from worries.'

So, the four friends lived there, each choosing his own meal-hours and diversions, as it suited their convenience. Each day they met at the noon hour beside the lake, under the trees, in the thick shade, where they entertained one another in talk and discussion on various texts on the Law, on economics and other related subjects. So the days passed in mutual affection. And this is quite natural:

For the wise, poetry and science suffice (170)

> *to keep the mind occupied.*
> *It is only for fools that time passes*
> *in sleep, squabbling and hatching mischief.*

Moreover:

> *Their skin tingles, their limbs thrill, relishing*   (171)
> *the savour of witty, well-turned phrases;*
> *men of intellect experience pleasure*
> *though they lack the company of women.*

One day when Speckle failed to appear at the usual place at the usual time the others became worried. Fear gnawed at their hearts, especially when just that instant an ill omen appeared. The friends concluded that the deer was in some sort of danger; peace of mind eluded them until Slowcoach and Goldy turned to Lightwing and said, 'Friend Lightwing, you know very well that we two are creatures of slow gait, and for that reason it is hard for us to go in search of our dear friend, Speckle. So it is up to you to go in search of him and find out what has happened. Perhaps he has been killed and eaten by some lion or the other; or he has been consumed in a forest fire; or he might have fallen prey to hunters and the like. How aptly the saying puts it:

> *One's loved ones might only be strolling*   (172)
> *in a pleasure garden—yet,*
> *all on a sudden one fears for them.*
> *What if they are marooned in the midst*
> *of a wilderness*
> *Savage, filled with perils?*

'So, go wherever you think best; look for precise details of Speckle's whereabouts and return as quick as you can.'

Lightwing did so. He had not flown too far when he noticed Speckle at the edge of a pool. He had fallen into a sturdy trap held securely by strong pegs of acacia wood. Seeing him in such misery, Lightwing spoke sorrowfully, 'Ah! My dearest friend, how ever did you fall into this misfortune?'

And Speckle answered, 'Alas, my friend, there is no time to lose; so listen to what I have to say.

> *When life is nearing its end* (173)
> *the sight of a dear friend*
> *twofold happiness does bring:*
> *to the living and to the dying.*

'Forgive me, my friend, if at any time when we sat together, I uttered something in anger springing from affection.[62] And likewise speak to Slowcoach and Goldy on my behalf; say to them;

> *If ever I uttered a harsh word,* (174)
> *knowingly, or, unknowingly,*
> *forgive me, my friends, I beg you;*
> *remember only the affection.'*

Lightwing was quick to comfort the deer. 'O, my friend, you should not be afraid; not while you have friends like us. I shall fetch Goldy to cut your bonds: I shall return with him in no time.'

With a heavy heart, Lightwing flew back to Slowcoach and Goldy and described exactly how Speckle lay in captivity. Then he returned to Speckle carrying Goldy in his beak.

Goldy saw Speckle in this miserable plight and spoke sadly to him, 'Dear, dear, friend, you who ever had a cautious mind and a sharp eye, how did you fall into such a calamity as to be bound and fettered?' And Speckle replied, 'Why put such questions? Fate is all-powerful. Is it not said:

> *The wisest, most perspicacious* (175)
> *can do nothing face to face with Death*
> *—that great Ocean of Calamity—*
> *Unseen, he strikes, by night, or by day*
> *or any other time he wills:*
> *Who dares oppose Him?*

'So, my noble friend, as you are well aware of Fate's capricious tricks and turns, please cut through my bonds quickly, before those pitiless hunters arrive on the scene.'

'Now, now, don't panic, my friend, not while I am here by your side,' responded Goldy. 'But great anguish fills my heart; assuage that pain by recounting the events of your life, Your Honour. You possess the eye of wisdom. How did you allow yourself to be made captive?'

Speckle then rejoined, 'If you really wish to know, then listen to my story; how I have fallen into captivity once again, through Fate's power, although I have endured the pains of bondage once before.'

Goldy exclaimed, 'What? Do you mean to tell me that Your Honour found yourself once before bound in captivity? I am eager to know the whole story in all its detail.' And, the deer began the tale of *Speckle's Captivity*.

In the past when I was but six months old, out of childish exuberance, I used to go bounding off in advance of the rest of the herd. And going some distance ahead in playful spirits, I used to stop and wait for the herd to catch up with me. We deer follow two kinds of gait; one is the jump-up, the other is the straight-ahead. Of these two I was familiar with the straight-ahead, not with the jump-up.

While I was having fun one day, gambolling, I suddenly noticed that I had lost contact with the herd. I was terribly worried, wondering where they had all gone. Looking in all directions, I saw them standing at a distance ahead of me. They had all obviously gone ahead, avoiding a net by using the jump-up gait and were now waiting, looking fixedly at me. Unacquainted as I was with the jump-up gait I fell into the hunter's net and got all entangled in it. While I tried to drag the net along towards the waiting herd, the hunter came and bound my legs together. I fell on the ground, face down. The herd, seeing there was no hope of saving me, fled and vanished.

Now the hunter came close and said, 'Oh, but this is just a little fawn, fit only to play with.' And out of compassion he did not kill me, but took me home instead and then presented me to the prince for a pet. The prince was so delighted that he made the hunter a generous gift. The prince treated me with great affection, having me bathed and rubbed with oils and balms, brushed and massaged and perfumed with sweet-smelling creams, fed with fine food and adorned with beautiful garlands of pearls. But at the same time I was petted so much, passed from hand to hand by the women in the royal apartments and by eager young princes, that I was greatly vexed, even hurt somewhat, for they fondled and pulled my ears, stroked and scratched my neck and paws, even touched my eyes.

One day, during the rains, the prince lay reclining on a couch. I heard the clouds thundering: I saw the lightning flash; and I remembered my own people. My heart was deeply stirred by a longing to see them, to be with the herd. And I recited this verse:

> *'O, to run with the coursing herd of deer,* (176)
> *swiftly, with the wind in my face!*
> *When, O, when will that be?'*

'Who said that?' cried the prince, with fear clutching at his heart; and he looked all around. Then he saw me, 'Ah! These words were not spoken by a human, but by a deer; so this creature must be some sort of prodigy. I am undone—wholly undone.' Thinking thus, the prince ran out of the palace, tottering, like one possessed by a demon. Convinced that he was demon-ridden, he summoned various sorcerers and magicians and tempted them with great rewards, saying, 'Whoever rids me of this torment, I shall honour him no end.' I, too, on my part, was being hit and struck with sticks, bricks and cudgels by ignorant individuals. But being destined to live longer, I was rescued by a kind holy man who said, 'Why kill this poor creature?' He saved my life. Furthermore, understanding my state of mind, he advised the prince, explaining, 'Friend, now that it is the season of rains, this poor creature was only wistfully remembering his herd, and in longing recited this verse:

257

> *O, to run with the coursing herd of deer* (177)
> *swiftly, with the wind in my face!*
> *When, O, when will that be?*

'So, why does Your Honour distress yourself needlessly?' The prince, hearing this, was cured of his brain-fever and returned to his normal state of health. He then ordered his men to release me, 'Douse this deer profusely on the head with cool water; take him to the forest where he was captured and leave him there.' And his men did so. Having suffered captivity once, I suffered the same fate a second time because of Destiny's Will.

In the meantime, Slowcoach, urged by affection for his friend arrived on the scene, having trudged the whole way leaving reeds, grass and shrubs crushed in his wake. Seeing him, the friends became even more distressed. Goldy now addressed the tortoise, observing, 'Dear friend; you have not acted wisely by leaving your fortress and coming here, because you cannot protect yourself from the hunter if he should happen to arrive on the scene. Once his bonds are cut, in case the hunter is close by, Speckle can easily take one quick leap and flee. And Lightwing can fly up into a tree, while I, being tiny, can with ease slip into some little crevice or cranny. But what will you do if the hunter sees you?'

Slowcoach listened and then replied, 'No, no, do not say such things; for:

> *Parting from loved ones, loss of wealth—* (178)
> *Who can endure these*
> *if reunion with dear friends is not there?*
> *A veritable panacea?*

'And again:

> *Days spent in constant company* (179)
> *of men cherished for their learning,*

258

refinement, and discipline, are like clear paths
    opening out in life's wilderness.

To speak of one's sorrows to a virtuous wife,   (180)
a dear friend of like mind, or a master
who truly understands all one's troubles
is to build your heart a resting-place.

'Therefore, my dear friend,

The heart swells with longing,   (181)
    the eyes wildly wander,
the mind bewildered goes somewhere,
    one does not know where—
    because of the absence of a person
    of undiminished worth and affection.

'Oh! My friend!

It's far better to give up one's life   (182)
than be parted from friends like yourself;
life is regained when we are born again;
but friends like you are never found again.'

At that moment the hunter arrived, bow and arrow in hand. Right before his eyes, Goldy cut Speckle's bonds and as mentioned before immediately disappeared into a small cranny. Lightwing flew up into the sky and instantly disappeared while Speckle swiftly bounded away. The hunter, when he saw that the deer's bonds had been cut, cried out in amazement, 'Never have deer been known to cut their own bonds; it must surely be Fate's doing that severed his bonds.'

Then he noticed the tortoise in the most unlikely of places for a tortoise to be. And he reacted predictably. 'Ah, well,' he told himself, 'It is true that with Fate's help the deer burst his bonds and got away. But I sure have this tortoise right here; as it is admirably put:

259

Whatever flies in the air, (183)
whatever walks on the ground,
whatever courses over this earth—
> *nothing comes within your reach*
> *unless Fate wills it to be yours.'*

Ruminating in this manner, the hunter drew out his knife,
cut some spear-grass, wove it into a stout rope and securely tied
the legs of the tortoise together. He then slung the loop of the
rope round one end of his bow and started for home. Seeing his
friend being carried away in this manner, Goldy was woebegone
and cried out, 'Alas, alas, what a calamity!

No sooner was one great sorrow ended (184)
—it seemed I had crossed over the ocean—
than another looms ahead of me:
misfortunes are massed at the weakest points.

Fresh blows sharply fall on a wound; (185)
lack of food stokes the fires in the belly;
enmities spring up in the wake of woes:
> *misfortunes are massed at the weakest points.*

As long as you do not trip (186)
it's easy going on even ground;
but once you begin to stumble,
each step you take is full of pain.

'And again:

A bow, a wife, a friend, (187)
of good stock, fine quality,
strong, straight, yet supple,
> *not sinking, giving way*
> *in times of trouble . . .*
these are indeed hard to find.

Friendship is that which springs spontaneous, (188)

a blessing only good fortune can bring.
False friends who put on the mask of friendship
    why . . . they are a dime a dozen.

Not in a mother, not in a wife,   (189)
not in a brother, or in a son,
can that unalloyed trust be placed
unquestioningly, as in a true friend.

Not diminished by constant enjoyment,   (190)
not ravished by ignoble men,
but embellished by uprightness,
friendship is set at naught by death,
    and by death alone.

'Why, O, why does fate hurl its blows at me ceaselessly? First, it was the loss of resources, followed by humiliation at the hands of my people as a result of my poverty; then the depression arising from that led to the abandonment of my country. And now, Fate afflicts me with the loss of a friend. It has been said before:

In truth, the loss of wealth causes no great grief;   (191)
for wealth returns.
    It is this that burns me up—bereft
    of the support of wealth, good friends grow cold.

'And further:

Though my succession of actions good and bad   (192)
already played out have gained the other world;
yet I see them right here and now in action . . .
    life's vicissitudes seeming my former lives.

'Ah! How wisely it is said:

The body teeters on danger's edge;   (193)
Where fortune is, misfortune creeps in;

> *meetings end in parting;*
> *everything that is born is fragile.*

'Oh! Utter misery! I am undone by the loss of my friend. What does mine own matter now? What do my kinsfolk matter? As the saying goes:

> *A chalice of trust and affection,*   (194)
> *a sanctuary from sorrow, anxiety and fear—*
> *Who created this priceless gem, a friend?*
> *A word of just two syllables—MITRA![63]*

'And further:

> *Pure blessedness uninterrupted—*   (195)
> *a loom that weaves affection's single thread—*
> *sole companionship of noble minds—*
> *Then—Death's sentence of banishment,*
> *unbearable, breaks it all!*

'And again:

> *Close-knit companionship,*   (196)
> *mind-delighting treasures,*
> *and enmities as well—*
> *Death cuts short all at one single stroke.*

'Once again:

> *Were there no birth, or old age, or death;*   (197)
> *were there no separation from loved ones;*
> *were there not the transience of all things:*
> *who would not take delight in life in this world?'*

As Goldy, grief-stricken, was crying out aloud and lamenting in this manner, Lightwing, the crow, and Speckle, the deer, came and joined him.

'Listen, friends,' said Goldy to them, 'as long as our friend Slowcoach is within sight, there is some hope of saving him.

Therefore, dear Speckle, run; step past the hunter without being noticed and fall down somewhere close to water; pretend to be dead. And you, dear Lightwing, alight on Speckle's branching antlers, get your claws into their interstices and pretend to peck his eyes out. Then that wicked hunter, seized by greed, thinking to himself that it was great good fortune to have chanced upon a dead deer is sure to let go of the tortoise and grab the deer. At that point when his back is turned, I shall quickly step in and cut Slowcoach loose of his bonds so that he would be able to take refuge in the water. I, for my own part, will slide quickly into a clump of reeds. And take note, Speckle, you better plan to make a speedy escape when that wicked hunter is about to grab hold of you.'

The three friends then carried out the details of this plan. No sooner did the hunter notice a deer lying dead at the water's edge and a crow sitting on its antlers pecking his eyes out than he immediately threw the tortoise on the ground, and, raising his club high above his head ran towards the deer.

As soon as Speckle could tell from the tramp of the hunter's feet that he was very close, he rose up quickly and with a supreme burst of speed vanished into the dense forest. Lightwing at once flew up and settled on the branch of a tree. And Slowcoach, whose fetters had been cut hastily by Goldy's sharp claws, slid into the water. Goldy too scurried into a clump of reeds.

The hunter looked around, rubbed his eyes and almost believed that some magic was afoot. 'What on earth is happening?' he exclaimed in utter disappointment and hurried to the spot where he had left the tortoise. And what did he see there but the cords with which he had tied the tortoise up, all cut into small pieces, each a finger's length. Seeing that the tortoise had vanished like some sorcerer or saint, he looked at his own body, fearful that something strange might happen to his person. With a mind filled with deep misgivings, he hurried home, all the while casting troubled glances in every direction.

Meanwhile the four friends, free from all dangers to their persons gathered together once again and lived happily in mutual friendship and affection feeling that they had been granted a fresh lease of life.

Therefore, I say to you:

> *If creatures going on all fours display* (198)
> *Such friendship welded through worldly wisdom,*
> *what wonder then that men endowed*
> *with so fine an intelligence should do likewise.*

And now we come to the end of Book Two entitled the *Winning of Friends*, of which this is the opening verse:

> *Lacking resources, destitute of wealth,* (199)
> *wise men possessed of common sense and learning*
> *are quick to accomplish their desired aims*
> *as the crow and mole, the deer and tortoise did.*

BOOK III

Of Crows and Owls

And now begins the third book entitled *Of Crows and Owls* that treats of peace, war and other matters.[1] This is the opening verse.

Trust not a former enemy (1)
who comes professing amity;
Mark! The cave thronged by owls was burned
by deadly fire the crows kindled.

'Oh! And how was that?' asked the princes. And Viṣṇu Śarma began his tale *Of Crows and Owls* and their bitter enmity.

In the southern land there was a city named Earth Support.[2] Near the city grew a huge, many-branching banyan tree in which Cloud Hue,[3] King of Crows, nested, attended by hundreds of crow-retainers. He spent all his time there because that was home.

Now, another king, a great owl named Foe Crusher[4] lived secure in a fortress in a mountain cave, and he had countless numbers of owls serving him. This king of owls obsessed by some ancient enmity, invariably killed any crow that crossed his path as he made his rounds in that region. As time went by, a ring of dead crows encircled the tree on account of his daily forays. Things happen that way: for as it is wisely observed:

Whoever through sheer indifference (2)
disregards his foe, or a disease,
and lets them move unchecked
will, in no time, meet his end.

One day, Cloud Hue summoned his ministers of state and addressed them.

'Honourable gentlemen,' he began, 'we have an enemy whose power cannot be denied—a person of determination—and he knows how to choose his time too. For he comes at nightfall, each day, and wreaks havoc in our ranks. Now how do we retaliate? The truth is that we cannot see at night. And as we haven't a clue to the location of his fortress, we cannot go there during the day to attack him. Tell me, which of the following options should we make use of: start negotiations, or hostilities; begin a retreat or make a stand; seek alliance or sow discord in his ranks?'[5]

Then the ministers answered, 'Your Majesty has spoken wisely in posing this question. As it is wisely observed:

> *Even if his opinion is unsolicited,* (3)
> *a minister should speak his mind at such times;*
> *and when his advice is specially sought*
> *it should be for the good of the king . . .*

> *As for him who asked for advice* (4)
> *refrains from speaking what is right*
> *and in the royal interests as well,*
> *who offers soothing words instead, regard him*
> *as an enemy in minister's guise.*

'It is important, Your Majesty, that we confer immediately in private.'

Cloud Hue then began consulting with each one of his ministers whose names were, Live Again, Live Well, Live Along, Live On and Live Long.[6]

First the king asked Live Again, 'Dear friend, in the circumstances, what do you think we should do?'

To this Live Again replied, 'My lord; it is not wise to start hostilities against a powerful enemy. The enemy is not only powerful but one who knows when to strike. It is best to be conciliatory. For it is wisely said:

> *As streams do not flow against the current,* (5)
> *so too the prosperity of the noble*

who for the moment bow before
one more powerful, will not reverse its course.

'Moreover:

> *While the powerful foe, just, virtuous,* (6)
> *rich in kin and in resources,*
> *and victorious in many battles*
> *is a worthy ally indeed;*
>
> *Make peace even with the vilest* (7)
> *When your life is in danger;*
> *once life is well protected,*
> *the whole realm becomes secure.*

'And further:

> *He who gains a firm alliance* (8)
> *with the victor of many wars*
> *will soon find his other foes come to heel,*
> *awed into submission by his allies' power.*
>
> *Desire to make peace even with your equals;* (9)
> *for victory is never a certainty;*
> *better not take risks,*
> *counsels the sage, Bṛhaspati—*
>
> *Victory is ever uncertain, even* (10)
> *when warriors are evenly matched.*
> *Try first the other three expedients[7]*
> *before you opt for hostilities.*
>
> *Blinded by wounded pride,* (11)
> *reluctant to sue for peace,*
> *a man may be destroyed even by an equal;*
> *unable to make a stand*
> *he comes apart*
> *like an unbaked clay pot.*

Land, friends, gold: (12)
these are the three fruits of war;
if not even one of these is on the cards,
then, why in God's name
should anyone go to war.

Digging into a mole's burrow   (13)
all filled with bits of rock,
what does a lion get for his pains
but broken claws—at best a mouse.

Where no gain may be expected,   (14)
and only the fury of fighting is foreseen,
why start a war on your own
and carry it on at any cost?

If a stronger enemy assails you,   (15)
better bend like the reed by the stream.
Do not rear like an angry snake
if unremitting prosperity is what you seek.

Following the lowly manner of the reed   (16)
a man gains great prosperity in time.
Adopting the overbearing manner of the snake,
he is simply courting death.

Like the tortoise a wise man will retreat   (17)
into his shell and suffer cruel blows;
when the time is ripe he will rear up
ready to strike like a deadly serpent.

I know of no test that lays down   (18)
you ought to fight a powerful foe.
A rain cloud never moves ahead
if contrary winds prevail.'

Having listened to this view, Cloud Hue turned to Live Well
and asked, 'Gracious sir, let me have *your* opinion now.'

'Your Majesty,' replied Live Well, 'I am afraid this counsel does not appeal to me. In as much as the enemy is cruel, rapacious and unscrupulous, the prospect of peace with him should definitely not be entertained. For it is said:

> *At no cost should peace be proposed*   (19)
> *with one devoid of truth and justice;*
> *however binding the agreement you make,*
> *inborn viciousness will in no time change his course.*

'Therefore, my counsel is to go to war with the enemy, for it has been said:

> *To uproot a foe cruel and greedy,*   ·(20)
> *false and lazy,*
> *unprepared and cowardly*
> *and a blundering fool*
> *who despises warriors to boot,*
> *why, that is quite easy.*

'Another point that we ought to remember is, that he has humiliated us badly. Now, if we propose peace talks with him, he will be so exasperated that he is bound to resort to further violence. As the saying goes:

> *When it is clear a foe can be contained*   (21)
> *only by recourse to the final expedient,*[8]
> *conciliation proves a disservice:*
> *Would a wise man douse with water*
> *the initial stages of a fever*
> *that can only be sweated out?*

> *Conciliation merely serves to further inflame*   (22)
> *the man sputtering with violent rage;*
> *drops of water*
> *suddenly falling on boiling butter*
> *only makes it spatter.*

'And to consider what my honourable friend here has just

expressed, that the enemy is powerful . . . that is hardly a worth-while reason.

> *A smaller person of impetuous energy* (23)
> *may slay the larger and gain sovereignty,*
> *as the lion the lordly tusker.*

'Again:

> *Where force cannot overpower a foe,* (24)
> *guile might do the trick,*
> *just as Kīčaka was overthrown*
> *by Bhīma dressed in women's clothes.*

'Then again:

> *Foes crumble before a king* (25)
> *who wields like Death a cruel rod.*
> *But foes are all quick to fall upon*
> *a king by compassion ruled.*

> *If a man's valour fades* (26)
> *at the sight of others' heroic valour,*
> *he was born in vain indeed,*
> *born only to rob his mother of her youth*

> *Royal Glory whose limbs are unadorned,* (27)
> *with the bright saffron of enemy blood,*
> *though dearly loved does not bring high-souled men*
> *the taste of that pleasure they crave for.*

> *What glory can a monarch whose kingdom* (28)
> *is not drenched with blood of foes*
> *and tears of their wailing wives*
> > *truely boast of!'*

After listening to this view expressed by Live Well, the King of Crows next turned to Live Along. 'Gracious friend,' he said, 'now it is your turn to present your counsel.'

And Live Along replied: 'Your Majesty! I fear the enemy is vicious; he is superior in strength as well and unscrupulous in behaviour. Neither war nor peace ought to be considered in this situation. Our only option is withdrawal; moving out. As the saying goes:

> *Not peace, not war, neither course is right* (29)
> *when facing an enemy power-drunk*
> *and vicious, who lacks all restraint;*
> *nothing will work except withdrawal.*

> *Moving out takes two forms; retreat,* (30)
> *or flight, fearing for one's life, that's one;*
> *marching forwards thirsting for victory*
>   *that's the other.*

> *For a monarch exceedingly valorous* (31)
> *and set on conquest, December or April*
> *are deemed the best'months to set out*
> *marching into an enemy's land.*

> *But all times are deemed favourable* (32)
> *for a surprise attack on a foe*
> *dogged by disaster and vulnerable,*
> *the chinks in his armour clearly showing.*

> *Having first made his own realm secure,* (33)
> *well-guarded by warriors loyal and valorous,*
> *a king might then march against another*
> *once his trusted spies are in right places.*

> *Our present plight calls for withdrawal, O King!* (34)
> *No war, no, nor peace, is now possible*
> *with a foe both strong and evil-minded.*

'Furthermore, the texts state quite clearly that withdrawal should be effected with due regard to cause and effect. As the proverb says:

> *A ram draws back to butt more fiercely;* (35)

273

> the Lord of Beasts first crouches in cold fury
>> before he makes his deadly spring.
> Hiding enmity deep within their hearts,
> keeping secret their counsel and their moves,
> the wise wait biding their time
> and endure whatever happens to them meantime.

'Then again:

> Faced by a powerful foe (36)
> the king who leaves his realm,
> lives to see another day
> and rule the earth as Yudhiṣṭhira[9] did.

'Again:

> A weak king driven by overweening pride (37)
> who sets out to fight a powerful foe
> is in truth doing his enemy's bidding
> while bringing his own line to an end.

'Pressed hard as you are, my lord, at this point by a powerful foe, I suggest that this is a time for retreat, not for proposing peace or engaging in war.'

Having listened to these words of Minister Live Along, the King of Crows now turned to Live On and said, 'Gracious sir; come, now give us your advice on this matter.'

And the minister replied, 'Well, my lord; peace, war, retreat, none of these policies appeal to me; especially the last, the policy of retreat. For:

> At home in his own world a crocodile (38)
> can seize and hold a lordly elephant;
> but once dislodged from his habitat
> even a dog can beat him hollow.

'Once again:

> Attacked by a powerful foe, a monarch (39)

274

to his fortress should withdraw;
yet, persevere in his efforts
and stationed within send calls of distress
to friends to come to his aid.

Were a king to abandon his realm   (40)
panic-stricken at the sound
of enemy approach, there is not a hope
he can ever enter it again.

One man entrenched in his stronghold   (41)
can singly fight a hundred men,
each a powerful foe; therefore
a man should never give up his stronghold.

Making his stronghold secure with deep moat   (42 & 43)
and ramparts bristling with machines of war;[10]
well-stocked with arrows and other weapons,
with supplies and transport and reinforcements;
laying in a goodly store of provisions,
he should wait within, ready, resolved to fight.
        If he lives he gains great glory;
        dead, he goes to Paradise.

'It is also said:

As shrubs growing together   (44)
in close-knit clumps stay unscathed
though buffeted by contrary winds,
so too by banding together
the weak are unassailable
by however powerful a foe.

A lone tree firmly rooted,   (45 & 46)
and mighty, is yet no match
even for a moderate wind;
whereas trees densely packed in groves,
firmly rooted, stand tall

even when swift winds rip into them,
    because they stand together.

Likewise a lone man (47)
heroic in the extreme
is regarded easy prey
by foes who soon hem him in.'

Having listened to these views, King Cloud Hue now turned to Live Long and said, 'Worthy sir, pray let us now have your opinion.'

To which the minister replied, saying, 'Well, my lord, of all the six policy-expedients laid down, forming an alliance seems to be what is called for in the situation. Therefore, let us scout around for a suitable alliance. As the saying goes:

A man may be able and skilled; (48)
he may be bold, energetic;
    but if he lacks friends,
    what can he achieve?
Mark how a fire kindled in a windless spot
    soon dies down on its own.

'Therefore my lord, you should stay put right here and seek a powerful ally whose strength could offset the enemy's. If however you abandon your position and go elsewhere then no one is going to throw even a friendly word your way. You know the saying:

The wind is friend to the forest fire indeed; (49)
but the same wind puts out the flame of the lamp.
Who in the world honours one
    insignificant and weak?

'It is not the absolute rule however, that only those powerful are to be sought out as allies. Alliances with those weak can also provide one security. As the saying goes:

As a slender, swaying bamboo (50)

> *that grows in a thicket,*
> *encircled by other bamboos*
> > *is hard to uproot,*
> > *so too a monarch*
> *however powerless he may be.*

'So much the better if you find an ally truly great and noble. As it is observed:

> *Who is not ennobled*   (51)
> *by the society of the eminent?*
> *a drop of water on a lotus-leaf*
> *takes on the lustre of a pearl.*

'Therefore, my lord, nothing but a proper alliance can possibly offset our enemy's power; so let us go for an alliance. This is my advice.'

Thus advised, Cloud Hue now turned to an elder statesman, an ancient counsellor named Live Firm who had for a long time served as minister to his father and who was farseeing, and who possessed complete mastery of the texts on the political sciences. Bowing low, Cloud Hue addressed him as follows : 'Father,' he began, 'I solicited my ministers to offer their opinions on this matter in your presence so that several points of view may be put forward; and so that having listened to all the options available, you could advise me as to the best possible course. So now, instruct me in the proper expedients to follow.'

And Live Firm replied, 'Whatever your ministers have proposed here, my son, they have done so in complete conformity with the teaching of the texts on polity. Each, however, is appropriate for its own good time. But the present seems to be a time to practise double-dealing as the proverb puts it:

> *Towards an enemy powerful and evil*   (52)
> > *always harbour deep distrust;*
> *now offering peace, then again making war,*
> > *adopting a policy of duplicity.*

'Thus, by offering a tempting bait and thereby instilling confidence in him while remaining cautious oneself, the enemy can be easily extirpated. As we have heard:

> *Men skilled in diplomacy* (53)
> *do encourage the enemy*
> *they wish to see destroyed*
> *to grow and prosper a while:*
> *just as phlegm increased by molasses*
> *   vanishes without a trace.*

'Moreover:

> *A man who acts with candour towards a foe,* (54)
> *   a false friend, or towards women,*
> *   especially those for sale,*
> *   will not long survive.*

> *With gods and Brāhmanas, however,* (55)
> *with oneself and one's preceptor,*
> *a man ought to act with candour;*
> *with all others double-dealing is best.*

> *Towards ascetics purified* (56)
> *by prayer and meditation,*
> *candour is ever extolled;*
> *not with men who lust after worldly things;*
> *with kings especially, never.*

'Therefore, my son,

> *By resorting to double-dealing,* (57)
> *you will remain secure in your own place;*
> *Death will quickly extirpate*
> *the enemy obsessed with greed and hate.*

'And what's more, if the smallest chink in his armour appears, you will notice it and destroy him,' concluded Live Firm.

'But, Father,' objected Cloud Hue, 'I have no idea where my enemy lives; how can I then be aware of chinks in his armour?'

'Ah! My son,' replied Live Firm, 'leave that to me. By despatching secret agents, I shall be able to reveal to you not only where he lives but his weak points as well. For, you see:

> Cows see things by smell;   (58)
> Brāhmaṇas see by the Vedas;
> Kings see everything through spies:
> And all others with their eyes.

'And in this connection, it is further stated:

> The king who knows well his own high officials   (59)
>   and his enemy's particularly well
> through the employment of secret agents,
>   will never find himself in distress.'

'Father,' queried Cloud Hue, eagerly, 'Tell me who these high officials are? How many are they? What kind of men are secret agents? Pray, tell me all.'

The ancient counsellor then explained: 'In this matter, my son, the revered sage, Nārada, consulted by King Yudhiṣṭhira informed him clearly as follows: there are eighteen officials of importance in the enemy's ranks and fifteen in one's own. Three secret agents should be detailed to investigate each of these. By following this procedure, the high officials or personages in one's own ranks and in the enemy's as well are kept under control. The proverb puts the matter in a nutshell:

> Eighteen dignitaries on the other side   (60)
>   five and ten on one's own;
>   three spies to each surreptitiously
>   keeping a wary eye.
> And you'll know everything you need to know
>   about each dignitary.

'By the term "dignitary" is meant an official appointed to

perform a particular job. If he performs ill, he will bring about his master's downfall; if well, he will bring prosperity to his king. Now, these are the dignitaries: the Chief Minister, the High Priest, the Commander-in-Chief and the Crown Prince; the Chief Usher, Captain of the palace-guards, and Commandant of sappers and miners; the Commissioner of revenue and the Keeper of the stores; the Chief Justice; the Officer-in-Charge of the royal stables and the Superintendent of elephants; the Clerk of the council, the Minister for defence; the Commandant of the fort and Warden of the marches; the Secretary to the king and others; these are the important dignitaries in the enemy's realm. By sowing dissension among them the enemy becomes vulnerable.

'Coming to our own realm, the important personages are: the Queen and Queen-Mother; the Royal Chamberlain and garland-maker; the Lord of the royal bed-chamber; the Head of the secret service; the court-physician and court-astrologer; the water-carrier and the keeper of the royal box of betel-leaf and spices; the king's preceptor; the royal bodyguard; the quarter-master; the bearer of the royal umbrella and the chief courtesan. It is through these persons that the realm might by destroyed. Further:

> *Preceptor, astrologer, physician*   (61)
> *are best employed to spy on one's own men;*
> *while snake-charmer and madman*
> *know everything about one's foes.'*

'Tell me, Father,' said Cloud Hue, 'What is the reason for this deadly feud between crows and owls?'

'Listen, my son, and I'll tell you how it all began,' replied Live Firm. And then he began the story of *How the birds picked a king*.

Once upon a time all the different species of birds gathered together in a grand conclave and began deliberating. Assembled there were wild geese and sarus-cranes, koels[11] and peacocks, crested cuckoos,[12] pigeons, partridges and turtle-doves; blue-jays, skylarks and demoiselle cranes: owls and jungle fowls; thrushes,[13] woodpeckers and many others.

'To be sure, Vinatā's son[14] is our lord and king,' they said. 'But he is so rapt in the worship and service of the blessed lord, Nārāyaṇa, that he does not think of us. What good is it to have a make-believe king who cannot protect us from all the dangers we are subject to such as getting trapped, which causes us such great distress. As it is wisely observed:

> *Let there be one, any one,* (62)
> *a king whom we pay homage to,*
> *who will renew our spirits*
> *when we are weak and weary:*
> *who will keep us safe, anxiety-free,*
>   *as the sun keeps the moon.*

'Anyone else will be a king only in name: as they say:

> *He who does not protect his subjects* (63)
> *terrorized by continual harassment of foes,*
>   *he is no king—no doubt on that score—*
>   *but Death masquerading as king.*

'And again:

> *Like a leaky boat at sea, these six* (64 & 65)
> *ought to be avoided at all costs;*
>   *a preceptor without learning;*
>   *a priest ignorant of ritual;*
>   *a king who provides no defence;*
>   *a wife whose speech is harsh and cutting;*
>   *a cowherd fond of sticking to the village*
>   *and a barber who hankers after wealth.*

'Therefore let us consider someone else to be the King of Birds.'

Then, observing that the owl had a gracious appearance,

they all said, 'Let this owl now be our king. Let all the essential requisites[15] for the anointing of a king be collected and brought.'

Waters of sacred streams were brought; the hundred and eight herbs including *cakrānkita*[16] and *sahadevi*[17] were arranged in a bouquet; the lion-throne was set up. A picture of the earth's circle with its seven continents, seas and mountains, was drawn on the ground; a tiger-skin was spread out. Golden jars filled with five kinds of tender sprouts and blossoms, and coloured grains of rice were placed in a row; offerings were made ready. Then bards began their praise-songs and Brāhmanas skilled in chanting the four Vedas correctly, began their recitations. Young maidens specially trained to sing songs of celebration lifted up their melodious voices. A sanctified salver containing white mustard, parched grain, grains of coloured rice, yellow pigment, flower-garlands, conches and other auspicious items were then placed in the forefront. Materials for the lustration rites were placed in readiness and drums began to be gently struck.[18]

As the owl graced the lion-throne set in the centre of a raised dais decorated with designs drawn with barley-flour, in readiness for his coronation, a crow flew in from somewhere announcing his arrival with raucous cawing, and entered the assembly. As he came he was thinking to himself, 'Aha! What festival is this where all the birds are gathered together!'

Seeing him all the birds started whispering among themselves. 'Look, we hear that of all birds, this one is the shrewdest. So let us hear what he has to say. As the proverb states it:

> *Of men, the barber is the smartest,*   (66)
>   *of birds the crow,*
> *of four-footed creatures, the jackal,*
>   *of mendicants, the white-robed.*

'Besides:

> *When many counsellors, wise and learned*   (67)
>   *frame after due deliberation*
>   *in close consultation*
>   *and thorough examination*

> *a policy and carry it through,*
> *under no circumstances will it fail.'*

Thinking in this manner, the birds looked towards the crow and said, 'Because we birds have no king we have all gathered together and decided unanimously that the owl should be anointed to reign as the supreme sovereign of birds. Since you have arrived at the right time you are welcome to express your views on the matter.'

The crow then laughed and said, 'Worthy gentlemen! What an idea! When you have among you wild goose and peacock, koel and greek partridge,[19] green pigeon[20] and sarus-crane and other pre-eminent birds to choose from, why on earth would you go and pick this fellow here and crown him king—a creature blind by day and hideous looking? I am afraid I cannot approve of your choice. Look at him:

> *Hook-nosed and squint-eyed,* (68)
> *fierce, with looks most unprepossessing:*
> *in a pleasant mood if his face looks like this,*
> *what'll it be like when he's angry and ranting?*

'Moreover:

> *By nature wild and fierce,* (69)
> *a most savage creature, cruel,*
> *every word he speaks is harsh*
>   *and extremely disagreeable:*
> *having crowned the owl your king,*
> *what good fortune do you expect to have?*

'Besides, with Vinatā's son himself as your sovereign, what good is this fellow? Even granting he possesses virtues, when you already have a king, why think of another? As the proverb says:

> *One monarch, one only,* (70)
>   *brilliant and lordly,*

283

is a blessing to the world.
Monarchs many—Ah! that's a calamity,
   like multiple suns blazing forth
   at the end of the world.

'Why! The very name of your sovereign serves to keep you unassailable by enemies. As it is wisely said:

> *Where a noble sovereign is present,*   (71)
>   *the mention of his mere name*
> *before evil men however powerful,*
>   *results that very moment*
>   *in producing peace and security.*

'It is also kr.own that:

> *By feigning greatly*   (72)
> *great success follows;*
> *the hares lived happily*
> *riding high on the moon's glory.'*

'Oh! And how was that,' asked the birds eagerly. And the crow began the tale of *The Hare who fooled the Elephant-King*.

In a wooded region lived an elephant-king named Four Tusks[21] surrounded by a large retinue of elephants. His time was all taken up with the protection of his herd.

Once a twelve-year drought fell on this region resulting in all the ponds, pools, swamps and lakes drying up completely. Then the elephants spoke to their lord, lamenting, 'Great lord, our little ones are tormented by extreme thirst; some are at the point of death while others are already dead. Pray devise some means of coping with this thirst.'

The elephant-king then despatched some of his fleet-footed and impetuous attendants in all directions to search for water. Those that went in an easterly direction came upon a lake beside a path that ran close to a hermitage, a lake brimming with translucent water and enchanting with wild geese, cranes and curlews, sheldrakes and other aquatic creatures. Branches of various trees drooping from the weight of blossoming sprays and a wealth of tender leaf-shoots, formed a protective screen enclosing the lake. Both banks were adorned with trees. Little waves of pellucid water, tremulous in the breeze, jostled against the margins to tumble on to the sandy shores in a profusion of foam-bubbles. The waters were perfumed by the scent of ichor streaming down the sloping cheeks of lordly tuskers whose temples had been swept clean of bees that flew up as the beasts plunged into the lake. The waters were perpetually shaded from the heat of the sun's rays by a canopy of hundreds of leafy parasols formed by clumps of trees growing by the lake-edge. The waters reverberated with the deep-toned music made by a host of gathering wavelets that retreated hastily from the assault of plump buttocks, sloping hips and heavy breasts of young hill-women diving with speed to hit the waters in full force. The lake shone with the rare beauty of thickets of fully-blossomed lotuses. But why expatiate further? This pool of water known as Moon Lake was nothing short of a piece of paradise. The elephant-scouts took a look at the lake and hurried back to their lord to inform him of what they had seen.

After receiving their report, Four Tusks accompanied by them went by easy stages to Moon Lake. Seeing a gentle slope all around the lake the elephants descended, and in the process the heads and necks, bodies and feet of thousands of hares who had made the lake shore their home for long, were crushed and pounded to a jelly. Having drunk his fill and soaked to his heart's content, the elephant-lord came out of the lake with his herd and entered his home forest.

The surviving hares now gathered and sat in serious deliberation. 'Whatever shall we do now,' they lamented; 'now that these fellows know the way, they will come here daily to our lake. So we ought to think of a plan by which these fellows may be prevented from returning.'

Now, one of the hares, whose name was Victory, spoke out

of compassion, perceiving the terror that gripped the community, and the utter grief that overwhelmed those whose wives, children and kinsfolk had been crushed to death. 'Now, now, friends,' he said, 'You should not be frightened; these beasts will never come here again, I promise you. For the divinity[22] who oversees my actions has bestowed his grace upon me.'

Then Dart Face, King of Hares, commended Victory. 'Dear friend,' he said, 'I have no doubts at all on this score; and for good reason; for:

> *Wherever Victory is despatched,* (73)
> *who is the acknowledged master*
> *of the essence of texts on polity,*
> *who knows as well unerringly*
> *the right time and place for action;*
> *there, lies success unsurpassed.*

'Moreover:

> *The man whose speech is measured;* (74)
> *whose speech is always for the good;*
> *whose speech is wise and well-wrought;*
> *who never speaks in excess,*
> *and only after deep reflection; he*
> *is the one effective every time.*

'Receiving the full measure of Your Honour's profound wisdom, the elephants are sure to become aware of my three powers[23] even at a distance. For:

> *Judging from the messenger or the missive,* (75)
> *though I have never set eyes on him,*
> *I know what kind of king he is;*
> *whether he has any wisdom or none.*

'It is also said:

> *A messenger alone knits together;* (76)

> *a messenger alone breaks what's well-knit;*
> *a messenger does what is needed*
> *to make enemies come to terms.*

'Your going there serves the same purpose as my going personally; the reason being this:

> *When you speak and say all that needs to be said,* (77)
> *what men of virtue deem correct,*
> *articulating well what you speak,*
> *it is as if I myself have spoken.*

'And again:

> *In brief the object of a messenger* (78)
> *is to fit words to the facts of the case,*
> *communicating as best as he can*
> *and bringing about the desired aims.*

'So, my good friend, be on your way and may this mission be a second overseer of your actions.'

As Victory started on his mission, he saw the King of Elephants coming towards that very lake, surrounded by thousands of lordly elephants whose flapping ears looked like silken pennons dancing gaily in the breeze. His whole frame tinged yellow from masses of pollen of flowering golden čampā whose tender twigs made a carpet for him to rest on, made him resemble a rain-swollen cloud streaked by flashes of lightning. His trumpeting had the deep-toned resonance of thunderbolts clashing in the rainy season and emitting fiery, scintillating gleams of lightning. Having the sheen of radiant blue lotuses veiled in their leafy sheaths, he displayed the majesty of Airāvata, the celestial tusker. His trunk was beautifully coiled to resemble the foremost lord of serpents. Honey-coloured and glistening, his two pairs of tusks, grown to their full length looked gorgeous. The round of his face with the hum of bees drawn by the heady scent of ichor trickling down the sides of his temples was most captivating.

Victory thought to himself, 'A direct encounter with this person is inadvisable for persons like myself; the reason being,

> *A tusker kills by a mere touch;* (79)
> *a serpent by a simple sniff;*
> *A king has only to smile to kill;*
> *a knave by just paying honour.*

'I should therefore find some impregnable ground to stand on before I present myself to him.' With this idea, Victory clambered on to a very high and jagged pile of rocks and called out, 'O, Lord of Elephants! I trust all is well with you.'

Hearing this greeting, the elephant-king looked carefully around and demanded, 'Pray, sir, who are you?'

'An envoy,' replied the hare.

'And who has sent you, sir?' asked the tusker.

'I come from the blessed Lord Moon,' was the reply.

'And what may your business be, sir?' asked the Lord of Elephants.

'Your Honour is aware I am sure, that an envoy coming on a mission is not to be harmed; for envoys are the mouthpieces of all rulers. As the proverb says:

> *Even if weapons are drawn, ready;* (80)
> *even if kinsmen lie slaughtered;*
> *even if the messenger prates, harsh-tongued;*
> *a king should not take his life.*

'It is by the command of Lord Moon that I say this to Your Honour: "How is it, O, mortal, that without a true reckoning of your own powers and your enemy's as well, you have chosen to indulge in violent acts against others? Have you not heard that;

> *Whoever embarks on a venture* (81)
> *in a moment of rash folly*
> *with no thought of the strengths and weaknesses,*
> *his own and those of his enemy*
> *is simply asking for trouble.*

"You have cruelly violated the sanctity of Moon Lake, celebrated because it bears my name. And there, you have slaughtered those who belong to the race of the King of Hares who is dear to me because I bear the mark[24] of that animal and hares are for that reason under my special protection. This is unbearable provocation. What! Don't you know that I am celebrated in the world as the hare-marked divinity? But what good is it to pile charges against you? I warn you; if you do not desist from such acts, you will certainly meet with dire punishment at my hands. However, if from this very day you abstain from such conduct, you will receive a special mark of distinction. Your body shall be nourished by the moonlight that is a part of me and you shall live happily in these woods with your whole retinue roaming at will. But, if you do not heed the warning, by withdrawing my cooling rays, your body and the bodies of your people will be scorched by heat and you will all perish.'"

These words filled the heart of the King of Tuskers with intense agitation. After brooding over it for a long time, he addressed Victory, 'Good friend; all this is true; I have offended the blessed Lord Moon; and in future I shall not indulge in unfriendly acts against your people. Now quickly show me the way so that I can go to the gracious moon god and ask for forgiveness.'

'Come with me then, but alone, so that I can reveal the god to you,' said Victory.

So saying the hare led the way to Moon Lake and showed King Four Tusks, the glittering, lustrous disc of the full moon, a perfect circle, complete with all its digits shedding its enchanting radiance in the dark of night. Surrounded by the planets, the Seven Sages[25] and a whole host of stars all gleaming in their splendour in the vast expanse of sky, the moon god shone reflected in all its brilliance in the waters. When Four Tusks beheld it, he said, 'Let me ritually purify myself and offer worship to the divinity.' Then he dropped his huge trunk long enough to encircle two men round the waist, into the waters which became agitated by this sudden movement; and as the moon's disc whirled around here and there in the circling ripples as if mounted on wheels, he saw a thousand moons.

Victory started back as if in great agitation and spoke to the elephant-king, 'O, lord, misery, a great misery indeed! You have doubly angered Lord Moon.'

'Why is the blessed Lord Moon angry with me now?' asked Four Tusks.

'For touching this water,' was Victory's pat reply. Hearing this poor Four Tusks, with drooping ears, bent low down to touch the earth with his forehead and humbly begged the moon for forgiveness. And again addressing Victory he pleaded, 'My good friend, in all other matters also, request the blessed Lord Moon on my behalf to forgive me and bestow his grace upon me. I swear, I shall never again come here.' Saying this, Four Tusks returned the way he had come.

'And this is why I said to you, "By feigning greatly . . . " and the rest of it.

'But there is more to it. This fellow, this owl, is a mean, wicked and evil-minded chap; and also quite incapable of protecting his subjects. Not only is the protection of the people beyond his reach, there is the actual danger that you may need protection from him. For you must have heard this:

> *Engaging a scoundrel for a judge,*   (82)
> *what comfort can disputants expect?*
> *You know how both the hare and partridge*
> *perished at the hands of the cat.'*

The birds prompted by curiosity asked, 'Oh! How was that?' Then the crow began the tale of *The Cat's Judgement*.

Once in the past I lived in a certain tree. At the base of the same tree a partridge had its home. From sharing a common residence a firm friendship sprang up between the two of us. Everyday, after having our food and taken our airings, we spent the evening together sharing our diversions such as retailing witty sayings, telling each other tales and legends from old chronicles, setting each other problems to solve, posing riddles and exchanging gifts.

One day the partridge went foraging with other birds to a place where abundant rice grew ripening. But he did not return at the usual time. I was sick with worry wondering what had happened, repeatedly asking myself; 'Oh, why has my friend, the partridge not returned this evening? Has he been trapped? Has he been killed?'

Many days passed with such thoughts churning in my heart as I grieved in my loneliness, suffering the privation of separation from my friend, until one day a hare named Speedy[26] came along and went into the hollow where the partridge had nested. And I did nothing to stop him because I had lost all hope of ever seeing the partridge again.

Then, one day, the partridge, now grown nice and plump after eating a lot of rice, returned, remembering his old home. How wisely is it observed:

> *Not even in paradise* (83)
> *do living beings find the happiness*
> *they had in their own land, in their own home,*
>   *however poor and humble it was.*

When the partridge saw the hare now settled comfortably in his old home he chided him bitterly. 'Hey there, you hare; you have done a mean thing in occupying my home. Come now, get out, leave at once.' To which the hare replied, 'You bumbling fool! Don't you know that a residence belongs to its current occupant?'

'Is that so?' retorted the partridge. 'Let us go and ask our neighbours; for it is stated in the lawbooks:

> *Where pools, ponds, wells, houses* (84)
>   *and groves are concerned,*
> *the neighbour's testimony holds good:*
>   *that is Manu's dictum.*

'Moreover:

> *Wherever a dispute arises* (85)
> *over land, house, well, grove or field,*

the claim will always be settled
on the testimony of a neighbour.'

'Oh, you blockhead,' retorted the hare: 'And have you not heard what the precedent laid down in memorial law says?

Any place occupied personally   (86)
by one for ten years successively
belongs to him, legal texts
and eyewitness, notwithstanding.

'And further, you fool; you don't seem to have any knowledge of Nārada's opinion:

In the case of men   (87)
title to possession
is ten years occupation:
    in the case of birds
    and four-footed creatures,
    mere current habitation.

'So, even if this was your home, the fact is that it was unoccupied when I moved in. Therefore it is mine and mine alone.'

'Really?' exclaimed the partridge, 'So you take the laws of tradition as authoritative, do you? Well, then, come with me and let us go and consult the experts on the laws of tradition. Let them decide as to whether this residence is yours or mine.'

'Very well,' said the hare. And both set off to seek adjudication of their claim. I too possessed by eager curiosity followed them, thinking, 'Now let us see what happens next.'

They had not gone too far when the hare asked the partridge, 'Listen, my good fellow; tell me who will pass judgement in our dispute?'

'Certainly,' replied the partridge, 'On the sandy banks of the sacred river Gaṅgā whose waters murmur melodiously with the sound of waves jostling and clashing as her waters are swept by strong breezes, there dwells a cat named Curd Ear[27] who sits there unshaken in the observance of strict vows of penance and self-restraint. He is one possessed of great compassion for all living things. We shall go to him.'

However, when the hare saw the cat his innermost being shrank in fear and he blurted out, 'Oh! no, no; let us have nothing to do with this scurvy knave. You know the proverb:

> *Never trust the rogue who sits pretending* (88)
> *to be absorbed in severe penance;*
> *you see them around in places of pilgrimage*
> *fake-ascetics gorging themselves with food.'*

When he heard these words, Curd Ear, who was dissembling only to follow an easy way of making a livelihood, prepared to instil confidence in the minds of his visitors. Standing upon his hindlegs with his forelegs raised up to the sky and eyes closed, he faced the sun directly and steadfastly; and the better to deceive the visitors with a display of a holy and virtuous cast of mind, he delivered the following moral discourse: 'Alas! Alas! How vain and unprofitable are the things of this world! How fragile and transitory is life! Like dreams are our relationships with those who are dear to us. Illusory like a magician's tricks are family and possessions. No way of escape there is except the path of the Law.[28] As the saying goes:

> *The man whose days come and go* (89)
> *undistinguished by righteousness*
> *is like a blacksmith's bellows:*
>   *he breathes but does not live.*

'Moreover:

> *Learning divested of righteousness* (90)
> *is as useful as the tail of a cur*
> *that neither covers his nakedness*
> *nor serves to whisk off fleas and gnats.*

> *As chaff among grain* (91)
> *and bat among birds;*

293

as gnat among mortal things
are those who do not perceive
>*the Law as the Prime Cause.*

Better than a tree are its flowers and fruit; (92)
better than curds is butter held to be;
>*better than the oilcake is the oil indeed;*
>*better than worldly concerns is the Law.*

Firmness in all deeds is extolled (93)
>*by experts on right policy;*
many are the hurdles that beset
>*the rapid course of the Law.*

Why drag it out at great length (94)
when the Law is stated concisely as follows:
>*virtue lies in helping others;*
>*evil in injuring them.'*

Having listened to the cat's moral discourse, the hare exclaimed, 'Hey! Friend Partridge; on this river-bank stands a holy person expounding the Law; let us ask him.'

'Don't forget that he is our natural enemy,' replied the partridge. 'Let us stand at a distance and question him.'

So they both began to question the cat. 'O, learned ascetic and instructor in the Law,' they began, 'There is a dispute between us; so give us your judgement based on your knowledge of the Law. Whichever of us is speaking falsely can be your food.'

'Perish the thought,' replied the cat, 'Pray, don't say such things. The very thought of cruelty to others makes me shrink in abhorrence; for it leads straight to perdition. As it has been said:

As kindness is the Law's prior command, (95)
>*be devoted to universal good;*
>*protect even stinging insects*
>*such as the gad-fly, louse and bug.*

He who injures even beasts of prey (96)

he too is deemed merciless
    and plunges into a terrible hell:
what to speak of those who harm the harmless!

'As for those who slay animals in sacrificial rites, they are indeed misguided for they do not understand the true meaning of the sacred texts. When a text says "Sacrifice goats—*ajah*—" what is really meant in that context is rice grains seven years old, grain that is not gone—*a-jah*—not used up. It is not "goats" that are meant; the etymology of the word makes that quite clear. And how apt is the saying:

By cutting trees and slaying animals,   (97)
by fighting wars that create bloody slime,
if this is the way men go to Heaven,
who in that case goes to Hell?

'Therefore, I shall eat nobody. However as I am rather old I cannot tell the difference between your voices quite clearly from a distance. In that case how can I declare who wins and who loses? In view of this, please do come closer to me and ask me for my judgement, so that I can understand the facts in dispute and pronounce a judgement that will not obstruct my gaining the other world. As the saying goes:

If a man decides unjustly   (98)
    through pride or through greed,
through anger or through fear
    he goes straight to hell.

A wrong judgement over a goat   (99)
    is like killing five;
a wrong judgement over a cow
    is like killing ten;
a wrong judgement over a maiden
    is like killing a hundred;
a wrong judgement over a man
    is like killing a thousand.

'Therefore have complete trust in me and explain everything clearly, standing close to my ear.'

To cut the story short that knave of a cat succeeded in thoroughly bamboozling those two creatures. And then, when the hare and the partridge drew close to him, he seized them both simultaneously, one with his paw and the other in his saw-toothed jaws. And so were both creatures killed and eaten.

'And therefore I say to you, "Having engaged a knave for a judge . . . " and so on. Similarly, you too, sirs, who are blind by night, by making this knave your ruler will go the same way as the hare and the partridge. Reflect on it and then do whatever you think is right.'

The birds after listening to the words of the crow, talked among themselves, 'Yes, he does speak wisely; so let us meet again some other time and hold consultations on the matter of choosing a king.' So saying they dispersed and each went his own way. Only the owl who was blind by day was left sitting on the throne with his consort, awaiting his coronation. He called out, 'Hey there, hallo! Who is out there? Why has the coronation ceremony not begun as yet?' At this his consort spoke: 'Dear lord! This crow here has found a way to obstruct your coronation. The birds are all gone, flown in all directions as they pleased. Only the crow is hanging around for some reason or other. Now rise quickly and let me take you home.'

Hearing his wife's words, the owl, filled with deep disappointment, addressed the crow, 'O, you black-hearted fiend! What harm have I done you that you have prevented my coronation? Because of this action of yours, from this moment there shall be enmity between us. As the saying goes:

Pierced by arrows (100)
cut down by the hatchet,
a forest heals and again grows.
But what words cruelly hew,
cutting, abhorrent,
never heals to put forth shoots anew.'

While the owl and his wife went home, the crow, wise after

the event, reflected: 'Alas! Alas! By speaking in this manner I have incurred great enmity for no good reason. For as we have heard:

> *Words spoken without a reason,* (101)
> *without due regard to place and time*
> *and benefit in the future;*
> *words unpleasant that serve to lower*
> *one's own self in others' estimation*
>   *are not words but simply poison.*

'Therefore:

> *Though endowed with strength and power,* (102)
> *if he is wise, a man will not on his own*
>   *make an enemy of another.*
> *What man of sense for no reason*
> *goes and swallows poison thinking:*
>   *'Why not, I have a physician'!*

> *A person with sense and good feeling* (103)
> *should never defame others in public*
> *and make statements that cause distress,*
>   *even if they happen to be true.*

'Besides:

> *Wealth and glory dwells with the man* (104)
> *who acts after careful deliberation*
> *more than once with trusted friends;*
> *and after pondering deeply over the actualities.'*

Having reflected thus, the crow flew away.

'So, my son,' resumed Live Firm, 'this is the history of our feud with the owls.'

'Father, under the circumstances, what do you think we should do?' asked Cloud Hue.

To which Live Firm answered: 'Even under such circumstances, there is an alternative other than the six classic expedients. I

shall adopt that and myself lead the way to victory. By deceiving
the enemy, I shall put them in a vulnerable position where they
could be destroyed easily. As the story goes:

> *The crafty rogues, quick-witted,* (105)
> *swaggering in their strength, outwitted*
>   *the Brāhmaṇa with the goat.'*

'And how did that happen?' asked Cloud Hue. Then Live
Firm began the tale of *The Brāhmaṇa and his Goat*.

In a certain settlement a Brāhmaṇa named Mitra Śarma lived
persevering to keep the Sacred Fire alive. Once, in the month of
February on a day when a light breeze was blowing and the rain
fell gently from an overcast sky, he walked to another village to
beg for a sacrificial victim. Approaching a certain rich man he
said, 'O, sacrificer[29] I am performing a sacrifice this coming new
moon: so gift me an animal to offer as sacrifice.' And the man
gifted Mitra Śarma a plump animal as laid down in the ritual
texts. Mitra Śarma put the animal through its paces to check that
it was healthy and then lifting it on to his shoulders started
walking back briskly to his home town. On the way, three
dyed-in-the-wool rogues, who were famished, came walking
towards him. When they saw the plump animal being carried on
the Brāhmaṇa's shoulders they whispered among themselves,
'Hey, look; if we could only dine off this plump creature we could
stave off today's biting chill. Come, let's play a trick on this chap,
take his animal and protect ourselves against the cold.'

So one of them stepped off the road, changed his clothes and
coming out from a bylane stopped the Brāhmaṇa[30] and
addressed him thus, 'Oh, sir! Keeper of the Holy Fire! What is
this ridiculous and unconventional thing you are doing? Why are
you carrying a dog, an unclean creature on your shoulders?
Surely you are familiar with the saying:

> *A dog, a cock, a hangman, all three* (106)

> *are equally defiling, so it is held;*
> *a camel especially and an ass;*
> > *therefore avoid any contact with them.'*

This made the Brāhmana furious. 'What?' he burst out, 'Is Your Honour blind that you call this animal a dog?'

'Pray do not lose your temper, sir; go in peace,' said the rogue and walked off.

When Mitra Śarma had gone a little further, the second rogue came up to him and exclaimed 'Oh! Misery, misery! What is this, Your Holiness. This dead calf may have been the apple of your eye; still, isn't it highly improper to carry it on your shoulders? We all know what the purification rites for such defilement are:

> *For the fool who is defiled by the touch* (107)
> > *of the corpse of a beast or a man,*
> > *purification is twofold:*
> > *the use of the cow's five products,*[31]
> > *and observance of the lunar fast.'*[32]

And now the Brāhmana spoke in anger: 'What? Is Your Honour blind to call this animal a calf?'

'Oh! Please do not be angry, Your Holiness,' replied the rogue, 'I spoke through ignorance. Do as you please, sir.'

As the Brāhmana walked a little further, the third rogue having changed his clothes came in front of him and said, 'Oho! What gross impropriety! Carrying an ass on your shoulders, sir! It is said:

> *The man who touches an ass knowingly* (108)
> > *or out of ignorance may be,*
> *is instructed to have a ritual-bath*
> > *fully-clothed, to be rid of defilement.*

'Drop this animal at once, sir, before anyone else sees you.'

The poor Brāhmana concluded that the animal was in reality

299

a demon. He dropped the creature precipitately on the ground and in great fear ran home as fast as his legs could carry him.

And as for those three rogues, they met as planned and picking up the goat carried out the purpose they had in mind.

'Therefore, I say to you: "crafty rogues quick-witted . . . " and the rest of it. And is it not wisely said:

> There's no man in this world who is not duped   (109)
>   by the cheerful efforts of new servants to serve;
> by flattering praise of visitors or of guests;
>   by the crocodile tears of wanton women,
> and the voluble speech of confidence men.

'Moreover, one should not invite the enmity of the weak if they form a crowd. As we have heard:

> You should not pit your strength against a mob;   (110)
>   It is hard to win against the masses;
> the little red ants killed and ate the great snake
>   in spite of all his twisting and twitching.

And Cloud Hue exclaimed, 'Oh! Really? And how was that?' Then Live Firm began the tale of *The Ants who killed the Snake*.

In a certain anthill lived an enormous black snake named Haughty. One day instead of following the usual path he attempted to crawl out of his hide-out through a very narrow crevice. Because his body was so huge and the crevice so narrow and because Fate willed it to be so, he suffered a gash in his body as he was wriggling out. The smell of the blood oozing from the wound drew a whole host of small red ants to that spot. They surrounded the poor snake from all sides and their assaults on his body tormented him beyond all endurance. He thrashed around killing many and crushing many more. But they were such a large and formidable force that they stung him all over until his body was a mass of wounds; and Haughty died.

'This is why I advised you saying, "Do not pit your

strength . . . " and so on. There is one more thing I have to tell you, my lord; listen carefully, ponder over what I say and then carry it out.'

Cloud Hue replied reverentially, 'Yes, Father, do tell me what is on your mind.'

And Live Firm replied, 'Pay attention, my son; I have figured out a fifth expedient that is superior to the four classic expedients of statecraft such as peaceful negotiations and the rest. And it is this: adopt a hostile attitude towards me, threaten me in the harshest terms, smear my body with blood—which you have to procure from somewhere—and then throw me down to the base of this tree; all this in a convincing manner so that the enemy's spies are deceived. Then, you fly off to Antelope Hill with your whole retinue and stay there until such time as I have done everything in my power to gain the confidence of our enemies. Having done that I shall discover the heart of their stronghold and kill them: for as we know, owls are daytime-blind. This plan works on the assumption that their fortress must be of simple construction lacking a rear exit for escape. As the wise point out:

> *Experts in statecraft call a fortress* (111)
> *a stronghold possessing an escape route.*
> *A fortress lacking means of escape*
> *is but a euphemism for a trap.*

'And listen to me, my son; feel no pity for me; as it is well put:

> *Care for your retainers,* (112)
> *pamper them all you can,*
> > *consider them dear,*
> > *dear as your very life;*
> *but once the battle is begun*
> *regard them as so much dry tinder.*

'There is another thing I shall mention; pray do not try and dissuade me: for:

> *A king ought always to protect his men* (113)

301

> *as he would his own precious life;*
> *cherish them, nourish them each day*
> *as he would his own dear person;*
> *And all that against that one day*
> *when he joins battle with a foe.'*

With these words, Live Firm started a mock quarrel with his king. Seeing him ranting and raving at his king in such an unbridled fashion, the rest of the royal retainers rose up ready to despatch the offending minister when the King of the Crows restrained them saying, 'No, no, get out of my way all of you; leave; I shall punish this scoundrel myself; teach this evil-hearted traitor who has gone over to the enemy's side, a lesson.'

Having firmly checked his men, Cloud Hue then jumped peremptorily on to Live Firm's back. He pecked him lightly all over, smeared blood on him that he had already procured, threw him down and then set off as instructed for Antelope Hill with all his retinue.

At this juncture, the Queen of the Owls who had been acting as a spy saw what had happened and flew off to her lord to report in detail the misfortune that had befallen Cloud Hue's minister and the ensuing flight of the crows. As it was now sunset, the owl-king was already preparing to set out on a crow-slaughtering mission with his retinue.

When he heard what his queen had to say, he exclaimed with great glee, 'Well, well, hurry fellows, hurry up; it is solely through meritorious actions done, that a person has the good fortune of coming upon an enemy in flight: as we have all heard:

> *An enemy fleeing*   (114)
> *first hands you the opening*
> *you seek on a silver tray;*
> *next, seeking shelter elsewhere,*
> *in a dreadful scare,*
> *the royal retainers all in disarray,*
>   *to have him in your grasp*
>   *is simply child's play.'*

302

Urged on by the words of their king all the owls set out in the direction of the banyan tree. When they arrived there not a single crow was to be seen. King Foe Crusher with great satisfaction alighted on a branch of the tree and as his bards began their songs of praise in his honour, he spoke thus to his retainers, 'Hey there, fellows! Find out their line of retreat. Whichever route they might have taken they are all now finished for good, for I shall be at their heels in hot pursuit; and so long as they do not gain sanctuary in some fort, I shall surely kill them.'

At this point, Live Firm began to reflect thus; 'Now, if these enemies having got wind of what we have done simply return the way they came, then nothing would have been accomplished. For as the saying goes:

The first mark of intelligence (115)
   is to leave things well alone;
the second mark of intelligence
   is to see to its proper end what is begun.

'It is better not to undertake a project than have it fail right at the beginning. I think I had better call out and let them know I am here.'

Deciding on this line of action, Live Firm started cawing in the feeblest manner possible; and hearing him caw, the owls prepared to kill him.

'Alas! Alas!' lamented Live Firm at this point, 'Look at me; here I am, King Cloud Hue's minister, reduced by him to this miserable plight. Go and inform your king that I have much to say to him.'

Advised of this by his retainers, the King of Owls came close to Live Firm and seeing him covered with bloody gashes exclaimed in utter amazement, 'Oh, sir! What is this? How come you are in such a pitiable state? What happened? Tell me.'

'Ah! My lord,' replied Live Firm, 'Pray listen to me. Last evening, seeing a large number of crows slaughtered by you and your men, Cloud Hue was driven to distraction with great anger and grief; and the evil-hearted rascal was all set to pursue you to your fortress. Seeing that, I remonstrated with him, pointing out the facts, "No, no, Your Majesty," I said, "Do not proceed to their stronghold, for they are all very powerful and we are weak. As it is wisely said:

> If he values his own good, the weak man (116)
> will never contemplate a hostile act
> against an enemy exceeding strong,
> an act certain to be his utter ruin
> as a moth's that flies into a flame,
> while his foe of great power remains unscathed.

"Therefore, my lord, your best bet is to sue for peace, offering the enemy tribute." Hearing my words of advice and incited by evil-minded counsellors, Cloud Hue, suspecting me of being in your pay, reduced me to this plight. So, my lord, your royal feet are now my sole refuge. As long as I am capable of some movement I shall serve you by leading Your Majesty to Cloud Hue's whereabouts and thus bring about the destruction of all the crows.'

Hearing Live Firm speak thus, King Foe Crusher thought it best to consult his ministers who had served in succession his grandfather and father. There were five of them named: Red Eye, Fierce Eye, Flame Eye, Hook Nose and Rampart Ear.[33]

The owl-king turned first to Red Eye and addressed him courteously, 'Noble sir! What is to be done in the circumstances?'

'Why stop to think at all, Your Majesty,' replied Red Eye. 'Kill this fellow without the least compunction. For, as the saying goes:

> Kill a foe when he is down (117)
> before he grows in strength;
> Once he gains his fullest vigour
> he will become invincible.

'And further, my lord, you know what the world says: "If Lady

Fortune comes a-wooing and you turn her down, she will fall to cursing." It is also said that:

> *The right moment comes once only*   (118)
> *for him who waits for it eagerly.*
> *To find the moment once again,*
> *to do the thing you wish to do,*
>   *that is by no means easy.*

'We have also heard this; as the snake said:

> *Look at the blazing pyre*   (119)
> *and look at my battered hood;*
> *Love once broken, then glued together—*
> *what oil or balm can make it grow and thrive!'*

'Ah!' said King Foe Crusher, 'How did that happen?' Then Red Eye began the tale of *The Serpent who paid in gold.*

In a certain settlement lived a Brāhmana who however hard he tried his hand at farming found all his labour a fruitless waste of time. Now one day at the close of summer, exhausted by the heat, he lay down in the shade of the tree standing right in the middle of his field. Not far off was an anthill and as the Brāhmana looked towards it, he saw rearing on top of it an awesome sight, a fierce snake with a fully expanded hood. As he watched it, he reflected, 'Aha! That is the reason for it all. This snake is certainly the divinity that guards this field and I have never once offered it due rites of worship. And that is why all my toiling in this field turns out fruitless. So, today, I should pay it my respects and offer worship.'

With such thoughts in his mind he went and begged for some milk, poured it into a clay bowl and coming close to the anthill, addressed the snake. 'Oh! Guardian of the Field! All this time I have not been aware that you resided at this spot. Only for that reason have I been remiss of my duties and not paid you your

due rites of worship. Forgive me, I beg of you.' And with these
words he offered the snake the bowl of milk and went home.

The next morning the Brāhmaṇa came to the field and what
did he see but a gold coin nestling in the clay bowl. From that day
on he always went alone to the anthill to offer the snake milk
every day; and each day he was rewarded with a gold coin.

One day the Brāhmaṇa, who had to go to the neighbouring
town on business, instructed his son to take the bowl of milk to
the anthill. The boy did as he was instructed and placing the bowl
of milk went home.

The next morning when he went to the field, he noticed the
gold coin in the bowl; and he thought to himself; 'Ah! this anthill
is chock-full of gold coins; I am certain of it. So why don't I kill
this snake and take all the coins?'

With this intention, while offering the snake milk the next
morning, he fetched a hefty blow on its hood with the wooden
cudgel he had brought with him. But it was Fate's will that the
snake should not lose its life. Instead, it dug its sharp fangs into
the boy's flesh with venomous fury and bit him so hard that he
died instantly. His relatives found him and having built a funeral
pyre not far from the field, they cremated him with proper rites.

When the father returned the next day, his kinsfolk informed
him of how his son had died and been cremated. Reflecting
deeply on what had happened he spoke these lines:

> *He who shows no compassion for living things,* (120)
> *who grabs instead that which seeks sanctuary,*
> *is certain to lose all that he possesses*
> *as did the wild geese that lived in Lotus Lake.'*

'Oh! Did they really? And how was that?' asked the
Brāhmaṇa's kinsfolk. And then the Brāhmaṇa began the tale of
The Golden Geese of Lotus Lake.

In a certain kingdom lived a king by the name of Bright Chariot[34] who possessed a lake named Lotus Lake which his warriors guarded with the greatest care, for it abounded with golden, wild geese that paid the king the tribute of one tail-feather apiece, every six months.

Now, it happened that a great bird, all golden, flew into that lake one day. At once the wild geese spoke sharply to it saying, 'Look here, you have no right to come here and live in our midst, because we live in this lake by right of giving the king a gift of one golden tail-feather apiece once in six months.' And they went on in this manner. To make it brief, soon, a raging dispute rose between the two parties.

The great bird now sought the king's presence to plead for his intercession. 'Lord,' it began, 'this is what the birds in your lake say: "Go, we shall not give you an inch of space here to stay. What can the king do to us?" Then I answered them, lord, and said this, "It is not right that you speak so discourteously. I shall go and complain to the king." Now it is for His Majesty to make his decision.'

The king summoned his attendants and commanded them as follows: 'Fellows! Go; kill all those birds in the lake and bring them to me without delay.'

Receiving the royal command, the attendants left at once and set out for the lake. Seeing the king's men come marching, cudgel in hand, one ancient wild goose spoke as follows: 'Well, my dear kinsfolk; this is not at all a pleasant prospect. So, let us all be of one mind and fly away altogether.' The wild geese did precisely that.

'Therefore I say to you, "He who shows no compassion for living things . . . " and the rest of it.' Having said this the Brāhmana left.

Early the next morning he went with the bowl of milk to the anthill and in order to regain the snake's trust, called out, 'It was through his own fault that my son met his death.'

And the snake answered him thus:

'Look at the blazing pyre,   (121)
and look at my battered hood;

307

Love once broken, then glued together—
what oil or balm can make it grow and thrive!'

'Once the crow is put to death, then Your Majesty will without any effort on your part enjoy your realm, rid of all its thorns.'

Foe Crusher having listened to the advice of Minister Red Eye, turned to Fierce Eye, 'So, good sir, what is *your* opinion on this matter?' To which the minister replied, 'My lord; what my honourable friend here has just spoken strikes me as merciless, the reason being that a person seeking sanctuary ought not to be killed. You know the fable, my lord, that puts the moral excellently:

> *The dove it's told welcomed the enemy*　　　　(122)
> *who came humbly pleading for sanctuary;*
> > *offered him all guest-rites customary*
> > *and furthermore, his own flesh as a meal.'*

'Really? How was that?' asked Foe Crusher with interest. And then Fierce Eye began the tale of *The Dove who sacrificed himself*.

> *A fowler of fierce aspect, forbidding,*　　　　(123)
> *Death incarnate to every living thing,*
> *roamed wide the great forests, pursuing*
> > *his nefarious doings.*
> *No friend he had to call his own, no kin*　　　　(124)
> *by blood or by marriage;*
> *shunned by one and all for his deeds, savage.*

And is it not so, that:

> *Those vile and venomous who strike terror*　　　　(125)
> *into the heart of every single creature,*
> *killers, they truly become like serpents cruel.*
> *Each day, without fail, armed with cage and cudgel,*　　　　(126)
> > *with snares, traps and ropes as well,*
> > *this executioner universal*
> > *would frequent the great forests.*

One day the fowler in the forest prowling,   (127)
saw the skies grow dark with rain clouds menacing;
a mighty storm raged and roared, catapulting
    fierce torrents of rain pelting:
it seemed the end of the world was coming.
His heart shuddered and twisted with terror;   (128)
his limbs would not stop trembling; the cruel fowler
groped his way searching wildly for some shelter,
to one of the great lords of the forest.
He cowered for a while under that great tree;   (129)
the stars shone bright as the skies cleared suddenly.
A ray of wisdom glimmering, he spoke softly:
'O divinities! You are my sanctuary.'

A turtle dove who lived in a hollow   (130)
in the tree-trunk sat drowned in deepest sorrow;
not seeing his dear wife for a long time,
he began lamenting in mournful rhyme.

'O! What a terrible rainstorm!   (131)
And my sweet love has not come home;
deprived of her dear presence, how
deserted seems my house right now.
A house is no home; where the wife stays,   (132)
that is called home as the proverb says;
what is a house without its mistress?
To me it is simply a wilderness.
A virtuous and devoted wife   (133)
whose husband is her very life
Whose sole joy is his well-being—
the man who can boast of such a wife,
to him life is indeed a blessing.'

Trapped in the murderous fowler's cage   (134)
the female dove heard her husband's words,
    filled with such grief and tenderness.
    She thrilled with supreme happiness.
And then she spoke the following words.

'No woman deserves the name of wife   (135)
who brings no happiness in her husband's life;
   when the husband is pleased
   all the gods too are pleased.
Let her be burnt to ashes entire   (136)
like a blossoming vine by forest-fire;
the woman who does not make her husband happy.'

And she continued in a nobler strain:

'Pray, pay heed, my beloved, to what I speak   (137)
for I speak only what is for your good.
Protect always the suppliant at your feet
even at the cost of your own dear life.
Here lies this bird-catcher at your doorstep,   (138)
seeking shelter, stricken by cold and hunger.
Pray welcome him and attend to his needs.

'As we have heard:

Whoever honours not as best as he can   (139)
the guest who arrives at sunset, loses
the merit entire of his virtuous acts
and takes the burden of the other's sins.
Harbour no grudge towards him, my lord, thinking: (140)
'Ha! This man has snared and bound my beloved.'
Snared I am by my own misdeeds and bound
with the fetters of acts done in former lives.

'And so it is:

Poverty and sickness, sorrow and bondage   (141)
and diverse calamities, these are all
the fruits of the tree of their own misdeeds
that all living beings commit constantly.
Abandoning therefore all thoughts of hate   (142)
welling up by reason of my captivity,
fix your mind on virtue, on the path of duty;
offer this man the prescribed hospitality.'

The dove heard her speak; her words flowing (143)
    from living goodness and virtue practised.
Heartened, he boldly hopped down from the tree,
    approached the bird-catcher and addressed him thus:

'A warm and sincere welcome to you, sir! (144)
    what service can I do for you; tell me.
Feel at ease, consider yourself at home.'
These kind words of the turtle dove brought forth (145)
    this cold reply from that murderer of birds.
    'I am chilled to my bones, indeed, O dove!
    Do something to protect me from the frost.'

The dove flew off; he returned with lingering (146)
    embers of a forest-fire; and soon
in a bed of dry leaves he kindled a fire.

'Come, come warm your limbs freely, have no fear. (147)
But alas! I have no means whatsoever,
to still your hunger-pains,' said the turtle dove.
'One man maintains a thousand, another (148)
a hundred men, yet another ten men.
But I, with little merit to my credit
can barely maintain my puny little self.
What use is it leading the householder's[35] life (149)
fraught with a million hardships and sorrows
if one lacks the wherewithal to feed even
one single guest who comes to one's door?
Let me therefore dispose of this body (150)
racked by sorrow, so that never again
need I say with shame, "I have nothing"
to a needy guest who comes to my door.'

Himself he blamed, that noble dove; no word (151)
harsh did he utter against that fowler.
Only he said, 'Wait just a little while,
I may yet satisfy your need, my friend.'
And then that magnanimous soul, thrilling (152)
inwardly with rapture went right round the fire
    and entered it as if it were his home.

Seeing the poor dove plunge into the fire, (153)
tortured by searing pity, the fowler
    spoke these words:

'The man who does evil (154)
can have no love for himself, that's for sure.
One eats the fruit all by oneself
of evil done by one's own self.
I am nothing if not evil-minded, (155)
one who always delights in evil deeds.
It is certain that I am headed
for the deepest and most terrible hell.
By offering me, evil beyond compare, (156)
his own flesh for food, this high-minded dove
has held up a mirror for me to see
a reflection in reverse of myself.
So, from this day on I'll make my body (157)
deprived of all its comforts, dry up
like tiny pools of water in summer's heat.
Cold, wind and heat I shall endure, (158)
grow gaunt of face and frame, unkempt,
keeping many different fasts; thus,
I shall walk Virtue's highest road.'

Then the fowler broke his cudgel, (159)
and stick; his nets and cage as well.
    And the forlorn female dove
    he released from captivity.
Freed by the fowler, the dove in horror (160)
beheld her lord burning in the fire.
Her heart was gripped by sorrow and fear;
    desolated, she began to lament.

'O! My dearest love! Without you (161)
    I have nothing left to live for.
Bereft of her husband, forlorn,
    what profits it a woman to live.

Self-respect, the esteem of others,   (162)
a sense of one's own identity,
pride of birth, honour paid by one's kin,
authority over servants
command of dependants;
all vanish with widowhood.'

Lamenting thus most piteously,   (163)
    over and over again
    in immeasurable sorrow,
that virtuous wife walked straight ahead
    into that blazing fire.

Then clad in garments celestial,   (164)
    adorned with gems and jewels divine
the turtle-dove beheld her lord
    seated in a chariot divine.

He too having assumed a form divine   (165)
    spoke these words enshrining highest truth:
        'Joy! O joy indeed!
        My gracious lady!
Oh! What an admirable deed
is this you have done in following me!

As many hairs grow on human body   (166)
    three crores and a half, that many
years shall those wives live in the World of Light[36]
    who follow their husbands in death.'

Thus transported with joy the saintly dove helped his wife to mount the chariot, clasped her in an embrace and lived happily with her. As for the fowler, he was sunk in the deepest despondency. Setting his face towards death, he entered the great forest.

There, he saw a great forest-fire blazing.   (167)
All desires extinguished he entered it.
His moral blemishes all burnt away,
    he rejoiced as an immortal would
    in the World of Light.

'And hence, I say to you, "We hear of the turtle dove . . ."'
and the rest of it.' Having heard the tale, King Foe Crusher, now
turned to his third minister, Flame Eye, and asked him, 'Now,
what is Your Honour's opinion, as things stand at this moment.'
The minister answered thus:

> *She who constantly shrank from me*   (168)
>   *Now clasps me in close embrace.*
> *O! Benefactor! May you be blessed!*
>   *Take what you will of mine.*

'To which the thief's reply was:

> *Nothing worth taking of yours I see,*   (169)
> *if sometime there should be a thing*
> *worth taking, I'll come for it, you bet;*
>   *but not if she will closely cling.'*

'Who is she who will not embrace? And who is this thief?'
asked Foe Crusher. 'I'd like to hear this tale in all its detail.' And
Flame Eye then began the tale of *Old Man, Young Wife*.

In a certain town there once lived an old merchant named
Lovesick.[37] So besotted with love's passion was he that when his
wife died, he straight away married the young daughter of a very
poor merchant, paying a great deal of money for her. But the poor
girl was so heart-broken that she could not even bear to look at
the old merchant; which was quite predictable:

> *When Age places its frosty foot*   (170)
>   *upon a man's head*
>   *turning his hair all white,*
> *that itself marks it the fittest place*
>   *for his disgrace.*
> *For young women shun him and flee*
>   *miles away, as if he were*

> the hangman's hollow, chock-full
>> of fragments of whitening bones.

And furthermore:

> When the body is shrivelled (171)
>> and the steps falter;
> when the teeth are decayed
>> and the face smeared with slobber;
> when the sight fails
>> and the figure is no longer trim;
> then, kinsfolk find no time for conversation,
> and the wife pays scant attention;
> even the son despises the man
>> overcome by old age, alas!

One day as the young girl lay in the marriage bed with her face averted, a thief happened to enter the house. Seeing the thief the girl became mortally afraid and embraced her husband closely, clinging to him. He on his part, was taken completely by surprise. His whole body thrilled with pleasure as he reflected, 'Amazing, this . . . what makes this girl embrace me tonight, hey?'

Then peering around, he noticed the thief skulking in one of the corners of the bedchamber. 'Ah!' he exclaimed, 'I see now what it all is. My wife clings to me in fear of this thief and for no other reason, I bet.'

Seeing how matters stood, the old merchant called out to the thief, thus:

> 'She who always shrank from me (172)
>> now clasps me in her close embrace.
> Oh! Benefactor of mine! Blessed may you be!
>> Take what you will of mine.'

To this, the thief's reply was:

> 'Nothing of yours I see worth taking, sir: (173)

if sometime there is a thing worth taking
I shall be back for it, you bet,
but not if she should closely cling.'

'So, an advantage, even if it is provided only by a thief, has value; so much the better if it comes through a suppliant seeking sanctuary.

'And besides, when we consider how grossly mistreated this fellow has been by his own people, we can expect him to work zealously for our prosperity; or perhaps reveal to us their weak points. For these reasons, I recommend that his life be spared.'

Having listened carefully to these arguments, Foe Crusher turned to another of his ministers, the Honourable Hook Nose.

'My gracious friend, what do you think ought to be done in the present situation?' he asked.

And Hook Nose responded warmly, 'Ah! My lord, on no account should this fellow be killed, the reason being:

Even enemies at times might do one some good, (174)
especially if discord springs up in their midst.
The robber granted the gift of life
and the fierce demon, a pair of cows.'

'Ah! And how did that happen?' asked Foe Crusher with interest. And Hook Nose then began the tale of *The Brāhmana, the Robber and the Demon.*

In a certain settlement there lived a Brāhmana in abject poverty, surviving solely on gifts made by donors on festive and other occasions. His life was one of total privation; deprived of fine clothes and adornments, precious oils and ointments, perfumes and garlands, scented betel, creams and so on; in fact he lacked all the good things of life. From enduring heat and cold and rain, his frame had grown gaunt and covered with rough, bristling hair. The hair on his head and his beard were long and unkempt; his nails had grown long and horny.

Some kind person taking pity on the poor Brāhmana had once gifted him two little calves. From the time these creatures were tiny, the Brāhmana had tended them with affectionate care; feeding them melted butter, sesame oil, grass and other nourishing fodder that he had got by begging, until, in no time they grew sleek and plump.

A certain robber happening to notice these fine animals thought immediately, 'I shall steal this pair of fine cows from this Brāhmana.'

He set to work on the idea. He got hold of a rope and at night he set out towards the Brāhmana's house. Halfway, he met a fellow who had a row of pointed teeth set with wide gaps between them and a high-bridged nose and hollowed-out cheeks. He was cross-eyed to boot; his body was tawny in colour like a blazing fire amply fed with butter and looked as if it had been strung together with knotted veins and sinews.

Trembling horribly with terror, the robber quavered, 'Who might Your Honour be?'

'I? I am the demon-spirit[38] of a dead Brāhmana who had led an execrably evil life. My name is True Speech.[39] Now it is your turn, Your Honour, to introduce yourself,' answered the demon.

'A robber, sir,' the man replied, 'At your service, sir; one delighting in acts of cruelty. Right now, I am on my way to a poor Brāhmana's place, to steal his pair of cows.'

The demon felt greatly relieved hearing this and said to the robber, 'Oh, my friend; I am one of those who eats only every sixth meal.[40] So I might as well make a meal of that same Brāhmana you mentioned. The arrangement seems to be working out beautifully, I think, since we appear to be headed in the same direction and for an identical purpose.'

They proceeded together to the house of the poor Brāhmana and hid in a secluded corner waiting for the proper time to carry out their evil designs. When the Brāhmana had fallen asleep, the demon, True Speech, decided it was time to come out of hiding and start on his dinner. The robber noticed his move and restrained him, saying, 'No, you don't. Oh, no, sir; this is not right, my good friend. You had better wait until I have stolen the cows and departed. Then you can go ahead and have your dinner and eat the Brāhmana.'

To which the demon retorted, 'Now look here, my good sir; supposing the sounds you make awaken the Brāhmana, what then? My enterprise would fail even before it has begun.'

At this point, the robber observed rather testily, 'On the other hand, if there is some interruption during the course of your meal; if some hindrance or other crops up, I shall not be able to make away with the pair of cows. You see that, don't you? Therefore, I shall first steal the Brāhmana's pair of cows; then you can have your dinner.'

And so, the pair of them carried on, wrangling, arguing as to who should do his thing first, each crying, 'I first, then you, I first . . . .' They made such a racket that the unholy noise woke the Brāhmana. As he sat up, the robber lost no time informing him what the demon was up to, 'Hey there! You Brāhmana! You see this demon here? He is planning to have you for his dinner tonight.' The demon at once countered with. 'This fellow here, he is a robber and what do you think he is up to? He is after your fine pair of cows.'

Hearing them both, the Brāhmana became alert to the dangers facing him. He rose at once and by meditating on his chosen deity and silently articulating the requisite incantation, he saved himself from the demon's dreadful designs. Then lifting up a stout cudgel he sent the robber packing and saved his cows.

'Therefore, I said to you, "Even enemies at times . . . " and so forth. And besides:

> *As the chronicles tell it, saintly Śibi,* (175)
> *eager to earn holy merit, offered*
> *the hawk his own flesh unhesitating,*
> *as ransom for the dove that sought refuge.*

'To slay a supplicant, my lord, is to go against the Law.'

Having ascertained Hook Nose's views, Foe Crusher then turned to Rampart Ear and asked him courteously, 'Tell me, sir, what advice does Your Honour have for me?'

'No, my lord,' answered the minister, 'This crow ought not to be slain. For by sparing his life, affection might develop between the two of you; who knows? And then you might spend pleasant hours in each other's company. As the story retails it:

> *Creatures who do not keep secret*   (176)
> *the traits that make each vulnerable,*
> *surely perish, like the two snakes whose homes*
> *were the anthill and the prince's belly.'*

Foe Crusher asked in surprise, 'Really? And how was that?' And Rampart Ear then began the tale of *The Snake in the Prince's belly*.

In a certain city there ruled a king named Shining Power whose son wasted away in every limb because a snake had made his belly its home in place of an anthill. Overcome by acute depression, the prince decided to leave home and go to some distant land. He made his home in a great temple in one of the cities of the kingdom he came to and lived by begging for alms.

The ruler of that kingdom, King Bounteous,[41] had two daughters who had just entered womanhood. One of them approached the king each morning and bowing at his feet greeted him with, 'May His Majesty be ever victorious!' while the other simply said, 'Enjoy your just desserts, Your Majesty!' This greeting finally angered the king so much that he summoned his ministers one day and said, 'Honourable Counsellors, take this princess away, for her words grate on my ears. Marry her to some foreigner and let her enjoy *her* just desserts.'

Acquiescing in the royal whim, the ministers took the princess waited upon by a mere handful of attendants, to the temple where the unfortunate prince had taken sanctuary; and they gave the princess in marriage to him.

The princess joyously accepted the ailing prince as her husband and looked upon him as a god. She accompanied him to another country. There, in one of the great cities, they found

319

a dwelling house situated at the edge of a large pond. Leaving her husband in charge of the house, the princess accompanied by her maids went to the market to buy butter and oil, salt, spices and rice and other necessary household supplies.

When the princess returned with the maids after completing all her shopping, what did she see but the prince fast asleep with his head resting against an anthill. And from his mouth emerged the hooded head of a snake taking the air. Likewise another snake had emerged from the anthill and was also taking the air.

As the two snakes confronted each other their eyes reddened with anger. The snake that had emerged from the anthill, was the first to speak. 'Oh! You vile creature! How can you torment this prince, who is so perfectly handsome, in this cruel manner?' The snake standing within the prince's mouth hissed furiously and said, 'Vile creature yourself! How can you defile those two pots filled with the magic drink, that are hidden within the anthill?'

And so, the two snakes lashing out at each other revealed each other's secrets. The anthill snake continued, 'Oh! You vile creature! Do you really believe that nobody knows the simple remedy by which you can be destroyed? That by drinking a decoction of black mustard seeds, you can be easily killed?'

The snake in the prince's belly angrily hissed back, 'Ha! And you believe that nobody knows the way to get rid of you! Why, by pouring boiling water into the anthill, you can be destroyed.'

The princess who had been listening to all this, concealed behind some bushes, now did exactly as the angry exchange between the two snakes had conveyed to her. Following the treatments that she had overheard when the snakes revealed their mutual weak points, she restored her husband to sound health and also gained great prosperity. She then set out towards her native land where she was joyously welcomed and honoured by her parents and kinsfolk. There she lived happily ever after with the prince, enjoying all the pleasures allotted to her by Destiny.

'That is why I said to you, "Creatures that do not keep secret . . . " and the rest of it, my lord,' concluded Rampart Ear.

King Foe Crusher being convinced by the arguments he had just heard followed the advice conveyed in them and spared the life of the crow Live Firm. Red Eye who had been watching it all laughed bitterly in his heart and he spoke again, thus, 'Alas! What a terrible calamity! Our lord stands ruined, completely ruined by the perverse and evil advice given by you honourable gentlemen. As the saying goes:

> *Where honour is paid to those* (177)
> *who deserve none;*
> *and those worthy of honour*
> *are contemned;*
> *there, Fear, Famine and Death, these three*
> *prevail, unabated, free.*

'Besides:

> *Before his eyes he sees a foul act done* (178)
> *yet the fool takes no offence, but is pleased.*
> *The chariot-maker bore high on his head*
> *his errant wife and paramour as well.'*

The other ministers at once chorused, 'Tell us; how did that happen?' And the Honourable Red Eye then began the tale of *The Chariot-maker cuckolded*.

In a certain settlement lived a chariot-maker whose wife was a loose woman with a bad reputation. It occurred to him once that he should put her character to the test. 'But how shall I carry it out?' he asked himself. 'We know the saying:

> *If ever fire feels cool* (179)
> *and the hare-marked god*[42] *burns;*
> *if ever knaves are good,*
> *then women will be true.*

'That she is unfaithful I know from general report. For we have heard it said:

> *What is not seen, what is not heard* (180)
> *in texts secular and sacred,*

321

if it is found anywhere in this world
people are sure to know all about it.'

Having reflected in this manner, the chariot-maker told his wife, 'Dearest, tomorrow morning I am leaving for the next town on some business which will keep me away for several days. Why don't you prepare something nice for me that I can take for the journey.'

His wife was delighted to hear this. Quickly she dropped everything she was doing and quivering with excitement started preparing delicious food that was all butter and sugar for her husband to take with him. The jingle puts the facts neatly:

> *Foul and rainy days* (181)
> *when dark, heavy clouds lowering*
> *make the city's highways*
> *dangerous for walking,*
> *are happy days*
> *for lascivious women*
> *with heavy hips swinging,*
> *whose husbands are journeying*
> *in far-off places.*

The chariot-maker left his house early next morning. Having made sure that her husband had left, the woman, her face all wreathed in smiles, spent a good part of the day beautifying herself. Then she went to the house of a former lover and said, 'Listen, that scurvy knave, my husband, has left town on some business. When everyone is asleep, you can come to my house.' And it was all arranged.

In the meantime, the chariot-maker who had spent all day in the forest, returned home at dark and quietly slipped into his house by a side door. He entered the bedchamber and crawling under the bedstead, lay still.

At this point, the lover, Devadatta, also entered the chariot-maker's house and got into bed. Seeing the fellow in his bed, the chariot-maker's heart burned with anger; furious thoughts raced through his mind. 'Shall I get up and kill this fellow, right this very moment?' he asked himself, 'Or, shall I wait till they are in each other's embrace and engrossed in love-making? Or, wait a minute, shall I bide my time and see how she acts towards her lover? And listen to their lovetalk?'

Meanwhile, the wife came in: quietly locking the door securely, she was about to get into bed when her foot accidentally struck against the body of her husband lying hidden under the bedstead. She grasped the situation immediately, 'Ah! I see,' she said to herself. 'It is that husband of mine under the bedstead: no doubt he is planning to test my fidelity. Well, let me give him a real, good taste of womancraft.'

As she was mulling over what precisely she would do, her lover, Devadatta, was impatient to start the loveplay. The chariot-maker's wife now folded her hands in respect and pleaded with her lover. 'Oh! Noble gentleman! You should not touch me.'

'Not touch you?' spluttered the lover quite miffed, 'then why in god's name did you invite me over?'

'Oh! Sir,' she said, 'You see, I went early this morning to Candikā's [43] shrine to offer worship to the goddess. Then, quite unexpectedly, I heard a voice in the air, saying, "Alas! My daughter! What can I do? I know you are my ardent devotee. But in six months' time, Fate's hand will strike a blow against you and you will become a widow."

'And I humbly suggested, "Great Goddess! Since you have knowledge of the impending calamity, you must also know of a remedy to prevent it. There must be some means to adopt by which my husband will live to be a hundred years."

"Yes, indeed, there is," replied the goddess, "but only if you are prepared to adopt that remedy."

'Hearing her words I replied immediately, "O! Divine Lady! Even if it should cost me my life I shall willingly do it; please instruct me."

'The divine lady spoke gently, "If you go to bed with another man and embrace him in love, then the untimely death that threatens your husband will pass on to that other man; and your husband will live to be a hundred years."

323

'Only for this reason, sir, did I approach you and requested you to come over. And now do what you have been so eager to do; the words of divinity can never prove false.

Her lover's face shone, lit up by secret laughter; and he straight away began performing as required. As for the chariot-maker, colossal fool that he was, he thrilled in every pore of his body listening to what his wife had said. He leapt out from his hiding place under the bed crying, 'Well done! Well done, my faithful wife; well done, Gladdener of the family! Giving credence to the town's malicious gossip I pretended to leave town to put your fidelity to the test. Returning home stealthily, I crept under the bed. So, come, come, my dearest love; embrace me.'

So saying he took his wife in his arms and then lifting her on to his shoulder turned to the lover, Devadatta, to say, 'Oh! Large-hearted and noble soul; it is as a reward for my past meritorious works that you have come here this night. For it is by your favour that I have this day obtained the full measure of life of a hundred years. Let me honour you; you should also mount my shoulder.' And he forcibly lifted the reluctant lover on to his shoulder. Bearing both his wife and her paramour on his shoulders, the foolish chariot-maker went out dancing in the street, stopping at the doors of the houses of each of his relatives.

'Therefore, my lords, I say this to you,' concluded the Hon. Red Eye. '"Before his eyes he sees a foul act done . . . " and so on. We have been pulled up by the roots and completely destroyed. What more is there to say! And what wisdom is contained in these lines:

> *The wise and experienced regard*   (182)
> *those who disregard good advice*
> *to follow policies perverse and hostile*
> *as foes in the guise of friends.*

'Furthermore:

> *Served by impolitic counsellors,*   (183)
> *a king who fails to act*
> *as time and place dictate, sees destroyed*

advantages that he already possessed;
they vanish like darkness at sunrise.'

However, disregarding Red Eye's sage counsel, the owls got ready to pick Live Firm up and transport him to their fortress. As he was being carried there Live Firm began protesting in hollow terms.

'Ah! My lord,' he told King Foe Crusher. 'Considering that I can serve no useful purpose, the state I am in, why is Your Majesty taking me under your wing with such solicitude? The truth is that I earnestly desire to enter the blazing fire. You can serve me best by providing me with the fire that will be my deliverance.'

Red Eye at once caught on to his inmost thoughts and realized what Live Firm's true intent was. 'Why would you want to immolate yourself, sir?' he queried.

Live Firm's prompt reply was, 'It is only for your sakes that I have been reduced to this pitiable condition by Cloud Hue, King of the Crows. I wish therefore to be reborn as an owl to have my revenge on him.'

Hearing his words, Red Eye who knew the twists and turns of *realpolitik* in and out, retorted, 'My dear fellow, you are not only crafty in your actions but skilled in the use of deceitful speech. Granting that you are born again as an owl, I know that you will still think highly of your corvine origins. There is a tale that well illustrates my point:

> *Having spurned the sun and the rain,* (184)
> *the wind and the mountain,*
> *who came as suitors for her hand,*
> *the mouse-maiden picked on one of her own kind.*
> *In the end a person's true nature*
> *will speak out loud and clear.'*

'I see; and how was that?' asked Live Firm. And then Red Eye began the tale of *The Mouse-Maiden who wed a mouse.*

On the banks of the river Gaṅgā whose waves were flecked with white foam churned up by the confused whirling of fishes frightened by the sound of her waters stumbling and dashing on the jagged, rocky shores, there stood a hermitage thronged by a host of ascetics clad in nothing more than loincloths of bark. These ascetics chastened their bodies severely by subsisting entirely on a diet of roots, fruits and bulbs and the saivala[44] plants. They drank only hallowed water in measured amounts and spent their days engrossed in the proper performance of various sacred rites and rituals: silent prayers and meditation, penance and yogic exercise, recitation and chanting of vedic texts to themselves, fasting and performance of sacrifices. The patriarch who headed this hermitage was the great sage Yājnavalkya.

One day he went down to the Jāhnavī[45] to bathe and perform his ablutions. As he was about to carry out the ritual sipping of water[46] a tiny baby mouse fell from the beak of a hawk right into his hollowed palm. He gently placed the tiny creature on a banyan leaf, bathed again in the river and repeated his ablutions to purify himself of the defilement. Then by his ascetic powers, the sage changed the little mouse into a baby girl, picked her up and took her with him to his own dwelling in the hermitage.

Addressing his wife who was childless, he said, 'Gracious lady: here, take this little child who has come into our lives and bring her up as your own daughter with tender care.'

His wife was pleased, and accepted the foundling and reared her with love and care, petting and pampering her no end.

When the girl was twelve years of age, the mother noticed that she was nubile and pointed it out to the sage. 'My dear lord,' she said, 'How is it that you have not become aware that the right time for our daughter to be married might soon pass?'

To this the sage replied, 'Yes, my dear wife, what you have said just now is perfectly true. As we have heard:

> *Women are first wed by the Immortals,* (185)
> > *by Fire and Moon, and the Genius[47]*
> > *of the Waters of Life and Light;*
> > *and only after, by mortals.*
> > *Thus no wrong is done.*

326

For the Moon gives them radiant purity (186)
       of mind and body,
and the Fire all the holy perfections;
       the Gandharva makes their speech
              pleasant and decorous;
therefore are women free of all blemishes.

Before the monthly flow appears, (187)
a pure brilliance is hers;
and after, it is passion's redness.
Without breasts or a sense of shame,
a girl shows no distinguishing gender-signs.

As womanly allure buds and blossoms, (188)
it is the Moon who does the bridal rites.
The Fire's glow is in the monthly flow,
the Gandharva is enshrined in her breasts.

A girl ought to be wedded (189)
before she enters womanhood.
Marriage is highly commended
for girls just eight years old.

The first signs bring death to the elder brother, (190)
       the budding bosom to the younger;
passion consummated to all near and dear,
       the monthly flow is death to the father.

Once a girl is nubile (191)
she gives herself to whom she will;
so marry a girl off at a tender age
said Manu, the self-begotten sage.

The girl who sees her monthly flow (192)
while still in the paternal home, living
unconsecrated by the marriage vows
will never have a chance for marrying.

But despised she will remain, looked upon
as unfruitful and lowest of the low.

To avoid wrongdoing, a father   (193)
should seek out and arrange a bridegroom
    for his nubile daughter
from among his equals, or the noblest,
or pick even one of the vilest.

'I shall give this girl in marriage to one of equal status with her.
As we have heard:

Between those well-matched in wealth,   (194)
between those well-matched by birth,
a match may be arranged and friendship grow;
but not between the prosperous and the penniless.

Family and fortune, learning and virtue,   (195)
good looks and good health and good connections,
    these seven have to be weighed
    when a girl is to be wed,
other things being of little consequence.

'Therefore, I shall call upon the blessed sun and offer our
daughter in marriage to him, if she is pleased to accept him,'
concluded the sage Yājnavalkya.

'Yes, why not; it seems all right to me; do so accordingly,'
said his wife.

The holy ascetic then invoked the Sun who appeared before
him immediately and enquired courteously, 'Your Holiness; for
what purpose have I been summoned?'

And the sage replied, 'This is my daughter whom you see
here. Pray, marry her.' With these words, the sage turned to his
daughter and asked her, 'Dear daughter, does this suitor, the
blessed lord who is the light of the triple-world please you?'

'Dear father,' answered the daughter-elect,[48] 'this one? He
is one compounded all of blazing heat; he does not please me.
Let someone superior to him be summoned.'

Upon hearing her words the sage enquired of the luminous godhead, 'Blessed Lord, is there someone greater than you?' To which the Sun replied, 'Yes, there is. The Cloud is greater than I am; for when he veils me, I become invisible.'

The sage then called upon the Cloud and spoke tenderly to his daughter, 'My dearest child; I'll give you in marriage to the Cloud.'

However, she demurred, 'Oh, Father dear; he is dark-complexioned; leaden in form and spirit. Marry me to someone more excellent than him.'

The sage now inquired of the Cloud, 'O, Cloud; is there someone greater than you?'

'Certainly, sir; the Wind; he is much stronger than I am,' answered the Cloud.

So the sage called upon the Wind and addressed his daughter 'My darling child; let me marry you to the Wind.'

She objected saying, 'But, dearest Father; this man is restless and wayward. Please summon someone much better than him.'

The ascetic now said to the Wind, 'O, Wind; tell me if there is someone superior to you.'

'Oh yes, sir, the Mountain; he is far superior to me.'

The ascetic next summoned the Mountain and said to his daughter, 'My beloved daughter; I shall marry you to the Mountain.'

But she baulked at the very idea, 'O! How hard-hearted he is, and stiff-necked, dear father. O, please find me some other suitor.'

The ascetic wearily asked the Mountain, 'Oh, great Mountain-King; tell me if there is someone more powerful than you.'

The Mountain replied, 'Gladly, Your Holiness. Much more powerful than I are mice.'

Finally, the great sage called a mouse and presented him as a suitor to the maiden. And he said with affection, 'My dearest little one; does this suitor find favour in your eyes?'

She took one look and thought, 'Ah! At last; one of my own kind.' And her whole frame thrilled with joy as she looked at her father and said, 'Oh! Yes! Dearest father; turn me into a mouse-girl and let me marry this mouse-boy, so that I can follow the ways of my own people, and keep house accordingly.'

The sage smiled and using his great powers gained through penance, changed the maiden back into a mouse.

'Therefore, I said to you, "Having spurned the Sun for her husband . . . " and the rest of it,' concluded Red Eye.

But the owl-king and his followers, bent upon their own line of action, disregarded Red Eye's sage counsel and took Live Firm, the crow to their fortress, thus preparing the way for the destruction of their whole race. As he was being carried to the fortress of the owls, Live Firm, chuckling to himself, reflected with deep satisfaction:

> 'There was but one amongst this whole lot (196)
> who had expert knowledge of statecraft
> and understood its essential truths;
> who had his master's best interests at heart
> and advised that I should be slain forthwith.

'If these fellows had heeded his counsel and followed it, then not the slightest misfortune could have touched them.'

When the owls had arrived at the fortress-gate, their king, Foe Crusher, ordered his attendants thus. 'Hey there, fellows, make available to the Honourable Minister, Live Firm, any chamber in our fortress that he asks for; for he is our well-wisher.'

Hearing the words of the King of Owls instructing his attendants, Live Firm, highly gratified, pondered over the next step. 'I had better devise a good plan now for the destruction of these owls. Obviously, I cannot accomplish my purpose by living in their midst. For, if they should notice the slightest detail of my preparations and gain a hint of my intentions, it is certain to start them thinking. Then they would be on their guard. My best bet would be to stay close to the fortress-gate. Only by doing so can I hope to carry out my plan.'

Concluding that this was the best arrangement possible he addressed the King of Owls: 'My lord,' he began, 'what Your

Majesty has spoken just now is most laudable. But I am one who possesses sound political wisdom; and I am your sincere well-wisher. Even though I am lóyal and true, it is inappropriate for me to live within your fortress, right in its very heart. So, kindly permit me to take up my residence right here at the fortress-gate where I can serve you daily without fail with my body hallowed by the dust of Your Majesty's lotus feet.'

The King of Owls assented to this proposition. Day after day the royal attendants gathered the best possible foods and by the command of their lord, they fed Live Firm on sumptuous meals of flesh so that in a few days he became strong as a peacock.

Now, Red Eye, who was keenly observing the manner in which the crow, Live Firm, was being fed, nourished and pampered, was truly amazed. He felt bound to speak out, to the owl-ministers and to the king himself. 'Alas! Alas!' he cried in despair, 'What a pack of fools you ministers are; and you too, my lord. I am quite convinced of it. As the story tells it, the bird said:

> *First it was I who was a fool* (197)
> *then the man who snared me, the fowler,*
> *next it was the king himself*
> *and then his minister*
> *Oh! We were all a pack of fools.'*

The entire court asked eagerly, 'Oh? And how was that?' Then Minister Red Eye began the tale of *The Bird who dropped golden turd*.

On one side of a certain mountain grew a mighty tree in which nested a fabulous bird whose droppings turned to pure gold. One day a fowler came along to that spot and right in front of him, suddenly, the bird let fall its droppings. And imagine his amazement when the droppings turned into gold as soon as it fell on the ground. 'Good gracious,' exclaimed the fowler. 'For eighty long years, right from the time I was a mere child I have pursued my favourite pastime of snaring birds. Yet, in all this time, never have I seen bird droppings that turned to gold.' He decided to snare the bird, and set a trap in the tree.

Later, the unwary bird came to its accustomed place with complete confidence and sat there only to find itself trapped. The fowler cut the strings in which it was entangled, shut it up in a cage and took it home. Then he fell to thinking. 'This bird bodes evil for me; what am I doing bringing it home? Supposing that at some time or other someone finds out about the strangeness of this bird and reports it to the king. My life would be in danger then. I had better take this bird to the king myself and report the strange fact about it.' Having decided that this was a wise course to follow, he took the bird to the king. No sooner had the king set eyes on it than he became ecstatic, with his eyes widening in delight like newly blossomed lotuses. 'Who's there? Hey guards, come quick,' he called out, 'See that this bird is looked after with the utmost care; give it whatever it needs to eat and drink, as much as it wants.'

The minister interposed at this point. Oh! My lord! What's all this! What do you want with this thing hatched from an egg that you have accepted on trust based merely on some preposterous claim made by some fowler that its droppings turn to pure gold. Let this bird be released from its cage and set free.'

The king taking his minister's counsel seriously, opened the cage and let the bird out. The bird flew up to the topmost arch of the gateway, sat on it just long enough to drop some turd which immediately turned to gold and spoke the following verse:

> 'At first it was only I who was a fool! (198)
> Then it was the man who snared me, the fowler;
> > then it was His Royal Majesty
> > and then the prime minister!
> Oh! What a pack of fools were we!'

Having recited this verse the bird happily winged his way through the air.

'Therefore,' concluded the Honourable Red Eye, 'I too

repeated the lines, "At first it was only I who was a fool . . . "
and so on.'

But once again, the King of Owls and his entourage disregarded Red Eye's words of wisdom, for they were driven by a
hostile fate, and continued to sumptuously feed and nourish Live
Firm on ample supplies of different kinds of flesh.

Red Eye now gathered his own kin and loyal henchmen
round himself and spoke in secret with them with grave
deliberation. 'Alas! How lamentable! The well-being of our
monarch and the security of our stronghold is no more. I have
spoken out and counselled well as a hereditary minister of the
dynasty is bound to do. Now it is time for us to depart and take
shelter immediately in some other mountain-fortress. For, as we
have heard:

> He rejoices who carefully prepares (199)
>   for events yet to come.
> He sorrows who is caught unawares
>   by events when they come.
> Living in these woods I have grown old;
>   but, never ever before
> has a cave been heard to roar.'

'How was that ?' clamoured his followers all together. And
then Red Eye began the tale of *The Talking Cave*.

In a certain wooded region lived a lion named Razor-sharp Claws.
Once he was roaming all through the woods looking for prey but
he did not find a single creature, and his throat was pinched by
hunger. At last at sunset, he chanced upon a cave and entering
it, sat deep in thought.

'Some creature or other is bound to find its way into this cave
at night; no doubt about that. So let me lie here, quietly
concealed,' thought the lion.

And not long after, the master of the cave, a jackal named
Curd Ear came and stood at the entrance, puffing and blowing.

'Cave! Oh Cave! Oh Cave!' he called out thrice. And then

again he called out thrice to the cave. Then he fell silent. Again, he called out to the cave, this time he followed his calls with, 'Don't you remember me? Oh Cave! Don't you recall the agreement we made once, you and I? That when I came from the outside world I would call out to you, and that you would respond in kind? And today you do not return my greeting. Well, all right then; I shall leave and go to that other cave which I am sure will respond to my greeting.'

The lion listened to what the jackal had just said and began to think, 'I see; obviously, this cave always calls out a greeting to welcome its master home. But today, out of fear of me, it remains silent. How aptly the wise saying phrases it:

> *When fear grips the heart hard,* (200)
> *then hands and feet refuse to move;*
> > *great trembling seizes every limb*
> > *and the voice fades far away.*

'If I call out to the jackal and greet him, he will enter the cave according to the agreement and I can have him for dinner.'

Having come to this conclusion the lion roared out a tremendous greeting. The cave magnified the sound of his roaring until the echoes set up filled all directions right up to the far horizon. Even creatures living at a great distance hearing the sound were terrified and the jackal took to his heels, muttering the verse:

> *'He rejoices who with care prepares* (201)
> > *timely action for coming events.*
> *He sorrows who is caught unawares*
> > *by events when they come upon him.*
> *Living in these woods I have grown old:*
> > *but never ever before*
> *has a cave been heard to roar.'*

'Taking this to heart, you had all better go with me.' With these words, Red Eye, who had made up his mind, went to another far region followed by his family and adherents.

With Red Eye gone, Live Firm was overjoyed at the way things were working out and reflected with much satisfaction: 'The departure from the fortress of Red Eye and his men is indeed a piece of great good fortune for us crows. For he was a truly far-sighted minister; the others are blithering fools. And they will become easy prey; I can despatch them with little trouble. As this verse states it with such wisdom:

> *A monarch's ruin is certain,* (202)
> *   and it is not too distant,*
> *if he is not served by ministers*
> *   lineally-descended and far-sighted.*

'Moreover, it is wisely observed:

> *The learned and wise consider* (203)
> *him who discards right policy*
> *to follow courses contrary,*
> *a foe masquerading as minister.'*

Having run through all these reflections, Live Firm started bringing faggots one by one each day to lay them in his own place, with the intention of setting fire to the owls' cave-fortress. Nor did those incorrigibly foolish owls realize that the crow was building up his own place to burn down theirs.

> *He who makes his foe a friend,* (204)
> *hates a friend and destroys him,*
> *   suffers the loss of all his friends:*
> *   a foe is a loss from the start.*

Once Live Firm under the pretext of building his home at the fortress-gate had gathered a great pile of wood in it, he rose early one morning at sunrise when the owls were blind and flew quickly to meet Cloud Hue. 'My lord,' he began, 'I have made the enemy's cave vulnerable to fire. So arrange to come there with all your retinue, each one with a burning twig from the woods, and throw the twigs into my house at the enemy's fortress-gate, so that all our enemies will die in torment like those baked in the Potter's-Fiery-Oven-Hell.[49]

Hearing this Cloud Hue was overjoyed, 'Faiher,' he enquired, 'Tell me everything that happened to you; for I haven't seen you in ages.'

Live Firm replied, 'My son; this is not the time for talk, in case some spy or other of the enemy reports my arrival here to his master, and that blind fellow having gained that information makes his escape by flying away to some safe spot. So, hurry, hurry up. As we have heard:

> The man who is tardy acting (205)
> where utmost speed is called for,
> rouses the ire of gods who would set up
> obstacles in his way; you can bank on that.

'And besides:

> Time sucks the marrow (206)
> out of any enterprise
> planned but not done with promptitude,
> especially one about to bear fruit.

'I shall tell you everything there is to tell, once all our enemies are slain and you are back home,' concluded Live Firm.

Cloud Hue listened attentively to the minister's advice and gathering his retinue flew to the cave of the owls where they threw one after the other the burning twigs from the woods that each one of them had carried in his beak, right into Live Firm's house that stood at the fortress-gate. All the owls being blind by daytime now remembered Red Eye's sage counsel as they were roasted alive like sinners in the hell known as Potter's-Fiery-Oven. Having completely exterminated his enemies in this manner, Cloud Hue returned to his banyan-tree citadel once again.

Mounting the lion-throne, his heart bursting with exultation, he questioned Live Firm in the full assembly. 'Father, how did you pass your time in the enemy's midst? Tell us; for it is the truth that:

Men of meritorious works deem it better (207)
  to plunge into a blazing fire
than pass even a single hour
  mingling in enemy-society.'

Hearing Cloud Hue speak these words, Live Firm explained;
'My gracious lord, listen,' he said:

'From fear of being laid low, a man (208)
has recourse to any means that presents itself,
noble or mean that serves his interest best,
to follow it with fine-honed intelligence.
The diademed prince[50] *with a pair of arms*
resembling the trunks of noble tuskers,
and deeply scarred by the recoiling bowstring;
that wielder, skilled, of the mighty bow,[51] *bound*
with bracelets, like any woman, his wrists.

Expecting better times, O, my king, the wise (209)
though powerful, should always be prepared to dwell
even with persons, evil and vile, whose speech
falls fierce as thunderbolts: for did not Bhīma
of prodigious strength, toil in the kitchens
smoke-begrimed, of the fisher-king's[52] *palace,*
employed in wearisome, menial tasks, a cook
  wielding a greasy ladle in his hand?

A prudent man does the formidable deed (210)
cherished in his heart, whatever it might be,
noble or despicable
with an eye to the future;
Did not the two-handed[53] *archer with palms*
hardened by the flashing, far-stretched,
  throbbing bowstring
of the mighty Gāndīva, wantonly dance[54]
  wearing the dancer's flashing jewelled belt?
A wise man praying fervently for success (211)
hides deep within, the fire of his spirit,
though possessed of courage and vigour;

he should stay his course keeping a close eye
on the workings of Fortune.
Did not the glorious son of the Law[55] wander,
carrying the triple-staff of the mendicant,
although his was high honour paid by brothers,
each the equal of the immortal lords,
Lords of War, Wealth and Death?[56]

So too, Kunti's twin sons, of immense strength, (212)
rich in beauty and of noble birth, served
at Virāṭa's court doing menial tasks,
tending and herding cattle and horses.

Did not Draupadī of matchless beauty, (213)
blessed with youth, born of the noblest family,
radiant as the Goddess Herself of wealth
and beauty, struck by the turn of Fate
and fallen into a miserable state,
grind and rub sandal-paste
in the palace-courts of the fisher-king,
ordered around by haughty maidens
calling out, 'Ho there! Sairandhri.'[57]

'Father,' exclaimed Cloud Hue, 'dwelling in the midst of enemies is like taking the vow of lying on the razor-sharp edge of a sword-blade, I think.'

'So it is,' replied Live Firm. 'But I have never seen such a pack of fools as those owls, anywhere. Not one of them had any sense or imagination with the sole exception of Red Eye, who indeed possessed a keen intellect capable of ranging unobstructed over many fields of knowledge. I know this because I could see that he understood what my true intent and purposes were. As for the others, they were all such unmitigated fools merely making a living pretending to be wise counsellors, while in fact they possessed no expertise in statecraft. For they were even unaware of a simple fact such as this; that:

A retainer from the enemy's camp, (214)
a deserter anxious to become part

338

of those he tries to curry favour with,
is a villain, false and malcontent,
untrue to his own nature and kin.
Enemy spies scarcely show themselves; (215)
ever watchful for signs of negligence
displayed perchance by an enemy as he
takes his ease or sleeps, or walks around;
in what he eats and drinks as well, and strike him down,
A wise man should therefore make every effort (216)
    to be vigilant; and protect his self,
that abode of the three[58] existential pursuits:
It is through negligence that men come to naught.

'And how full of wisdom is this observation:

What bad minister is not guilty (217)
    of bad diplomacy?
Who living on unwholesome foods
    does not fall prey to disease?
Whom does Fortune not make haughty?
    whom does Death not lay low?
Who addicted to inordinate pleasures
    does not burn with pain and sorrow?

The stubborn forfeit fame, (218)
the irritable friendship;
those who labour fruitlessly
    lose their family;
Obsession with money
    is virtue's bane;
the miser loses peace of mind;
those out of luck the rewards of learning;
and the monarch whose minister
    is negligent loses his sovereignty.

'Therefore, O King! I took upon myself the vow of lying on the razor-sharp sword-blade by associating with the enemy. What

Your Majesty expressed in words I experienced in person. How wisely it is said:

> *Biding his time the wise man bears*   (219)
> *even his enemy on his shoulders.*
> *That is what the mighty black serpent did*
>   *and ended up devouring countless frogs.'*

'And how did that happen,' asked Cloud Hue. And then Live Firm began the tale of *The Frogs that rode snakeback*.

In a certain region lived a black serpent of a ripe old age, named Weak Venom. He deliberated over his sad situation thus: 'How in the world can I now manage to have a comfortable living?' He then crawled along to a deep pool inhabited by a great assemblage of frogs. There he flopped down as if he were infirm.

As he stayed thus, one of the frogs swimming near the edge of the pool asked, 'Uncle, how is it that you are not gliding around today, as you normally do, hunting for food?'

'My good friend,' replied the serpent. 'What desire for food can someone like myself have whose fortunes are at their lowest ebb? Just now, in the early hours of the night, I was crawling around looking for food and noticing a frog I duly prepared to grab him. He too having noticed me, slipped in somewhere where a group of Brāhmanas were intent on reciting the sacred texts to themselves; nor could I make out which way the frog had slithered away. But at the edge of the pool the son of one of the Brāhmanas was standing and mistaking his great toe for a frog, I bit it hard; the boy died instantaneously. The father, stung by grief, cursed me in the following words: "Oh! You! Villainous creature! Because you stung to death my innocent son, you shall suffer for this evil act by becoming a vehicle for frogs; and you shall live entirely on what the frogs allow you for food." So here I am, your vehicle, O, you frogs.'

The silly frog immediately carried this news to all the other frogs. They were all so excited about it that they approached the frog-king, Watertoes, in a body and told him of it. He, in turn, thinking what a wonderful happening it was, swam out of the pool in a great hurry and accompanied by his ministers went to where Weak Venom lay and climbed on to the serpent's outspread hood. The other frogs in order of seniority also climbed on to the serpent's back. Why say more; yet others, not finding any room on the serpent's back hopped behind Weak Venom as best as they could as he started moving. Weak Venom for his part keen on securing a comfortable living for himself, showed them many different fancy turns and movements that he knew, so that King Watertoes enjoying the contact with the serpent's body exclaimed with delight:

> *'Oh! What fun it is to ride on Weak Venom!*   (220)
>   *No horse or lordly elephant*
>   *no fine chariot, or palanquin*
>   *can at all compare with him.'*

The next day, Weak Venom, wily rogue that he was, barely managed to crawl at a snail's pace, which prompted Watertoes to remark, 'Why, friend Weak Venom, why are you not carrying us nicely as you did before?' To this Weak Venom promptly replied, 'My lord, through lack of food, I do not have the strength to carry you properly today.'

'Well, my good chap, why don't you eat a few of these low-born commoner frogs?' said Watertoes casually.

The sound of these words made Weak Venom thrill with delight in every limb. But then he made haste to observe, 'You see, my lord, I have this curse of the Brāhmana hanging over my head. But now that you have issued this command for me to eat a few frogs, I am simply delighted.'

Weak Venom now started eating frogs and he continued to do so without interruption, so much so that in a few days, he grew strong.

Gratified by the happy turn of events, he laughed to himself, as he reflected:

> *'Through a clever stratagem*   (221)
> *have I killed and eaten,·*
> *many varied kinds of frogs.*

341

> *Now, as I keep devouring them,*
> *how long will the supply last;*
>   *that is the big question.'*

As for Watertoes, a real simpleton, he was effectively fooled by Weak Venom's glib and deceitful talk, so that he did not have a clue as to what was going on.

Then one day, another huge black serpent happened to come that way. Seeing Weak Venom acting as a vehicle for frogs he was totally amazed; and he remarked, 'Friend, these frogs are our food; yet they ride on your back. This is contrary to all accepted practice; it is disagreeable, sir.'

Weak Venom answered his kinsman, saying:

> *'I know quite well it is not right*   (222)
> *I should let the frogs ride me piggyback.*
> *I'll put up with it for a while, my friend,*
>   *as did the Brāhmana butter-blind.'*

'And how was that?' asked the other snake. And Weak Venom then began the tale of *The Brāhmana's Revenge*.

In a certain settlement lived a Brāhmana named Yajnadatta whose wife was a loose woman constantly chasing other men. She was forever making delicious sweetmeats[59] of butter and sugar and taking to a lover, behind her husband's back.

One day the husband spoke to her as she was preparing these sweets. 'Dear wife,' he began, 'What is it that you are making? And where are you forever taking the delicious sweets you make? Now, tell me the truth.'

The woman who possessed a ready wit told her husband a string of lies. 'Not far from here is the shrine of the Great Goddess,' she said, 'I go there fasting and take the Goddess an offering of the finest, most delicious sweets that I can make.'

Then, even as her husband was looking on, she picked up the dish of sweets and started towards the shrine of the goddess, imagining that after what she had told him, her husband was certain to believe that she always took the delicious sweets she made, to the goddess, as an offering.

While the woman after her arrival at the shrine went down to the river for a ritual bath, her husband who had taken a different road now entered the shrine and- stood concealed behind the image of the goddess.

Meanwhile, the wife having completed her bath and ablutions now entered the shrine and performed all the prescribed rituals that were part of the worship of the goddess; lustration with holy water, anointing the image with sandal-paste, burning incense before it, offering the oblation and so on. Having done all this, the Brāhmana's wife bowed low with folded hands and reverently made her wish. 'May my husband go blind some way or the other, Great Goddess,' and she prayed.

The Brāhmana standing concealed behind the image heard his wife's prayer and changing the tone of his voice, intoned as follows, 'Give your husband butter, and sweets made of butter and sugar every day regularly; he shall soon become blind.'

And that woman of easy morals being deceived by the Brāhmana's false utterance in the shrine, duly began feeding him those very rich sweetmeats as instructed.

Then, one day, the Brāhmana spoke in a diffident tone to his wife, 'Dear wife, I simply do not seem to be able to see at all,' he confided.

The wife, overjoyed, told herself, 'Ah! The blessing of the goddess is being fulfilled.'

The paramour too, knowing what was happening, thought to himself. 'Ha! What can this blind Brāhmana do to me now,' and began frequenting the Brāhmana's house daily to approach the wife.

Then one fine day, seeing his wife's paramour entering his house, the Brāhmana, as soon as the man was within reach, seized him by the hair and administered some hefty blows with a stout cudgel and added a few sharp kicks. Next, he caught hold of his wife, chopped off her nose and turned her out.

'Therefore, I say to you, "I know quite well it is not

right . . ." and the rest of it, as I said before.' Weak Venom chuckled to himself noiselessly and spoke again, muttering: 'Frogs come in different flavours . . . ta-ta-ta tum-tum . . . .' and murmured once more to his friend the verse he had recited before:

(223)

'Through a clever stratagem
have I killed and eaten
many varied sorts of frogs.
Now, as I keep devouring them,
how long will the supply last?
  that is the big question.'

Watertoes hearing this verse intoned softly by Weak Venom became, uneasy; with his mind haunted by misgivings he asked himself, 'What in the name of all the gods is this fellow muttering?' And turning to Weak Venom he asked peremptorily, 'Now look here, my friend, what is the meaning of these odious lines that you are intoning?'

'Oh! Nothing; nothing at all,' hissed Weak Venom attempting to mask his real purpose. And Watertoes, once again thoroughly fooled by the serpent's ingenuous manner, was unable to see through the beast's treacherous plans.

To cut the tale short, Weak Venom succeeded in gobbling up every one of the frogs. Not a single frog was left; not even for seed.

'Therefore, I repeat to you, "Bearing on his shoulders even a foe . . . " and so on, as I said before,' concluded Live Firm.

'Thus, O King,' continued Live Firm, 'Just as the black serpent, Weak Venom, destroyed the whole host of frogs through the sheer power of his superior intelligence, I too, have destroyed all our enemies. Indeed, it is wisely observed:

The blazing forest fire rages   (224)
through the woods, but spares the roots of trees;
but cool and gentle waters flooding
rapidly in, uproot trees, roots and all.'

344

Cloud Hue responded to this, saying, 'Ah! Yes, that is so; besides:

> *This is the greatness of the truly great*   (225)
> *who wear wise policy as an ornament,*
> *that they never give up what they have begun,*
> *even when hard times bring swelling calamities.'*

Live Firm matched this, exclaiming, 'This is so; and it is also said:

> *He who pays off a debt to the last coin;*   (226)
> *who extinguishes the last spark of a fire;*
> *who extirpates the last of his enemies;*
> *who eradicates the last trace of a disease;*
> *he is the wise man who never faces ruin.*

'My lord, you are indeed fortunate, for the enterprise that was begun, has been crowned with success. No enterprise is accomplished by valour alone; what brings final victory is the wisdom[60] with which it is carried out. As we have heard:

> *It is not weapons that strike down the foe;*   (227)
> *it is wisdom that in the end lays him low;*
> *the arrow strikes the body; just that; no more;*
> *wisdom strikes at the root; destroying all;*
> *family, fame and sovereignty.*

'For that reason, success in all actions comes effortlessly only through the marriage of wisdom and valour. For:

> *When a man's stars are on the rise,*   (228)
>   *Intellect expands at the start*
>   *of an enterprise;*
> *Memory becomes firm; Advantages*
>   *on their own offer themselves;*
>   *Counsels do not flounder;*
> *Judgement shines with the promise of success;*

> *Mind attains to lofty heights;*
> *the man exults in doing laudable deeds.*

'Sovereignty, therefore, is his who possesses wisdom, valour and magnanimity. As it is aptly said:

> *A person having a keen zest* (229)
> *for consorting with the bravest,*
> *most learned and magnanimous,*
> *becomes virtuous;*
> > *the practice of virtue brings wealth;*
> *Wealth gains him glory;*
> > *Glory begets Authority.*
> > *and from that he gains Sovereignty.'*

Cloud Hue impressed, remarked, 'How admirable it is that the knowledge of statecraft brings immediate results. Possessing this knowledge you were able to infiltrate the enemy's ranks as a person favourably inclined to them. Thus you exterminated Foe Crusher with all his retinue.'

Whereupon Live Firm commented:

> *'Though extreme measures might be demanded* (230)
> > *to ensure ultimate success;*
> *to begin gentle measures are better suited.*
> *The Lord of Trees, the choicest in the forest*
> > *with soaring top, sky-high, is worshipped first*
> > *before he is felled.*

'On the other hand, my lord, what good is it holding forth on a future event that requires no action or requires great effort to accomplish? Indeed, it is wisely said:

> *Words spoken by indecisive men shying* (231)
> > *timidly away from persevering*
> *in their efforts—instead, at each step pointing*
> > *to a hundred odd stumbling blocks—*
> *sound hollow when the fruits they yield*

346

> *turn out disappointing,*
> *and turn them into the world's laughing stocks.*

'Nor for that matter do intelligent men show any negligence even
in the most trivial of tasks to be done; for:

> *Some there are negligent, who say,* (232)
>   *'Ah! such a trivial little thing!*
> *That I can do without the least effort:*
>   *why worry over it now?'—*
>   *And they pay no attention*
>   *to what has got to be done.*
> *Bitter repentance comes soon enough,*
> *Calamity's invariable companion.*

'But for my lord who has conquered his enemy, the soundest
sleep he ever enjoyed is awaiting him; as it is wisely observed:

> *One sleeps in peace in homes,* (233)
> *where no serpents are;*
> *or serpents seen, are caught.*
>   *But when a serpent appears*
>   *and then disappears*
>   *uneasy is one's sleep.*

'And then again:

> *When enterprises are afoot, momentous* (234)
>   *from calling forth efforts prodigious,*
> *and persevering for their perfect consummation;*
> *urged on by loved ones with many a blessing,*
> *directed by loftiness of conception,*
>   *shrewd policy and wild daring,*
> *men bestride the heights of Ambition.*
>   *What man who passionately loves*
>   *Honour, Valour and Self-esteem,*
> *can rest content with an unrealized dream?*

347

> *Where is his heart packed with brooding impatience*
> *can space for peace be found?*

'And now, my heart is at peace, knowing that the enterprise I mounted has been brought to a successful conclusion. Therefore, my lord, may you now long enjoy your kingdom completely cleared of thorns. May you now rule long, ever intent on the protection of your subjects; and may the long succession of sons and grandsons and others after them, and the stability of your Royal Umbrella and Throne and the Grace of Royal Glory ever remain assured. It is said:

> *If a monarch his subjects does not please* (235)
> *fulfilling his responsibilities,*
> *protection and other royal duties,*
> *his rulership is of little use,*
> *like teats hanging from the necks of ewes.*

'What's more:

> *Passion for Virtue, aversion for Vice,* (236)
> *Affection for men of good conduct:*
> *Such a monarch for long enjoys*
> *Royal Glory resplendent,*
> *with the white umbrella,*
> *waving plumes and pennant.*

'Nor should you, intoxicated by the access of Royal Glory,[61] betray the integrity of your character, thinking, "Ah! I have regained my sovereignty." I say this, my lord, because the splendours of monarchs are passing. The goddess, Royal Glory, is hard to climb as a bamboo's stem. She is prone to fall precipitately; a million efforts are required to possess her securely; still she is hard to hold fast to; worship her as reverently as you may, she deceives you in the end; hers is a mind desultory as a monkey's; wobbling as a water-droplet on a lotus leaf. She will stick with no one; restless in the extreme as the wandering winds; unreliable as an alliance with knaves; hard to control as snake-venom; momentarily gleaming bright like a fine curving line of sunset-clouds; naturally fragile like bubbles floating on waters; ungrateful as humankind; glimpsed in a dream like a treasure-trove, only to vanish once seen. Moreover:

> *The moment a monarch is consecrated,* (237)
> *his intelligence has to be enlisted*
> *in solving impending troubles; for sacred*
> *pitchers let fall on royal heads, disasters*
> *as well as holy waters.*

'Who in the world is safe from the clutches of misfortune! For it is wisely observed:

> *Rāma's*[62] *banishment, Bali's*[63] *binding,* (238)
> *the long exile of Pāṇḍu's sons*[64] *in far forests;*
> *the Vṛṣṇis' tragic annihilation*[65]
> *and Nala's forfeiture of his kingdom;*[66]
> *the heroic Arjuna's term*
> *as a teacher of dancing*[67]
> *and the downfall of Laṅkā's great lord.*[68]
> *Remember these—Life's vicissitudes, O King!*
> > *All brought about by the power of Time;*
> > > *Mankind has to endure all.*
> > *Who can be a saviour? And whom save?*
>
> *Where is Daśaratha*[69] *who rose to the Realms of Light*[70] (239)
> *to dwell beside its great lord*[71] *as his friend?*
> *Where too is the great King Sāgara*[72] *who set*
> *the bounds of the mighty Ocean?*
> *Where is Vena's son*[73] *churned from his father's right arm?*
> *And Manu,*[74] *where is he, the child of the Sun?*
> *Ah! Powerful Time alone awakened them*
> *and closed their eyes again.*

'And again:

> *Where is King Māndhātā*[75] *gone now,* (240)
> *once victorious over the Triple World?*

And where is he now who swore a solemn vow
to be ever truthful and pure?[76]
Nahuṣa[77] *too, chosen to rule over the Shining Ones?*[78]
Ah! Where is he now? And where Keśava,[79]
Divine Lord, Knower of the Way of Truth?
All these, possessing chariots and finest elephants,
even seated beside Indra on his celestial seat—
All these splendours conferred on them by Time alone.
All driven into endless oblivion by Time alone.

'Further:

Gone the king, gone the ministers; (241)
those beautiful woods and groves
and all those lovely women,
all gone, passed away; each one lost,
mortally stung by the Great ender.[80]

'And so, my son,' concluded Live Firm, counselling Cloud Hue, 'now that you have secured for yourself Royal Glory who restlessly goes to and fro like the ears of an elephant in rut, enjoy her; but make it your principal aim to rule your people justly.'

And now ends this book entitled *Of Crows and Owls*, the third in the *Texts on Policy* dealing with the six expedients in statecraft, such as peace, war and the rest; and the first verse of this is as follows:

Trust not a former enemy (242)
who comes professing amity.
Mark! The cave thronged with owls was burned
by deadly fire the crows kindled.

350

BOOK IV

Loss of Gains

And now begins the fourth book entitled *Loss of Gains*; and this is its opening verse:

> *He who foolishly lets himself be wheedled*   (1)
> > *into parting with his gains,*
> *is a dolt thoroughly bamboozled,*
> > *like the Crocodile by the Ape*.

The princes asked eagerly, 'How did that happen, O venerable sir?' and Viṣṇu Śarma then began the tale of *The Ape and the Crocodile*.

By the ocean-strand grew a great rose-apple tree, which was perennially laden with fruit. An ape named Red Face[1] lived in it. One day, a crocodile named Hideous Jaws[2] swam out of the waters and lay basking on the lovely, soft sands by the strand, right beneath the tree. When Red Face saw him, he accosted him thus: 'Sir, you are a guest here: as such do me the honour of accepting this divinely delicious fruit of the rose-apple that I offer you. For it is laid down:

> *Be he pleasant or be he hateful,*   (2)
> > *be he a scholar or a dunce,*
> *a guest[3] at your door at mealtimes[4]*
> > *is your stairway to the Worlds of Light.[5]*

> *Ask not the lineage or profession,*   (3)
> > *learning, or country of origin*
> *of the guest at your door at mealtimes*
> > *or at rites performed for ancestors[6]—*
> > > *so Manu rules.*

'Besides:

> By welcoming a guest at the door (4)
> who arrives at mealtimes proper,
> from far, travel-weary, the householder
> attains the state of Final Bliss.

'But:

> If a guest unwelcomed leaves a man's house (5)
> deeply sighing, gods and ancestors alike
> turn their faces away from him.

With these words Red Face offered the crocodile some rose-apple fruit. The crocodile having eaten the fruit sat for a long time conversing with the ape and enjoying his company, after which he went back to his own home.

After this, each day the ape and the crocodile resorting to the shade of the rose-apple tree sat together and passed their time happily in mutual discourse on matters virtuous and edifying. And always the crocodile took home with him some of the rose-apple fruit left over after he had eaten, to give to his wife.

Now one day, the wife said to the crocodile, 'My dear lord, where do you find such delicious ambrosial fruit?' And Hideous Jaws replied, 'Dearest lady, know that I have a bosom friend who provides me with this fruit with the greatest affection, an ape named Red Face.'

'I see,' declared the wife, 'A person who always eats this ambrosial fruit must possess a heart that is all ambrosia. So, my lord, if at all you value your wife, then bring me his heart, so that I may eat it and never be subject to sickness or old age,[7] but enjoy life with you for ever and ever.'

'Ah, my dearest lady,' objected Hideous Jaws, 'For one thing the ape is now my sworn brother; and for another, he is the source of this rare fruit. For these reasons, I cannot possibly kill him. So, please, my beloved, do give up this perverse craving. For it is said:

> First, we are born brothers of one mother; (6)

then as brothers of the Word[8] we are born again.
The bond of the Word is praised as greater
than the natural bond uterine.'

To this the crocodile's wife retorted, 'You have never before
crossed my wishes. I know this creature is certainly a female ape.
And because you are infatuated with this female, you go and
spend the whole day there and that is precisely why you will not
accede to my wishes. And for the same reason, when you lie with
me at night you breathe out great burning sighs that are like the
flames of a blazing fire; your kisses and embraces too are cold and
passionless. There is no doubt in my mind that another woman
has installed herself in your heart.'

Poor Hideous Jaws stood before his wife in utter misery and
humbly expostulated with her:

'Even as I fall at your feet, dear wife, (7)
your willing slave, Oh! Life of my life!
why go into this tearing rage of passion?
Oh! My Passionate One?'

At these words of her husband, the female crocodile spoke
with tears streaming down her face:

'The beloved, of whom you dream (8)
with a hundred fond imaginings,
Oh! you clever cheat! She alone
dwells in your heart, ensnaring
with what fascinations of pretended love!
What place have I now in your heart?
Mock me not falling at my feet:
enough of these vain protestations false.

'Moreover, tell me this; if she is really not your beloved then why
won't you kill her when I am asking you to do so? Again, if the
creature is truly a male ape, as you say, what kind of affection is
this that you feel for it? But why labour the point; suffice it to say

that if you do not bring the creature's heart for me to eat, I swear I shall sit here and fast to death.'

Realizing how determined his wife was, poor Hideous Jaws, racked by anxious thoughts, said miserably: 'Aha! How admirably did the ancients put it:

> For fools and fishes, woman and crab,   (9)
> for fresh-mixed lime-mortar and indigo,
> and drunks as well, a single grab
> suffices: they hold fast and won't let go.

'What shall I do now? How can I kill him who is my friend?'

Anxiously revolving these thoughts in his mind, the crocodile went to meet his friend, the ape. Red Face seeing him come after a long time and looking as if he were in great distress, asked, 'Hello, my friend! Why has it taken all this time for you to come today? And why are you not talking cheerfully? And not repeating wise and witty maxims?'

'My friend,' answered Hideous Jaws, 'I have been soundly berated today by your sister-in-law. "You ungrateful wretch," she cried, "don't you show me your face again; for, day after day, you have been living off your friend; and yet you do not show him the simple courtesy of even inviting him to your home in return for his kindness. What amends can you possibly make for this ingratitude of yours? For is it not said:

> For a toper or a Brāhmana-slayer,   (10)
> for a robber or a promise-breaker,
> the sages have prescribed rites of expiation,
>   but for the ingrate none.

"So, my lord, you had better invite my brother-in-law forthwith to our home to repay his kindness to us; otherwise you and I will meet again only in the other world." Thus enjoined by my wife, I come now to invite you to our home. As it is, much time has been wasted with the two of us, my wife and I, wrangling over you. So, come, let us go. Having decorated the courtyard, arranged all the proper guest-offerings such as fine garments, rubies, emeralds and other precious gems, hung garlands of welcome over the doorway, my wife awaits your arrival with keen and eager excitement.'

'My friend,' observed the ape, 'My brother's wife has indeed spoken wisely and well, for you know the verse which says:

> To give, to receive
> to dine, to be dined, as well;
> to talk, to listen in secret:
> these six are sure signs of affection. (11)

'But—as you know, we are forest-dwellers, while your home is deep in the waters. So, how can I go there? Instead, why don't you bring our sister-in-law here, so that I may bow down at her feet and receive her blessings.'

Hideous Jaws countered this observation: 'Listen, my friend,' he said, 'our home is on a lovely stretch of sand on the other side of the ocean; and you can go there quite easily and in comfort riding on my back; there is nothing to fear.'

Red Face readily agreed; with great delight he exclaimed, 'My good fellow; if that is the case, then let us do it; make haste; why delay? Look, here I am, already mounted on your back.'

With Red Face seated on his back, Hideous Jaws started swimming along in the unfathomable waters at a great pace. Seeing this the ape was terrified, 'Hey, hey, brother, take it easy; go slow, won't you?' he cried, 'My whole body is drenched by the rolling, sounding billows.'

At these words, the crocodile began to reflect, 'Now, this poor fellow, in case he slips off my back cannot move a hair's breadth in these unfathomable waters. He is completely in my power. So why not reveal to him my real intentions; he can at least pray to his chosen deity.'

With this idea, Hideous Jaws said to the ape, Red Face, 'My friend, if you must know, having tricked you I am taking you to your death at my wife's express bidding. Therefore, you had better say your last prayers to your chosen deity.'

Poor Red Face, thunderstruck, asked piteously, 'Brother, in

what way have I wronged you or your wife that you should gratuitously plan to kill me.'

To this the crocodile replied, 'It is like this, my friend: my wife after tasting that delicious rose-apple fruit you provided us with, began to show an obsessive craving[9] for your heart which she decided must be even more delicious from your constant diet of ambrosially delectable rose-apple fruit. I hit upon this plan for this reason.'

The ape, fortunately, had the presence of mind to cope with this shocking revelation. 'O, dear, dear! What a pity,' he remarked, 'if that were the case, why didn't you say so before, right at the start? Then I would have brought with me that other wonderfully sweet heart I keep safely tucked away in a hollow in the trunk of the rose-apple tree. Now see what has happened; you have brought me to this point for no useful purpose. For here I am, heartless, lacking my sweet heart.'[10]

The crocodile's joy knew no bounds when he heard these words of the ape, Red Face, 'Dear, dear friend,' he exclaimed, 'if that is the case, please let me have your other heart so that after eating it, that wicked wife of mine will be satisfied and desist from starving herself to death. Look, I shall take you back this instant to the rose-apple tree.'

With these words, Hideous Jaws turned around and raced back in the direction of the rose-apple tree, with poor Red Face murmuring a hundred prayers to many a god. The ape could hardly wait to reach his side of the ocean-strand. No sooner were they at the ocean's edge than Red Face quickly leaped off the crocodile's back and with swift leaps and bounds went up the rose-apple tree. And when he reached its top he said with great relief, 'O, all you blessed gods; at last; my life has been restored to me. O, what wisdom is in this advice:

> *Trust not one unworthy of trust,*   (12)
> *nor even one in whom you repose trust;*
> *such trust might breed many a peril*
> *that destroys a person root and all.*

358

'O, blessed gods! This indeed is the day of a second birth for me.'

Now Hideous Jaws looked up and called out to Red Face, 'Hey, hey there! My good friend; where is this heart you talked about? Give it to me so that your sister-in-law may eat and break her fast.'

Red Face laughed loudly and mocking the crocodile, cried out, 'You perfidious villain! You incorrigible idiot! Does any creature in this world possess a second heart? Fool! Go home, and don't dare come near this rose-apple tree ever again. As it is wisely observed:

> Once a friend turns faithless, (13)
> to trust him once more,
> is to court certain death;
> like a she-mule when she conceives.'[11]

Red Face's reproachful words made Hideous Jaws feel quite disconcerted. 'O, what an ass I was to have disclosed my real intentions to this fellow. But if I can somehow regain his trust, I have to be more careful.'

So, Hideous Jaws tried again. 'Dear friend, listen; think what earthly use can a heart be to my wife. It was all a joke. Whatever I said before was said all in fun; just to test your real feelings for me. So please come to our home as a guest. You cannot imagine how eager your brother's wife is to meet you: eager beyond all measure,' he pleaded.

'You scurvy knave,' burst out Red Face, 'go home; go this instant. I am not going with you; as the moral in the tale points out:

> What crime will a man famished not commit? (14)
> For ruthless indeed are those down and out.
> Go, fair lady; tell Sir Handsome[12] from me
> Gaṅgādatta[13] will never appear at the well again!'

'What is that tale? Tell me,' importuned Hideous Jaws. And

Red Face then began the tale of *The Frog-king who overreached himself*.

Once, in a well somewhere, lived Gaṅgādatta, King of the Frogs, who being pestered day in and day out by various kinsmen, decided he would leave the well. By climbing on to bucket after bucket of the circle of buckets attached to the water-wheel in the well, Gaṅgādatta managed to get out. Then he fell to thinking: 'Now, how shall I avenge myself on these kinsmen? As we know, there is a saying:

> *Paying back a person in the same coin,* (15)
> *him who helped during hard times*
> *and him who jeered as well, each one*
> *as he deserves, a man is born again!'*

As he sat reflecting in this manner, Gaṅgādatta noticed a black serpent entering his hollow. The serpent was known in the neighbourhood as Sir Handsome.

Watching the serpent, an idea came to the frog-king: 'What if I lead this deadly black serpent into my well and have him extirpate all those kinsmen of mine who made my life miserable? For we have heard the saying:

> *The wise root out one fiery foe* (16)
> *by means of another more fiery,*
> *as a sharp thorn by one sharper,*
> *so that pain turns to ease.'*

Gaṅgādatta thought this over and then going up to the entrance of the snake-pit, stood there and called out, 'Come out, Sir Handsome, come here.'

The serpent on being called like this by name, became wary, 'Who is this?' he asked himself. 'Whoever it is who is calling out to me does not seem to be of my race. For this is no serpent-voice. Moreover, I have no connections with any other kind in this

world of mortal beings. So, I shall just stay right here until I find
out who this person is. For:

> *Until you possess full information* (17)
> *of someone's conduct, lineage, strength,*
> *make no alliance with him,*
> *is Bṛhaspati's*[14] *sage counsel '*

'For who knows if this is not some snake-charmer or someone
skilled in preparing medicines who is summoning me, to bind
and put me in a cage. Or it may be someone perhaps who has
revenge on his mind; who may be summoning me to enlist my
aid in the interests of a friend or faction.'

Sir Handsome, the serpent, cautiously called out, 'Ho, there!
who are you?'

'I am Gaṅgādatta, King of Frogs,' answered the frog-king,
'and I have come here seeking your friendship.'

Hearing this statement, Sir Handsome snorted, 'Friendship?
Incredible! Does the grass make friends with the fire? You know
the wise saying:

> *You do not come too close to a foe* (18)
> *if you are made to be his prey;*
> *no; not even in a dream; so,*
> *why talk in this absurd way?'*

'Sir, listen, please; what you say is prefectly true,' answered
Gaṅgādatta, 'But, I tell you truly; I swear, I swear, I have come
to you for help because I am smarting under great humiliation.
How wisely it is said:

> *When you are about to lose all that you own,* (19)
> *and your very life hangs in the beam,*
> *you grovel even at the feet of an enemy*
> *to save your life and property.'*

'All right then. tell me, who has humiliated you?' asked the
serpent.

'My kinsmen,' replied, the frog-king.

Sir Handsome next asked: 'Well, where is your home? A pool, a pond, a lake or a well?'

'My home is in a well,' replied Gangādatta.

'I cannot enter a well, you know,' remarked the serpent; 'and even if I could, there would be no space inside where I could lie comfortably and kill your kinsmen. So go away. As the proverb puts it:

> *Persons mindful of their well-being* (20)
> *Had better eat a mouthful at a time;*
> *eat what is easily digestible;*
> *eat food that is good and nourishing.'*

'Just come with me, sir,' insisted Gangādatta, 'and I shall show you the easiest way to get into the well. Further, I shall show you a most comfortable hollow in the well at the water's level for you to stay. Settled there, it would be mere child's play for you to finish off my kinsmen.'

The serpent thought this over; he said to himself, 'It is true I am getting old; now and then with great effort, I am able to catch a mouse; at times not even that. We should learn from the wise saying:

> *When life is drawing to a close* (21)
> *and a wife and friends are lacking,*
> *the wise man reaches out for ways*
> *to ensure for himself a good living.*

Having considered the matter carefully, Sir Handsome said to Gangādatta, 'Well, Gangādatta, if it is as you say it is, then lead the way; let us go to your well.'

Gangādatta was delighted, 'Come, come, Sir Handsome; I shall take you into the well by a very pleasant way and show you the hollow which will be your residence. But . . . ' he added a cautionary note, 'but you must not harm my family or my close friends. You should eat only those frogs that I point out to you.'

'Come, come, dear fellow; have no fear,' said Sir Handsome,

reassuringly, 'now that we are such good friends, I shall do whatever you say.'

So saying, Sir Handsome slithered out of his hole, and closely embraced the frog-king; and they set off together.

Reaching the well's edge, the serpent closely followed the frog, entering the well by way of the round of circles on the water-wheel. After settling the black serpent in the hollow at the water's level, Gaṅgādatta indicated to him who his kinsmen were who were harassing him, all of whom Sir Handsome gradually gobbled up. When no more of the frog-king's hostile kinsmen were left to eat, Sir Handsome quietly picked a few of the royalty and ate them on the sly.

After that, the serpent told the king most courteously, 'Dear friend, I have exterminated all your enemies: now give me something to eat, for it was you who brought me here.'

To this Gaṅgādatta replied loftily, 'My dear fellow, you have done what a friend should do. Now you had better go back the way you came, climbing up the well by the buckets strung on the water-wheel.'

But the serpent was not one to be put off in this manner; 'Hey, Gaṅgādatta, you have not given much thought to what you said just now, have you? My hollow which was my fortress must certainly be occupied by others now. No, I shall stay right here and expect you to provide me with frogs, one after the other even if they happen to belong to your own family. And if you don't, why . . . I shall eat them all up.'

Hearing these ominous threats, Gaṅgādatta was deeply troubled as he reflected, 'Alas, alas; what is this that I have done bringing this fellow here? And if I refuse him, he is going to swallow every single frog here. Oh! How admirably these lines express it:

Whoever makes friends with a foe (22)
far more powerful than himself
is feeding himself poison;
of that I am by no means uncertain.

'I daresay I have to give this fellow a frog a day even if it has to be one of my friends : as we well know:

> *Prudent men please with some trivial gift* (23)
> *an enemy who has the power to seize all,*
> *just as the ocean pacifies*
> *the fiery mare lying in its depths.*

'Moreover:

> *When loss of the whole threatens* (24)
> *the prudent man parts with a half,*
> *to carry on with the other half:*
> *for total loss is hard to take.*

'Besides:

> *Men with practical sense will not expend* (25)
> *too much for too little profit:*
> *Prudence consists in this: protect*
> *a great deal at little expense.'*

Having decided that this was the best possible course, Gangādatta alloted one frog a day to the black serpent, who ate that and another besides behind the frog-king's back. What wisdom is contained in these lines:

> *As a man in soiled clothes sits here,* (26)
> *there and any where,*
> *so also he who strays from Virtue's path*
> *cares not to preserve mere tatters of good conduct.*

Now one day, while eating some frogs, Sir Handsome happened to gobble up Prince Sunadatta, Gangādatta's son. Seeing this the frog-king set up a howl, wailing bitterly in shrill, high-pitched tones. Then his wife, taunting, reproached him thus:

> *'Why, why shriek so shrill?* (27)
> *You, whose cry no one hears!*

You, the bane of your whole race!
Gone are all your kinsfolk;
Who can give you sanctuary now?

'Therefore, think of a way for our escape, this very day; or think of a scheme to kill this black serpent.'

And the days went by: one by one, all the frogs in the well were eaten up; all except Gaṅgādatta.

Then, Sir Handsome turned to him and said, 'Friend, Gaṅgādatta, all the frogs here are gone, finished, and I am hungry; so find me something to eat.'

'Listen, friend,' replied Gaṅgādatta, 'don't you worry about a thing while I am still here. If you permit me to leave, I shall go to many other wells and lure all the frogs dwelling in them to this well.'

Sir Handsome thought it was a splendid idea: 'Since I cannot dine off you because you are like a brother to me, go; if you succeed in bringing off this scheme of yours, then you will be like a father to me,' he said.

With his plan clearly thought out, Gaṅgādatta made good his escape by slipping out of the well, while Sir Handsome sat within waiting, eagerly expecting his return.

After a long time, Sir Handsome addressed a lizard who also resided in the well in a hollow near his own. 'Fair lady,' he said, 'do me a small favour. Since Gaṅgādatta is a very old acquaintance of yours, pray go and look for him in some pool or other and give him this message from me. Say to him: "Friend, come back quickly, alone if need be; even if no other frogs accompany you. I cannot live here alone without you. And if I do you the least harm, may all the merit I have gained in my life be wholly yours, I swear."'

The lizard scurried off at Sir Handsome's bidding. Looking high and low for him, she finally found Gaṅgādatta, 'Gracious Lord,' she said to him, 'your friend, Sir Handsome is waiting impatiently for your return. So please hurry and come back. Furthermore, he has sworn that if he does you any harm, all the merit he has earned in life will be wholly yours. Come home without the slightest fear.'

Gaṅgādatta listened to what the lizard had to say; then he recited this verse:

> *'What crime will a man famished not commit?*   (28)
> *Ruthless indeed are those down-and-out,*
> *Go, fair lady; tell Sir Handsome, the snake;*
> *Gaṅgādatta will never again be at the well.'*

And with these words he sent her back.

'So, you wicked water-dweller, like Gaṅgādatta, I shall never, never enter your home.'

Hearing these harsh words, the crocodile pleaded, dissembling, 'Oh! My dear friend! what a thing to say! Please come to my home and by that act wipe off my sin of ingratitude. Otherwise, I shall sit here and starve myself to death.'

'You blockhead,' retorted Red Face. 'You think I am like the fellow named Long Ears to go to a place in full sight of danger and get myself killed?'

The crocodile asked, 'Who is this fellow named Long Ears? How did he die even as he saw danger staring at him? Pray, tell me that tale.'

And then Red Face, the ape, began the tale of *Long Ears and Dusty*.

Once there was a lion named Flaming Mane[15] who lived in a certain forest. He had a jackal named Dusty[16] who was his faithful follower and factotum. Once, the lion suffered many deep gashes in his body as a result of a fight with an elephant; so wounded was he that he could hardly move. And as the lion could not bestir himself, Dusty grew famished. His throat was pinched by hunger. So one day he said to the lion, 'My lord, so tormented am I by acute hunger that I can scarcely place one foot before the other. So, how can I attend on you?'

And the lion replied, 'My good Dusty, you go and hunt out some creature which I can slay even in the sorry state I am in.'

Obeying the lion's command, Dusty, the jackal, went searching for prey. As he was searching he came to the nearby village

366

where he saw an ass named Long Ears struggling to crop a thin and scanty patch of *dūrvā*[17] grass growing at the edge of a pond.

Dusty walked up to the ass and greeted him. 'Uncle, please accept my respectful greetings. My goodness! what a long time it is since I saw you last, and why have you grown so feeble?'

'Oh, my dear nephew,[18] what is to be done? The dhobi[19] treats me cruelly laying heavy loads on my back. And in return he hardly gives me a mouthful of grass to eat. Subsisting on this dust-coated *dūrvā* grass what nourishment does my body get?' replied the ass.

'Ah! I see,' observed the jackal, 'I tell you what: there is an absolutely charming spot by the river all lush with emerald green grass. Come, live with me there and enjoy witty conversation and pleasant company.'

'Ah! Dear nephew; you speak nicely indeed. But, as you know, creatures of the fields are the natural prey of dwellers in the woods; so what good is that charming spot you talk of?'

'No, no, don't talk like that,' remarked Dusty. 'You see, that is a spot protected by the strong fence of my arms. No stranger dares enter it. Besides, there are three female asses there who have also been cruelly tortured by dhobis. They are in need of a husband. They have grown sleek and plump and frisky, bursting with youth's ardour. And do you know what they told me: "Uncle dear, listen, please go to some village or other and find us a nice husband"; that is what they said. Now you know why I came to fetch you.'

These words of the jackal filled every limb of Long Ears' body with aching passion. He readily agreed. 'My good fellow, if that is the case, then, let us hurry there. Lead the way, my friend. Ah! How well the poet expresses it:

> *Nothing there is in this world,*   (29)
> *that is neither nectar, nor poison,*
> *except one . . .*
> *a lovely woman.*
> *We live by her presence,*
>   *we die from her absence.'*

And with these fancies the silly ass went along with the jackal into the lion's presence. But the lion being a greater ass took one leap as soon as the ass came within the range of his spring and went right over Long Ears' back to land on the far side and fall on the ground.

The ass was taken by surprise and wondered: 'O, Gracious Gods! What could this be?' For it seemed as if a thunderbolt had shot over him. Though confounded by all that had happened, he somehow came through unhurt by the grace of a kind fate perhaps. Then as he looked back he saw a creature he had never seen before; a terrifying creature with cruel, bloodshot eyes. Seized by intense fear, he beat a hasty retreat and galloping swiftly with his feet responding to his terror, raced back to town.

The jackal, who was watching, now taunted the lion. 'Ho ho! What is this! I have witnessed a piece of your heroism today, it seems!'

Totally dumbfounded the lion whimpered, 'But . . . the position I took to make my spring was not well-prepared. So, what could I do? Could an elephant have ever escaped once he came within the range of my spring? Hm . . . ?'

'Then, you had better have your spring well-positioned the next time, because I am planning to bring this ass once again into your presence,' replied Dusty, curtly.

'My good fellow,' exclaimed Flaming Mane, 'Once the ass saw me face to face he ran for his life; how can you then make him agree to come again?'

'You leave that to me; why are you bothered about it? It is up to me to be circumspect on this point.'

With these words, Dusty followed the tracks made by the ass and found him grazing at exactly the same spot as previously.

When Long Ears saw Dusty, the jackal, standing there, he remarked drily, 'Well, dear nephew; that was indeed a charming spot you took me to. And was I not lucky to escape with my life! So tell me; what was that terrible creature, extremely ferocious, from whose thunderbolt blows I was glad to escape?'

At this, Dusty laughed and said, 'Oh, that . . . that, Uncle,

was the she-ass, dressed up in all her finery. Seeing you
advancing towards her, she rose up in a flurry of passion to
embrace you. But you . . . you were so timid that you fled. Even
as you disappeared she stretched out a hand to stop you. That's
all; there is nothing else to it. So come back, for she has resolved
to starve to death on your account; and she says, "If I cannot
have Long Ears for my husband, I shall enter the fire or water or
take poison. But I simply cannot bear to be separated from him."
So be gracious and return, otherwise, mark you, you incur the
sin[20] of causing a woman's death and the God of Love[21] will be
enraged. As these lines express it well:

> *If misguided men desiring Paradise,*　　　　　　　　(30)
> *or Final Bliss, elect to shun outright*
> *the dolphin-bannered god's[22] victorious emblem*
> *and provider of all things good—WOMAN,*
> *for this error Love hurls cruel blows at them;*
> *post-haste some become naked mendicants,*
> *or shaven monks; others wear matted hair,*
> *or garlands of skulls, or robes of saffron.'*

The ass, convinced by Dusty's words and trusting him
implicitly, prepared to go with the jackal once again; for indeed,
it is wisely said:

> *A man, knowing better, may do a deed*　　　　　　　(31)
> *most horrid driven by a fate most unfavourable.*
> *For who in the world can relish a deed*
> *the whole world regards reprehensible!*

As Long Ears, taken in completely by a hundred deceitful
words spoken by the rascal Dusty as they went along, came once
again in to the lion's presence, Flaming Mane, who had
positioned himself suitably for his spring, killed him instantly.

Having slain the ass, Flaming Mane instructed Dusty to
stand guard over the beast and himself went down to the river to
have a bath. The jackal, overcome by intense craving for food,
ate up the donkey's ears and heart. When the lion returned after

completing his bath, and all the prescribed rituals[23] following it, he noticed that both ears and the heart of the ass were missing. Flaming Mane's whole being was blazing with fury as he demanded of Dusty, 'Ha! You blasted villain! What is this dastardly act of yours? Turning my royal share of this food into your leavings[24] by eating of it before I did? For you have eaten this animal's heart and ears.'

Dusty replied humbly and respectfully, 'O, my lord, please, please do not speak so harshly. This ass was born without a heart or ears. Or else, how would he have come here, seen you, fled in terror, only to come back again? For it is very wisely observed:

> *He came, he saw, he bolted, having seen,*   (32)
> *having glimpsed your horrible mien.*
> *He ran; yet he came back again,*
> *the fool . . . he surely lacked heart and ears.'*

Flaming Mane being mollified by Dusty's words, believed them to be true. He divided the carcass with the jackal and ate his own portion.

'This is why I said to you that I was not an ass like Long Ears,' said Red Face wryly. Then he added in a burst of anger, 'You nincompoop, you played a mean trick on me, but, like Yudhisthira, you spoilt your game by blurting out the truth. As these lines say:

> *The fake who unmindful of self-interest*   (33)
> *spills the beans, is slow-witted;*
> *another Yudhisthira at best;*
> *he is certain to lose what he gained . . . .'*

'How did that happen?' enquired Hideous Jaws. And then Red Face began the tale of *The Potter who played the hero*.

In a certain settlement there once lived a potter named Yudhisthira. [25] One day as he was entering his courtyard at a very fast pace, drunk, he carelessly stumbled on a half-broken pot with sharp edges and fell down head-on. The jagged rim of the pot made a deep gash on his forehead cutting it open. With blood flowing profusely and drenching his whole body, he somehow managed to get on to his feet. As the wound was treated without any skill, it festered and healed badly leaving a horrible scar on the potter's forehead.

Some time later, a cruel famine struck that region and the potter pinched by terrible hunger left his place and in the company of some palace-guards he went to another land where he too took up service as a palace-guard. The king of that land noticed the thickened, ragged and horrid-looking scar left by the potsherd and thinking, 'O, what a great hero this man must be for he has taken a wound in front, on his brow,' looked upon our fake hero, the potter, with even greater favour, giving him greater honour and finer gifts than to all the others. Even the princes became intensely envious seeing the exceptional favour shown to the potter, but said nothing in the palace about it for fear of the king.

Now one day a great review was being held in honour of veteran heroes; elephants were arrayed, horses caparisoned and warriors stood in line for the royal inspection. The king turned to the potter at his side during the introductory ceremony and asked, 'O, prince, what is your name? And your clan? And in which battle did you receive the blow that left honour indelibly printed on your brow?'

To this the potter replied, 'My lord, I am a potter by birth, and my name is Yudhiṣṭhira. And this scar that you see is not a sword-wound. One day as I was hurrying through the courtyard littered with broken pots, being drunk and unsteady, I stumbled over a broken pot and fell flat on my face. The jagged potsherd made a deep gash which festered and left this hideous scar.'

The king was flabbergasted, 'O, you gods; how badly deceived have I been by this potter whom I took to be a brave prince. He deserves a good cuffing,' and straight away gave orders for that to be done. When a good cuffing had been administered, the potter observed, 'My lord, it is not right that you should treat me in this manner; you should first observe the dexterity of my actions in battle.'

371

'No, no, my fine fellow,' replied the king, 'you may be a veritable treasury of excellent qualities; but you had better leave; remember the well-known saying:

> *You are brave, your looks too are fine,*   (34)
> *dear boy; you have acquired knowledge;*
> *but you come of a lineage*
> *where no elephant is slain.'*

'And what is that all about?' asked the potter. Then the king began the tale of *The Jackal mothered by the Lioness.*

Once, a lion and his wife lived in a certain forest. One day the lioness gave birth to twins. Every day the lion went hunting, killed deer or some other prey and brought it to the lioness. But once it happened that though he roamed.all through the forest, the lion failed to find anything. The glorious divinity, the sun, was already behind the Western Mountain.[26] As he was on his way home, the lion came upon a baby jackal lying on the trail. Looking at it he thought, 'It is just a baby,' and picking it up gently, he carried it between his teeth with great care and brought it home alive. He then handed it over to the lioness.

'Have you brought any food, beloved?' asked the lioness.

'No, my dearest,' answered the lion, 'I could find nothing today except this tiny jackal cub; and I could not find it in my heart to kill him, thinking, "After all, he is one of our own kind and a baby at that." There is a saying which goes as follows:

> *Even when your life is in great peril*   (35)
> *never strike a woman, a child, a Brāhmana,*
> *or an ascetic wearing Śiva's symbol,*[27]
> *specially not those who place their trust in you.*

'Have this little creature for your wholesome diet[28] for the time being; I shall see what I can find and bring you something else at dawn.' And the lioness at once remarked, 'Beloved: you spared his life because you thought, "he is a baby". How can I then kill and eat him to fill my belly? For we have been taught this:

> *Refrain from what is prohibited*　　　　　　　(36)
> *even when life itself is at stake;*
> *do not abandon what is prescribed;*
> *this the Eternal Law states.*

'So, this fellow shall be my third son.' Saying this she started nursing him at her own breast and soon he became very strong and healthy. So the three cubs grew up together unaware of any genetic difference and spent their childhood acting the same way and indulging in the same amusements.

Now, one day, a wild elephant roaming around came to that part of the forest. Seeing the elephant, the two lion-cubs quivering with fury started towards him, eager for the kill. But the jackal cub restrained them saying, 'Oh, no! This is an elephant, an enemy of your race; so don't go near him, brothers.' With these words, he ran home as fast as he could. Seeing their elder brother turn tail, the two lion cubs became dispirited. Ah! How admirably put:

> *One single doughty warrior*　　　　　　　(37)
> *with fiery courage headed for battle,*
> *fires an army entire,*
> *but if there is one broken blighter,*
> *the entire army is routed.*

And so:

> *For this reason, the Earth's rulers*　　　　　　　(38)
> *look only for mighty warriors,*
> *valiant, resolute, fiery-spirited;*
> *and steer clear of the faint-hearted.*

On reaching home, the twin lion cubs, laughing heartily, reported all that had happened to their parents with real zest, describing how their elder brother had behaved. 'You know what,' they said, 'the moment he saw the elephant, he couldn't run fast enough to put a safe distance between himself and the beast.'

The jackal cub heard this and his heart distended with anger; his blossom-lip quivered, his eyes reddened; his brows twisted into triple-arched curves. And he spoke harshly, severely reprimanding his siblings.

The lioness then took the little cub aside and gently admonished him. 'Now, now, sweet child; you should never talk like this to them; they are your brothers.'

But her gentle, calming words only made the jackal cub even angrier and he turned on her in a fury chiding her bitterly, 'What?' he exclaimed, 'Am I inferior to these two in courage and beauty, in learning and skills? Or in discipline and use of the mind? Am I? That they should ridicule me in this manner? I shall kill them; don't you doubt that.'

The lioness laughed quietly at this outburst; as she did not wish to see him die she recited this verse:

> *'Brave you are, handsome too, my boy,*　　　　　　　(39)
> *and you have acquired knowledge;*
> *but you come of a lineage*
> *where no elephant is slain.*

'Now pay close attention to what I have to tell you. My darling child, you are the son of a jackal mother, whom out of compassion I reared, feeding you with my own milk to make you strong. So, while my two sons are still babies, and do not know that you are a jackal, you had better make haste and run away to live among your own people. Otherwise, once they know the truth, you can be certain that you are walking the path to death.'

When he heard this the jackal cub was terrified to death; and he quietly stole away to join his own people.

'Therefore, good potter, you too had better quickly take yourself off from here before these seasoned warriors find out that you are a potter. Otherwise, you will be scorned, hooted at and killed.'

The potter got the message and quickly made himself scarce. 'Therefore I say to you, "The fake, unmindful of his own interests . . . " and so on. Oh, you blockhead, shame on you! To undertake a deed like this for your wife. Never trust a woman. The moral is aptly pointed out in this little tale:

My family I forsook for her,   (40)
I was deprived of half my life for her;
and now she leaves me, cold, uncaring;
Oh! What man can trust a woman!'

'Ah! How was that?' asked the crocodile, Hideous Jaws. And the ape, Red Face, then began the tale of *The Ungrateful Wife*.

Once in a certain settlement there lived a Brāhmaṇa who loved his wife more than his life. She quarrelled daily with all his family without rest and to such an extent that he found life unbearable. So he forsook his family and taking his wife with him departed to some distant land.

In the middle of a great forest, the Brāhmaṇī, said to him, 'My lord, I am dying of thirst. Can you find some water?' So, the Brāhmaṇa went searching for water but when he came back with some, he found her lying dead. Since he loved her dearly he was grief-stricken and began to lament. As he was bewailing his loss, he heard a voice in the air say, 'If, O, Brāhmaṇa, you are willing to part with half your life, then, the Brāhmaṇī will live again.'

At once the Brāhmaṇa did the prescribed purifying rites and by repeating the words 'I give life' three times he parted with half his life. No sooner had he said the three words than the Brāhmaṇī revived.

The pair then drank some water and having eaten some wild fruits continued on their journey. In due course, they reached a certain city and entered a garden of flowers situated at the gates. The Brāhmaṇa said to his wife, 'Dear lady, you wait here while I go and fetch some food for us.' Having advised her thus, he left.

Now, in that flower-garden there was a cripple turning a

water-wheel and singing divinely as he did so. Listening to his singing, the Brāhmaṇī was smitten with love for him and went up to him saying, 'Gracious friend, if you do not love me, the sin of slaying a woman will cling to you.'

'What do you want with a handicapped man like myself?' asked the cripple.

But she insisted: 'Not one word more; you must make love to me.'

And the cripple agreed and did so. After her passion was consummated, she told him, 'Listen, from this moment I am yours for life. With this understanding, Your Honour must now go with us.'

'So be it,' said the cripple.

When the Brāhmaṇa returned with some food and started eating with his wife, she said, 'This cripple is hungry; give him a bit of this food.'

The Brāhmaṇa did so; then his wife suggested; 'Look you are without a companion and when you go alone to some village or other, I am left without anybody to talk to. So why not take this cripple along with us?'

To this the husband replied, 'Lady, it is hard enough for me, I find, to carry my own body, what to say of this cripple.'

'All right, then I shall carry him myself if he sits in a basket, retorted the wife.

Bewildered by her crafty words, the Brāhmaṇa was agreeable to her suggestion and they walked on in this fashion.

One day as they rested close to the mouth of a well, the Brāhmaṇī, with the help of the cripple, gave her sleeping husband a push so that he tumbled into the water. Then picking up the basket with the cripple in it, the woman entered the city where the king's officers of law, who were in charge of preventing thefts and robberies and seeing to the collection of toll at the gates, were making their rounds. Seeing a woman with a basket on her head, they forcibly seized it and took it into the king's presence. On opening the basket the king found the cripple.

Presently, the Brāhmaṇī arrived there weeping and wailing, for she had followed close on the heels of the royal officers of law.

'What is all this?' demanded the king on seeing her.

And the woman said, 'This is my husband, my lord, a cripple so harassed by a whole host of his kinsmen that distracted in mind by my love for him, I placed him on my head and was coming to you.'

The king was moved by what he heard; 'You are like a sister to me,' he said, 'I grant you two villages; enjoy all delights with your husband and live happily.'

At this point her husband, the Brāhmana, who by a fortunate turn of fate had been rescued from the well by some holy man, and been wandering around for a while, had finally arrived in the same city. His wicked wife, seeing him, denounced him straight away to the king. 'Oh great king,' she cried out, 'there, he is one of my husband's kinsmen; he has come here.'

The king immediately ordered the Brāhmana to be put to death. The Brāhmana now interposed with a request, 'My lord,' he said, 'this woman has in her possession something she received from me. If you love justice, then ask her to restore that thing to me first.'

'Lady,' said the king, 'if you have something belonging to this man, return it to him.'

'But, my lord, I have taken nothing from this man,' she replied.

'I gave you half my life, making it yours by uttering thrice the words, "I give life". Give that back to me,' said the Brāhmana with determination.

Fearing the king's anger, the Brāhmani uttered the very same words 'I give life', thrice, and instantly dropped dead.

The king, in great astonishment, demanded, 'What is the meaning of all this?'

The Brāhmana then told the king the whole story as it had happened.

'This is the reason why I recited those lines to you: "My family I forsook for her . . . " and the rest of it.'

And Red Face continued, 'There is yet another tale, my friend, which also points out the moral quite neatly:

What will a man not do (41)
what will he not grant too,
when asked by a woman.
Where those who are not horses, neigh,
there, heads are shaven[29] out of season.'

'Oh ? And what is that tale: tell me,' said the crocodile. And then Red Face began the tale of *Two Henpecked Husbands.*

A long time ago there was a great emperor named Delight,[30] of great power and prowess who was sole lord of the sea-girdled Earth; whose footstool scintillated with the intermingled rays radiating from the lustrous gems on the crowns of countless hosts of kneeling princes; whose glory spread clear and dazzling as autumn moonbeams. Now the emperor had a minister named Splendour[31] who had complete mastery of the knowledge contained in all the treatises on statecraft.

Once, Splendour's wife threw a tantrum as the result of a lover's quarrel and would not even look at him. Splendour, who absolutely doted on his wife, tried his best to please and cajole her in many different ways, but on no account would she relent. In desperation he begged her saying, 'Fair lady, what can I do to please you, tell me and I shall do it.'

After a great deal of persuasion she deigned to say, 'Well, if you shave your head completely and then come and fall at my feet. I might cast a gracious glance or two in your direction.'

Poor Splendour did as she wanted and she became pleased with him.

Now, the queen of Emperor Delight also became annoyed with him in much the same manner and however hard he tried to pacify her she would not be pleased. Finally, the emperor pleaded, 'Gracious Lady,' he said, 'I cannot live even an instant without you. See, here I am, falling at your feet to beg your forgiveness.'

The queen replied, 'If you take a horse's bit in your mouth

and if you let me mount you and make you gallop, and if you
neigh like a horse as you are galloping, then I shall become
pleased with you.' The emperor did accordingly.

Next morning Splendour came into the council chamber
where the emperor was seated. Seeing him, the emperor asked,
'Why, good Splendour, why have you had your head shaved
when there is no occasion for it?' To which Splendour replied
with these lines:

> *'What will a man not do,* (42)
> *what will he not grant too,*
> *if asked by a woman.*
> *Where those who are not horses, neigh,*
> *there, heads are shaven out of season.'*

'You simpleton! You too are henpecked just like Delight and
Splendour were. You tried to find a way of killing me because
your wife asked you to; and that fact was revealed to me by your
own words, and mark how well the saying puts it:

> *Parrots and myna birds are caught* (43)
> *and caged through the fault of speaking;*
> *while herons and cranes are not:*
> *Silence leads to success in everything.*

'Then again:

> *Though the secret was well-guarded* (44)
> *and he presented a horrid sight,*
> *the ass in tiger-skin attired*
> *was killed as soon as he descanted.'*

'Oh! Tell me about it,' said Hideous Jaws. And then Red Face
began the tale of *The Ass in tiger-skin*.

There was once a washerman called Clean Clothes[32] who lived
in a certain settlement. And he owned a single donkey.[33] For lack
of fodder this donkey grew very feeble.

As he roamed in the forest, the washerman once found the skin of a dead tiger. And that started him thinking, 'Ah! what a piece of good luck. I can wrap this tiger-skin round my poor old donkey and let him loose in the barley fields at night. Taking him to be a tiger the farmers will be afraid to drive him off.'

The washerman carried out his plan and his donkey grazed in the fields and ate barley to his heart's content. Early in the morning the washerman led the donkey back home. And as time went on he grew so plump that his master found it hard to lead him to the tying-post.

One day, the donkey, while grazing, heard the sound of a she-donkey braying in the distance. The instant he heard that, he too started braying loudly in response. The farmers heard him and talked among themselves: 'Good heavens! This is a donkey in disguise.' Realizing the truth, they killed him with stones and arrows and blows from wooden staves.

'Therefore, I say this: "Though the secret was well-guarded . . . " and the rest of it.'

Now while the ape was retailing these stories to the crocodile, some water-dwelling creature came up to Hideous Jaws with important information. It said, 'Hey there! Friend, Hideous Jaws, listen, your wife who had undertaken a vow to fast unto death is gone.'

Stricken to the heart with sorrow the crocodile began to lament for his wife. 'Alas! What has come upon me; what an unfortunate person I am! As we have heard:

A house where no mother dwells (45)
or wife whose speech is loving
is no home but a wilderness;
so why not go live in the wilds!

'So, dear friend, forgive me for I have wronged you somewhat. Having lost my wife I shall now enter the fire.'

Red Face listening to these words of Hideous Jaws, laughed heartily and said, 'Come, come, my friend. I knew from the beginning that you were henpecked and completely under your wife's thumb. And right here is the proof. O, you dunderhead. When happiness comes knocking at your door you sit drowned in despair. When a wife like yours dies, it is an occasion to celebrate. Surely you know the wise saying:

> *A wife whose conduct is vicious,* (46)
> *a wife who is cantankerous,*
> *is no wife but Old Age incarnate,*
> *cruel, horrid, as the learned state.*

> *So, make every effort you can* (47)
> *in this sorry world of man*
> *to shun WOMAN's very name,*
> *if happiness is your aim.*

> *What's within them appears not on the tongue;* (48)
> *What's on the tongue finds no expression;*
> *What is expressed is not acted upon;*
> *Ah! How strange are the ways of WOMAN!*

> *When we have one classic instance before us* (49)
> *of the depravity of women,*
> *why cite others? Without a single qualm*
> *they can slay their own children,*
> *even those they carried in their womb.*

> *To see true affection* (50)
> *where no kindliness is;*
> *to look for softness in a rock's hardness;*
> *to find sentiment in the insensate . . .*
> *these are a callow youth's fancies*
> *pining for nubile girls.'*

Then Hideous Jaws commented ruefully; 'Ah! Yes, my friend; all this is true. But what can I do now that two calamities have hit me? First, the break up of my home; next, the unfortunate misunderstanding with a dear friend. When one is out of luck such things happen to one. As the verse expresses it so well:

Sure I could boast that I was clever;   (51)
but you were doubly clever, you shameless hussy;
yet now you have neither husband nor lover;
so why do you sit and stare vacantly.'

'Oh? And what is that story?' asked Red Face. And then Hideous Jaws began the tale of *The Unfaithful Wife*.

A farmer lived in a certain settlement with his wife. Because her husband was old the farmer's wife had her thoughts constantly flitting around other men, and could not bear to stay at home. Her mind was forever occupied with her lovers and she went about here and there looking for men. A certain rogue who lived by thievery once saw her. Coming up to her, he said, 'Fair Lady; my wife is dead; now that I have seen you I am head over heels in love with you. Please grant me love's supreme treasure.'

The farmer's wife was delighted and answered, 'Oh! you handsome gentleman, if that be the case, let me tell you this; my husband has immense wealth and he is so old that he can hardly stir. So this is what I shall do; I shall gather all his wealth, each and everything he has and come to you. We shall go away somewhere together and enjoy all the pleasures of love.'

'A great idea,' replied the thief. 'Why don't you hasten to this very spot at dawn tomorrow so that we might go to some beautiful city or other where I shall obtain the complete fulfilment of my life in this beautiful world.'

'Very well,' said the woman and went home, her face wreathed in beatific smiles.

At night, when her husband was fast asleep the farmer's wife gathered together all the wealth in the home and went with it at dawn to the appointed meeting place. The rogue making the woman walk ahead of him started in a southerly direction. Gaily conversing with each other they covered some two leagues when they came to a river.

When he saw the river the rogue began reflecting on the

situation, 'Now, what on earth will I do with a middle-aged woman? Besides, I shall be in deep trouble if someone or other suddenly appears coming after her in hot pursuit. I think I had better take all her wealth and be on my way leaving her in the lurch.'

With this idea in his mind he addressed the woman: 'My dearest one, look, this great river is difficult to cross. So, why don't I first take all the wealth safely across, and then come back for you. That way I have only you to ferry across and that I can do easily enough carrying you on my back in comfort.'

'Oh, my handsome lover, do what you think is best,' said the besotted woman.

When she had thus agreed to his plan, the rogue took hold of all her wealth, to the last coin and then he said again, 'Dearest, perhaps you should take off both your upper and lower garments and hand them over to me so that when I am carrying you across you would feel perfectly at ease, unencumbered, in the waters of the river.'

The foolish woman did as he said, handing over both her garments to the rogue who took off with her wealth and clothes and headed towards the particular place he already had in mind.

As for the farmer's wife, she sat utterly woebegone on the river bank, with both hands clutching at her throat.

As she sat like this, there came along a vixen carrying a chunk of raw meat. As she stopped and looked around, the vixen saw a huge fish leap out of the river and lie stranded on the river bank. Dropping the chunk of meat the vixen darted towards the fish. But before she could grab it a kite swooped down from the sky, seized the gobbet of meat and flew up again.

The fish too seeing the vixen coming towards it somehow managed to struggle back into the river.

As the vixen, disappointed because all her efforts had come to nothing, gazed up disconsolately at the kite, the farmer's wife addressed her, smiling mockingly:

> 'O vixen, little vixen, bereft (52)
> of both fish and flesh

what are you staring at?
The kite has got your lump of flesh,
the fish is back in the water.'

The vixen, when she heard this and knowing full well that
the woman had lost her wealth, husband and lover, jeered at her,
taunting her with these words:

'Whatever cleverness I could boast of (53)
of that you had double, you wanton!
but now, without husband, without lover,
you sit naked[34] *beside the river.'*

As Hideous Jaws was telling the ape this tale, there came
another water-creature, with yet another bit of distressing news:
'Oh, friend, listen; your home has been occupied by another huge
crocodile.'

Whereupon the crocodile became extremely despondent and
began to ponder over ways and means of kicking the intruder out
of his home.

'O, misery upon misery,' he lamented, 'how I am kicked
around by a cruel fate; mark:

A friend has turned unfriendly: (54)
a dearly-loved wife is dead:
my home too is invaded
what else will happen to me?

'How true is the well-known maxim: misfortunes never come
singly. What should I do now? Should I fight this intruder? Or
should I call out to him in gentle words of conciliation and request
him to leave my house? Or, should I try intrigue? Or resort to
offering him a bribe? Let me ask my simian friend, Red Face, for
some good advice. For we are told:

Whatever be your task first ask (55)
those whom you should ask:
those with experience who have

your best interests at heart:
no obstacle will then cross your path.'

Having mulled over the problem, Hideous Jaws again addressed Red Face who was sitting on the tree. 'Ah! My friend,' said he, 'look at me: my luck is at an all-time low; for I have lost even my house to another powerful crocodile. So now I turn to you for advice; please tell me what I should do. Should I resort to conciliation, or to one of the other three expedients of policy?'[35]

Red Face retorted in a huff, 'You ungrateful wretch! I have told you already that I wish to have nothing to do with you; then why come to me again? I would not care to offer good advice to a fool like you. The old tale points out the moral quite plainly:

> *Good advice should not be provided* (56)
> *to just anyone you meet; See!*
> *The foolish monkey dispossessed*
> *her who had built her home cozy.'*

'Oh! How did that happen? Tell me,' insisted the crocodile. And Red Face then began the tale of *The Officious Sparrow*.

In a certain forest a pair of sparrows lived in a nest they had built on the branch of a tree. One chilly day in the month of February, a monkey who had been caught in an unseasonable hailstorm came to the foot of that tree, his body trembling like a leaf in the lightest breeze. As he sat crouched with teeth making music like the plucked strings of a lute, and knees and feet, arms and hands tightly locked, he looked the very picture of misery.

The hen-sparrow watching him, spoke out of compassion:

> *'With hands and feet provided* (57)
> *you have a human form, almost;*
> *by wind and cold buffeted*
> *why don't you build a house, you fool?'*

The monkey listened to her and thought to himself: 'Ah!

Well: that is how the world is: full of folks who exude smugness.
What a high opinion of herself does this miserable little bird have!
These lines express it admirably:

> *Who on earth does not have his share*   (58)
> *of a sense of self-importance!*
> *The lapwing lies with legs upstretched*
> *to prop a falling sky!'*

Thereupon he told the little hen-sparrow:

> *'Oh! Needlebeak! You ill-bred tart!*   (59)
> *You think yourself mighty smart!*
> *Hold your tongue, you slut . . . or else,*
> *I shall make you homeless.'*

Though the monkey thus expressly forbade her from doing
so, the sparrow would not desist but repeatedly offered him her
good advice on building a house. Finally, the monkey was so
exasperated that he dashed up the tree and broke the nest of the
sparrows into smithereens.

'This is why I said before, "Advice should not be thrown
away . . . " and so on,' concluded Red Face.

Having heard what Red Face said, the crocodile would still
not take no for an answer. 'Ah! My friend: I am guilty of
wrongdoing, I know. Still, remembering our past friendship,
please give me some good advice.'

But Red Face was adamant; he answered resolutely, 'Listen.
I will not give one word of advice, believe me. Because you were
planning to plunge me in mid-ocean, obeying your wife.
Granting you loved your wife dearly, was that any reason to
drown friends, kin and others in the deep ocean? Just because
she asked you to? Eh?'

Hideous Jaws replied, 'All that you say is true, my friend.
But you are well aware of the maxim that says, "Seven steps
make friendship".[36] Consider this, and give me a bit of advice.
You also know this saying:

> *Men who offer sage counsel* (60)
> *wishing others well,*
> *will never suffer pain and sorrow*
> *in this world or in the other.*

'Though I di!' you great wrong, my friend, be gracious and do me the favour of counselling me. As we are told:

> *What is there so commendable* (61)
> *in returning good for good;*
> *the virtuous seek those just and noble*
> *who for ill return good.'*

Red Face was touched by these words and he relented, 'Well, my good fellow, perhaps there is something in what you say. You had better go and fight this fellow. The wise have said that a person succeeds by:

> *Humbling*[37] *himself before the noble,* (62)
> *intriguing against the valiant,*
> *bestowing trifling gifts to lackeys*
> *and fighting boldly with equals,*

as the tale tells it.'

'How does the tale tell it?' asked the crocodile. And Red Face, the ape, then began the tale of *The Smart Jackal*.

Once in the deep woods there lived a jackal named Smart Aleck. One day he found an elephant that had died from natural causes lying in a part of the woodland. He walked right round the animal but found himself unable to bite through the thick hide and get at the flesh.

At this moment, a lion who had been roaming around in the woods appeared there. Seeing the lion, the jackal immediately bent low till the crown of his head touched the dust on the ground, clasped the lion's lotus-claws and spoke with great humility: 'My lord, here I am, serving as your sentry and standing guard over this elephant. Let His Majesty now partake of this food.'

'Hey, fellow,' roared the lion with a lordly air, 'I never eat what has been killed by another. So, here, take it, for I am pleased to make a gift of this animal to you.'

'Indeed, my lord,' said Smart Aleck beaming with joy, 'the magnanimity shown by His Majesty towards his servants is most commendable.'

When the lion was gone, there came along a tiger. On seeing him, Smart Aleck did some quick thinking. 'True, I got rid of one low-down villain by making deep obeisance to him. Now, how shall I deal with this second rascal, for he is valiant to be sure, who can be tackled only through cunning manipulation; intrigue is the only right approach here. For we have heard this:

> *Where gentle persuasion and offers of gifts* (63)
> *are of no avail*
> *in making someone do your will,*
> *try intrigue; that should not fail.*

'And to tell the truth, who in the world is not caught by intrigue? As we are well aware:

> *Even a pearl flawless, whole, inviolate,* (64)
> *a compact and exquisite, lustrous globe,*
> *becomes vulnerable to bondage*
> *once it is pierced through the heart.*'[38]

Having thought this over, Smart Aleck faced the tiger with his neck thrust out a bit, acting scared. 'O, Uncle, how could you venture like this into the jaws of death! For this elephant was slain by a lion who has just this minute gone down to the river for a bath having charged me with the task of standing guard over his kill. And further, as he was leaving, he admonished me strictly, thus: "Listen, if any tiger should come by, you had better slip away quietly and inform me; do you hear? For I am determined to clear these woods of all tigers, the reason being that once after

I had killed an elephant and left it unguarded, a tiger sneaked up and helped himself to its meat, and I had the leavings. From that day I have sworn vengeance against tigers."'

The tiger was terrified hearing these ominous words. 'O, dear nephew,' he whimpered, 'make me a gift of my life. Even if the lion takes ever so long, please do not say a word about me to him.'

Having made this request the tiger ran for his life.

No sooner had the tiger disappeared than a leopard arrived there.

'Well, well,' chuckled Smart Aleck. 'If it is not our friend the spotted leopard arriving in good time! And doesn't he have powerful teeth! Just the person to cut into this elephant-hide!'

Smart Aleck called out to the leopard, 'Come, come here, dear nephew. Oh, it has been a long time since we met; where have you been? And why are you looking so famished? Come and be my guest. You know the maxim: "A guest is one who arrives at the right moment." Here lies an elephant slain by a lion; and here am I, duly appointed to guard it. Be that as it may, so long as the lion does not get back, you are welcome to a square meal of elephant-meat and then run.'

The leopard however demurred. 'As things stand, Uncle, this meat is not my cup of tea, I am afraid. As you are well aware of that other maxim:

If a fellow lives, he lives to see   (65)
a hundred happy occasions, surely.

'It is best to eat just what one can well digest. Therefore I had better be on my way.'

'Oh, come, come, you faint-hearted fellow! Where's your courage? Eat. I am here to warn you when the lion is still at some distance.'

Tempted, the leopard followed Smart Aleck's suggestion and started to bite through the elephant-hide. But no sooner had he made a deep cut than Smart Aleck cried out, 'Go, oh, go quickly, dear nephew; here comes the lion.' At these words, the leopard took off and disappeared.

Now, as Smart Aleck began eating the flesh of the elephant, through the gash the leopard had made there came another jackal and he seemed to be in a terrible rage. Smart Aleck quickly sized him up and knew him to be his equal whose strength he could gauge correctly. Muttering these lines:

> 'Fall flat on your face   (66)
> before your superior:
> employ devious ways
> against the valiant;
> > throw a crumb or two
> > to a fawning menial
> > but . . . show your mettle
> > to your equal . . . .'

Smart Aleck crashed headlong into the intruder and tore at him with his fangs scattering his flesh and bones in all directions.

Having done this he happily enjoyed the elephant-meat for a long, long time.

'In the same way, you too should fight your foe who is one of your kind: overcome him and scatter his limbs to the far horizon. If you do not do that, he will put down deep roots and end up destroying you,' concluded Red Face. Then he added. 'My friend, you know the saying:

> From cows we expect sustenance,   (67)
> and from Brāhmanas penance;
> frailty one expects from women
> and cause for alarm from kinsmen.

'There is another saying too on this score:

> Fine foods in plenty   (68)
> and in great variety
> you may eat when you go abroad;
> and in the cities

> *the sweet young ladies*
> *are easygoing, really,*
> *in a foreign land;*
> *but there's just one thing wrong*
> *in your foreign land*
> *your kith and kin who live abroad*
> *hate your guts quite sincerely.'*

'What you say sounds quite intriguing; tell me more,' said the crocodile. And then Red Face began the tale of *The Dog who went abroad*.

There was once a dog named Spotty[39] who lived in a certain settlement which at one time suffered a prolonged famine. As food became scarce, all the dogs and other animals were dying and their families were becoming extinct. Afraid of what might happen, Spotty, already drawn and pinched by hunger, decided to go abroad. In a certain city in the foreign land he went to, he discovered a house where the lady of the house was careless and easygoing.[40] So Spotty started going in there regularly and each day he ate to his heart's content enjoying a variety of fine foods, dainties and the like until he was replete with satisfaction. But, as he came out of the house he was surrounded by a number of powerful dogs, all puffed up with pride, who came from all sides, fell upon him and tore at his limbs with their fangs.

After a while when this became too much, Spotty began to do some serious thinking. 'This is just a bit much,' he told himself. 'It is better to live in one's own land; there might be a famine raging there, but at least one lives in peace. Nobody comes and fights you. I had better return to my own city.' So, Spotty made up his mind to return home.

Seeing him come home from abroad, his kinsmen and friends crowded around him plying him with questions. 'Hi, Spotty. What was it like? What kind of land was it? What were the people like? What was the food like; tell us; tell us every thing . . . .' and so on.

And poor Spotty replied, 'What can I say about that land?
Except this:

> Fine foods in plenty   (69)
>   and a great variety
> I found when I went abroad:
>   and in the cities
>   the sweet young ladies
>   are easygoing, really;
> but there's just one thing wrong
>   in your foreign land;
> your kith and kin who live abroad
>   hate your guts quite sincerely.'

The crocodile, Hideous Jaws, having listened attentively to
the advice given by Red Face, resolved to fight and die if need
be. Bidding farewell to his friend, the ape, he returned to his own
house where he fought with the intruder who had taken forcible
possession of it. Pinning his faith on his own resolute valour,
Hideous Jaws killed the intruding crocodile and regained his
residence. And he lived in it happily for many, many years.

As it is said with admirable wisdom:

> What use is wealth acquired   (70)
> without manly effort
> and enjoyed in idleness?
> Even an antelope enjoys its fill of grass
> that fate drops into its lap.

Now here ends Book Four named *Loss of Gains* of which this
was the opening verse:

> He who foolishly lets himself be wheedled   (71)
>   into parting with his gains
> is a dolt thoroughly bamboozled,
>   like the Crocodile by the Ape.

BOOK V

Rash Deeds

Now here begins the fifth book entitled *Rash Deeds*; and this is its opening verse:

> *Let no man undertake a deed* (1)
> *ill-conceived and ill-considered,*
> *ill-examined and ill-done*
> *as the barber was guilty of.*

And Viṣṇu Śarma began the tale of *The Barber who slaughtered the Monks.*

In the southern land flourished a city named Trumpet Flowers[1] where lived a merchant prince named Precious Gems.[2] Though he led a life devoted to the pursuit of the four existential aims, Virtue, Wealth, Love and Salvation, somehow through the cruel play of Fate, he lost his fortune. The loss of material wealth led to a series of humiliations and he was plunged into deep despondency as a result.

One night as he lay awake thinking, 'Curse upon this cruel poverty,' he told himself; 'and how true are these verses :

> *Virtue, purity of conduct, forbearance,* (2)
> *kindliness, sweetness of disposition, noble birth,*
>   *what are all these worth?*
> *They lose their lustre when a man loses his wealth.*

> *Self-esteem, true pride, judgement and learning* (3)
>   *wit, social graces and understanding:*
> *all seem to vanish precipitately*
>   *when a man loses power and authority.*

Day by day the wisdom even of the wise   (4)
wanes chipped away by constant household worries,
as the beauty of the season of dews pales
touched by the breath of Spring's warming breezes.

Deprived of wealth and power; preoccupied   (5)
        with nagging problems of procuring
the family's wherewithal for mere existence
—butter and oil, grain and salt, fuel and clothing—
even the minds of men with sweeping intellect,
reaching far horizons, start to decay.

Like bubbles on flowing waters,   (6)
        ever-forming, ever-dissolving,
men down-and-out and weak from lack of fortune,
become insignificant, beneath notice,
even if they are one's neighbours.

Here in this world, the opulent may indulge   (7)
with impunity in many a shameless act :
yet who dares point a finger at them?
Mark how the Lord of Waters[3] bellows no end:
the world does not snigger saying, "How unmannerly!"'

Having rehearsed such observations in his mind, Precious
Gems reflected, 'What good is this life full of troubles. Let me
abandon it by starving to death.' And then he fell asleep and
started to dream. In his dream he saw before him a hoard of ten
crore[4] gold coins appear in the shape of a monk.[5] And the
monk-shape spoke to the dreamer, 'Oh! Merchant prince, do not
give up, do not harbour such loathing for worldly goods. I am a
treasure-trove of ten crore gold coins your ancestors earned. In
the morning I shall come to your house in this very shape. Then
you must club me on the head and kill me so that I will turn into
a hoard of inexhaustible gold.'

In the morning Precious Gems woke up and remembering
his dream sat pondering over it. 'Hm . . . let me think. It was only

a dream; whether it will turn out true or false, one cannot say. Oh . . . ! There is no doubt it will prove to be an illusion; for the simple reason that nowadays my mind being preoccupied with money, day and night I think of money and money only. As the proverbial saying goes :

> *The dream of the ailing and grief-stricken,* (8)
> *of the anxiety-ridden, the love-sick,*
> *and the drunk, is a mere illusion*
> *bearing no real fruit.'*

In the meantime, a certain barber came to the house to manicure his wife's nails. And as the barber was engaged in manicuring the lady's nails, the monk-shape of the merchant's dream suddenly materialized. Precious Gems, on seeing it, was transported with joy and picking up a stout wooden cudgel, he gave the shape a good hard blow on the head; and that very instant the monk-shape turned into gold and fell on the floor.

Precious Gems having stowed away the golden shape safely inside took the barber aside and giving him a handsome tip cautioned him, 'Now, my good fellow, pray do not report any of what happened here in my house to anyone, do you understand?'

The barber readily agreed and went home. Then he began to reflect on what he had seen. 'It must be that all these naked mendicants turn to gold whenever they are hit on the head. So, I, too, shall invite a number of them and hit them on the head with a cudgel so that I can gain a whole store of gold.'

Having passed the rest of that day and the night on tenterhooks meditating on his plan, the barber rose early in the morning and went to the monastery. There he draped his upper cloth in the manner prescribed, went thrice round the image of the Victorious,[6] got down on his knees, folded his hands in reverence and covering the gateways[7] in his face began intoning the following chants in a high-pitched voice.

> *Virtuous are the anchorites* (9)
> *radiant with highest knowledge*

397

who make their minds' soil infertile
for the seed of worldly existence.

'Furthermore:

Blessed is the tongue that praises the Victorious (10)
and blessed the mind fixed on Him;
those two hands that offer worship to Him,
they alone deserve praise glorious.'

And the barber chanted many more praises in the same vein, after which he sought the presence of the abbot. Dropping on his knees on the floor he spoke with great reverence, 'My salutations, Your Holiness.' In return he received the benediction of the abbot for the increase of virtue in him, and instructions for the inflexible vow of perpetual celibacy as well. Then he devoutly made this request: 'Do me the favour, Your Holiness, of directing today's walk for alms towards my home accompanied by all the monks.'

The abbot, bristling, replied, 'O, devotee, why do you speak such words, though you are conversant with the precepts of our order? What! Do you think we are Brāhmanas[8] to go running to households to eat that you invite us to your home? We walk around as the will prompts us and if we happen to meet a Jaina devotee distinguished for his piety, we enter his home and ask for alms. So, begone; never again speak to me this manner.'

To this the barber replied, 'I am certainly conversant with the precepts that govern your order, Your Holiness. But, there are many pious devotees who honour you with invitations to their homes. We too have ready, pieces of cloth to wrap manuscripts in, and funds set apart as well, for the writing of manuscripts and for the payment of scribes employed in such activities. So bearing this in mind, it is for His Holiness to make his decision.'

With these meaningful words, the barber went home and got ready a stout cudgel of acacia wood which he hid in a corner behind the door. Close to noontime he went again to the monastery and stood waiting at the gates. As the monks filed out in due order, he importuned them to visit his home. And all of them tempted by the prospect of manuscript covers and money, passed by their most pious devotees and trooped happily behind the barber. How true the saying is:

> *Alone in the world having abandoned* (11)
> *home and family, he is clad in space,*[9]
> *and eats out of the bowl his cupped palms make;*
> *even he is led astray by Desire.*
>   *Is that not something to wonder at?*

The barber led the monks right inside his house and started hitting them on the head with his cudgel. A few died instantaneously; others with heads broken set up a terrible howling. At this point, the soldiers on duty in the city-fort hearing the awful sounds of shrieking, exclaimed, 'Good heavens! What is this terrible hullabaloo coming from within the city. Let us go and investigate.' And they dashed post-haste in the direction from which these unholy sounds were coming; and what did they see but the holy monks rushing out of the barber's house with blood streaming down their limbs. Seeing the horrid sight the soldiers asked, 'What is the meaning of all this?' And the monks came out with accounts of the barber's dastardly act.

The soldiers seized the barber, bound and fettered him and conveyed him along with the monks who had survived the slaughter, to the courts of justice where the judges questioned him thus, 'Why have you done this horrendous deed, sir?'

'Your Honours,' the barber responded, 'In the circumstances, what else could I do?' and retailed the whole story of what had taken place in the house of the merchant, Precious Gems.

The judges immediately despatched a person to summon Precious Gems; and when he was brought before them, the judges questioned him, 'Sir merchant, did you kill a monk?'

Precious Gems then disclosed to the judges the events surrounding his dream and its sequel. Whereupon the judges gave their judgement, 'Ho there, guards; take this villainous barber away and have him impaled; for he is guilty of a blood-curdling deed of horror.'

When the sentence had been carried out, the judges spoke severely:

'Let no man ever contemplate (12)
an act ill-conceived and ill-considered,
ill-done without proper scrutiny
like the hare-brained barber in our city.

Inspect a matter with utmost care (13)
before jumping to conclusions
and rushing headlong into actions;
else, bitter remorse is let loose,
as in the tale of lady and mongoose.'

'And what might that tale be, Your Honours?' inquired the merchant, Precious Gems. And the judges began the tale of *The Brāhmani*[10] *and the faithful Mongoose.*

Once a Brāhmana named Deva Śarma lived in a certain settlement. His wife gave birth to a little boy and on the same day a female mongoose died after giving birth. As the Brāhmani tenderly loved little creatures, she took up the baby mongoose as if it were her own child, nursed him at her breast, bathed him, massaged him with oils and generally reared him with affection. But there was always a little doubt, a little fear lurking in her mind regarding the little animal. 'After all,' she told herself, 'this fellow comes of a family of predators; and sometime or other he might attack and harm my little son; who knows? For there is truth in what is commonly held:

Folks might have a bad son, wayward, (14)
and wilful, even ill-favoured;
an idiot may be, or even a rogue,
one addicted to vice, yet he brings
joy and delight to the hearts of his parents.'

Once, having tucked her son into his cradle, the Brāhmani picked up her water-pot and said to her husband, 'Hey, great preceptor, I have to fetch water; see that the mongoose does not harm the child,' and left.

As soon as she had left, the Brāhmana too went off on his rounds to beg for alms, leaving the house empty. Just then, as Fate would have it, a black serpent emerged from its hole and started crawling towards the child's cradle. The mongoose recognizing him to be a natural enemy and fearing for the life of his baby brother, met the serpent halfway, joined battle with him and tore him to pieces, scattering the bits far and wide. Then delighted with his own heroism, he ran, blood smeared all over his face, to meet his mother, eager and proud to show her what he had accomplished.

But when the mother saw him come running towards her in great excitement, and saw his blood-spattered face and bloody mouth, she grew frightened thinking; 'Aha! This vicious beast has killed and eaten my darling little boy.' And without a second thought and with her mind seething with suspicion, she angrily dropped the water-pot on the poor little mongoose who died instantly. Leaving the little mongoose lying dead at that very spot, without giving it another thought she hurried home, only to see the baby safe and sound; and near the cradle a great black serpent torn to bits. Overwhelmed with grief and remorse at having thoughtlessly killed the son who had proved a true benefactor, the Brāhmani beat her head and breast wildly.

At this moment the Brāhmana returned from his daily round of seeking alms, with a pot of rice-gruel and saw his wife bewailing the loss of her son, the little mongoose. As soon as she saw her husband, the Brāhmani reproached him bitterly, crying out: 'Shame! O, shame on you, sir, overcome by an excess of desire for food, you did not listen to me and do as I asked you to. Experience the sorrow of the loss of a child now; taste the bitter fruit borne by the tree of your own ill deeds; for that is what happens to those blinded by excessive desire; as it is observed:

Neither give rein to excessive desire, (15)

401

nor abstain from desire altogether.
A wheel whirls over the head of one
   overcome by excess of desire.'

'How is that?' inquired the Brāhmaṇa. And then the
Brāhmaṇī began the tale of *The Four Treasure-seekers*.

In a certain settlement lived four Brāhmaṇas who were the best
of friends. Beset by abject poverty they talked among themselves.
'Oh! What a terrible curse is this poverty! And how beautifully it
is said:

> A man's strengths might be grounded in justice,   (16)
>   but if he has no money in his purse,
> he might provide good and faithful service,
>   yet his employer hates his guts;
>   his close kin leave him all at once,
>   high and dry; and his sons,
>   his own flesh-and-blood forsake him too;
>   the wife though nobly-born
>   grows cold and pays him no honour;
>   good friends shun his very sight;
>   virtues do not glow forth bright,
>   and miseries wax and grow apace.

'Moreover:

> Brave, handsome and eloquent   (17)
>   a man may be,
> with grace of manner and mastery
>   of all the fields of learning;
> yet in this world of ours, if money
> does not back all these qualities,
> the crowning laurels of Art are not his.

'Death is far better than a state of penury. As it has been
admirably expressed in this little vignette:

402

> *A pauper hastened to the burning-grounds,* (18)
> *and addressed a corpse: 'Stand up a moment,*
> *my friend, and lift off and bear this burden*
> *grievous, of my grinding penury;*
>> *for of late I have grown weary,*
>> *and I long to have instead*
>> *the peace and comfort you have dead.'*
> *But the corpse remained silent, knowing well*
>> *a man is better dead than poor.*

'So, we should strive at all costs to acquire wealth; as we have heard:

> *Nothing in this world there is* (19)
> *that wealth cannot accomplish;*
>> *so, let the sole aim be*
>> *of men of sense, to make money.*

'This wealth that we are talking of can be acquired in six ways, as follows: by begging; by serving kings; by farming; by teaching; by money-lending; and by trade. But of all these only one, trade, is best suited for the acquisition of wealth with no curbs or controls. As the saying goes:

> *Crows can peck at what is gathered by begging:* (20)
> *and changeable is the mind of a king:*
>> *farming, alas, is such hard labour;*
>> *a teacher's living is beset cruelly*
>> *by the need to bow and eat humble pie;*
> *You remain poor lending to your neighbour;*
>> *for your livelihood, your life*
>> *—your wealth, that is—is held in other hands.*
> *So, no occupation compares with trade;*
>> *nothing's more worthwhile, I conclude, in life.*

'As we are now talking of trade as the best means of gathering wealth, let it be known that trade is sevenfold, as follows: use of

403

false weights and measures; boosting prices; running a pawn-shop or mortgage firm; retail trade; stock companies; perfume-ries; and export and foreign trade. But it has been said:

> *Not weighing a full measure;* (21)
> *always quoting false prices;*
> *swindling consistently*
> *one's regular customers,*
> *are despicable practices*
> *followed by wild tribes of the hills.*

'Besides:

> *When goods in a household are pledged,* (22)
> *the pawnbroker prays hard each day;*
> *'Lord! Let the houseowner be dead,*
> *and I will give you whatever you say.'*

'Also:

> *The director of a stock company* (23)
> *imagines, rejoicing inwardly;*
> *The whole world is mine, and all its riches,*
> *so what matters all else?*

'Further:

> *Of wares for trade, perfumes are right on top;* (24)
> *why deal in other stuff, gold and such?*
> *Whatever the cost you buy perfume at*
> *you sell for a thousand times that.*

'Only men with great fortunes are able to engage in foreign trade. As it is observed:

> *Men who possess immense fortunes* (25)
> *and advertise that far and wide,*
> *they with their wealth capture greater wealth*
> *as tuskers lure great lordly tuskers.*

> *In life, those expert in buying and selling* (26)
> *who travel to distant lands for trading,*
> *double and triple their fortunes*
> *through their unflagging exertions.*

'Moreover:

> *Afraid of foreign lands,* (27)
> *crows, deer, and cowards*
> *shiftless and lacking energy,*
> *stay and die in their own country.'*

Having resolved thus and decided to go abroad, the friends, all four of them, left their homes, families and friends and set out. Remember what is wisely observed:

> *A man preoccupied by need for wealth* (28)
> *gives up values, forsakes his family,*
> *abandons his mother and land of birth,*
> *leaves his own place disadvantageous*
> *and quickly goes to foreign places;*
> > *what else?*

Travelling by stages, the friends reached the kingdom of Avanti[11] where they bathed in the waters of the river Śipra and worshipped the Lord in His shrine of Great Time.[12] As they continued their journey they met, on the way, a master magician, named Fierce Joy.[13] Greeting him in the proper Brāhmanic manner, the four of them then accompanied the magician to his monastery where they were courteously asked by him; 'Where are you from, noble sirs? And where are you bound for? What may your purpose be?' To which the four Brāhmanas replied, 'We are pilgrims in search of magical powers, and we are bent on going to such a place where we shall find all the wealth we seek, or death. This is our firm decision; for as we all know:

> *Water falls at times from the skies;* (29)

at times by digging, it gushes
from deep within the bowels of the earth.
Fate, as you might think, is not all-powerful;
manly exertion is equally so.

It is through true manly exertion (30)
that cherished aims achieve perfect fulfilment;
even what you might describe as Fate,
is simply manliness unmanifest.

In this world, joys come not easily (31)
without the body's painful striving.
Madhu[14] Himself embraced Lakshmi
with arms grown weary from ocean-churning.

'So, reveal to us some effective way of gaining wealth; whether
it is entering the earth's insides; or summoning through magic
powers mysterious spirits of woods and waters; or incantations
in burning-grounds; or even selling and offering the flesh of
humans and other higher orders of animals. You, sir, are celebrated for possessing marvellous power; and we, are men of
extraordinary daring. As it is said:

Only the great can accomplish (32)
the aims of the great.
Who else but the ocean can bear
the fierce submarine[15] Fire?'

Recognizing their fitness as worthy disciples, the magician
formed four magical quills and gave one to each of the four
Brāhmanas, saying, 'Now, go, and travel north in the direction
of the Himālaya Mountains. Wherever your quill happens to fall,
there you will certainly find your treasure.'

As the four of them went onwards following the directions
given by the magician, the quill of the Brāhmana who was in the
forefront, fell on the ground. When he started to dig at that spot,
he discovered the soil to be all copper. 'O, look,' he exclaimed,
'take all the copper you want.' The others sneering at him,

retorted, 'O, you fool! What use is this stuff that even in great quantity cannot make a dent in our poverty! Come, get up, and let us go forward.' But the first traveller replied, 'You three go on if you wish, but I shall go no further.' So saying he took all the copper he needed and turned back, the first to do so.

The other three continued on their journey north. When they had travelled just a little way onwards, the quill of the Brāhmana in front dropped down, and when he started digging at that spot he discovered the soil to be all silver. Seeing it, he was delighted and turned to the other two, 'Look, friends, here is silver; take all you need; let us go no further.' But the other two travellers ridiculed him saying, 'O, you fool! Behind us the soil was all copper; before us it is all silver. If we go further we shall certainly come upon soil that is completely gold. And as for this stuff, even in great quantity it will not destroy our poverty.' Then the second Brāhmana remarked, 'You two can go on if you wish; as for me, I shall not go with you.' With these words, he gathered all the silver he could take and turned back.

Now, as the two remaining friends continued their journey, the quill of one of them fell down. As he started digging at that spot the third Brāhmana discovered that the soil was all pure gold. With great delight he spoke to his companion, 'Look, my friend; this soil is all gold; take as much of it as you like, for nothing that comes after this can be superior to it.'

And his friend, the last and fourth Brāhmana replied scornfully, 'You idiot! Don't you see? First it was copper, then silver, and now gold. After this is there any doubt that we shall find precious gems? So, get up; let us go on. Why carry home large quantities of this heavy stuff that is a burden?' And the other man answered: 'You go, Your Honour; I shall stay right here and await your return.'

So the last Brāhmana went on alone. The summer sun beat down on him and scorched his limbs; his wits became disoriented from intense thirst and he wandered here and there by the paths in that land of magic. At last, he saw in front of him, a whirling platform on which stood a man with his whole frame drenched in blood, for a whirling wheel was set on his head. He went quickly up to the man and accosted him, 'Sir, why do you stand there with a wheel whirling on your head? And pray tell me if there is water anywhere around here. For I am dying of thirst.'

The moment the Brāhmana spoke these words, the wheel left the other man's head and settled on his own. In dismay, the Brāhmana interrogated the other man, 'My good sir; what is the meaning of this?' To this the man replied, 'Sir, the wheel settled on my head in precisely the same way.' And the Brāhmana asked again, 'Then tell me, sir, when will this wheel leave my head; for I suffer intense agony.'

Then the man reponded thus: 'Only when someone like you comes holding a magic quill in his hand and speaks as you did, the wheel will become mounted on the head of that person.'

'I see,' remarked the Brāhmana, 'now tell me, how long have you been here?'

'Ah! Who is the king ruling the earth at present?' inquired the man.

'Why, it is King Vatsa of the Lute,'[16] answered the Brāhmana.

'I see,' observed the man, 'When Rāma was ruling over the earth,[17] I came here driven by poverty and like you holding a magic quill in my hand. On reaching this spot, I also saw a man standing with a wheel mounted on his head and asked him a question. As soon as the words were out of my mouth the wheel flew off the man's head and settled on mine. But I am afraid I have lost count of time.'

The Brāhmana who was now the wheel-bearer put another question to the other man. 'Then tell me, sir, how do you manage to get food, standing as you are in this position?'

'It is like this, my good fellow,' explained the man, 'afraid that his priceless treasures might be stolen, the Lord of Wealth,[18] formed this mode of torture to keep persons with magical powers from coming this far. But if any man manages somehow to come here, he feels no hunger or thirst; is not subject to old age or death; he experiences this torment, and this alone. Now, permit me to leave, sir. You have released me from what can only be described as the ultimate in torture. Let me go home.' With these words, the man departed.

In the meantime, the Brāhmaṇa who had found gold was waiting for his friend who had gone forward on his quest for wealth. Wondering why his companion was delayed and anxious to find him, he set out in search, following the line of his friend's footprints. When he had gone some distance, he saw a man whose body was drenched with blood and on whose head was mounted a cruel wheel that whirled constantly. To his horror he recognized this man, in the throes of agony, as his friend. He came close and with tears welling up in his eyes, asked, 'O, my dear friend; what is this? What does it mean?'

'The cruel play of Fate, what else?' answered his friend.

Goldfinder asked again. 'Tell me, how did this happen?'

In reply, Wheelbearer related the whole story of the wheel. Having listened to it, Goldfinder reproached his friend, 'My friend, time and again I advised you against going on your quest. But, lacking judgement,[19] you would not pay heed to my words. How wisely is the moral pointed out in this tale:

> *Better common sense than erudition;*   (33)
> *good sense is superior to book-learning;*
> *absence of sense invites destruction;*
> *as with the scholars who made a dead lion living.'*

'And how was that?' asked Wheelbearer. And Goldfinder then began the tale of *The Scholars who brought a dead lion to life*.

In a certain settlement lived four Brāhmaṇas in close friendship. Three of them had mastered all the branches of knowledge but they lacked one thing—common sense. One, however, the fourth among them, who had decisively set his face against scholarship possessed just this—plain and simple good sense.

Once, the four of them sat discussing among themselves; and one observed, 'What use is scholarship to a man who does not travel to other lands to earn wealth by gratifying kings? So whatever we do, it is imperative that we travel abroad.' And they set out.

When they had gone some distance, the eldest said, 'Look,

the fourth among us is an unlettered fellow. What does he have but just common sense. Without scholarship, depending on mere good sense, how can anyone gain the favour of princes. So, we shall not share the wealth we earn, with him. Let him therefore part company with us and go home.'

The second Brāhmana chimed in with, 'All right, friend Commonsense you have no scholarship; so you had better go home.'

But the third Brāhmana courteously interprosed, 'No, no, this is no way to talk; we have played together since we were small children.' Turning to the fourth Brāhmana, he said, 'Come along, my good friend; you shall share equally with us.'

With this understanding, the four of them continued their journey. In a forest they chanced upon the bones of a dead lion. And one of them remarked, 'Look, here is an opportunity for us to demonstrate the value of our learning and put it to practical use. Here lies a creature dead. Let us bring it back to life using the knowledge we have gained by diligent study.'

Immediately one of them rose to the occasion. 'Oh, I know how to assemble the bones and make the skeleton.'

A second added, 'And I can provide it with skin and flesh and blood as well.'

The third capped this with, 'But I can give it the breath of life.

So, when one had assembled the bones properly, another furnished flesh and blood and covered it with skin. Just as the third Brāhmana scholar was going to infuse life into the form, the fourth stopped him, saying, 'Look; this is a lion; if you give it life, it is going to kill us all.'

But the third scholar retorted bristling, 'Shame upon you! You wretched fool! What! You think I am the one to make my learning useless and unfruitful, do you?'

The fourth man's reply came pat, 'Well, all right then; go ahead; but just wait one moment while I climb this tree nearby.'

As Commonsense climbed up the tree, the third scholar breathed life into the form which straight away rose up as a lion and killed all the three scholars. When the lion went elsewhere the fourth Brāhmana, the man of sense, climbed down and went home.

'Therefore I told you, "Better common sense than erudition . . ." and the rest of it,' concluded Goldfinder.

Whereupon Wheelbearer retorted, 'O, no, not at all; for your reasoning here is faulty. And I tell you that even those with ample good sense may perish if Fate strikes a blow at them. On the other hand, if Fate is kind, even those with meagre wit succeed in living happily; the following lines make the point clear:

> *While Hundredwit sits on someone's head* (34)
> *and Thousandwit hangs limp and dead,*
> *I, who am plain simple Singlewit, you see, my love*
> *playing in these clear waters, happily.'*

'And how was that?' asked Goldfinder. And then Wheelbearer began the tale of *Thousandwit, Hundredwit, Singlewit.*

Once, two fishes named Hundredwit and Thousandwit lived in a certain lake. A frog named Singlewit made friends with them. All three would sit together at the water's edge and enjoy the pleasures of conversation interspersed with wise and witty sayings for a while, then dive back into the water.

One evening at sunset as they were engaged in such conversation, some fishermen carrying nets came there. Looking at the lake they said to one another. 'See this lake? It abounds with fish and the water is shallow. We shall come here at dawn.'

These words struck the three friends like a bolt of thunder. They started consulting one another. The frog was the first to speak: 'Did you hear that, my friends Hundredwit and Thousandwit? What should we do now? Flee, or, stay put?'

At this Thousandwit laughed heartily and said, 'Ah, my dear friend, don't be alarmed just hearing some words. I doubt if these fellows would really make an appearance, as they say they would. And even if they do, why, I will protect you and myself by using my wits. For, I must tell you, I know a host of tricks in the water.'

Hundredwit agreed, and added, 'Come, come, my friend;
Thousandwit has spoken admirably; for:

> *Where the wind cannot go in to blow* (35)
>   *nor the sun's rays find a way,*
> *even there the wise man's wit*
>   *always enters and without delay.*

'From merely hearing some words spoken we cannot abandon
the place of our birth and everything that has come down to us
from our ancestors in due succession. So, do not go from here; I
shall protect you by the power of my wit.'

However, the frog said determinedly, 'Listen, friends, I have
but one single wit, and that tells me to flee. I am taking my wife
and going right this day to some other lake.' Having said this,
the frog taking advantage of the night departed and went to some
other lake.

Early next morning, the fishermen arrived looking like the
henchmen of Death. They threw their nets over the water,
enclosing the lake. Fishes and turtles, frogs and crabs and all the
other lake-dwellers were caught in the nets and taken. And those
two fishes, Hundredwit and Thousandwit fell into the nets,
though they tried many a fancy twist and turn to save their lives;
and were killed.

Next day, the fishermen satisfied with their catch started
home. Hundredwit, being heavy, was carried on the head of one
of the fishermen, while Thousandwit was carried tied to a rope,
by another man. The frog sitting pretty in an inlet in a pool, saw
it all and called out to his wife, 'Look, look, my beloved,

> *While Hundredwit sits on someone's head* (36)
> *and Thousandwit swings from a rope limp and dead,*
> *I, plain, simple singlewit, am sitting pretty here,*
> *my love, playing happily in waters clear.'*

'Therefore, I say to you, my friend, "Even intelligence or wit
cannot be the sole measure of things."'

'That may be so,' replied Goldfinder, 'but is it not wrong to disregard the advice of a friend? But what can be done now? In spite of my dissuasion, you would not desist, such was your inordinate greed and self-opinionatedness born of scholarship. How well the following verse says it all:

> *Well sung, dear uncle,* (37)
> *you would not stop your song*
> *when I told you to hold your tongue;*
> *now you wear round your neck a jewel*
> *never seen before—a medal*
> *for being so musical!'*

'How was that?' asked Wheelbearer. And then Goldfinder began the tale of *The Singing Ass*.

In a certain region lived a donkey named Pushy. In the daytime he had to carry loads of washing, but at night he was free to roam wherever he wished. Once, as he was roaming about in the fields, he met a jackal with whom he struck up a friendship. The two of them once broke through a fence and got into the cucumber beds where they ate as much cucumber as they could and each returned to his own place in the early morning.

One night, the donkey, puffed up with conceit, stood in the middle of the field of cucumbers and said to the jackal: 'My dear nephew, see how bright the night is, so clear, I feel like singing. Now tell me which raga shall I sing?'

'Uncle dear,' answered the jackal apprehensively, 'why do you wish to stir up trouble? For, we are engaged in the business of thievery. Thieves and lovers should go quietly about their business, as you know. And as the jingle expresses it aptly:

> *Any man who wishes to keep alive,* (38)
> *would be wise to give up thieving*
> *if racked by a cough;*
> *to give up whoring*
> *if he tends to doze off;*
> *and to curb his eating*
> *if he is full of ailments.*

'Besides, Uncle, your singing is not mellifluous like the tones of conches. Further, the farmers who keep watch in the fields can hear you even at a distance; they will come and bind you with ropes, or even kill you. So why don't you eat quietly?'

When the donkey heard this he was outraged. 'You are a dweller of the woods and for that reason, you can have no musical sensibility; which is why you speak like this. But have you not heard it said:

When autumnal moonlight (39)
puts the darkness to flight
and the beloved stays near,
music's tones murmurous,
    sweet as nectar,
breathe softly upon the ear
of those blessed with Fortune's favour.'

'True enough, dear Uncle, but you bray so harshly. So why do something against your own interests?' urged the jackal.

And the donkey bristling with indignation rejoined, 'Shame, shame on you, you blockhead! What? Do you think I do not know any music? All right then; listen, I'll tell you the basic principles of musicology. They are as follows:[20]

Seven notes and three scales there be (40-42)
    with one and twenty modes in use,
all weaving music's golden tones
    nine-and-forty distinct ways.
Music moves bound by measures three,
in registers three, in strict accordance
    with tempos too and pauses three.

Six singing styles express beautifully
the nine moods[21] and emotions forty,
enhanced skilfully by shading and colouring
six and thirty ways, varied exquisitely.

One hundred and five-and-eighty songs and more

414

> *of golden sound most melodious,*
> *with subtle phrasing, delicate flourishes*
> *and many a graceful embellishment,*
>   *are found set down for the skilled vocalist.*

> *Nothing is to be found here in this world*   (43)
> *nor in the world of Immortals above*
> *nobler than the art of song.*
> *The Great Lord Himself[22] Rāvaṇa enthralled*
> *with throbbing music he drew with such art*
> *out of bare wizened sinews taut.*

'So now tell me, how can you think that I am not a musicologist? And restrain me from performing?' demanded Pushy peremptorily.

'Very well, Uncle, if you think so, go ahead and sing to your heart's content while I stay by the gap in the fence and keep an eye on the men guarding the fields,' observed the jackal.

As soon as the jackal had stationed himself near the gap in the fence, the donkey with out-thrust neck began his performance. When the watchmen stationed in the fields heard the braying, they gnashed their teeth in rage, and picking up their cudgels ran to the spot where the donkey stood. They fell in a body and belaboured him so hard that he fell to the ground. Then, picking up a millstone, they tied it round his neck; then they lay down to sleep. In a few moments the donkey stood up forgetting the pain and soreness as donkeys normally do. As expressed in the following lines:

> *With a dog, a mule, or a horse,*   (44)
> *and an ass most of all,*
> *after the first few moments,*
> *the pain from sound drubbings, is hardly felt at all.*

With the millstone still hanging round his neck, the donkey crashed headlong through the fence and galloped away while the jackal watching from a safe distance smiled to himself as he muttered this verse:

'Well sung, dear uncle,   (45)
you did sing your song,
though I told you to hold your tongue;
and now, you wear this jewel
never ever seen before
at your neck . . . a medal
for being so musical.'

'You too, my friend,' concluded Goldfinder, 'in the same manner, you too would not refrain from what you had decided to do.'

After listening to his friend's reproach, Wheelbearer admitted ruefully, 'Ah, my friend, what you say is true; and the proverb says it too:

He who has no wit of his own   (46)
nor sense to listen to a friend,
like Dull the weaver in the tale
will meet a miserable end.'

'And how did that happen?' asked Goldfinder. And then Wheelbearer began the tale of *The Dull-witted Weaver*.

Once, a weaver named Dull lived in a certain settlement. It happened one day that the wooden frame and pegs of his loom simply broke. So, picking up an axe, Dull went looking for wood, and wandering everywhere, he finally came to the seashore where he saw a great śiśam tree growing. He looked up at it and started thinking, 'O, what a mighty tree. If I cut it down I would be able to make as many tools for my trade as I would ever need.' As he lifted up his axe to hit the first blow to fell the tree, he heard a voice speaking to him. It was the tree-spirit who had his home in the śiśam: 'Sir, this tree is my home; please spare it at all costs, for I live here in utmost comfort and happiness because the breezes cooled by the ocean-spray refresh my limbs.'

To this the weaver replied, 'O, tree-spirit, what can I do?

416

Without my tools which are all of wood, my family will be subject to hunger and starvation. Why don't you leave this tree and go and live elsewhere; for I must cut this tree down.'

The tree-spirit answered, 'Well, Sir Weaver; indeed I am pleased with you. Ask for anything that you wish and I shall grant it; only spare my tree.'

'Well,' observed Dull a little hesitantly, 'if you say so. I shall go home first, consult my friend and my wife and then come back.'

The tree-spirit agreed and the weaver started home. As he was entering the settlement whom should he see but his good friend, the barber. 'Well met, my friend,' said Dull accosting the barber. 'I have won the favour of a tree-spirit who has offered me the choice of a boon. So, advise me, what shall I ask for?'

'Is that so?' exclaimed the barber surprised. 'Ask for a kingdom, I'd say. You shall be king and I shall be minister. Together the two of us shall enjoy all the pleasures of this world and go on to taste happiness in the other.'

'Splendid idea, my friend,' said the weaver, 'now let me also consult my wife.'

'No, no, don't do that, Dull, my friend,' the barber hastened to say, 'Women should never be consulted, you know. For surely you are aware of the common observation:

> *Give a woman fine foods and clothes,* (47)
> *ornaments as well; and be nice;*
> *most of all, approach her at proper times;*[23]
> *but never ask her for advice.*

'And further:

> *Where a young boy, where a woman,* (48)
> *rules the roost; or a charlatan,*
> *that house goes to rack and ruin:*
> *such is sage Bhārgava's*[24] *opinion.*

'Moreover:

> *Only so long as a man pays no heed* (49)

417

to women's secret whispers,
will he remain devoted to elders,
and a man of importance, indeed.

Wholly self-centred are all women; (50)
self-gratification their sole concern:
no one, not even their own sons
are truly dear to them
except as part of their own well-being

'That may well be,' retorted Dull, 'but I still ought to consult her because she is a loyal wife.'

With these words, Dull made haste to get home and said to his wife, 'My dearest wife, today we have won the favour of a tree-spirit who is willing to grant us anything we ask for. So I have rushed home to ask for your advice. Tell me, what shall I ask for? My good friend, the barber, advised me to ask for a kingdom.' And his wife replied with a lofty air, 'Ah, my lord, what sense do barbers have? Pray do not heed his advice. We are all aware of the common saying:

Never consult with bards and boys (51)
and wandering minstrels,
or with barbers and base-born churls,
with hermits and mendicants as well.

'And further, consider how onerous is the government of a kingdom with all that it involves; a host of problems relating to war and peace, invasions, and containments, alliances and intrigue and other matters of policy, that a man can never have peace and happiness. And in addition, as we know:

Since his very own brothers and sons (52)
wish to kill a king to gain his realm,
it is wise to keep one's distance
from the business of ruling.'

'Your ladyship has indeed spoken wisely,' replied the

weaver, 'then tell me, what shall I ask the tree-spirit for?' His wife then made this suggestion; 'My lord, as of now, you weave one length of cloth a day; and all our household expenses are met from the sale of that cloth. Now, if you ask the tree spirit to give you an extra pair of hands and a second head, you will be able to weave one length of cloth in front and another behind. While the price of one will meet all our daily expenses comfortably, the sale of the other will provide you with the money to spend on special activities and on luxuries, so that you can live in style among your peers.'

Dull was delighted with his wife's suggestion and congratulated her, 'O, my faithful wife, what a splendid idea!' he said, 'Believe me, I shall do just that.'

Pleased with it all, Dull now returned to the tree-spirit and made his request: 'O, great spirit, if you wish to show me favour, pray grant me a second pair of hands and a second head to go with it.' The moment the words were out of his mouth, Dull, the weaver, was transformed into a double-headed, four-armed person. His joy knew no bounds as he walked home. But, alas, as he neared the settlement, people saw him and muttered ominously. 'Look, look, this is a demon,' and they started stoning him and beat the poor man with sticks and staves until he dropped dead.

'Therefore I say to you again, my friend, "The man who has no wit of his own . . . " and the rest of it, as I said before.'

Wheelbearer added, 'Yes, it is true, my friend; any man who is seized by the demon of preposterous hopes and desires becomes the butt of ridicule. How well this is expressed in these lines:

> *Whoever indulges in day-dreams* (53)
> *of an unattainable nature,*
> *will be on the floor, whitened all over*
> *by flour, like the father of Moonbeams.'*[25]

'And how did that happen?' asked Goldfinder eagerly. And then Wheelbearer began the tale of *The Day-dreaming Brāhmana*.

Once, in a certain city, there lived a Brāhmana named Misery.[26]

The Pancatantra

By begging for alms, he collected barleymeal and after eating part of it stored the rest in a clay jar which he hung on a peg in the wall. Placing his cot right under the jar he gazed up at it for hours each night until he fell into a reverie.

Night after night he created a scenario in his reverie, which went as follows: 'Sometime this jar will become completely filled with barleymeal: then a famine will strike this land and the barleymeal will fetch a hundred silver coins. With that money I shall purchase a pair of goats; as goats have kids every six months, I shall soon be able to build up a herd of goats. With those, I shall purchase a pair of cows whose calves I shall of course sell to purchase some mares. As the mares start to foal I shall soon acquire a whole lot of horses. By selling the horses I can amass a great store of gold. With the gold I shall acquire a mansion with a courtyard and large halls. Then someone will come to my mansion and offer me his beautiful daughter blessed with all excellences. A son will be born to us whom I shall name Moonbeams. When he is old enough to crawl on all fours, I shall be sitting one day in the garden behind the stables with a book in my hand and be lost in contemplation. Meanwhile, Moonbeams, my boy, will see me sitting there and getting out of his mother's arms, will make for me in his eagerness to ride on my knee; but he will go too near the horses. This will make me angry and I shall shout to the Brāhmani, his mother, "Hey, you! catch hold of the boy, pick him up." But being busy with household chores my wife will not hear. Whereupon I shall rise straight away and give her a good kick on her behind.'

One night sunk as he was in a deep reverie, Misery let fly a good strong kick upwards and caught the jar, smashing it. All the flour spilled out and fell on poor Misery turning him white all over.

'Therefore, my friend, I say to you: "Whoever indulges in day-dreams . . . " and the rest of it,' concluded Wheelbearer.

Goldfinder responded with, 'O, yes, how true, my friend,' and matched it with another tale:

'Whoever acts possessed by greed,   (54)

420

and does a deed,
with no thought of its consequence,
like King Moon will be rewarded with vexations.'

'O, really, how was that?' asked Wheelbearer. And then Goldfinder began the tale of *The Ape's revenge.*

In a certain city there once ruled a king named Moon.[27] He had acquired a troop of monkeys as pets for his son's amusement. Fed daily with fine foods and various kinds of delicacies, the monkeys were in great shape, sleek and frisky. A herd of rams was also kept in the palace for the amusement of the prince. One of the rams, a real gourmand, was in the habit of entering the kitchens day and night and eating up everything in sight; and the cooks would hit him with a stick or anything else they could lay their hands on to drive him away.

The Chief of Monkeys who had been observing this for a while began to give it serious thought. 'Well, this is not good; this perpetual bickering of the cooks and the ram is bound to lead to the destruction of us monkeys. For, this ram is obsessed with eating and cooks are irritable fellows. Supposing at some time or the other the cooks, not finding anything handy, reach out for a burning piece of wood to drive the ram away and hurl it at him, the broad, woolly back of this ram might quite easily catch fire. And then if this creature on fire rushes headlong into the stables nearby, the stables will also catch fire because they are stocked with bundles of hay. The horses are certain to suffer burns. Now, as we know, the sage who has written the standard treatise on veterinary science prescribes monkey-fat as *the* specific to treat burns suffered by horses. That means certain death for us.'

Having thought this matter over carefully, the monkey-chief summoned his troop and explained the situation to them. 'Listen friends:

This quarrel of cooks with the ram, (55)
lately risen and waxing strong,

promises to become a serious threat
to us monkeys; no doubt about that.

So, if senseless fights should arise (56)
in a house each and every day,
people who wish to stay alive,
should decide to move far away.

'Moreover:

Bad blood ends all great houses; (57)
bad words end all friendships;
bad government is the end of a country;
and bad deeds of manly glory.

'Therefore, let us leave the palace and resort to the woods before we are all destroyed.'

But the monkeys intoxicated with their life of ease, listening to his words, ridiculed him saying, 'Hey, Grandpa, you are old and your intellect is losing its edge. We are definitely not foregoing the ambrosial delicacies the prince feeds us with his own hands, to live in the woods, eating wild fruit, sharp and bitter, acrid and rotting.'

Hearing their foolish words the monkey-chief gave them a dirty look and exclaimed; 'O, you pack of worthless fools! Little do you know how this comfortable existence is going to end. This is happiness for the moment, all sweetness at present that in the end will turn to poison. As I simply cannot bear to witness the destruction of my whole clan, I shall leave right this moment and set out for the woods. Mark the wisdom in these lines:

Blessed are they, dear boy, who do not see (58)
family decay, and country in ruin,
a friend in trouble, and a wife stolen.'

Having warned them, the chief abandoned his troop of monkeys and set out for the woods.

After his departure from the palace it happened that one day the greedy ram entered the kitchen as usual to eat. The cook was enraged, and not finding anything else at hand, picked up a half-burnt but still blazing piece of wood and struck the ram with it.

Bleating piteously the ram with his woolly coat on fire rushed out and into the stables close by. As he lay rolling on the ground, the bundles of hay stacked there caught fire and burst into flames. Blinded by the blaze, some of the horses tethered in the stables died, while others with bodies badly burned and whining in agony, broke their halters and stampeded, making the attendants run around in consternation. The king became deeply dejected seeing the state of affairs and had the veterinary physicians and surgeons summoned; he addressed them vehemently, 'For god's sake, prescribe something to ease the pain of my horses that have suffered deadly burns.'

The veterinarians recollected the texts they had studied and delivered their expert advice: 'Lord, the celebrated author, Sālihotra, has clearly stated the specific treatment for such an emergency; he says:

> *The pain of horses from burns* (59)
> *will soon be gone*
> *like darkness at dawn,*
> *with salve of monkey-fat.*

'So, my lord, let this treatment be administered immediately, before the horses perish from infection.'

Following their recommendations, the king ordered an immediate slaughter of monkeys. Why describe the events at great length? Suffice it to record that every one of the troop of monkeys was slaughtered. The chief did not see the outrage perpetrated on his troop with his own eyes. But as the news of the event spread by word of mouth, it came to his ears and he could not bear the pain it brought. As the saying goes:

> *Vilest of the vile is that man* (60)
> *who bears patiently through greed or fear,*

423

the outrage perpetrated on his clan
by outsiders; so we hear.

As this elderly monkey-chief wandered about tormented by thirst, he came to a lake radiant with lotus-clusters. He looked carefully at the lake and noticed footprints leading into the lake, but not out, which started him thinking: 'How odd; there must be some monstrous aquatic reptile living in these waters. I think I had better stay at a safe distance; I can easily drink water through the hollow stem of a lotus.'

As he was thus engaged, quenching his thirst, there emerged from the middle of the lake, an ogre wearing a fabulous necklace of rubies who declared; 'Hear, O Ape, I eat whoever enters these waters. There is no one shrewder than you, I must say, sir, who drinks water in this manner. For this reason, I am pleased with you. You may now ask for what your heart desires.'

'O, sir,' replied the monkey-chief, 'tell me, sir, how many persons can you eat?'

'O, I?' guffawed the ogre, 'Why, I can eat any number; hundreds, thousands, tens of thousands and lakhs of beings if they enter the waters. But, once I come out, even a jackal can overpower me.'

The monkey observed, 'Sir, I asked because I entertain a bitter enmity towards a certain king; an enmity which has gone into my very bones. Now, if you will only loan me your necklace I shall rouse the cupidity of this king by my artful words and persuade him to enter your lake with his whole retinue.'

The ogre thought that this was an excellent idea and handed over his ruby necklace to the monkey-chief who began roaming over treetops and palace roofs with the ruby necklace beautifully adorning his throat. The people noticing him asked, 'Hey there, monkey-chief, where have you been all this time? And where did you get such a splendid ruby necklace? That dims even the sunlight with its dazzling lustre?'

To these questions, the monkey-chief replied, 'Deep in the woods in a certain spot lies a well-hidden lake formed by the God of Wealth.[28] Anyone who dives into the middle of that lake at daybreak comes out with a necklace like this radiantly adorning his throat, a sign of the favour of the God of Wealth.' The news of the necklace spread like wildfire and came to the ears of King Moon who sent for the monkey-chief and questioned him: 'Well, sir, Chief of the Troop, is this true what I hear?'

'My lord,' answered the chief, 'you see the proof right here before your eyes; the ruby necklace encircles my throat. If you fancy one like this for yourself, all you have to do is to send someone with me and I shall show him the place where he can find it.'

'In that case, I shall myself accompany you with all my retinue, so that many such ruby necklaces might be obtained,' observed the king.

'A splendid idea, indeed, my lord,' remarked the monkey-chief.

King Moon then set out of his capital surrounded by his retinue, driven by greed to possess ruby necklaces. He travelled in a palanquin with the monkey-chief seated on his lap to whom he showed great honour as they went along. As the proverb expresses it well:

> *Greed alone befuddles the minds*   (61)
> *of even the learned and the rich;*
> *it drives them to do horrendous deeds*
> *and roam in strange, impassable regions.*

Consider this besides:

> *One with a hundred longs for a thousand;*   (62)
> *one with a thousand yearns for lakhs;*
> *and lords of lakhs for rulership of a kingdom;*
> *monarchs aim to gain Paradise[29] itself.*

> *The hair ages along with aging years;*   (63)
> *with aging years the teeth age and decay;*
> *eyes and ears age with aging years;*
> *One thing alone, GREED, never ages.*

In the early morning when the king and company reached

the lake, the monkey said to the king, 'Lord, fulfilment comes to those who dive into the lake at the moment the sun is just over the horizon. So, instruct your retinue to plunge all together at that instant into the waters; you and I will enter the lake together afterwards and go to the spot that I have already been at and I will show you the profusion of ruby necklaces lying around.'

No sooner had the attendants of the king entered the waters of the lake than the ogre ate them all up. Seeing that his people were delaying inordinately the king turned to the monkey and asked, 'Well, Chief, Lord of the Troop! Why do my attendants linger?'

The monkey quickly climbed up a tree and told the king, 'Well, wicked-hearted Lord of Men! All your people have been eaten up by the ogre who lives in the lake. I swore vengeance against you for having encompassed the extirpation of my whole clan; that vengeance has now been accomplished. You may go. Regarding you as my lord and master I refrained from leading you into the lake. Know this, my lord:

A deed begets a counter deed: (64)
injury is met with injury:
I see nothing wrong with it
if someone repays evil with evil.

'You wrought havoc with my people; I have done the same with yours.'

When King Moon heard this he quickly returned the way he had come, totally devastated; while the ogre, replete, rose out of the lake and exclaimed joyfully:

'An enemy slain, a friend gained, (65)
the necklace of rubies not lost,
you have done well, my monkey-friend
drinking water through hollow lotus-stalk.'

'Therefore, I said to you, my friend, "He who acts out of greed . . . " and the rest of it,' concluded Goldfinder. Again he spoke to his friend: 'Permit me to leave so that I can go home.'

Whereupon Wheelbearer pleaded, 'How can you go, my friend, leaving me in this miserable plight? You know what is said:

> *Prompted by sheer hard-heartedness* (66)
> *a man who forsakes a friend in distress*
> *is an ingrate, nothing less:*
> *for this sin he is certain to go to Hell.'*

And Goldfinder replied, 'Yes, my friend, what you say is true; but it is valid only in cases where a man who has the ability to aid his friend abandons him and that too in a situation where help can be provided.[30] But this is a situation[31] beyond all human remedy. As for me, I can never gain the power to set you free, remember that; more than that, even as I watch you twisting in the agony created by the whirling wheel, even as I see your face distorted with pain, I feel afraid that the same calamity might perchance befall me. And the more urgent then is my desire to leave and go far away from this place. The following lines from a tale illustrates my point aptly:

> *To judge from the look on your face,* (67)
> *dear monkey, it is quite plain to me,*
> *you are caught in Twilight's cruel grip;*
> *he lives long who flees far.'*

Wheelbearer asked his friend, 'What is that tale?' And then Goldfinder began the tale of *The Credulous Ogre*.

In a certain city there once ruled a king named Fine Forces who had a daughter named Jewel, a maiden blessed with all imaginable beauties.[32] A certain ogre lusted after her and wished to carry her off. Every night he came to her chamber, forced himself upon her and took his pleasure of her; but he could not carry her off because she was protected by a circle of magical spells and charms. At the hour when the ogre was enjoying her body, the poor princess displayed all the certain signs of demonic possession, such as feverishness, trembling, and so on. As the days passed, one night, the ogre stood in a corner of the bed-chamber and made himself visible to the princess. 'Look, look, dear friend,' the princess exclaimed, turning to her lady-in-waiting, 'do you see this ogre who each evening come twilight, arrives to torment me this way? Do you think there is some means of warding off this evil-hearted demon?'

Hearing the princess speak, the ogre began thinking anxiously, 'Oho! So, there is another like me who comes to her every night and like me wishes to carry the princess away. And his name is Twilight, I see. But it looks as if he is also not able to carry her off. So, let me assume the form of a horse and stand among the horses and watch to see what form this other fellow takes and judge what power he has.'

So he went and stood in the stables among the horses having assumed an equine form. At dead of night, a horse-thief stole into the royal stables. He looked around and carefully examined each horse there. Deciding that the horse which was in fact the ogre, was the finest of them all, the thief fitted a bit into that horse's mouth and mounted him. As all these preparations were going on, the ogre in horse-shape thought to himself, 'So, this is the fellow the princess calls Twilight; presuming me to be a villain, he has become enraged and has come here to kill me. What the hell am I to do?'

While the ogre was lost in such thoughts, the horse-thief picked up a whip and struck him hard. Terrified, the ogre took off and started galloping at a terrific speed. Having ridden him for a long distance, the thief pulled sharply at the bit to slow him down and make him keep a steady pace; but to no avail.

The horse-thief reflected; 'If this creature were really a horse then he would understand my tugging at the bit, and respond; instead, he goes faster than ever.'

Seeing that the horse was not in the least paying heed to the control exerted through the bit, the thief grew apprehensive: 'Well, well; horses do not act like this,' he thought to himself; 'This must surely be some demon or other who has taken the form of a horse. I had better watch out for some spot where the dust lies thick so that I can drop down. There seems no other way of staying alive.'

As the horse-thief rode on, anxiety-ridden, praying fervently to his chosen deity, the demon-horse galloped under a spreading banyan tree. The thief caught hold of one of the aerial roots of the tree and clung to it for dear life. The two of them, thief and ogre, thus fortuitously separated, now had their hopes for life restored and were filled with supreme delight.

Now, a certain monkey, the ogre's close friend, lived in that tree. Seeing the ogre rushing away, he called out : 'Look here, why on earth are you running away like this from an imaginary danger? This is a man, your natural prey; eat him.'

Hearing the monkey's words, the ogre resumed his natural form and turned around, but remained dithering, perplexed and uncertain. As for the thief he became so furious at the monkey for having recalled the fleeing ogre that seeing it sit right above him, he caught hold of its tail that was hanging down, put it in his mouth and chewed very, very, hard on it. The monkey concluding that here was a person much more powerful than the ogre, was too frightened to make a sound. All it could do was to sit there in dreadful pain, with eyes closed tight and teeth clenched hard. The ogre marked how the monkey sat there looking quite miserable and recited this verse:

> 'To judge from the look on your face (68)
> dear monkey, I see quite clearly
> that you are held tight in Twilight's grip;
> he lives long who flees far.'

Once again Goldfinder said to his friend, 'Give me leave to depart; I wish to return home. And as for you, my friend, you had better remain here, tasting the fruit of the Tree of Heedlessness.'

To this Wheelbearer, stung by his friend's criticism, retorted: 'Look here, my friend, I cannot accept what you say; this is not simply a question of prudence or the lack of it. For good luck and ill luck come to men, allotted by fate, as these lines aptly point out:

Blind man, hunchback, princess with three breasts, (69)
all three won, and gained the right ends,
even though they used the wrong means :
for Fortune did wait upon them.'

Rather put out, Goldfinder said, 'Oh? Is that so? Tell me how?' And then Wheelbearer began the tale of *The Three-breasted Princess*.

In the north country is a place named Honey City which was ruled by a king by the name of Honey Forces. At one time a daughter was born to him, but the baby princess had three breasts. When the king heard about this, he at once summoned the royal chamberlain and commanded him thus: 'Listen, sir, take this baby to the forest and abandon her there so that no one will ever know of this strange birth.'

Hearing his command, the chamberlain suggested: 'O, King of Kings, it is well-known that even though the birth of a girl with three breasts is a calamitous event, still, the learned priests should be summoned and asked for advice as to what ought to be done so that there would be no likelihood of any transgression of the Law in this world and in the other. For we know the saying:

A prudent man is ever (70)
an inveterate inquirer;
a Brāhmana of old
as the tale is told,
seized by a demon king
managed to go scot-free
simply by making an inquiry.'

'O, really? How was that?' asked King Honey Forces. And then the chamberlain began the tale of *The Brāhmana who asked*.

Once, in a forest somewhere, there lived an ogre named Violent.

As he was roaming around one day he met a Brāhmana, on whose shoulders he promptly mounted and ordered, 'Now, go ahead.'

The Brāhmana, terror-stricken, set out as ordered, carrying the ogre on his shoulders. By chance he noticed something of interest; the ogre's feet were tender and delicate as the heart of a lotus. Curious, he put a question to his passenger: 'How is it that your feet are so tender, Your Honour?'

'Because,' replied the ogre, 'I never allow my bare feet to touch the earth; this is a vow I have taken.'

The poor Brāhmana struggled on with the ogre riding on his shoulders, while various ways of escaping from his predicament revolved in his mind, until they came to a lake. The ogre stopped him, saying, 'Hey, you are not to stir from this spot until I come out of the lake after I have had my bath in its waters and offered worship to the divinities.'

When the ogre had entered the lake the Brāhmana started thinking as he waited: 'It is quite plain to me that this demon, once he has had his bath and worshipped the divinities, will eat me up: I am certain of that. I had better leave this place quietly and quickly too; for this wicked fellow will not come after me on bare feet.' And he ran away as fast as he could. The ogre afraid of violating his own vow refrained from pursuing him.

'Therefore, my lord, I say to you, "A prudent man always enquires first . . . " and the rest of it,' concluded the chamberlain.

The king heeded the chamberlain's advice and sent for the learned priests and declared to them : 'O, learned priests, a daughter with three breasts has been born to me. Are there any remedial measures to be adopted or not in this case?'

The priests replied, 'Listen, O, King:

> *Born without a limb or with one too many,* (71)
> *a girl is a threat to her virtue*
> *and to the life of her husband too.*

> *What's worse, my lord, a three-breasted daughter* (72)
> *who comes within eyeshot of her father*

431

dooms him to a speedy death;
there is no doubt in this matter.

'For these reasons, our advice is that His Majesty should shun
the very sight of this princess. If any man is willing to marry her,
let her be given to him, after which he should be banished from
the land with her. By following this procedure, His Majesty
would be acting in accordance with the Law, human and divine.'

The king accepted their advice and ordered that a proclamation be made throughout his kingdom by beat of drum, as
follows: 'Hear this, all you people, hear this, whoever offers to
marry the princess with three breasts, to him will the king freely
offer a hundred thousand gold pieces; and banish him from the
land.'

For a very long time this proclamation was made but no one
came forward to marry the unfortunate princess who remained
in seclusion until she reached the point of stepping into womanhood.

In that same city a certain blind man lived and he had a
hunchback for a companion, who guided him around with a
stick. One day these two heard the royal proclamation made by
beat of drum and it started them thinking. They talked about it
and took counsel with one another. 'Listen, supposing we touch
the drum,[33] we get the girl and the gold. With the gold we can
lead a life of comfort and happiness. And even if the girl's
deformity brings death with itself, it will put an end finally to the
misery of abject poverty. As we have heard:

> *Wit, kindliness and modesty,*   (73)
> *sweetness of speech and youthful beauty,*
> *liveliness too and vitality,*
> *freedom from sorrow, and joviality,*
> *uprightness, knowledge of sacred texts,*
> *and wisdom of the Preceptor of the Immortals,[34]*
> *purity as well, of mind and body,*
> *respect too for rules of right conduct:*
> *all these fine attributes arise in people*
> *once their belly-pot is full.'*

Having talked it over, the blind man went up to the town-crier and tapped the drum. The king's men went straight away and informed the monarch: 'Lord, some blind man walked up to the drum and touched it. Now it is up to His Majesty to take a decision.'

The king replied immediately: 'Listen, sirs:

Blind man or deaf, or even a leper, (74)
or an outcast even, whoever,
let him but marry the girl, take the gold,
all hundred thousand pieces, and leave the land.'

Immediately, on receiving the royal command, the king's officers took the three-breasted princess to the river's edge where they married her to the blind man after handing over a hundred thousand gold pieces to him. Then putting all three of them into a small fishing boat they instructed the fishermen: 'Take this blind man with his wife and hunchback companion to some foreign land and let him settle there.' The boatmen followed these instructions. The three of them, when they reached a foreign land, travelled to a town there and with part of their wealth, purchased a house and settled down to live comfortably. The blind man, however, spent all his time lazing on a couch while the hunchback managed the household.

As time went on, the princess became involved in an affair with the hunchback. And one day she whispered to him. 'My beloved, if only this blind fellow can somehow be murdered, we could then have a wonderful life together, just the two of us. Try and find some poison which I can administer to my husband to put an end to his life; I would be the happiest woman alive.'

The hunchback, accordingly, began looking around and one day he discovered a dead black serpent lying somewhere, which he picked up and, with great joy, brought home. Giving it to the princess, he murmured: 'Beloved, here, take this; I found this black serpent; cut it up into small pieces; flavour well with fine spices and serve the dish to this eyeless fellow, telling him it is fish, eating which he will perish in no time.' Having instructed

433

the princess in this manner, the hunchback went off in the direction of the market.

The three-breasted princess cut up the deadly serpent, put the pieces in a pot with some buttermilk and placed the pot on the fire. Having a number of household chores to attend to, she called out lovingly to her husband. 'My lord, I have got some of your favourite fish today and put it on the fire to cook. While I am attending to some household chores, will you pick up the spoon and stir it now and again?'

The blind man was so delighted to hear this that he began licking his chops. Rising with alacrity from his couch, he took a spoon and began stirring the stuff cooking in the pot. As he kept stirring, the poisonous vapours rising from the pot got into his eyes. And imagine his surprise when the thick film that had covered his eyes began to melt and peel away gradually. Noticing this beneficial effect of the steam on his sight, he opened his eyes wide and did his best to let the steam impinge on them. Soon his vision cleared completely so that he could look into the pot. And what did he see at the bottom of the cooking pot but a chopped up black serpent. And he pondered over this: 'Sure she said it was fish; but this is no fish cooking; it is chopped black serpent! Well, well, I have to get to the bottom of this. Is this the doing of the three-breasted princess? Or of the hunchback who is planning my murder? Or someone else's?'

Determined to get to the truth, the blind man concealed his real emotions and acted as usual as if he were blind. In the meantime the hunchback returned. Without the least suspicion he went up to the princess, took her in his arms, kissing her passionately, caressing and indulging in other forms of loveplay and soon started making love to her. The blind man was watching it all. Not finding any weapon he could lay his hands on, he slowly went towards the hunchback, feeling his way as he used to previously. When he was close enough, he grabbed the feet of the hunchback and blinded by anger, whirled the man round and round over his head with all his strength and then dashed him against the chest of the princess. The force of the impact of the hunchback's body on her chest pushed her third breast in, while her lover's hump dashing against her bosom, straightened out.

'Therefore, I said to you, my friend, "Blind man, hunchback, three-breasted princess . . . " and the rest of that verse,' concluded Wheelbearer.

To this, Goldfinder answered, 'Well said, my friend, what you said is perfectly true, that good fortune comes if fate favours a person. Yet, while accepting the power of Fate, no man should desert prudence, as you did rejecting my advice.'

With these final words, Goldfinder bid his friend farewell and started home.

And here ends the work known to the world as the *Pančatantra*[35] and by its other name of *Pančākhyānaka*,[36] a treatise on the art of living wisely and well.

This work on polity, composed by the celebrated Viṣṇu Śarma, consisting of stories linked by wise and good sayings of a good and true poet aims to be of service to others here in this world, and to lead the way to the World of Eternal Light, as the wise and learned declare.

Notes and References

Introduction

1. The term *nīti* like other Sanskrit terms such as *dharma*, cannot be translated into English by a single word; it conveys the ideas of conducting one's life and affairs wisely and well, using practical wisdom. The concept of *nīti* is explained in detail later in the introduction.
2. Antonio Francesco Doni (1513-1574).
3. See pp. 34-71 in the 1938 reprint, op. cit. This is the first reprinting of North's translation after the second edition of 1572.
4. This term is used once in the *Pañćatantra*; I. 174, 3.
5. An English version of *Bidpai's Fables*, based upon Ancient Arabic and Spanish manuscripts; published by Juan de la Cuesta, Newark, Delaware, 1980.
6. It is conjectured that al-Muqaffa who rendered Burzoë's Pehlevi version of the *Pañćatantra* into Arabic (*Kalilah wa Dimnah*) in AD 750, also used an earlier Arabic version of the work by a Jew who knew both Sanskrit and Arabic.
7. It is suggested that the work was carried into Africa by Arab traders who were the great entrepreneurs of the early Middle Ages and that it (or stories from it) went with the slaves to America.
8. *A History of Sanskrit Literature*. OUP. 1928 ed. p. 359.
9. Op. cit. intro. p. vii.
10. Adopted later as a surname or family name, as Vājpeyi or Vājpayee; a modernized form, Bajpai, is also in use.
11. Epic is an English word used rather loosely to signify the literary genre that Sanskrit poetics describes as *Mahākāvya* (The Great Poem). The principles and classification, and the terminology used in Sanskrit poetics, are different from those in Western poetics. For instance, rigid distinctions are

not made in Sanskrit poetics between fairy tale, folk-tale and fable.

12. In my childhood, storytelling sessions (*Kathākālakṣepam* and *Harikathā*) were fairly frequent and were held in a temple or in people's houses. They have been revived of late, as part of literary conferences, for example.

13. We see this in our own times where contemporary artists in the oral tradition of storytelling, such as the fabulous Teejan Bai and Rekha Nishad, both from Madhya Pradesh, introduce little touches that bring the past and the present together—a word, a gesture, a topical allusion or reference to a current issue, sometimes political—into their narration of episodes from the *Mahābhārata* (known as Pandavani) or of ancient ballads. Sauli Mitra, another artist in the oral tradition who brings a fresh point of view, a 're-vision', to her narration of the stripping of Draupadī in the Assembly Hall (*Mahābhārata*, Book II), questions the values of the patriarchal society of the epic. By inference the questioning is addressed to contemporary society.

14. Franklin Edgerton attempts a *re-construction* of 'the original', in his *The Pañćatantra Reconstructed*, in two volumes. (American Original Series, vol. III, New Haven, Connecticut 1920). But it is a hypothetical text; a construct.

15. This text derives from three earlier recensions of the *Pañćatantra* that are designated as *Tantrākhyāyikā*, Simplicior, and an unknown (obviously lost and untraceable) recension. It is Hertel's opinion that the first recension mentioned is closest to 'the original'. Keith and Macdonell concur; Edgerton disagrees, though he acknowledges that the greater part is close to the original.

16. For example, M. R. Kale's edition, reprinted many times (Motilal Banarsidass, Delhi). Unfortunately, Kale does not specify the recension/s on which his text is based.

17. '*Simhasakāśe samupaviṣṭah Karaṭakah Damanakam prati abravit . . . .*'

18. Modern theatre in the West, stretches the limits of formal theatre: for example, Samuel Beckett's *Krapp's Last Tape*.

19. For example, Gilda in Verdi's *Rigoletto*.

20. Amṛtamaya: *Amṛtam* signifies paradise and the drink of immortality, ambrosia. In mythology, gods and titans seeking immortality, churn the Milky Ocean for ambrosia.
21. This stanza is also found in Bhartṛhari's *nītiśataka*. Who borrowed from whom, or whether both had a common source is difficult to tell.
22. I use the term Law (capital 'L') to signify the moral law and order of the universe as it is seen operating in creation; and law (small 'l') in the strictly legal sense.
23. Exegetical texts for the sacrificial ritual; composed around 900-800 BC.
24. *The Great Tale*, date uncertain, perhaps the AD first century.
25. *Tantra* has several meanings: text, a chapter of a text, a loom or frame.
26. Another name for *Mahilāropya; pramadā* and *mahilā* both mean young and beautiful women.

Preamble

1. Undying Energy.
2. Rich Energy; Fierce Energy; Endless Energy.
3. Sumati.
4. Indra, Lord of the Immortals.

Book I

1. Increase or Flourishing Prosperity.
2. Nandana; Sanjīvaka.
3. Piṅgalaka.
4. Bṛhaspati, the preceptor of the gods.
5. *Hālāhala*, the deadly poison that emerged when the Milky Ocean was churned at the beginning of Time and which Śiva swallowed to save the world.
6. Himālaya mountains.
7. Deva Śarma.
8. Āshāḍha bhūti: a name for the planet Mars; literally, born in June-July, i.e., late summer.

9. God's gift.

10. The Sanskrit word for *vyāsana* has several meanings: distress, misfortune and evil practices.

11. Manda-Mati.

12. Viśvakarma—Divine Architect and framer of the Universe.

13. Paraśurāma or Rāma-of-the-Axe who slew the whole lot of princes in revenge for the slaying of his father.

14. A fallacy in logic: because once a palm fruit fell down the moment a crow alighted on the palm tree it does not mean that the crow caused the fruit to fall.

15. Garuḍa, the golden eagle.

16. The Creator.

17. These are the five flowers of springtime: red lotus, aśoka and mango blossoms, jasmine and blue lily.

18. Eros or Cupid.

19. Excellences both physical and moral.

20. Kālidāsa: *Śakuntalā* 1.21.

21. A contract entered into by two persons in love, of their own free will, with mutual vows of fidelity; it is legal and carries the rights and responsibilities of marriage and the penalties for breaking the marriage vows, just as the sacramental marriage performed by the priest in an assembly of family, friends and relatives, before the sacred fire as witness does.

22. A literary convention; the depth of love and ardour of passion were believed to be indicated by bruised lips, nail marks on the limbs. It should not be construed as some form of sadistic enjoyment.

23. Vikramasenā; literally, the monarch with victorious armies.

24. A lakh is a hundred thousand.

25. Words such as *kāla*, *kṛtānta*, are used for both Time and Death.

26. The ancient Indian army was divided into four sections: elephants, chariots, horses and infantry.

27. The Cosmic Mountain, centre and support of the world.

28. Mother of Garuḍa, the golden eagle; she was rewarded by having her son chosen as Viṣṇu's mount.

29. The three powers of the state are: the army, the treasury, and the council of ministers.

30. The Himālayas.
31. Yajna-datta: literally, 'one who is preserved by sacrifice'.
32. A Brāhmana.
33. Modern Broach, a port city on the Rann of Kutch on the west coast, an arm of the Arabian sea.
34. The Sanskrit word guru refers to elders, a parent and a preceptor.
35. The three ends of life: the pursuit of virtue, wealth and love.
36. Mandasarpiṇī is slow-creeping.
37. Candarava.
38. Madarakta.
39. Sāgaradatta—literally, 'ocean-preserved'.
40. Madotkata.
41. The Realm of Light, Heaven, Paradise.
42. God-Preserved.
43. Vimala.
44. That is, himself; he regards the lion as his brother.
45. In *realpolitik*, four expedients are available for princes: conciliation, bribes, intrigues and the last, war.
46. Uttānapāda—literally, 'outstretched feet'.
47. Pativratā—'the chaste wife'.
48. A bull elephant in rut is dangerous.
49. God of Death.
50. Death.
51. Probably refers to the Fire at the end of Time.
52. The zodiacal sign Libra.
53. Vīṇārava.
54. Meghadūta.
55. Death: dissolution of the cremated body into the five elements it is constituted of: Ether, Air, Fire, Water, Earth.
56. That is, they have to spend much time away from their nests, foraging.
57. Literally, 'Dweller-in-the-Water', i.e., the Waters of Creation; Nārāyaṇa, Viṣṇu and many other words are epithets for the Supreme One.
58. Celestial City; City of the Gods.

59. Hyenas feed chiefly on carrion; the Sanskrit word is *kravyamukha*, literally, carrion-in-the-mouth.

60. Dharmarāja; Death, who is the upholder of Law, both moral and physical, of the universe.

61. That is, of eating before his master does.

62. The lion has to have his share of his kill first and takes the choicest parts.

63 That is, they belong to the same family and to eat the flesh of kin is taboo.

64. Or, 'a forest tumultuous with fires blazing'.

65. Also known as Kimśuka; the flame-of-the-forest that blooms at the beginning of summer. The flowers appear before the leaves in clusters of big, brilliant, crimson blossoms, five-petalled with one forming a keel that resembles a parrot's beak. Nectar-bearing, it attracts many birds, especially parrots.

66. *Sāma*, one of the four expedients of policy; the first and most esteemed.

67. *Daṇḍa*, war, the last and most extreme measure in *realpolitik*.

68. The four expedients stated in the maxim, *sāma-dāna-bheda-daṇḍa*; or peace (conciliation); bribes; intrigue; war.

69. Here, political acumen.

70. Here, machismo implied.

71. Words in Sanskrit signifying knowledge, wisdom, learning are mostly in the feminine gender.

72. This verse implies two things; the dangers that surround a king, especially if he is alone; that aspect of royalty as a focal point for social needs and forces.

73. Magnanimity, sagacity and so on, all royal virtues.

74. Conciliation, bribes, intrigue, war: *sāma*, *dāna*, *bheda*, *daṇḍa*.

75. Virtue, wealth, happiness.

76. The Impregnable.

77. Suratha.

78. Balabhadra: literally, blessed with strength.

79. Antahpura—Inner Apartments, the part of the palace

reserved exclusively for the residence of the queens and princesses and their attendants.

80. The traditional greeting to a monarch.

81. *Deva* is a word with several meanings: god, child, fool; the phrase *devanam priyah*, 'beloved of gods', also means a stupid idiot or prize-fool, the meaning implied in the context.

82. Literally, the Royal City, ancient capital of Magadha (modern Bihar); it was situated near Pāṭaliputra (modern Patna).

83. The first two lines of verse 376 may also be rendered as follows:

Time, the Ender, determines the act;
And what will be will be;

84. *Sūkta*, this word can also refer to wise and pithy sayings.

85. Ketakī—Pandanus.

86. Āmalakā(Āmlā)—Myrobalan.

87. *Āhāranirgamasthānam*—literally, the place from which food is excreted.

88. Dharmabuddhi, Duṣṭabuddhi

89. A *dinara* is variously computed in weight, but obviously it is a large gold coin.

90. Brahmahṛdayam—literally, the heart of the world; i.e., gold.

91. The Sanskrit term, *jihvādvayam*, means 'double-tongue' or 'forked tongue'.

92. Men possessing qualities of majesty, nobility, magnanimity and so on, attributed to lions.

93. The implication seems to be that Nāduka borrowed money for his business ventures from the guild-president.

94. The traditional guest-offering consisted of a number of articles of welcome offered as part of hospitality: water to wash the face, hands and feet: a refreshing drink of blended milk, honey, curds, fruits, etc.

95. Negotiation and parleys; battle; logistics, consisting of the modes of advance, lying in wait (ambush), battle-formation; and alliances or coalitions.

96. Kubera, Lord of Yakshas.

97. Indra, Lord of the Immortals.

98. Or bias, or vested interests.

Book II

1. Laghupatanaka; literally, little one who flies and alights
    lightly.
2. Citragrīva; literally, iridescent-necked.
3. Hiraṇya.
4. A *yojana* is equal to eight to ten miles.
5. The bright star Arcturus, in the constellation Boötes; a red
    giant.
6. One of the six systems of philosophy based on the exegesis
    of Vedic texts.
7. The first to write on prosody.
8. The great Titan, archetypal enemy of the gods.
9. Mother of the Titans.
10. An allusion to the seven steps taken round the sacred fire by
    bride and bridegroom that makes them comrades for life.
11. Literally, I lay my head on your lap.
12. An easy, even flight.
13. Maheśvara—one of the many epithets given to Lord Śiva.
14. Bootakarṇa.
15. Some monastic orders prescribe this as a daily routine.
16. Crumbly, unrefined brown sugar.
17. Brhadsphik.
18. Or it could mean telling stories on religious themes.
19. A lady belonging to the Śāndilya clan.
20. Monks went into retreat for the rainy season; at other times
    of the year they travelled about.
21. Greed, avarice; the Sanskrit word *tṛṣṇā* means thirst,
    craving, lusting after things as well as desire in the sense of
    motivation.
22. A hill tribe who were hunter-gatherers.
23. Hunting; the chase is set down as one of the eight deadly
    sins; snaring birds is considered a sin.
24. Peacocks usually walk backwards, 'When the young
    peacock, whose tail has not yet grown, has drunk water, he

does not turn around but walks backwards just like an old bird. The latter must do so in order not to soil the feathers of his tail.'–Buhler (cited by M. R. Kale) in his edition of the *Pancatantra*.

25. Empty ears of barley without the kernel inside the husk.

26. *Vyartha*, i.e., without wealth, also means, useless, unprofitable, insignificant.

27. Or Fate.

28. Exile; or, renunciation of the world, the third stage in the life prescribed in sacred texts and known as *vanaprastha*, the ascetic life.

29. The Himālayas.

30. Like a monk.

31. Literally, Gift of the Ocean.

32. Candramatī.

33. Brahmaghātaka; literally, 'Brāhmana-slayer', held to be the most heinous crime.

34. Perdition, Hell.

35. One of the six recognized forms of marriage, entered into by mutual consent of a man and woman without sacramental rites; it was legal and binding.

36. The groom puts his right arm round the bride during some of the marriage rites, or, holds her right hand.

37. Tṛṣṇā (Desire) is in mythology, the daughter of Kāma (Eros, Love); but here it is inordinate desire: lust, passion, greed, that is castigated.

38. Viṣṇu contracted His enormous size that filled the three worlds, to that of a dwarf to trick the magnanimous Emperor Bali, to grant Him three feet of land.

39. Holy men belonging to certain sects on the fringe of Śaivism, Kāpālikas and others carried around a half-skull as their almsbowl and ate out of it; they were not part of the mainstream of Śaiva faith.

40. In strictly legal terms, motive and proof.

41. Heaven, Earth, Underworld; or Air, Earth, Water.

42. Or, life's vicissitudes.

43. The preceptor of the Immortals and epitome of intellect, wisdom and learning.

44. Literally, the tiny depression made by the hoof of a cow that fills with dirty water.
45. The Himālayas.
46. The man who will marry her.
47. That is, the Earth; Indian cosmography figures the landmass on the planet as seven enormous islands—*saptadvīpa*.
48. His best is not good enough because of Fate, circumstance, what you will.
49. Vardhamānapuram; modern Burdwan.
50. That is, whether he may use and enjoy the returns, or not.
51. Darbhā; spear-grass; its narrow leaves have sharp points.
52. A small shell used as currency.
53. Pralambavṛṣaṇa, literally, Pendulous-Testicles.
54. Pralobhika.
55. The cātaka or crested-cuckoo is believed to subsist only on rain-drops; however thirsty it is firmly resolved not to drink any other water.
56. Indra, Lord of the Immortals, is the rain-god.
57. Mahouts train and direct an elephant by pricking the sensitive part of its ear with the sharp point of the goad.
58. The Himālayas.
59. *Niyati*, is the fixed order of things in the world.
60. The Sanskrit phrase is *'Vidhinā likhitam lalāṭe yad'*, meaning 'the writing of Destiny on the brow'.
61. Ćitrānga—the spotted antelope.
62. Or from feigned anger.
63. Mitra is a friend.

Book III

1. These are the classic expedients of a policy laid down in texts on statecraft; these are meant for princes and others involved in government; they are *sāma*, *dāna*, *bheda*, *daṇḍa*, (peace, bribes, discord, war).
2. Prithiviprathishttana.
3. Meghavarṇa.
4. Arimardana.

5. The expedients of policy: *sandhi, vigraha, yāna, āsana, samsraya, dvaidhibhava.*
6. Ujjīvi, Sanjīvi, Anujīvi, Prajīvi, Ćiranjīvi.
7. Negotiations, gifts and bribery, sowing dissention.
8. The fourth and final expedient is the use of force.
9. The Pāṇḍava who went into exile and returned to fight and conquer. *(Mahābhārata)*
10. Catapults, battering rams, moving towers, etc.
11. Kokila or nightingales.
12. Ćātaka, also known as hawk-cuckoo.
13. Śyāmā.
14. Garuda, the golden eagle.
15. The Abhiṣeka.
16. Marked by the figure of a wheel.
17. A special collection of holy herbs used in consecrations.
18. The coronation of the owl as King of Birds: the details that follow are based mainly on details found in the Brāhmana literature in the sections dealing with the *Abhiṣeka* rites of Indra and earthly kings such as Bharata, son of Śakuntalā, and the *Rājasūya* sacrifices of the Vedic age; for instance in the *Aitareya Brāhmana,* (Panćikā VIII Adhyāya II – Keith).
19. Ćakora.
20. Hārīta.
21. Ćaturdanta.
22. Nine divinities are said to watch over all actions, good and bad: the sun and moon, death and time, and the five elements.
23. The three regal powers, of majesty or the personal power of a ruler; of diplomacy or the power of the counsellors; and the power of action, or military power.
24. In Indian mythology the disfigurations on the moon's surface are perceived as forming the shape of a hare; the 'hare-in-the-moon' is similar to the English phrase 'man-in-the-moon'.
25. Ursa Major; constellation of the Great Bear.
26. Śīghraka.
27. Dadhikarṇa.

28. *Dharma*—the Law; here it refers to law in the narrow sense which is based on moral law or ethics, as well as to righteousness, virtue and so forth.
29. Yajamāna, the man who arranged for a sacrifice to be performed and paid all the expenses.
30. *Āhitāgni*—literally, one who tends the sacred fire on the altar.
31. Milk, butter, curds, urine, dung.
32. Regulation of the diet according to the waxing and waning of the moon: one mouthful increased daily to fifteen mouthfuls at full moon and decreased to one mouthful at new moon.
33. Raktākṣa,   Krūrākṣa,   Dīptākṣa,   Vakranāsa, Prākārakarṇa.
34. Citraratha, i.e., one who had bright chariots.
35. The second of the four stages or ashramas of life and considered the most meritorious.
36. Svarga, Paradise.
37. Kāmātura.
38. Brahmarākṣas.
39. Satyavacna.
40. That is, once every three days.
41. Bali.
42. The moon.
43. Durgā.
44. A species of aquatic plant, probably duckweed.
45. Born of the sage Jahnu; another name for Gaṇgā.
46. A small amount of water is held in the hollow of the right palm and sipped after certain prayers are uttered to sanctify it.
47. Gandharva; the Gandharva is a spirit whose dwelling is in the air or in the space-ocean, the Waters of Life; he also guards Soma, the sap of life.
48. Putrikā, is the term used for a daughter chosen to raise male issue to parents without a son.
49. One of the many hells in which sinners are baked like clay pots in a furnace.
50. Arjuna, the third Pāṇḍava brother. During their last year of

exile, the five brothers and Draupadī lived incognito in the kingdom of the Matsyas (also known as Virāṭa), disguised and performing menial tasks at the court. Arjuna, disguised as a eunuch, was teacher of dance and music to the princess. Bhīma, the second Pāṇḍava, was the cook.

51. Gāṇḍīva, Arjuna's bow, a gift from Agni (Fire) for helping in the burning of the Khandava forest.
52. King of the Matsyas.
53. Arjuna, who could shoot with both hands.
54. Arjuna.
55. Dharma, the Law personified. Yudhiṣṭhira, the eldest of the Pāṇḍavas was the son of Kuntī and Dharma.
56. Indra, Kubera, Yama, respectively.
57. A slave or maid doing menial tasks in the apartments of queens and princesses.
58. Dharma, Artha, Kāma: Virtue, Wealth, Love.
59. Sweets made of flour, sugar, butter, milk and coconut.
60. Here and in other passages, 'wisdom' refers to political wisdom, shrewd diplomacy, knowledge of *realpolitik*.
61. Sri or Rājyalakshmī: Sovereignty and Royal Glory personified.
62. Hero of the epic *Rāmāyana*, banished to the forests.
63. The magnanimous *daitya*-monarch bound by Viṣṇu by a trick and pushed down into the underworld.
64. The five Pāṇḍavas who lost the game of dice and lived in exile for thirteen years.
65. The clan of which Kṛṣṇa was the chief; they ran amok and killed one another through a curse.
66. Nala, King of the Nishadas, who forfeited his kingdom to his cousin in a game of dice.
67. Arjuna, the third Pāṇḍava brother; see note 50, above.
68. Rāvaṇa, King of Laṅkā, who abducted Rāma's wife, Sītā, and was killed in the battle for her rescue.
69. Rāma's father, who had to banish his son to keep his promise to his junior queen, Kaikeyī.
70. Svarga—Realm of the Immortals or the Shining Ones (Devas) ruled over by Indra.

71. Indra.
72. An ancient emperor of the Solar Race of kings, ruler of Ayodhyā, Rāma's distant ancestor.
73. Pṛthu, after whom the Earth is named Pṛthvī; he was born from the right arm of his dead father, a mythical first emperor.
74. The primal ancestor of mankind, born of the sun.
75. A mythical king, born of his father without a mother and nursed by Indra himself; conquered the whole world and ruled it from the eastern to the western oceans.
76. Satyavrata—literally, one who vows to speak the truth; Bhīṣma, or the eldest Pāṇḍava, Yudhiṣṭhira, may be referred to; also a name for Triśaṅku who tried to ascend bodily to heaven but remained suspended midway in space.
77. Nahuṣa, chosen temporarily as Lord of the Immortals he became arrogant and was cursed to become a serpent.
78. Devas: the Immortals.
79. One of Viṣṇu's names; literally, one who has long and beautiful hair.
80. Time.

Book IV

1. Raktamukha.
2. Vikarālamukha.
3. The Sanskrit word *'atithi'* signifies one who comes unannounced, uninvited and unexpectedly; literally, it means one who comes without a date, *a-tithi*, date-less.
4. The text specifies this as Vaisvedevante: at the close of the twice-daily rites when offerings are made into the sacred fire to all the divine powers before the morning and evening meals.
5. Svarga.
6. Śrāddha ceremonies to the Pitris or Manes.
7. Ambrosia is believed to confer eternal youth and life.

8. The words that establish a relationship or articulate a binding oath.
9. The word *'dauhrda'* in the text suggests the uncontrollable craving for certain foods during pregnancy.
10. Note the wordplay on *heart*.
11. A she-mule is believed to die the moment she gives birth.
12. Priya darsana, literally, beautiful to look at.
13. Literally, Gaṅgā's Gift.
14. An important writer on law; author of a treatise on policy with special reference to mistrust.
15. Karalakesara.
16. Dhūsaraka—thecolourofdust.
17. Sacred grass used in religious rites.
18. The terms 'uncle' and 'nephew' for an elder and a younger person are modes of friendly and courteous address.
19. Laundry man or washerman.
20. Killing a woman is a deadly sin.
21. Kāma, Eros.
22. Kāma or Love.
23. Prayers to gods and to ancestors and purificatory rites, etc.
24. According to the rules of hierarchy, the master eats first then the servant.
25. We see here a play on the name. Yudhiṣṭhira, the eldest of the Pāṇḍava brothers in the *Mahābhārata* who was renowned as a speaker of truth as a matter of principle; the potter, however, tells the truth because he is dim-witted.
26. There are two mythical mountains, the eastern and western, where the sun is believed to rise and set respectively.
27. Linga.
28. A woman who has given birth is given a special diet.
29. Heads are shaved completely on certain occasions as part of the ceremonies.
30. Nanda.
31. Vararuchi.
32. Śuddha pata.
33. The donkey is a beast of burden for the dhobi to carry the washing back and forth.

34. The word *nagnikā* has the double meaning of a naked woman and whore.
35. *Sāma, dāna, bheda, daṇḍa*: conciliation, bribery, intrigue, war.
36. Or by exchanging seven words; see note 10 on p.444.
37. Literally, throwing oneself at the feet of someone.
38. When it is bored and strung.
39. Spotted.
40. That is, she did not bother to put things away and lock the doors, etc.

Book V

1. Pāṭaliputra: Pāṭali is the pale-pink, fragrant blossom of the trumpet-tree, a species of Bignonia.
2. Maṇibhadra, a yakṣa who was the patron saint of merchants.
3. The ocean, or rain clouds.
4. A trillion.
5. Jaina monk.
6. Mahāvira, founder of Jainism, who conquered the ills of existence.
7. The mouth and nose.
8. Priests who officiate at ceremonies and rituals in households and are fed as part of those rites.
9. Digambara Jain monks go about naked.
10. A Brāhmaṇa lady.
11. Region round Ujjain, in Madhya Pradesh.
12. Śiva's shrine of Mahākāla in Ujjain on the banks of the Śiprā.
13. Bhairavananda.
14. Viṣṇu; the myth alluded to is that of the churning of the Milky Ocean, from which rose a number of objects of beauty, Lakshmi or Beauty being one of them.
15. One of the forms of Agni or fire, in the form of a mare.
16. According to Wilson, Udayana of the Vatsas may be referred to here; he was celebrated as a skilled player on the lute or Vīṇa.

17. Rāma, epic hero; there is a time lapse of several centuries between the two kings mentioned.
18. Kubera, Lord of Yakṣas.
19. *Buddhi* includes the meanings of good sense or common sense, judgement and wit.
20. These are all listed in all treatises on music, e.g., the *Sangitaratnākara* of Śāraṅgadeva and earlier works on the subject.
21. Rasas.
22. The story tells of how Rāvaṇa in his pride tried to uproot Mount Kailāsa itself with Śiva and Pārvatī sitting on it. Feeling the mountain shake, the goddess grew afraid and the Great Lord knowing what caused it, pressed down with his big toe, crushing the trapped Rāvaṇa, who cut off one his ten heads and making it into a stringed instrument drew such divine music from it that the Lord, enchanted, relented and let him go.
23. For sexual union.
24. Uśanās or Śukra, a celebrated law giver and author of the famous treatise on *realpolitik* or statecraft.
25. Soma Śarma.
26. Svabhāva-Kripaṇa: literally, a man naturally mean or pitiable.
27. Chandra.
28. Kubera.
29. Svarga or the Immortal Worlds of Light.
30. Alternately, in a place easy of access.
31. Alternately: it is a place inaccessible to human beings.
32. There are thirty-two marks of beauty listed.
33. To signify acceptance.
34. Bṛhaspati.
35. The five chapters or threads.
36. The five short narratives.

PENGUIN CLASSICS

THE BHAGAVAD GITA

'In death thy glory in heaven, in victory thy glory on earth.
Arise therefore, Arjuna, with thy soul ready to fight'

The Bhagavad Gita is an intensely spiritual work that forms the
cornerstone of the Hindu faith, and is also one of the masterpieces of
Sanskrit poetry. It describes how, at the beginning of a mighty battle
between the Pandava and Kaurava armies, the god Krishna gives
spiritual enlightenment to the warrior Arjuna, who realizes that the
true battle is for his own soul.

Juan Mascaró's translation of *The Bhagavad Gita* captures the
extraordinary aural qualities of the original Sanskrit. This edition
features a new introduction by Simon Brodbeck, which discusses
concepts such as dehin, prakriti and Karma.

'The task of truly translating such a work is indeed formidable. The
translator must at least possess three qualities. He must be an artist in
words as well as a Sanskrit scholar, and above all, perhaps, he must be
deeply sympathetic with the spirit of the original. Mascaró has succeeded
so well because he possesses all these' *The Times Literary Supplement*

Translated by Juan Mascaró with an introduction by Simon Brodbeck

THE ANALECTS   CONFUCIUS

'The Master said, "If a man sets his heart on benevolence, he will be free from evil"'

The Analects are a collection of Confucius's sayings brought together by his pupils shortly after his death in 497 BC. Together they express a philosophy, or a moral code, by which Confucius, one of the most humane thinkers of all time, believed everyone should live. Upholding the ideals of wisdom, self-knowledge, courage and love of one's fellow man, he argued that the pursuit of virtue should be every individual's supreme goal. And while following the Way, or the truth, might not result in immediate or material gain, Confucius showed that it could nevertheless bring its own powerful and lasting spiritual rewards.

This edition contains a detailed introduction exploring the concepts of the original work, a bibliography and glossary and appendices on Confucius himself, *The Analects* and the disciples who compiled them.

Translated with an introduction and notes by D. C. Lau

THE STORY OF PENGUIN CLASSICS

Before 1946 ...'Classics' are mainly the domain of academics and students, without readable editions for everyone else. This all changes when a little-known classicist, E. V. Rieu, presents Penguin founder Allen Lane with the translation of Homer's *Odyssey* that he has been working on and reading to his wife Nelly in his spare time.

1946 *The Odyssey* becomes the first Penguin Classic published, and promptly sells three million copies. Suddenly, classic books are no longer for the privileged few.

1950s Rieu, now series editor, turns to professional writers for the best modern, readable translations, including Dorothy L. Sayers's *Inferno* and Robert Graves's *The Twelve Caesars*, which revives the salacious original.

1960s The Classics are given the distinctive black jackets that have remained a constant throughout the series's various looks. Rieu retires in 1964, hailing the Penguin Classics list as 'the greatest educative force of the 20th century'.

1970s A new generation of translators arrives to swell the Penguin Classics ranks, and the list grows to encompass more philosophy, religion, science, history and politics.

1980s The Penguin American Library joins the Classics stable, with titles such as *The Last of the Mohicans* safeguarded. Penguin Classics now offers the most comprehensive library of world literature available.

1990s The launch of Penguin Audiobooks brings the classics to a listening audience for the first time, and in 1999 the launch of the Penguin Classics website takes them online to a larger global readership than ever before.

The 21st Century Penguin Classics are rejacketed for the first time in nearly twenty years. This world famous series now consists of more than 1300 titles, making the widest range of the best books ever written available to millions – and constantly redefining the meaning of what makes a 'classic'.

The Odyssey continues ...

The best books ever written

PENGUIN ✺ CLASSICS

SINCE 1946

Find out more at www.penguinclassics.com